Our Norman
Slander'd King

Our Norman Slander'd King

George Vass

UPFRONT PUBLISHING
LEICESTERSHIRE

ISBN 1-84426-295-2

Published 2004 by
UPFRONT PUBLISHING
Leicestershire

Printed by Lightning Source

"…fancy hears the ring
Of harness, and that deathful arrow sing,
And Saxon battle-axe clang on Norman helm.
Here rose the dragon-banner of our realm;
Here fought, here fell, our Norman slander'd king."

Alfred Lord Tennyson

Chapter One

Destination Dover

T he astounding, virtually incredible disclosure of his supposed birthright staggered Edmond Edwysson. He felt as if he had been rammed in the chest by the leveled lance of a charging Norman knight.

"Men rightly hold you as though you were born of kingly stock, my son. Your blood is that of Alfred, the most renowned of our royal line, that of his son Edward the Elder and of his grandson Athelstane. Yes, also that of my unhappy father, your grandfather King Ethelred, whom traitors derided as the redeless, the ill-advised."

His dying father's words reverberated in Edmond's turbulent thoughts. Despite endless repetition, they remained as astonishing and vibrantly vivid as when first uttered, yet their speaker had been buried for a month or more in an obscure grave in a distant western shire across the breadth of England.

"You were born to be a king..." Edwy Ethelredson had whispered with almost his last breath.

Edmond revolved the extraordinary declaration in his mind, unable to accept its full implications yet fascinated by the premise. Was it the fruit of an expiring man's prophetic vision or merely the feverish meandering of a fading intellect? Whatever the cause, it tantalized and almost burdened him. It required the exertion of all his willpower to shake off abstraction and focus on the ancient Roman highway leading to Dover.

He was already breathing in the salt-spiced sea breeze, its scent new but pleasing to his senses. Ever nearer, though draped by a light, was the drifting fog. He beheld the hoary Roman lighthouse, lancing the sky atop the white cliffs that overawed the humble buildings of Dover huddled at their feet. The crumbling walls of the decayed fortress that frowned over the River Dour soon emerged into view from the shrouding mist. His father had accurately described the river as winding between lofty chalk bluffs to a rendezvous with the sea. When the sun suddenly burst through the fog and glared fiercely upon the vaulting ancient tower he realized he would reach the town by mid-afternoon.

The road to Dover was strangely lonely on this pleasant September day in the Year of Grace 1051. The highway was usually a throbbing

1

artery of the England that already bustled with commerce that was ever its lifeblood. Recently, there had been frequent incidents of outlaw savagery on the road, and most of the merchants, churchmen, pilgrims, tinkers and travelers of all stripes who customarily thronged the route had been frightened off. By the time Edmond approached Dover he had tramped several miles without meeting anyone. The last passerby had been an old tradesman plodding inland who had glanced fearfully at him until Edmond had nodded reassuringly, if absent-mindedly—still deeply engrossed in his father's solemn final admonition.

"When I die tomorrow—no, don't shake your head at me, God wills it, and I know it will be so—see that I'm laid to rest beside your mother, my dearest Christina. Pray for me, Edmond. I shall need prayer—may the saints forgive me. Would that I had died like my brother Edmond in the prime of life before the golden days of my youth were tarnished with defeat and disappointment.

"When I'm laid to rest, leave these wild western marches, this wasteland of gorse and broom. Depart altogether from England and seek your fortune in other, happier lands. Perhaps your destiny lies in that great city of Constantinople, which they say surpasses all others in size and wealth, and to which so many of our people have fled. I've heard that the great emperor always welcomes men of our nation as recruits to his guard, the noble Varangians. If true, you may still gain honor, rank and riches despite your unhappy father's failure to provide for you. Here in England, gold, estates and distinction go only to the Normans whom my saintly brother King Edward favors in his court."

The dying man sighed disapproval, then continued.

"So hasten to Dover, dear son. Seek out the merchant Osgood, a dealer of woolen cloths. Whisper to him that you are Edmond, son of Edwy Ethelredson, and he will know what is to be done. You'll need no countersign, no monk-written message from me. He'll recognize you without fail. Twins couldn't look more alike than you and I—that is, when I was your age. My loyal old shield-bearer will embrace you for the love he bore me in a happier season. Trust him as you would a second father. He'll furnish you with weapons and armor, and arrange for your passage abroad."

His father's reassuring and confident tone had impressed Edmond, but he could not shake lingering doubts. What if Osgood were dead? What if the merchant failed to recognize him as Edwy's son, or preferred not to do so? What then? Where could he, the almost penniless son of an obscure country thane, obtain the means to go abroad and seek the honorable career denied to him in England? Money had been scarce in Thane Edwy's house. He had left his only child a scant handful of silver pennies, two nearly broken-down nags and a battered, if serviceable and once richly-adorned, old sword, which unfortunately had long lost its jewels. In respect to his father's memory, Edmond had girded on the sword, but not even filial piety could persuade him to mount either jade. He sold both to discharge part of his father's debts, and disposed of the rest of his legacy by leasing the paternal cottage and its patch of land to a neighbor. He then set out on the long, arduous trek all the way across England from Bosbury to Dover.

Even now, with his destination in sight, he was beset by misgivings. Yet his father had been so certain that Osgood was still alive and would joyfully welcome his old master's son, that even to question his confidence seemed disrespectful to his memory. Most likely they had maintained a secret correspondence. In any event, Edmond's doubts would soon be quickly resolved. He could already hear the lively sounds of Dover, and he was soon passing through muddy streets and narrow lanes, kicking aside the pigs rooting in the heaps of refuse that bordered them. Suddenly, the sea burst into view and he saw the waterfront, cluttered with small boats tied to the piers or drawn up on shore, and ringed by a wall of larger ships swaying rhythmically at anchor.

He had never beheld such a broad expanse of water; it far surpassed the River Severn, which as a boy had awed him with its breadth and swift current. He had marveled at the Thames and the Wey, but this vastness of turbulent liquid stretching into seeming infinity astonished him. Despite straining his eyes, he was unable to pierce the mist veiling the eastern horizon until the sun finally vanquished it and a grayish bulk gradually emerged into view. That must be Baldwinesland, as his father had termed the French coast. He saw an approaching ship with billowing sails bobbing on the heaving whitecaps. In his naiveté, he marveled that the great surges of tumultuous waves did not swallow up the seemingly fragile craft. But the vessel skimmed along the creaming billows in apparent defiance of nature's elemental force.

"A gladsome sight, by the holy rood?" boomed a deep, good-natured voice. Startled, Edmond spun around sharply to discover at his elbow a huge barrel of a sailor, red-faced with three chins resting snugly on an enormous chest, smiling with obvious delight as he gazed on the oncoming craft. "There's a ship that's a proper sight for a sailorman," the sailor bellowed admiringly, turning to Edmond as if for confirmation of his verdict.

"I've never seen a ship before, but it's a handsome craft," Edmond politely agreed.

"Never seen a ship before?" The sailor echoed astonishment, the words ascending his three chins to emerge in a rumble. "No matter, you'll be seeing all sorts—a fleet and more—if you linger long in Dover, though none will be so trim and well-behaved as that saucy craft." He nodded toward the oncoming vessel. "By all the saints, it's well that she's coming into harbor. It'll be sharp work for many a poor seaman this night, and to some, no doubt, a heavy chore to stay afloat, or off a lee shore. I sniff a storm coming on. Let's hope the lighthouse keeper has laid in a good supply of fuel for that beacon." He glanced upward to the ancient lighthouse high above the town on the crest of the chalk cliffs. Edmond's eyes followed, and then swept down toward the base of the tower to examine the remains of the crumbling fort.

"What think you of our lighthouse?" the sailor asked. "A fair sight, isn't it? Even handsomer when you finally discover its bright eye on a hellish night during a storm out there." He thrust a stubby finger seaward. "Many a poor seaman would be rotting at water's bottom if it weren't for that God-given beacon. And the body of many an honest Englishman," his voice falling to what he apparently considered a whisper though it came out as a dull roar, "will be moldering on land if that fort below isn't repaired."

"What do you mean?"

The sailor gestured across the water to the south of the grayish bulk Edmond supposed to be Baldwinesland. There lay Normandy, and Edmond understood.

"Come now," resumed the sailor, shaking off his momentary solemnity, "never let it be said that Wiglaf ever parted dry-throated from a friend. There's a goodly ale-shop just a step or so away if you're of mind to share a horn or two with me."

"With all my heart," Edmond agreed, reflecting that it was early in the afternoon, and that it might be preferable to look up Osgood closer to nightfall to avoid attracting too much attention. Besides, he was anxious to learn as much as he could in advance about the merchant. Perhaps the sailor knew him, at least by reputation. He fell in willingly beside Wiglaf, who ambled along with surprising grace and agility for so huge a man, his enormous bulk almost dwarfing the shorter yet powerfully-built Edmond.

Wiglaf nodded perfunctorily to the innkeeper as they found seats in the dark, dingy, low-ceilinged tavern. The sailor demanded two tankards of ale and as many huge portions of cake bread. Without drawing a second breath, he tossed off his ale, wiped his lips on a sleeve of his well-worn tunic, then looked inquiringly at Edmond even while booming for a refill. "I didn't catch your name, friend, though I'd guess from your manner of speaking that you hail from the West Country."

"They call me Edmond Edwysson, and I come from Bosbury." Seeing that Wiglaf was puzzled, Edmond hastily added, "It's near the Malvern Hills, north of Gloucester."

"Ah well, that's better. I know Gloucester like the back of my hand, as I do most any seaport you might name. I've knocked about a great deal the past thirty years, and there aren't many tavern keepers who haven't called for a reckoning from Wiglaf. What brings you so far from Gloucester, friend Edmond?"

"I mean to go much farther yet, to Constantinople, God willing."

Wiglaf whistled surprise. "Aye, that's farther indeed, about as far as you can go without sailing off the edge of the great ocean sea. I should know, though it's been twenty years since I've cursed the lack of good ale there."

"You've been to Constantinople?" Edmond's respect heightened. "What's it like? Is it true a man can make his fortune in the great emperor's guard?"

"Aye, make or mar, there've been many who have, I'm told, though I can't speak for myself, having left that cursed place as poor as when I arrived." Wiglaf drained his second tankard, smacked his lips, then leant forward as if to confide a secret. "You've heard of Harald Sigurdson, he who is king of Norway nowadays? Aye, well who hasn't? I was with him when he led the Varangians, the Greek emperor's corps of guards."

Edmond almost stammered astonishment. "You were with Harald Hardraade?"

"Aye, I served with him for years. Ah, those were rare, happy days, when I was young and supple, a mere slip of a lad, my waist no bigger than yours." Wiglaf sighed. "Hardraade, hard counsel, they call Harald Sigurdson, and so he is; stern and ruthless. For all that, there is some humor in him. I could tell you about the birds." He called for another tankard, drank half, wiped his lips, and ran a finger contemplatively about the rim.

"We were in Sicily besieging a fortress, cursing the defenders, stubborn knaves who kept us twiddling our thumbs outside for many a weary day. The besieged dogs of hell had plenty of food and drink, while we were dying of thirst, and almost starving. There were many among our people—and they grumbled more loudly each passing day—who pleaded with Hardraade to let them stow their gear into the baggage carts and bid the accursed stronghold and its obstinate defenders go to the devil, but Harald wouldn't hear of lifting the siege.

"He roared, 'The first one of you bastards I catch deserting I'll spit on my sword like a partridge and roast.' We knew he'd carry out his threat, that's the sort of devil he was—and is. But even as he threatened his frown melted into a cunning smile and that was even more frightening, most of us fearing he was about to make an example of one man so the rest would realize he wasn't trifling. Luckily, he had a better idea.

"He turned to me and shouted, 'Wiglaf, you're not quite as stupid as the rest. You must have noticed the flock of birds that nest around the castle?' I was so terrified when he looked at me I scarcely heard his words, and blurted out like a fool, 'Aye, my lord, there are a great many.' In truth, thousands of birds had swarmed into the air during each of our attempts to breach the castle walls, but I hadn't given them a thought.' Harald barked, 'A great many indeed, you big dolt. How many doesn't matter. What's important is that they must feed in the countryside during the day, and return to their nests at night. Wouldn't you agree, Wiglaf?' I squirmed, uneasy at how he had fixed his attention on me, and wondered like everyone else just what was on his mind. He didn't bother to explain, merely ordering us to set out snares and capture as many birds as possible, taking care not to damage their wings. When we had collected three or four dozen, Harald showed us how to prepare splinters of tarred wood and fasten them to the birds' backs. Next, he had some Greeks among us smear the splinters with wax and sulfur, stocks of which they always carried in their supply carts. It finally dawned on us what he intended to do, and we finished the task with a will.

"'Now set fire to the wood, and free the birds,' he ordered. In no time, the poor creatures, their backs alight, were winging like so many huge fireflies toward the castle. They returned to their straw nests, most of which were just below the reed-covered roof. Ah, what a despairing cry rose from the besieged when they realized what was about to happen. Soon the roofs of almost every building within the castle walls were ablaze, and the people swarmed out of the gates, begging for mercy. Harald granted them quarter for he was a fair man, if a hard one, and esteemed bravery even in a dogged enemy."

Edmond shook his head admiringly. "How many men would think of such a scheme? It's wonderful."

"There aren't many soldiers equal to Harald Sigurdson," Wiglaf agreed, wiping his mouth with his soggy sleeve. "Not that he's always wise for all his cunning. He's a bit too rash for my taste, though there's no denying he's clever enough. Just ask his enemies in Constantinople. He got away from them when they were sure he couldn't escape."

"You mean when he carried off the empress?" Edmond broke in. "My father told me he'd heard some such tale from a wandering minstrel."

Wiglaf laughed. "That just goes to show how a story can get twisted around. People have been asking me for twenty years if it's true that Harald Sigurdson carried off the Empress Zoe. As if he'd wanted to run off with that ugly old bag of bones! I tell you, as I've told everyone, that he abducted another woman, Zoe's cousin Marie. Not that the empress wouldn't make for a better story. But if you'd ever seen that old witch Zoe—and I have—you'd have chosen Marie without a second thought.

It's true Zoe was extremely fond of handsome young men, and she wasn't too squeamish about their backgrounds, so it's not unlikely Harald found favor with her. What's certain is that they fell out because Zoe became jealous of the attentions Harald was paying Marie. When he asked her permission to marry the princess, the old lady had him locked up, but we got him out before he'd spent a night in prison. He immediately led us to the docks where we found two large, unmanned galleys. We boarded them, and prepared to flee though most of us wondered how we could possibly get past the immense iron chain drawn across the mouth of the harbor. The barrier was intended to deny access to any attacker, as well as make it impossible for a vessel to leave without permission.

"Harald wasn't about to let any barrier, no matter how imposing or seemingly impregnable, hinder our escape. As soon as we pulled away from the quays, he ordered the oarsmen of each galley to stretch out full length on the benches, and told everyone else on board to shift to the stern with the baggage. With the bows of the ships almost out of the water, we rammed the chain at full speed in mid-channel until the keels hung fast on the huge iron links of the barrier. Then he ordered all those who had crowded aft to run forward. Luckily, I'd followed Harald, and his galley swung down over the chain until it floated free on the far side. Unluckily, the other galley broke in two, and many of our comrades drowned, though we were able to rescue a few before escaping from Constantinople with a fortune in treasure and the Lady Marie.

"That's the truth about Harald Sigurdson's escape from Constantinople. I was there. And it was not that old bag Zoe, but Lady Marie whom he carried off."

"Did he marry her?"

"Not likely! He put her ashore at the nearest landfall, and asked her to tell that ungrateful bitch, the Empress Zoe, that while she might treat her spineless subjects like slaves she had no power over Harald Hardraade, the son of King Sigurd of Norway."

"Where did you go from there?"

"As my infernal luck would have it, the rotgut Greek wine I was forced to drink in place of honest English ale gave me such a bellyache that Harald left me with the other sick and wounded at a God-forsaken little port in the Black Sea He promised to return soon to pick us up, but we never saw that stone-hearted bastard again. Three miserable years passed until I was able to touch the blessed earth of England once more. As for Harald, it's said he sailed all the way up a great river that empties from the north into the Black Sea to a city called Novgorod. He carried with him the great treasure he had seized in Constantinople, including my little share, which might have comforted me in old age."

Wiglaf sadly consoled himself by again draining his tankard. His spirits quickly restored by the ale, Wiglaf continued to entertain Edmond with other tales of his adventures, genuine or fabulous. He insisted that on one voyage in uncharted waters he had seen fire burning unquenched on the very surface of the water. On another, he had beheld sea serpents so huge that they dwarfed the long ships of the sea kings. The monsters had raised their frighteningly fierce heads high out of the depths to devour several terrified sailors at one swallow. He also described the strange customs of the Letts, a people who wooed their brides by competing in horse races, then carried them away at a gallop. He ran on and on, refreshing his memory with ale until the weary innkeeper finally refused to refill his tankard, pleading the lateness of the hour.

"Aye, he has the right of it," Wiglaf grudgingly admitted as he heaved his enormous bulk erect. "The hours are short and the reckoning long, as ever." He fumbled with a shriveled pouch at his girdle, then looked up sheepishly. "Strange," he mumbled. "I must've left my silver pence at home. Have you the reckoning, lad?"

Edmond suppressed a smile. The stories were well worth a bit of silver. He willingly diminished his slender inheritance even further.

"To bed, to bed we must," Wiglaf rumbled, then halted abruptly after lurching out of the tavern. "Ah, I've forgotten you're newly come to Dover. Have you a place to lay your head? I'd take you home but it'd be a sorry welcome my Hilda would give us with me being so late, let alone bringing a friend."

"Thank you, good Wiglaf, but I've come to Dover to call upon the merchant Osgood, my late father's friend. Do you know his house?"

"Aye, who doesn't? It's the finest in Dover, only a few steps from here." Wiglaf led the way unsteadily, his liquid cargo giving him a pronounced list to port.

They were soon in front of a large stone dwelling whose wings embraced a courtyard as well as an extensive garden. Here they parted, the sailor hauling up anchor and sailing bravely into the wind until he tacked out of sight around a corner. Edmond rapped tentatively on the door until, becoming impatient at the lack of a response, he began to hammer with one fist, then both.

The heavy door eventually creaked open to disclose a red-faced old man clad in a white night shirt, a nightcap pulled down over his ears. The enraged householder wielded a battle-ax in his right hand and carried a lighted rush taper in his left as he roared, "Whoever you are, I'll split your empty head for waking honest folk at this time of night."

Edmond retreated a step, then explained in a low but firm voice, "I'm Edmond, son of the Atheling Edwy, come to see Osgood the merchant."

"And I'm our lord King Edward's martyred brother, Alfred," jeered the old man as he thrust the flaming taper into Edmond's face, almost singeing his eyebrows. An intense glance, and the old man's ruddy countenance drained of color. He lowered the battle-ax with shaking hand, and gasped, "It must be truly so, young man. You're the image of your father as I knew him." Lost in wonder for a moment, he quickly recollected his duty as a host. "Come in, come in, my lord," he urged, bowing Edmond over the threshold. "Forgive me for not expecting you. Your father's last letter said it would be another year, or even longer, before he could bear to part with you. He's well, I trust."

"Edwy Ethelredson died more than a month ago."

"Holy Mother of God!" Osgood cried. "He was yet a young man."

"He was somewhat past fifty years, I believe."

"True, now that I think of it, and you would consider that old," Osgood mused. "I recall that he was only a year or two younger than me. Alas, we are frayed into old age without being aware of it. It's hard for me to think of Atheling Edwy other than in youth. When last I saw him, he wasn't much older than you now. A brave prince, yet a most unlucky one. May he fare better in heaven than he did on earth." Osgood crossed himself, then continued briskly, "But come, what an old fool you must think me to prattle on of such sad matters. You're weary. We'll find you a bed, and we can talk tomorrow."

With the taper fitfully lighting the way, the merchant led Edmond into a small enclosure curtained off from a great hall by thick, richly-embellished tapestries.

Osgood had barely wished him good night before Edmond was fast asleep, much too tired to wonder what the morrow might bring, or to reflect on the strange tales Wiglaf had told him on his first day in Dover.

Chapter Two

Adele

He heard her bell-like laughter as if in a dream, but when her sweet, low voice trilled out for a second time he became wide awake, and hesitantly, expectantly, opened his eyes to discover the source of such spontaneous merriment.

He was richly rewarded. She stood tip-toe at the entrance to his secluded nook, holding aside the tapestry shielding it from the great hall, red lips curved in impish glee, her direct gaze sparkling with a hint of mischievous spirit. Glossy black hair seething in shimmering locks set off the iridescent sea-blueness of a pair of elfin eyes. The raven curls falling to her shoulders floated like a veil against the milky whiteness of a long gown with wide-hanging full sleeves, its hem embroidered all around with sable-black dancing figurines. A golden girdle, scarcely greater in circumference than a brawny thane's upper arm torque of precious metal, embraced her minuscule waist.

"You're awake at last, sleepyhead," she said archly, then warned, "I was about to call for a pitcher of cold water so I could bring you to life."

"You wouldn't have the heart," he shivered. He was delighted at the mere sight of this beautiful child, scarce past fifteen years of age, whose emerging womanhood had not yet blunted the engaging coquetry of adolescence. "You wouldn't dare be so cruel to a humble wayfarer who is grateful for your father's kind hospitality."

"Humble indeed," she sniffed. "Father loves to tease me, and he claims you're a prince, and that I should treat you with the deference due to an atheling. As if one so high-born would come to our house, much less arrive unaccompanied at night."

"What do you know of princes, other than dreaming of them, as I imagine you must?"

She blushingly retorted, "Prince, or more likely churl, if you want to break your fast you'll have to hurry. Father may linger at table as long as he likes, but I'll not wait." She sent her ebony locks flying with a pert toss of the head, spun about with a pivot that swirled her gown, and vanished behind the tapestry.

He swiftly slipped into fresh garments he found laid out beside the bed, surprised at their perfect fit. Hunger lent impetus to the concluding touches of a toilet to which, nevertheless, he paid more attention than usual.

In spite of Edmond's protests, Osgood rose from the table in a corner of the great hall, and personally conducted his young guest to a chair of honor. Edmond was surprised, but hid his pleasure when he saw that the girl, despite her threat, had not left.

The old man smothered Edmond's objection to being treated so deferentially. "Nay, nay, my lord, I'm not so old, feeble or lacking in courtesy that I can't rise when my beloved master's son honors my house with his presence." He virtually thrust Edmond into the chair, and motioned to a servant to heap a platter with cold meats and freshly-baked bread. Edmond was astonished at the generous supply of food, and the ornate platters, utensils and drinking horns. He had grown up in the western marches where such lavish display were unknown even in most well-to-do households, much less the establishments of minor thanes, such as his father had pretended to be. Osgood's urging to fall to heartily was superfluous. Edmond's appetite was naturally robust. But he was embarrassed by his host's solicitous attention and relieved when the merchant finally yielded to repeated pleas to sit down. Even then Osgood kept an eye on the servants, making sure Edmond's plate and drinking horn were constantly replenished.

"You must forgive my Adele's rudeness in waking you," Osgood apologized, with a reproachful glance at his daughter, who seemed extremely subdued and picked fitfully at her food. "I asked her to see if you were awake, and if so to call you to the table, but I couldn't imagine she'd be so impertinent. I fear I've failed to teach her the good manners her dear, departed mother surely would have impressed on her."

Edmond stole a glance at Adele, not wishing to embarrass her further. Her father's rebuke for having been so saucy to Edmond had further flushed her naturally rosy cheeks. She took comfort in reflecting that it was hardly surprising to have laughed when Osgood had asked her to awaken the prince, as he had called the young guest who had arrived at their door the previous night. It was a standing joke between them that he would not let her marry until a prince sought her hand. Not surprisingly, she assumed he was just teasing her again when he spoke of Edmond as an atheling, a prince of the royal house of England. She had expected their visitor to be merely another merchant's son, sent on an errand by one of Osgood's many business connections. It was only when she saw how deferentially Osgood treated the newcomer that she began to suspect that for once he might have been serious, that Edmond might indeed be a prince. She flushed anew at having momentarily thought of him as "her prince", as if Osgood's habitual raillery was about to become reality. She stole a covert glance at Edmond, who was listening intently to her father while hungrily disposing of the stack of food on his platter. He appeared overly serious for someone so young. He certainly could be not much over twenty. Yet there was hint of a gentler nature in his somber brown eyes. His coarse sandy hair was close-cropped, and extraordinarily broad shoulders somewhat diminished his apparent height, though he was taller than average. She quickly looked away in confusion when his eyes momentarily met hers.

"Tell me, friend Osgood," Edmond began softly, pushing away his plate, and interrupting his host's vivid description of the battle of Assandun in which he had fought beside his guest's father, "where is the saucy girl who awakened me with such a brisk manner and pointed tongue? Such a chatterbox! An impudent maiden, if I've ever met one. Surely, this must be her timid sister, she's so quiet."

He grinned, and Osgood chuckled as Adele's face turned crimson with embarrassment. She shot to her feet, and with swishing skirts fled from the hall, leaving Edmond to reproach himself for having baited her. But he could not help smiling on comparing her embarrassment to her earlier impertinence.

"A forward girl, indeed," Osgood admitted. "Yet there is none more dutiful, even if her father is the one to say so. She comes by her impudent tongue honestly though. Her mother, a French lass, was just such a forward wench when I first met her."

"You were telling me about Assandun," Edmund prompted, suddenly eager to change the topic.

"So I was." Osgood suppressed a smile. "I was describing how your father, the Atheling Edwy, stood shoulder to shoulder with his brother, King Edmond, both dealing death with battle-axes such as the Danes use. If it had not been for your father, the king might have fallen that day. The Danes surged toward the king's standard, and twice beat down his shield only to be driven off by Edwy, who rushed to Edmond Ironside's rescue. The atheling defended his brother even when some traitors betrayed the king by deserting the battlefield. The brothers were an army in themselves. If all had fought as well as they, it might have been a different outcome for our cause." The old man's eyes dimmed at the dismal memory of an event so fatal to English arms.

"But why did my father mysteriously disappear after King Edmond died unexpectedly a few weeks later? Why did he not claim a throne to which he had as much right as anyone? Why did he fail to continue the struggle against that usurping Dane, King Cnut?" Edmond was bewildered and almost apprehensive. Had his father yielded to fear? He could not believe that. Edwy had proved his valor on other occasions besides Assandun. Why then had he fled to bury himself in a remote village during the remaining thirty-five years of his life after Cnut had seized sole power over England?

12

Osgood shook his head. "No one knows. Perhaps his brother's death took the heart out of him. For months thereafter he was like a man in a stupor. He ate little, drank less, and spoke seldom. When it was rumored that Cnut intended to hunt him down, it was all we could do to persuade him to seek refuge. Not that we ever suspected he would retreat from the world altogether, without ever returning to claim his rights. That was his decision. He was able to evade Cnut's agents in the early days after King Edmond died. Eventually the Danes thought him dead and gave up the search. For whatever reason, he chose to live out his life quietly and obscurely. He was able to do so without enemies discovering his whereabouts or true identity."

"Quietly and obscurely," Edmond whispered.

"Obscurely?" Osgood echoed almost wistfully. "Yes, to the world, to King Cnut and to the three kings since; that Danish usurper's sons Harold Harefoot and Harthacnut, and our present lord, King Edward. To them he was obscure, or rather forgotten, perhaps even altogether unknown. But to me, and to a few other loyal subjects, he remained the Atheling Edwy, the brother of Edmond Ironside, the young hero of Assandun. Thus shall I always remember him." The old man's eyes flashed momentarily with pride, then dimmed as quickly with sorrow.

They sat silently for a while before Osgood spoke again. "The past may haunt us, but you can be proud of your father, Atheling Edmond. Forget the many wasted years after Assandun, the long duration of your father's living death, if you can forgive me for calling it so. Remember only that the royal brothers Edmond and Edwy were warriors worthy of their ancestors. It's up to you now to take up the sword that fell from the hands of Edmond Ironside. His half-brother Edward—who rules now that the Dane has departed—has neither the will nor the strength to wield such a weapon. Who will defend us from the Normans, who soon may wrest England from the feeble grip of such a feckless, if godly king? He may even bequeath it to them. That it should come to this!

"You have as much right by birth to the crown of great Alfred as does this unwarlike Edward, who was enthroned by recognition of the Witangemot chiefly at the urging of Earl Godwin. The great council had no other choice when King Harthacnut finally paid the penalty for his wicked, impious ways. He was a monster, that son of King Cnut, a beast who disinterred his own brother King Harold Harefoot's body from its consecrated tomb and flung it into a ditch as if he had been a dog.

"Come, declare yourself! There are loyal men of noble birth, power and wealth who would eagerly rally to your side to make good your claim."

Osgood's enthusiasm made him seem almost young again. He gazed penetratingly at Edmond as if seeking to read his mind and discover whether he possessed the ambition and spirit of his greatest ancestors.

Edmond's heart pounded, his throat became dry, and the blood rushed to his head. He wanted to shout that Osgood should lead him to those whose support might enable him to reclaim his patrimony. His father had said he was born to be a king. If that were true then it would be betraying his forefathers not to seek the crown. Yet there was an insurmountable barrier to such a course, the promise to his father to leave England, to seek his fortunes abroad, something of which Osgood was unaware. He could not, would not disregard that pledge. He reluctantly repressed his surging pride and ambition.

"It may well be as you say, Master Osgood, but I am bound by a vow to my father to seek my fortunes abroad, not in England. He must have thought my cause to be hopeless, and feared that to press it would lead only to disaster for his people."

Osgood threw up his hands in despair, almost in horror. "He should not have extracted such a pledge from you. The will of God and the ancient customs of our people would enforce your claim. It is one thing for Edwy Ethelredson to have abandoned his rightful inheritance, his people, and his loyal friends. But it is another to deprive his true-born son of seeking what is rightfully his inheritance, the duties, honors and privileges of a king. It was wrong to do so. He wronged not only his son but his unhappy people."

Osgood's face brightened with a sudden hopeful thought.

"Was it an oath?" he demanded eagerly.

"It was a promise, but as sacred as an oath. My father insisted he could not rest in peace if I remained in England, and urged that I should give my word to leave. When I offered to take an oath, he declined to demand such a solemn undertaking. A promise is binding enough, he said, and there might be circumstances in which it might be necessary to delay or even disregard it if it did not incur dishonor to do so. But the breaking of a sacred oath would imperil my soul, and he would not bind me so irrevocably."

"Here is reason and duty, both strong and clear," Osgood cried. "Your father, were he alive and could hear my arguments, would not quibble about a promise."

Edmond hesitated momentarily as if tempted, then shook his head. As much as he wanted to tell Osgood, "Lead me to your friends. I am their man." he could not force himself to that point. True, it had been a promise not an oath, yet it had been a pledge voluntarily made by a dutiful son to a dying father. It was as sacred as if he had sworn it before the Archbishop of Canterbury.

Osgood sensed the struggle in Edmond's mind. He refused to be put off so easily and tried another approach. "How much did your father tell you of his history?"

"Virtually nothing until just during the last year," Edmond confessed. "Until then I thought of him only as a thane who for some reason had lost favor with the king, and had been forbidden his presence. He spoke very little of the past; I never dreamed that he was a son of King Ethelred, and a brother of King Edmond Ironside. When he first told me these matters just before his death I could scarcely believe what I heard."

"What did he tell you about me?"

"He told me of how you helped—nay, almost forced—him to escape King Cnut's men when they tried to find and imprison him. You warned him that they might take his life, and urged him to stay hidden until times changed for the better."

"So I did," Osgood agreed. "Didn't he tell you of the many occasions on which I implored him to declare himself? When Cnut died, Edwy had an opportunity to seize power. When that sot Harold Harefoot passed away, the people would have welcomed him instead of accepting Cnut's bastard son. When that bloodthirsty tyrant Harthacnut fell dead at Tofig the Proud's bride-ale, Edwy should have become king instead of this weak, priest-like, Norman-loving Edward."

Osgood groaned upon recalling the wasted opportunities. "Didn't he tell you about these matters? I'm not asking out of aimless curiosity, but because I want to know if you're aware of how many opportunities your father let slip away. Don't think he didn't have his chances. He did, but you may have only one, my son, if for the love I bore your father I may call you so, and now is the time to seize it."

"He mentioned some of these things," Edmond replied, his composure, if not his resolution, shaken by Osgood's vehemence. "He also told me that if I applied to the merchant Osgood, the one friend who had never failed him, his old shield-bearer would help me in whatever course I chose. I rely on that, and I ask only that you help me leave England as I promised my father I would."

Osgood still refused to give in.

"Your fortune lies here, Childe Edmond. What do you suppose will happen when this weak, timorous, and priestly shadow of a king dies? Who will take his place? He has no children by his queen, and will have none. He has vowed celibacy in his admirable but selfish piety. You are the last of the royal line of Wessex, the descendants of the great Alfred, left here in England, and none but I know of your true birth."

"What about my cousins, King Edmond Ironside's two sons?"

"Who knows if they're still alive. They are reported to be in Hungary, a remote land where it's said they've lived since fleeing England more than thirty years ago. Would they be more English than King Edward, that half-Norman, after they've been abroad almost their entire lives?

Forget about them. Your competitor lies much nearer at hand, and his growing power almost matches his boundless ambition."

"What competitor? Who?"

"Duke William of Normandy."

"He has no claim, no right."

"His strongest claim may be a mailed fist, but he does carry a dash of English blood, and he is cousin to our saintly King Edward, even if from the wrong side of the blanket. Enemies call him William the Bastard, scorning his right even to the rule of Normandy, but none can withstand him. He is a young man, bold, brave, and dominating, who knows what he wants and will stop at nothing to seize it." There was a hint of admiration in Osgood's voice, and Edmond felt the sting. It was unfair, he thought bitterly. He also knew what he wanted, but there was the promise to his father.

"It may be as you say," he said hoarsely, "but I must go abroad."

Osgood admitted defeat, sighing heavily, thinking of Edmond's father, the fire-breathing young Atheling Edwy who once had been bold to foolhardiness. What had come upon him to so cloud his spirit after the death of Edmond Ironside? He had abandoned all ambition, whether for the throne and the power it symbolized, of pomp and circumstance, and what was worst of all, the devotion to duty demanded of his descent. He had chosen to become an obscure thane living out an ordinary life far from the seat of power. Somehow this unfortunate son must have inherited the apathy and indolence of his latter years, or that of his grandfather, King Ethelred.

"Your father has wronged you, Childe Edmond," Osgood said haltingly, laboriously, as if the words stuck in his throat. "He has wronged you, and he has wronged his people, who will pay dearly before long for his desertion of them. I fear that I, a plain merchant, lacks the eloquence needed to persuade you to change your mind. Alas, we must yield to your father's demand, and bow to his wishes and yours."

"You will help me voyage to Baldwinesland?"

"Yes, though with a heavy heart. It's not far, which is all the more reason I fear the worst." The old man's voice became louder. "Mark you well; it will not be long before the Norman vaults across this narrow ditch to claim England's crown for his own. Only you could thwart him, Childe Edmond, only you."

Chapter Three

The Silver Ring

E dmond lingered alone at the table, struggling to sort out his confused thoughts and calm his emotions. Osgood's blunt talk about the duties and obligations required by his descent had hit home. Yet to face up to his heritage demanded far wider aspirations and greater dedication than called for by the modest objective of his journey to Dover. The merchant had urged him to follow a course that might lead either to disaster or the realization of the destiny inherent in his dying father's revelation. To embark on it would be to reject Edwy's command that he leave England, extracted the day before his deathbed revelation, "You were born to be a king, Edmond!" Had Edwy in his final moments regretted having insisted upon his son's solemn promise? Could he have been attempting to release Edmond from having to honor it by affirming his right to England's crown?

Edmond rejected the temptation to rationalize his father's final intention. Conjecture was useless, duty clear. His devotion to Edwy had been too strong to allow him to dishonor his memory by disregarding his wishes. There was no choice. He would obey and leave England.

Light footsteps and the soft swish of a gown interrupted his preoccupation. Adele stood before him. But such a change had come over her. Gone was the saucy tilt of nose, the arch smile, the laughing curve of roseate lips. Confronting him instead was a sad-faced girl with downcast glance and tear-reddened eyes. She struggled to speak, and when she did her voice dwindled to a whisper.

"Childe Edmond, forgive me if I've offended you," she murmured. "I didn't know who you were, and my father has teased me so often that..." She hesitated, unable to complete her self-abasement.

Astonished, Edmond jumped to his feet to clasp her trembling hands. "You needn't humble yourself before me, Adele," he assured her. "If there's any apology to be made, I should be the one to offer it. I mocked you thoughtlessly just to make sport. It was unkind."

"But how could I, a humble merchant's daughter, so forget myself with you, an atheling, a prince," she wailed, tears welling.

He gently grasped her chin and tilted it up the better to smile into those blue eyes as he wiped away her tears.

"You make too much of a trifle," he breathed. "If I am a prince, who knows it but your father, myself, and none beside. To the world, I'm a lesser thane like my father, a nobleman it's true, yet without influence, wealth, or even a tiny plot of land. So did my father leave me and so must I be content to stay. As for what happened today, why what sort of a world would it be if a pretty girl couldn't tease a foolish young man?"

Comfort lay in those friendly words, and Adele brightened. Suddenly aware that Edmond held her hands, she gently pulled away. He yielded reluctantly. She curtseyed as if to leave and he tried to detain her by capturing her hands again.

"I must return to my duties, Childe Edmond," she pleaded, but with only half a voice and less heart.

"Is not one of your duties to act as hostess to your father's guests, and am I not the sole visitor in his house?" he demanded. She could not and would not deny it. "Come, let's be friends. You needn't be so formal as to call me Childe Edmond. Let it be just Edmond, and I will call you, if I may, simply Adele. Is it agreed?"

She nodded, with downcast eyes.

"Then let it be Edmond and Adele. I have no grand title and seek none," he said, striving to accept the full sense of his declaration. "Come, show me about the house. My father and I lived in a simple, small cottage with few comforts. I would like to see how a merchant of Dover dwells."

She danced along beside him; her usual buoyant spirits restored, and chattered without letup. Osgood's house was splendidly furnished for that rude age. Richly embroidered silken hangings bedecked and partitioned the great hall, which had as its main feature an enormous fireplace. More chairs, benches, tables, beds, and other furniture, including many heavy pieces of plate, were gathered in that one house than Edmond had ever seen altogether. Osgood clearly had prospered enormously from trading in woolens, and other goods. Many a wealthy thane, and even the greatest nobles of England, the earldormen, would have been content with humbler surroundings.

Edmond, however, even while he nodded approval of everything Adele pointed out, and pretended to listen earnestly to her chatter, cared little about the house itself, impressive as it was. He was totally engrossed in her. The country girls of his western shire were not remotely like this feather-footed, cream-skinned delicate creature with such scintillating eyes. A few had been pretty enough in a suntanned, wind-swept way, but they were fated to wilt quickly under the strain of the coarse work and hard lives that were their inevitable lot.

This enchantress obviously came from a different race. She had been nourished like an exquisite blossom in a lovingly-tended garden. He could not stop marveling at her fair skin, blue eyes, scarlet lips, gentle swell of her budding breasts under the bodice of the neatly-fitting gown, and even the diminutiveness of her fluttering feet as she tripped through the hall and into the bower, pointing to this and that with infectious enthusiasm. He looked and listened but only her tantalizing image made any real impression.

"And this," she was saying, "this ring has hung upon this nail ever since I can remember."

She pointed toward a rusty nail projecting from a wall at a man's height above the floor. A ring hung from it, apparently of silver, though so tarnished as to be scarcely recognizable as precious metal. He unthinkingly reached for the ring, attracted by an inscription which was barely visible beneath the dark discoloration.

"No, no, don't remove the ring, Edmond," Adele cried in alarm. "My father has cautioned me that no one must touch it until its rightful owner comes to claim it. So many times I've longed to snatch it off that nail, but I dared not disobey Father."

"Well then, we'll respect his wish," Edmond agreed. Turning away on hearing approaching footsteps, he saw a smiling Osgood.

"Take the ring, Childe Edmond," Osgood urged solemnly. "Don't hesitate. It's yours. It has been kept for you, and you alone have the right to wear it."

Osgood's earnest, almost grand manner sent a shiver down Edmond's spine. He slowly, reverently reached for the circlet of blackened silver. Momentarily forgetting the inscription, he was about to slip the ring on his finger to try it on for size when Osgood interrupted, "Wait, my lord! Don't forget to examine the words engraved on it."

It was difficult to make them out even though Edmond had learned to read well. He inwardly blessed the monk Eanric, who had taught him his letters; a skill denied most nobles and even churchmen, let alone common people. He carefully rubbed off enough tarnish to be able to decipher the inscription, "AELFRED MEC HEHT GEWYRCAN", or "Alfred ordered me to be made." A writhing dragon, the royal ensign of the West Saxons, was engraved on the ring's inner surface.

"This is the regal ring of King Alfred, your ancestor," Osgood explained. "It was handed down to your uncle Edmond Ironside, who wore it as did his forefathers. When he was dying, he handed it to your father, who entrusted it to me for safekeeping until he chose to reclaim it. He hung it on that nail, directing me never to permit anyone other than its rightful owner to remove it. During all the many years it has been kept there, I've never permitted anyone to touch it, not even to clean it. Now it can be burnished bright once more because its true owner has come to claim it. Take it. Accept it. This precious, hallowed badge of the House of Wessex belongs to you alone, Childe Edmond."

"I may have the right to it, as you say, good Osgood, but am I worthy of accepting and wearing such a sacred heirloom?" Edmond whispered doubtfully, fingering the ring nervously, and reading the inscription over and over.

"Take it! You have it in you to become far more deserving of it than the priest-like weakling king who sullies our throne and mocks the very title by his supine inaction."

Osgood grasped Edmond's right hand, and reverently slipped the ancient ring on his index finger. It fit perfectly, yet it seemed to Edmond that this trifling circlet of silver was far heavier than the cumbersome shield he had carried when his father had taught him how to wield arms.

On completing what he obviously considered to be a sacred duty, Osgood silently retreated, leaving Adele and Edmond to resume their tour of the building. Edmond forced himself to appear attentive to her words as she explained some unusual feature, but his mind was in turmoil. The previous vague temptation to bid for the crown, come what may, which he had suppressed firmly despite all of Osgood's urging, suddenly became overwhelming. The ancient ring on his finger, a bauble worn more than one hundred and fifty years earlier by King Alfred, seemed to lend enormous weight to his claim. If the throne of Alfred was rightfully his by inheritance, as his father and Osgood had suggested it to be, then it was almost his sacred duty to unseat the Frenchified King Edward, who was distributing England's wealth to his Norman favorites with scant regard for his own subjects. Edmond involuntarily clasped the dagger at his side as he thought of his half-uncle, so unfit either by nature or disposition to rule.

Unaware of his inward turmoil, Adele interrupted his thoughts by asking, "Will you sit here, Edmond?" She had halted before a stone bench in the garden, which extended to an elevated prospect overlooking the sea. "This is my favorite spot. I love to linger here and look toward France, my mother's homeland."

He gazed in the direction to which she was pointing and discerned a gray mass looming over the water on the far edge of the eastern horizon. A brilliant sun made the continent seem nearer than it really was, and thus all the more menacing because it emphasized England's vulnerability to invasion. He wondered what Baldwinesland was like. He soon would know, he reflected with a tinge of regret. He could not break that promise to his father, no matter how earnestly he might wish to do so.

"Have you ever been across the water?" he asked Adele.

"Oh, yes, several times. Last summer my father took me along on business to the city of Caen in Normandy." Her eyes shone. "A wonderful town, and we saw so much; even a procession led by Duke William. Such a grim young man." She shuddered, but the Norman ruler obviously had made a great impression on her.

"Was he as handsome as he's said to be?" asked Edmond with a half-smile.

She crimsoned. "I didn't notice."

"If I ever chance to meet him, I'll inspect him closely, and tell you my opinion."

Adele changed the subject. "Will you stay with us long?"

"No. As soon as your father can arrange it, I'll cross the sea. I may journey a great way to enlist in the Greek emperor's guard, and rise to become a second Harald Hardraade. Or I may go to Rome, as many pilgrims do for the salvation of their souls, and seek the Pope's blessing before I venture farther."

"If only I were a man!" Her unfeminine outburst astonished him. "If only I could travel and see the world, make a pilgrimage to Rome, or wander in search of adventure. You're so lucky to be a man. You may go wherever you wish, do whatever you please. But what can a woman look forward to other than to marry or become a nun? I'll have to wed some dull son of one of father's merchant friends, and spend the rest of my life catering to him hand and foot."

"It can't be as bad as all that," he assured her, stifling an impulse to laugh. What a strange creature she was, so womanly in form but unfeminine in spirit.

"How would you know?" she retorted indignantly. "You can't understand how I feel. You're free to do whatever you like, to wander where you choose. You can seek adventures, explore distant lands. What can you know about how a poor young girl feels?" She was genuinely stirred up, a flush suffusing her cheeks, admirably setting off her blue eyes and sable hair.

"Nay, nay, I meant no harm or mockery by my careless words." He reached for her soft hands, and she made only token resistance before surrendering them. "I meant only that the young girls I've known—not that there have been many—would gladly change places with you. Marriage to a wealthy merchant would be far more than they ever could dare hope for or even dream of."

"I know," she admitted, her agitation subsiding, "I suppose it is willful and strange of me to wish it could be otherwise. I must inherit these strange notions from my mother, or so my father never tires of telling me."

"Was she as beautiful as you?" It was more than he meant to say, and more fervent and earnest than was proper. She was startled, and freed her hands from his grasp.

"I've neglected my duties far too long," she snapped, and sprang up to leave.

"No, stay a while longer, and talk to me," he pleaded. "I shouldn't have said what I did, though it was sincerely meant." He could not help adding the last, as if to extenuate his rashness. He gained his point, and she sat down again.

Even while they chatted more idly now, he realized how much he was attracted to her. The feeling was new for him. Though he had carried on several casual affairs with country girls in the neighborhood of Bosbury, none had gone beyond fulfilling an appetite, merely yielding to the pull of strong physical attraction.

This girl, however, was indescribably different. She was so bright, so intense, as well as so beautiful, that he could not regard her casually, but felt compelled to delve into her personality and way of looking at the world, as well as to marvel at the quicksilver fluctuation of her moods. Even more mysterious to him was that he derived such pleasure from merely being near her, let alone reveling in her lively conversation. Her father had seen to it that she had been educated far more carefully than was customary among women of her station in life. Edmond discovered that she knew more about some aspects of the world than he did, though he was ever hungry for knowledge and information.

If Osgood had not sent Vebba, a house churl, to summon them to the table they would have talked on far into the afternoon.

Chapter Four

Royal Armor

I f ever time flew it was during the agreeable days spent in Adele's company. Not that Edmond was entirely aware of how great a share of his thoughts she occupied while Osgood was completing preparations for his departure from England. He was content to enjoy the pleasures of her presence without dwelling on what drew him to her side. His infatuation, if that is what it was, made it easier to avoid rigorous, and possibly painful, consideration of the wisdom of his decision to go abroad. Whatever the cause, he felt himself at a loss when away from Adele. Whenever her household duties permitted, he clung to her side to share her laughter, enjoy her teasing, and playfully annoy her by speculating at length about what strange and wonderful sights and adventures he was likely to encounter across the seas.

It went no further than this innocent flirtation, even though Edmond tried occasionally to carry his attentions beyond an infrequent almost brotherly kiss. But if his hands strayed, she instantly stiffened, scolded him, and threatened to avoid him altogether. Or if a kiss became too prolonged, she broke into a gale of laughter which was sure to disconcert him. He would jump up, ready to leave her, but then would think better of it, resume his place beside her and promise not to blunder again.

In the aftermath, he was always relieved that she had not yielded to his imprudent surges of ardor. It would have been ill repayment for Osgood's devotion, loyalty and generosity. Yet her maidenly modesty surprised him because it was so unlike the free ways of the uninhibited country girls of his home shire, who had considered it an honor to lie with their thane's son. Lovemaking seemed as natural to them and him as eating and drinking. True the church had its inflexible mandates against fornication and adultery, but only the truly religious and those past caring took them to heart. It was also true that King Edward was revered by the clergy and the pious for allegedly having taken a vow never to lie with his wife, the Lady Edith. But Edmond, like most of King Edward's less unearthly subjects, was appalled at what he considered a strange, unnatural and unkingly pledge, a betrayal of a monarch's duty to his people to provide them with a successor to his throne. He might envy uncle Edward his kingship, but that was one royal resolution he would never imitate. Nevertheless, he was thankful that his half-hearted attempts to court Adele met invariably with a rebuff. To his wonder, he discovered that her resistance had the effect of making her seem all the more desirable.

As a result, he was surprisingly chagrined when Osgood finally announced that the arrangements for his departure were nearly complete.

"You spare me so little time, Master Osgood," he snapped almost petulantly. "I've scarcely had a chance to catch my breath and rest my sore feet from my long walk across the breadth of England, and now I must be off again."

"You've been with us a week, my lord, and I thought you impatient to set off," Osgood reminded him, with a hint of amusement. "You know it's not my wish that you depart. If I thought it would change your mind, as old as I am I would sink to my knees and beg you to remain in England, where you're needed."

"I know, my loyal old friend, I know," Edmond replied. "If I had the right to do so, I'd prefer to remain. There's much to keep me here—my land, my people, my friends," he added hastily. "Yet I suppose it's just as well that you've wasted no time in arranging matters for my journey. Believe me, I'm grateful, Master Osgood."

"What I've done, I can undo, my lord," Osgood said, sensing Edmond's inward conflict. "Stay and seek the lordship of England, which is your God-given birthright, your duty, your fitting ambition."

"I can't disregard my solemn promise to my father."

"Aye, that unhappy promise," Osgood groaned. "It seems there's no shaking your resolution, so if there's no help for it you might as well leave as soon as possible. First of all, go to the shop of the armorer Aegelsig, whom I've told to expect you. My brother-in-law will fit you out with the weapons and armor I've asked him to prepare for you. I trust they'll be acceptable. Equipped with those, I'd wager every lord in England will envy you—even such great men as Earl Harold Godwinson, and that devilish brother of his, Earl Sweyn Godwinson. Then, from Aegelsig's shop, proceed to the dockside tavern where you'll find a sailor, one Master Wiglaf. I've asked him to make arrangements for your passage across the Channel. By the bye, he says he has met you, though I never put much stock in anything that tun of a man tells me he's such a spinner of fantastic tales."

"It's true enough we met my first day in Dover. We lifted a horn or two of ale together, and he amused me with some wonderful stories."

"You paid the reckoning, that's certain," Osgood chuckled. "No matter. He's a good man for all that, especially about seafaring matters, though much too careless about money to my way of thinking."

Edmond readily found the armorer's shop. The din of metal forging metal, wheezing blast of bellows, and raging roar of a blazing fire melded into a deafening cacophony within a hundred yards of the building. Edmond picked his way through a courtyard littered with junked metal weapons, armor, tools and household utensils of every description to enter Aegelsig's smoke-filled workroom. A short, fat, sweat-bathed, red-faced, middle-aged workman wiped blackened hands on a leather apron, gave an encouraging box on the ear to an apprentice, and bustled forward to greet the visitor.

"What can I do for you, young man?" Aegelsig barked condescendingly. The master armorer often dealt with men of high rank, and Edmond's plain attire failed to impress him. "Is it a shield you want, or a fine hauberk? I've plenty of both in stock, as well as swords and helms of the best quality. Far too many, to tell the truth. The times are bad for our trade." He waved his begrimed hands toward the stacks of armor and weapons ranged along the walls of the room. His stock included dozens of shields both kite-shaped and round, and a large supply of helms, hauberks, swords, lances, battle-axes, and even more exotic military equipment.

"I suppose a period of peace would be ruinous to your business," Edmond sympathized, though he saw at a glance that Aegelsig had not missed many meals. "That should make me all the more welcome. I've been sent by Master Osgood, who calls me Thane Edmond."

The armorer's cool, supercilious attitude instantly became deferential, and his shrewd eyes lost their wariness as he snatched off his leather cap in respect. "My lord, I didn't expect you today, Osgood not having told me just when you were to honor me with your visit. No matter. Your equipment has been ready for many a day and, even if I am the one to say it, few can boast of carrying its equal, and I know of none better."

Aegelsig bustled into a corner, lifted the lid of a rude but substantial chest, and carefully removed an armload of weapons and armor under whose weight he staggered toward Edmond. He deposited the heavy burden on the floor as gently as if it consisted of fragile glass, then selected a piece to exhibit to his caller.

"Examine this shield if you care to, my lord," Aegelsig said almost reverently.

The glow of the armorer's face matched the gleam of the polished surface as he gazed with almost paternal pride on the kite-shaped shield of leather stretched tightly over a wooden frame. Its borders were decorated with brass studs which also adorned several bands radiating from a single boss projecting slightly from its geometrical midpoint. The bands were engraved with the figures of real and mythical beasts—lions, griffins, dragons, and unicorns.

"Have you ever beheld its like, Thane Edmond?" Aegelsig demanded.

"It's almost too fine to risk damaging in battle," Edmond replied, lost in admiration of the exquisite craftsmanship. "A work of art, a wonderful product of an artificer's skill." He hesitated momentarily, reluctant to risk offending Aegelsig, then plunged on. "But tell me, good Aegelsig, why is it shaped in the Norman style? A round buckler might be more suitable to a true Englishman."

"Not so, my lord, not so. Round no longer is in common use among the better sort." Aegelsig lifted his hands in dismay. "This shape is preferred by all the greatest noblemen, Saxons as well as Normans. Earl Harold favors such a one, though not nearly so fine, if I may be so bold as to say."

"You know best, I'm sure," Edmond said placatingly. "I do remember now that Earl Ralph, our king's nephew, carried a similar shield when I watched him lead his troop through Bosbury on his way to punish the Welsh raiders."

"Not so choice, my lord, not nearly so well crafted," sniffed Aegelsig, incensed at the comparison. "There's not another in England, nay not in the world, I'm sure, that can match it. The same, I can honestly claim, is true of the sword, the hauberk, helm, or the rest of the gear my good kinsman, Master Osgood, commissioned me to fashion for you."

"Especially for me? Osgood did this to prepare for my coming?" Edmond was astounded.

"Yes, my lord, for you alone, none else. A year or so ago Osgood asked me to prepare weapons and armor of the best quality, and to spare neither skill nor expense of material. He did not tell me for whom it was intended, but charged, 'Make them fit for a king.'" Aegelsig fondled the shield as lovingly as if it were a newborn baby. "I pride myself that I've done so. I assure you, my lord, that not King Edward, or that Norman bastard, Duke William, or Earl Godwin and any of his proud sons, not even Earl Harold, can boast of possessing the equal of the equipment I've fashioned for you."

Edmond was lost in admiration as Aegelsig successively displayed each item of his handiwork for inspection. So Osgood had been preparing for years against his coming! The merchant must have paid a fortune to this incomparably skillful artisan to make certain that he, Edmond Edwysson, an untried lad whom he knew of only as the son of the prince he once had served as shield-bearer, would be outfitted in royal style.

He was embarrassed at how ill he had repaid the unlimited and unselfish loyalty and devotion of his father's old attendant. He had rejected Osgood's repeated pleas to remain in England and struggle for his birthright. It was as if he were scorning the old man's unwavering support. He nervously twisted the bit of silver that once had adorned King Alfred's finger. In his father's hall, wandering minstrels had often recounted the legends of how Alfred, at times a fugitive with a mere handful of followers, never had yielded to misfortune, but with unbroken determination and courage had overcome all adversity to seat himself firmly on the throne that belonged to him by inheritance. The ring seared Edmond's finger as if made of white-hot iron rather than cold silver.

"How do you like this hauberk, Thane Edmond?" Aegelsig's question broke into Edmond's thoughts. "Have you ever held one so light, almost as if it were made of silk?"

Edmond shook his head in wonder after picking up the tangled warbyrnie, or hauberk as the Normans called the coat of mail, and shaking it out to examine it more closely. It was a long, narrow, blouse-like protective garment with three-quarter sleeves, formed of interlocked iron rings. He put it on to find it fitted perfectly, though it was hardly so light as Aegelsig claimed. The warbyrnie was divided at bottom so that its wearer could wrap it around each thigh when mounted, or when on foot would be able to cover his legs without impeding his stride.

"If it were made of linen, it wouldn't weigh much less," Edmond exaggerated, drawing another smile from the armorer. He laid down the hauberk to pick up and heft a battle-ax. "This is well-honed, with good balance," he commented of the deadly weapon with its short handle.

"Its temper is true, Thane Edmond," Aegelsig beamed, running a thumb along the sharp edge of the ax blade after Edmond handed it back. "But these are mere toys, my lord. Here's a weapon which has not its twin in all Christendom, or elsewhere, I wager."

He carefully lifted a long, narrow object wrapped tightly in thick cloth, which he meticulously removed to reveal a sword within its scabbard. But far from an ordinary scabbard! It dazzled Edmond with its damascening of delicate floral patterns of gold. Semi-precious stones glittered at the intersections of the gold tracery. The sword within the magnificent casing was tri-lobed like the battered old weapon hanging from Edmond's belt, and its hilt was damascened in a pattern complementing that of the scabbard. Pride and exultation swept Edmond as he unsheathed the sword and flourished it overhead to test its balance.

"You'll never see its mate, my lord," Aegelsig boasted. "It's fashioned after a rare skill I learned when I was a prisoner of the Saracens for long, weary years." He lovingly caressed the delicate pattern of the damascening, a process yet almost unknown in England but highly-developed among craftsmen in the East.

"You fought against the Saracens?" Edmond's interest shifted from the sword and scabbard to their maker.

"It was long, long ago, Thane Edmond. When I was a lad, younger even than you, my father apprenticed me to a master blacksmith. I soon became tired of being beaten black and blue every other day and ran off. I stowed away on a ship bound for Normandy, where I took service with William de Hauteville, a hard, cruel lord, but a brave and crafty soldier. He led us on campaign in Sicily, where I soon had good reason to wish I'd stayed at home because I fell into the hands of the Saracens. How was I to know that to become their prisoner was to be the making of me? My captor sold me as a slave to a wonderfully-skilled master craftsman in metal, and he taught me the secrets of the trade I've put to good use since my escape."

"You have no reason to regret your adventures then, Master Aegelsig?"

"Not now, but when I was first taken by the Saracens I would've given you a different answer, that's for certain," chuckled Aegelsig.

After lavishly praising Aegelsig's skill, and requesting him to send the accouterments to Osgood's house, Edmond headed for the inn at which he was to meet Wiglaf. He found the sailor surrounding a corner table.

"Good day, Thane Edmond," Wiglaf bellowed. "You'll have something to wet our parched throats before our good host runs out of his finest ale? By the holy rood, it's dry work waiting for you."

Edmond grinned on noticing an empty tankard on the table. Wiglaf's complaint about "dry work" was vastly overstated.

"A sip or two, if you like," he agreed. "But I'm eager to see the ship as soon as possible, Master Wiglaf."

"A sip? Two sounds better," Wiglaf laughed, then rapped the table and waited impatiently for the host to refill his tankard, before raising it joyfully. "Here, let me sip slow and easy to settle the stomach, then we'll be off to the quay to inspect the vessel, not that she's much to look at. My good friend, Master Lewin, who'll take you across in the *Eldrytha*, is probably impatiently awaiting us."

Edmond was as good as his word, taking only a single sip before setting down his tankard and expecting the sailor to do the same. Wiglaf refused to be hurried, however. He was bent on savoring the ale drop by drop. Edmond fell to musing about Adele until a strident, clamorous, rising voice caught his attention.

"No, by the thunderer, no!" A slim, pale, elegantly-dressed young man sprang to his feet at a table across the room, and thumped the floor with a scabbard. "You can tell your master I'll see him go to hell before I'll let you thieving Normans outwit me." He seized a tankard from the table and flung it at his companion, a huskily-built, older man dressed in the Norman fashion, who ducked just in time to avoid being struck in the head. His enraged companion, straw-colored mustaches bristling, face flushed, stalked out of the inn after flinging two or three silver pennies at the astonished innkeeper. The Norman settled back at his table, nursing a flagon of wine with a surly grin.

"Devil take me if I've ever seen that hot-headed young man before," Wiglaf commented. "Still, he reminds me of someone I've met. Some earl or thane, I imagine. Probably some nobleman's son."

Edmond shrugged. "Does it matter? Are you ready to leave?"

Wiglaf replied by hauling himself to his feet. "Never fear, the good ship *Eldrytha* won't sail without you. What a name for that old scow!"

Master Lewin proved to be a short, bandy-legged, weather-beaten seaman of indeterminate age. He invited Edmond and Wiglaf aboard the *Eldrytha* with a friendly hail. To call the *Eldrytha* a ship was to flatter her. She was little more than an oversized old boat built of planks laid with each one overlapping the upper edge of the one immediately beneath it. The craft carried a single yard and a lugsail that when new had been embellished with a colorful design which the ravages of wind, water and time long since had churned into a variegated mud-like hue.

"Aye, it'll be a pleasure to take you across, Thane Edmond." The weathered seams of Lewin's face crinkled into deep furrows intended for a smile. "Friend Wiglaf tells me that Master Osgood wants us to take good care of you, and so we shall. We might have to if it's true, as Wiglaf says, you've never been to sea." Edmond admitted that he had never boarded a ship, drawing a snicker from Lewin. "You've something to learn, my lord. Yet it's only a short haul to Baldwinesland, and with Wiglaf and my two knaves as crew, we'll fetch across in no time. If weather and wind favor us, and it's your pleasure, we can lift anchor at break of day."

Edmond nodded agreement, and cast a final, dubious glance at the little craft bobbing at anchor, then peered across the white-capped sea toward the horizon. The coast of Baldwinesland was concealed by mist but he felt it beckoning. He became aware of growing excitement. He was ready to obey his father's final wish.

Chapter Five

Battle of Dover

"You're determined to leave us then, my lord?" Osgood's husky voice expressed a regret mirrored far more gently and poignantly in Adele's downcast, misted eyes.

"If the wind blows fair, and Master Lewin is of the same mind as when I left him, we set sail in the morning." Edmond's eyes met Adele's. She immediately looked away, unwilling to let him suspect her emotion.

"Master Aegelsig's apprentice has delivered your weapons and armor, my lord," Osgood continued. "It may have been presumptuous, but when your father first intimated that some day he would send you to me, I thought it best to order the equipment against your coming. Even Aegelsig, with all his skill, needed time to fashion the fine accouterments one of your rank should carry. I hope they please and content you, and that you think them suitable."

"Why they're magnificent, matchless, good Osgood." Edmond searched for appropriate adjectives with which to express his gratitude. "Not even a king's wergeld would suffice to repay you for what you've done on my behalf, but, if God wills it, someday I hope to do so."

"No need, my son, no need," Osgood mumbled, so moved by Edmond's earnestness as to momentarily forget his customary deference. "I am glad these military baubles please you, but the liberality of your uncle and father long ago compensated me more than amply for their value." His upraised right arm swept around the ornately furnished hall. "God's blessing, King Edmond Ironside's bounty, Childe Edwy's generosity and an old soldier's thrift and good fortune have enabled me to prosper, as you can see."

Osgood left the hall as usual after supper, but not before promising to accompany Edmond to the ship at dawn. Edmond and Adele lingered at the table, as did Freya, a middle-aged serving woman whom Osgood obviously had delegated to be his daughter's chaperone. Adele was intent on a piece of intricate needlework, and frequently consulted Freya as to its progress. Edmond pretended to be lost in thought while stealing an occasional glance at her. He was astonished to realize how much he regretted leaving her the next morning, almost surely forever.

Adele finally looked up. "Will you send my father word of how you fare, Thane Edmond?" She was careful to sound unemotional, and hastily added, "I'm sure my father will want to know how you're getting along abroad."

"You, of course, wouldn't really want to hear about the rough life of a vagabond soldier, would you?" He felt compelled to tease her.

She did not rise to the bait. "I love hearing of the marvels travelers behold in foreign lands, and the strange, exciting adventures they encounter." she explained.

"Nothing more?" He sounded disappointed.

"Nothing more!" She was emphatic, if not entirely truthful.

"I owe your father a great deal, he has been so kind and generous. It would be ungrateful of me not to send him word of how I'm faring."

"Would that be your only reason for writing to him?"

"Could there be another one?" It was his turn to be less than candid.

"Oh, I suppose not."

"Perhaps you'll also want to read my letters?" he ventured.

"Perhaps." She was curt, pretending indifference. As if to be polite, she added, "Where are you going first?"

"Master Lewin said he would land me at a town called Boulogne. I'm not certain where I'll head from there. Eventually, I hope to join the great emperor's guard in Constantinople."

"Do you indeed?" Her eyes glowed despite her pretense of indifference. "They say it's a wonderful city, the greatest, the richest in the world, with towers reaching to the sky, and palaces extending out of sight. Master Aegelsig has often spoken of it. If only I could see it!" The conclusion was wistful.

"If only I could take you with me!" he blurted, astounded at his own impetuosity. It was a ridiculous thing to say, fantastic and unrealistic, but it had escaped his lips. She was startled, but did not speak.

He longed to pull her into his arms, but Freya sat impassively next to her, betraying no sign of having heard a word of their conversational duel. She was an insurmountable barrier to even innocent physical contact between him and Adele. To his delighted surprise, Adele suddenly asked the woman to fetch more thread from another part of the house. As soon as the domestic was out of sight, Edmond reached for Adele. She laughingly permitted him to wrap his arms around her, and their lips touched for an instant before she disengaged herself, a blush suffusing her cheeks. By the time Freya returned, she was placidly back at her needlework as if nothing had taken place.

A clatter of horse hooves, stomping feet, and shouts from outside the building penetrated their idyll. Someone was banging imperiously on the massive oak door of the great hall. Vebba quickly appeared and rushed into the entryway to find out what was causing the tumultuous commotion. As soon as the churl opened the door, he was shoved back, but then stood his ground to block the passage.

"You can't enter unless my master gives leave," he protested shrilly.

"Aside, churl! Summon your master!" The accent was French, and was accompanied by the clank of armor and the rasp of weapons. From where they sat, Edmond and Adele could not see who was at the door, but soon heard Osgood's familiarly slow and heavy footsteps as he approached the doorway from another part of the building.

"What's this all about, Vebba?" he asked.

"This Norman knight demands to see you, Master Osgood." Reassured by his master's presence, the servant spoke more calmly. "He says that his master, Count Eustace of Boulogne, intends to stay here overnight."

"Yes, that's my lord's command, so make ready for him immediately," the Norman at the door interrupted arrogantly. "Count Eustace will arrive soon from the ale shop by the wharf. It has been a tiring journey from King Edward's court at Gloucester. The count requires a good night's rest before we set sail in the morning for Boulogne. He's not accustomed to being kept waiting by insolent churls."

"By what right do you demand to stay in my house?" Osgood roared in outrage.

"Your king's command, merchant, and that should satisfy better men than you," the Norman snapped. "The count, as you surely must know, is your King Edward's brother-in-law. The king has commanded that all his subjects must regard and treat his brother as they would his royal self. Come, come, fellow, see to it that the king is obeyed, and do so at once. My master won't be defied without punishing such insolent behavior."

"Not even King Edward may cross my threshold without my permission," Osgood shouted, stung beyond endurance by the Norman's arrogance, "even though he wears England's crown. As for your count, he's no lord of mine, nor that of any Englishman. He can stay at the inn, and be damned!"

Enraged by Osgood's defiance, the Norman shoved him violently aside and forced his way into the hall, followed by two men-at-arms, who at his command seized the merchant. As soon as the commotion began, Edmond had urged Adele to withdraw to a distant portion of the hall, and she and Freya began to slip toward her secluded, curtained-off bower. As the women fled, the Norman knight caught a glimpse of Adele before she and Freya vanished behind the hangings at the far end of the building.

"By our lady, there's a tasty wench," the Norman shouted. "Count Eustace can warm his bed properly here tonight."

The insinuation enraged Osgood beyond endurance, and indignation gave him the strength to tear away from the grip of his guards. With surprising agility for one of his age and bulk, he tore a battle-ax from the wall, then rushed at the knight. But the old man's dexterity was unequal to his fury, and the ax stroke glanced off the dodging Norman's helm, without even stunning him. One of the men-at-arms clouted Osgood with a mace, and the merchant sank to the floor, his blood instantly staining the rushes.

By the time Osgood fell, Edmond had snatched up the nearest weapon from among the stack deposited by Aegelsig's apprentice earlier in the day in a corner of the hall, and begun to rush to Osgood's aid. He unsheathed his sword and confronted the intruders almost before they became aware of his presence. He was so enraged as well as heartsick at the sight of Osgood sweltering in his own blood, that he threw away all caution. His headlong rush drove the three Normans almost out of the hall, and he skillfully kept them at bay in the narrow entryway until a half dozen townsmen, summoned by Vebba, arrived to threaten the foreigners from the rear. Edmond finally penetrated the knight's link mail with a sword thrust.

"God help me," the Norman gasped in French as he twisted to the ground, bleeding copiously. Their leader fallen, his two men-at-arms fled toward the harbor, where the count and the rest of his retinue were as yet unaware of the deadly tumult.

Edmond hurried back into the house, heedless of the constantly increasing crowd of Dover's townspeople swarming by the door. A tearful, sobbing Adele and a distraught Vebba knelt beside Osgood, fumblingly attempting to stem the flow of blood by bandaging the merchant's gaping head wound. Osgood was conscious but it was obvious he would not survive.

"A priest, Vebba, go fetch a priest!" Edmond urged softly. The distraught servant obeyed mutely, and Edmond knelt beside Adele. Osgood's breath came in gasps. With great effort, he began to speak despite Adele's and Edmond's protests.

"No, no, I must have my say before it's too late," he whispered huskily. "My sweet Adele, my poor orphan child, go to your uncle Aegelsig. He'll care for you and do what's best. He knows my affairs. I've entrusted everything to him in the event of my death. He and good Maude will be a second father and mother to you." His voice weakened so that his words were scarcely distinguishable. "You'll leave England in the morning, my lord?" Edmond detected the reproach in the dying man's look. It was an appeal to remain, to help punish the Normans, to prevent other misdeeds such as this. Edmond felt a surge of hatred for the arrogant foreigners who had struck down his father's old friend in cold blood and without cause—no, his own friend, his faithful old counselor.

"I stay!" he replied. His declaration erupted on a spearhead of decision. He thrilled with a fierce joy at liberating himself so impetuously from the solemn, yet now seemingly ill-advised, pledge to his father.

With waning strength, Osgood fumbled for Edmond's ring finger. Edmond helped to raise the old man's head so he could kiss the silver insignia of royalty. "Your father in heaven will bless you as I do now," Osgood whispered. "The crown, King Edmond! The crown, my lord! I see you with a crown on your head." The words were his last.

Adele's sobs distracted Edmond from pondering Osgood's dying vision. She knelt in prayer beside the body, tears streaming. "It's my punishment," she moaned. "Oh God, pardon my transgression for having been tempted to sin. I would have sinned, and you have punished me. Father, forgive me, forgive your erring daughter." She flung herself across the corpse, sobbing as if her heart were broken. Edmond tried to comfort her, but she repulsed him with a look almost of hatred. All because of an innocent kiss? It could not be. Or could it? He was dumbfounded.

By this time, the crowd of townsmen around Osgood's house had increased to more than two hundred. The uproar was deafening as they raucously swore to wreak vengeance on the Normans. It diminished only as they entered the hall one-by-one to file in reverent silence past Osgood's body. Edmond thought it best to entrust Adele to the care of Vebba, Freya, the priest, and sympathetic women neighbors. He grimly armed himself completely to prepare for the battle he suspected might break out at any moment. As he adjusted the sword suspended from his baldric, Aegelsig arrived. A single tear ran down the armorer's cheek when he beheld Osgood's body. He brushed it away almost angrily as if embarrassed by the display of emotion, then turned to Edmond.

"By the heavens, I'm no longer young, yet I'm an old soldier and there's a blow or two left in my arm," he growled, brandishing the battle-ax he had seized on his way out of his shop. "I'll teach these murderous Norman curs a trick or two."

Turning on his heels, Aegelsig stepped out into the open and began to harangue the crowd that immediately gathered around him. "Who is with me?" he challenged. "You, Edda? How about you, Wulfhere? There they are, the bloodthirsty foreign bastards, sopping up wine by the waterfront, and laughing over the murder of one of our own, an old man who had done them no harm. Shall we let them get away with it? No, by St. Edward the Martyr's bones, we'll make them pay for it. Those who are with me, fetch arms, and we'll teach these Norman hounds they can't lord it over free-born Englishmen as if we were all slaves."

A few townsfolk hung back, then shamefacedly slunk away, but the majority rushed off to arm in preparation for a march upon the Normans. While waiting for them to reassemble, Aegelsig turned to Edmond.

"What about you, Thane Edmond? Will you lead us, as is your right, not to say your duty?"

"Yes, good friend, but you should leave the exaction of vengeance to me. You must not risk your life, not if you mean to honor Osgood's faith in you. He has entrusted his daughter to your care. Consider your family as well. Don't betray that trust by risking all. Let those who have less to hazard punish these bloodthirsty foreign dogs."

Aegelsig was torn between a hot-headed desire to personally avenge Osgood's murder, and the obvious common sense of Edmond's plea to avoid confrontation with the Normans for the sake of Adele and his family. Edmond tried to take advantage of his hesitation, keeping his voice low so that none but Aegelsig, whom he suspected was in on the secret of his royal ancestry, could hear him.

"I've asked you as a friend, but now I must command you as your lord. You owe me obeisance for my father's sake, or that of my uncle, King Edmond Ironside, if not on my own account. I have the right, Aegelsig, I have the right to demand this of you."

Aegelsig bowed his head in submission. "If you put it that way, Childe Edmond, I must obey." Edmond extended his hand, and Aegelsig reverently kissed the silver ring.

The armorer glumly entered the house. He soon reemerged with Vebba, Freya and Adele, who walked haltingly, still in a state of shock though no longer weeping. Edmond put a hand on her arm as they passed. She halted, but looked at him reproachfully.

"We part in sadness, Adele," he murmured, ignoring her censure by gazing lovingly and wistfully into her eyes. "But we shall meet again in better days, I promise."

As her companions led her away, he watched somberly until she disappeared around a corner. He then wheeled toward the townsfolk, several dozen of whom had gathered around him in the street. Before leaving, Aegelsig had urged them to follow the young man's lead, which they were more than willing to do on learning it was he who had struck down the Norman knight. The townsmen were poorly armed, a few carrying swords, daggers and lances, while the majority had snatched up whatever implement was handy, such as household axes, scythes, lengths of chain, and even skewers and pokers, anything that might wound or injure an enemy.

It was a motley, undisciplined troop, Edmond reflected ruefully. While the angry townsmen were spoiling for a fight, they were clearly at a loss as to how to organize a concerted attack on the Normans. Unless their ardor was properly harnessed it would be wasted in a haphazard, wild, almost aimless rush upon the alehouse, or merely dissipate in empty threats until they lost heart and retreated to their homes. It was up to him to provide inspiration and leadership. He unsheathed his sword, and vaulted onto a cart, his resplendently armored figure instantly riveting the crowd's attention.

"Listen to me, good, brave people of Dover." he exhorted. "Let's show these Norman butchers who slaughter old men that there's still iron in our English bones. Let's prove we haven't forgotten the great Alfred, who knew how to deal with foreign bandits. Let's follow the example of the valiant King Edmond Ironside, who never yielded to invading raiders. Let's give these Normans such a whipping that those who survive will scuttle back to their homeland and warn their kinsfolk that the rights and lives of Englishmen are sacred. They'll not be so eager to come over here to despoil us once they've discovered we're not sheep whose throats can be cut with impunity, but wolves that will send them howling back to Normandy."

He paused to let the words sink in as the crowd cheered, then outlined his plan. "Fetch furniture, tables and benches, bring wagons, tools, and stone. We'll erect a barricade across the street. Don't think of rushing them. That would be playing into their hands. Let them charge our barrier, and we'll give them a welcome such as they'll remember until their bones rattle into their graves."

Stirred into action by his words, the townsfolk scattered to carry out his bidding. They returned with whatever was movable, and raised a formidable barricade to block off the narrow street leading to Osgood's house. Edmond posted the best armed in front of the barrier, and stationed a second line of defenders behind it. The latter's task was to pull their comrades to safety when they fell back from the Norman charge. He stationed a few men on the roofs of the buildings fronting the street, instructing them to rain down rocks, weapons, utensils, whatever was handy, upon the Normans when they passed by.

The preparations were completed just in time because the Normans, finally made aware of the commotion among the townsfolk, surged out of the taverns fully armed and mounted their horses. Edmond estimated Count Eustace's entourage at more than two score knights, squires and men-at arms. They clearly represented a formidable threat as they formed up in preparation for an assault, which they obviously expected would easily scatter the townsfolk.

An impressive figure in full armor, Edmond took up his post at the head of the men in front of the barricade to await the Norman onslaught. He was painfully aware that the untrained townsmen on foot could not long stand up against a charge by such a powerful force of experienced mounted soldiers. The townsfolk's chief asset was their superior numbers which might exact a heavy toll of the Normans and repulse them before the defenders were driven back from the barricade.

Edmond was not conscious of the slightest fear. He was totally engulfed in the exultation and anticipation of impending combat, the pride of leadership, and the hope of being worthy of his heritage. Most of all, he was aware of an overwhelming desire to destroy the enemy who had murdered his faithful benefactor.

When Count Eustace judged his men to be ready, he ordered a charge, and the opposing forces soon collided in a pandemonium of clattering horse hooves, clanging weapons and furious war cries. A townsman at Edmond's left was the first to fall, spitted by a Norman rider's lance. Edmond seized the horseman's leg, pulled him off his mount, and stabbed him in the chest as he fell. Another Norman rushed directly at him, swinging a ponderous mace overhead as he prepared to strike. Edmond avoided the blow with a sidewise leap, then thrust his sword deep into the flank of the rider's horse.

"Hold fast, Thane Edmond! Hold fast!" roared a familiar voice by his ear. It was Wiglaf, armed with an ax that he twirled as if it were a twig. The ax struck home with a sickening thud, and the mace-bearing Norman shriveled to the ground from his wounded and screaming horse, his head split almost to his chin.

There was no time for gratitude. Edmond caught sight of a Norman clad in superb, gilded armor, who had just cut down a townsman with a sword thrust. "It must be Count Eustace," he cried, and sprang forward to confront the Norman leader. Their swords clashed for an instant but the whirl of battle immediately forced them apart.

Most of the surviving townsmen already had scrambled behind the barricade by this time. Only Edmond, Wiglaf, and three or four others, bolder than the rest, remained in front of it, ready to defend the barrier as long as they could stand. But the Normans had suffered severely, and Count Eustace decided he could not afford to lose more men in another assault on such a fiercely defended and formidable obstacle. He called for retreat, and withdrew his remaining followers toward the waterfront.

"The field is ours, my lord," wheezed Wiglaf, leaning his broad back against the barricade to rest from his strenuous efforts. He was correct. After a brief conference, the Normans rode slowly out of Dover, screaming dire threats in both French and broken English that they would quickly return to burn the town. It had been a costly battle for both sides. Nineteen Normans lay dead or mortally wounded. The people of Dover mourned eighteen members of their families in addition to Osgood.

Edmond watched the Normans ride out of sight as he leaned wearily beside Wiglaf. His heart was still pounding from the excitement of combat. Until now he had had no time to think, merely to slash, cut and thrust. It was only after the battle was over that he began to grasp its implications for him personally. What should he do next? How could he help protect these good people of Dover from the vengeance which the Normans would surely seek? King Edward was unlikely to permit an attack on his brother-in-law to go unpunished. What was to be his own next step? Would it be best to remain in Dover? Or would that just make the town's punishment more severe? Perhaps he could deflect the monarch's anger on himself by fleeing, thus softening the retribution against Dover? If he decided to remain in England and seek the crown, as Osgood had urged him to do, would it be better to begin in Dover or elsewhere? Unfortunately, all hope of learning the identity of the influential men who might support his claim had died with Osgood, who had intimated he knew several who were disaffected with King Edward's policies, most seriously by his preference for Normans.

"Thinking, even more than fighting, is hot, dry work, Thane Edmond," Wiglaf snorted impatiently. "What say we have a stoup or two of good, refreshing ale at the inn, now that those Norman dogs have scurried away with their tails between their legs," he frowned. "By the bones of holy St. Cuthbert! What if those curs have drunk the place dry? No, it's that sour vinegar they call wine they'd have lapped up."

Despite being bone-tired and saddened by the lamentations of the townsfolk as they mournfully cleared the streets of their dead and wounded, Edmond could not help but smile at the sailor's hangdog look.

"Come, have courage, my friend. Let's hope it's the latter, and there's a drop or two of good brew left for you. Shall we see?"

To Wiglaf's chagrin, his worst foreboding was realized. Not that the Normans had drunk all the ale. Instead they had turned the inn into a shambles. They had staved in every single cask, and the thirsty dirt floor had indiscriminately absorbed ale and wine without delicate distinction of taste. The sailor was near tears as he frantically searched the desolate scene of barbaric destruction in desperate hopes of finding a surviving pint.

"I wouldn't have thought it, not even of those sons of the devil," he groaned, grinding his teeth. A happy thought brought back a smile. "By the holy rood! How could I've forgotten. Master Lewin surely will be a good host to us. Quick! To his ship, if you will, Thane Edmond."

"But I've changed my mind, Master Wiglaf," Edmond protested. "I'm not sailing to Baldwinesland. I've decided to remain in England."

"I'm glad to hear it, that I am," Wiglaf replied heartily. "There's need of men like you, my lord. But why should that keep us from boarding the *Eldrytha*? It's reason all the more to visit Master Lewin. You can inform him of your change in plan, and I happen to know he always keeps a good supply of mettlesome ale aboard."

The sailor's throat may have been dry, but his head was clear. He concealed his real reason for wanting to lure Edmond aboard the ship. He had taken a liking to the young thane, an affection tempered only slightly by the respect due from a common sailor to a nobleman. Shrewd and experienced, Wiglaf knew a great deal more about the world than did his companion. He considered it probable that the Normans could not get King Edward's assent to harshly punish the entire community of Dover. Even if King Edward failed to protect the townsmen, Earl Godwin surely would do so. Dover lay in his jurisdiction, and as the most powerful magnate in England Godwin was not easily cowed by foreigners, no matter how highly placed. The king literally owed his throne to the great earl, and was unlikely to risk offending him.

Edmond was another matter, not being a resident of Dover but an unknown bypasser who had meddled in an affair that some might consider as having been none of his business. Thwarted of acting against the town and its people, the Normans were likely to single him out for vengeance. Earl Godwin might be happy to let them do so if it drew their anger away from the townsfolk. As Wiglaf saw it, Dover had little to fear from the Normans, but Thane Edmond had a great deal. He was best off on Master Lewin's ship, which could carry him to a safer destination.

Edmond reluctantly accompanied Wiglaf to the wharf. He heard footsteps behind him, followed by a whistle, and spun about to see Aegelsig, all out of breath from pursuing him. The armorer carried Edmond's battered old sword, the one bequeathed to him by his father Edwy.

"My lord, I thought you might have need of this. You left it at Osgood's house."

"I intended to return, though not for that sword. Your handiwork suits me much better."

Wiglaf was outraged. "Are we going to stand here and chatter like a bunch of washerwomen? Master Lewin is waiting for us. Come, Master Aegelsig, join us for a drink aboard ship."

Lewin greeted them with a whoop of joy. "Ah, lads, from what I've heard, you gave a good account of yourselves. One of my churls has told me all about it. I sent him to observe what was going on because I dared not leave the ship unguarded." The seaman poured a round of ale for his visitors, then looked inquiringly at Edmond. "You're sailing at dawn as we planned, Thane Edmond?"

"No, I'm staying here, good Master Lewin."

The seaman pursed his lips disapprovingly, and shook his head. "Nay, nay, my lord, if I may be so bold as to contradict you. If you fear for the men of Dover, dismiss the thought. When King Edward hears of this sad matter he's not likely to side with the Normans, much as he loves some of them. After all, the blame rests on Count Eustace. Besides, if it comes to that, Earl Godwin will look after his own."

Aegelsig and Wiglaf seconded Lewin's opinion, but Edmond remained unmoved.

"I have other reasons for wishing to stay in England," he said. Yet he was reassured as to the fate of Dover, believing that Aegelsig, as one of its leading citizens, was in a good position to judge. He had forgotten that the town was in Godwin's domain. There could be little doubt of the earl's stand. Still, this was all beside the point. He had made up his mind to pursue his destiny in England, though he could not tell these men his real reason for wanting to remain.

"The decision is yours, my lord," Aegelsig admitted, "but consider that while we of Dover have little to fear, you as a stranger to our town will be in great danger. Depend on it, there'll be questions asked as to why you intervened, and demands that you be punished, if only to satisfy the Normans' hunger for revenge. It's better that you leave."

"I stay!" Edmond declared firmly.

His three companions exchanged puzzled glances. They could not understand his obstinacy.

Lewin tried a different approach. "If my lord permits, I have a suggestion. Dover is not all England, and you'd be much safer as far away from here as possible. I can take you along the coast and land you wherever you choose to leave ship. No one will connect you with this affray if you're seen in a distant part of the country within a day or two."

Lewin's suggestion appealed to Edmond. He hesitated only a moment before agreeing. There could be no dishonor in taking a sensible precaution as long as it did not endanger anyone else. He could consider his next step later. He was sure, however, that he would not carry his new weapons and armor. Aegelsig helped him remove it.

"I charge you, friend Aegelsig, to store this wonderful equipment for me until I return to claim it," Edmond requested. "My father's battered sword will serve for now, and attract far less attention."

As Aegelsig turned toward the gangplank to leave the ship, Edmond caught his arm. "Tell me, how is the maiden Adele?"

"My niece is too grief-stricken to speak coherently even now. Somehow, for whatever reason, she holds herself responsible for her father's death, though I can't understand how she could have had anything to do with it."

"Tell her, I'll not forget her—for her good father's sake—and that someday I'll return. Tell her—no, just take good care of her, which I know you will."

Aegelsig nodded, and they shook hands warmly before the armorer left the ship. Edmond suddenly realized he was extremely tired. Lewin led him to a pile of dry straw in a sheltered area of the deck, and he immediately lay down. He was asleep before the ship weighed anchor, set sail, and beat out to sea.

Chapter Six

Prisoner in the Weald

It was a relief to tread dry land again. A single day aboard the *Eldrytha* had been enough to churn Edmond's stomach and to uncomfortably and thoroughly convince him of being unfit for a sailor's life. Two days after the affray at Dover, with heavy foot and light heart he was tramping the yielding, leaf-strewn byways of Sussex. He headed northward, away from the ill-tempered, wind-tossed whitecaps of the English Channel. The ruins of the ancient Roman city of Anderida slowly faded into the distance behind him. He vaguely remembered having heard that its crumbling walls ages ago had protected the beleaguered Britons from his marauding Saxon ancestors.

He had left ship at Pevensey, where Lewin and Wiglaf had wished him Godspeed and good-bye after promising to relay his best wishes to Aegelsig and Adele.

"We shall down a drink with you again soon, I trust, my lord." Wiglaf's booming voice did not entirely conceal his regret at parting. "It's not every day I meet a young carl who promises so well when it comes to lining his belly with good ale. By the holy rood, if it were not for my Hilda I'd accompany you. Then again, maybe Hilda's reason enough to go. If only I dared!" He turned serious. "I hope with all my heart you'll hurry back to Dover and put your legs under a table with me and our good friend here, Master Lewin."

"I shall do so, if God wills," Edmond pledged. "But for now my only companion must be this battered old blade." He slapped his sword hilt.

"I've another companion for you, Thane Edmond," shouted Lewin, diving into the *Eldrytha's* hold and emerging just as quickly. He flourished a stout quarterstaff, almost nine feet in length, which he thrust into Edmond's hands. "Take it, my lord. This may be as welcome a companion as that fragile sword if you know how to use it."

"Know how to use it?" Edmond delightedly tested the staff for balance and was satisfied. "I was born with one like it in my grip. I thank you, good Lewin."

So armed with sword, dagger and quarterstaff, and dressed in a gray rustic nondescript tunic provided by Lewin, Edmond set out, pausing only briefly to inspect the desolate yet still impressive ruins of Anderida, which he soon left behind.

The wild, uneven terrain, with its abrupt transitions from spreading lowlands and gentle valleys to serried ranks of hills, some formidably steep, hampered progress even for a young man bursting with energy. The going being slow, he pressed on, not pausing for rest until late afternoon, when he halted under the shade of an ancient apple tree crowning a high knoll. It was a fine vantage point. The prominence resembled an elevated peninsula thrusting inland from a cluster of lower hills nearer the seacoast from which he had come. Nearby was an isolated, lesser hill serving, as it were, as an outpost for the heights from which he surveyed the surrounding countryside. It was a desolate prospect, a wilderness with only occasional evidence of human habitation in view.

Feeling the chill of a sudden breeze from the sea, he wrapped himself snugly in his cloak. He was hungry after the vigorous walk, and sat down below the hoar apple tree to wolf the bread and cheese brought from the ship. His sparse meal finished, he got to his feet to resume his trek, but was struck by a whim. He unsheathed the dagger and painstakingly carved the letters "A-D-E-L-E" into the bark of the venerable tree.

Stepping back to admire his handiwork, he laughed. What a childish gesture! He was instantly sobered on recalling his last sight of Adele, overcome by grief and inexplicably guilt-stricken. How and why did she blame herself for Osgood's death? She apparently also reproached him, but why? No doubt, after the first excess of sorrow faded, she would take a more rational view of the tragic affair. He gloomily sheathed the dagger, not quite able to convince himself that it would be so.

He resumed his journey, pondering what to do next. His decision to remain in England had come on the spur of the moment, without considering the possible consequences. He had no real plan of action, nor even a definite destination. With Osgood dead, none but Edmond himself knew the entire truth about his origins, though Aegelsig and Adele were aware that he was somehow connected to the royal House of Wessex. He felt he could trust Aegelsig implicitly, but the armorer's status was too humble for him to exert much influence, other than among fellow artisans and the townsfolk of Dover. As for the young girl's knowledge, it was neither to be feared nor depended upon. It could have no weight with anyone of consequence.

Without influential friends and powerful allies to support his claim, his ancestry was best kept secret. There was no benefit in revealing it. Who would believe him? Some people would dismiss him as a madman, others as an impostor. He would either be laughed at or suspected of plotting treason. It was mere prudence to keep the truth of his origin to himself for the time being, if not forever.

He reverently pulled King Alfred's ring from off his finger and re-examined the inscription, "AELFRED MEC HEHT GEWYRCAN". He sadly shook his head. A king had ordered the ring made, and it had been handed down a long line of his successors, but it almost surely would never again be worn by a monarch. It was best to resign himself to accepting that bitter truth. He resolved to do so, and though uncertain about his immediate future, and cast adrift by Osgood's death, plodded steadily onward. He decided to head toward London for want of a more urgent destination.

Edmond strode along a trail that slashed through the darkening forest as directly as the flight of an arrow. His gait became more confident as he shook off his gloom, and he took little notice of the thickening growth threatening to overwhelm the narrow pathway. When leaving Anderida, he had met a peasant who had cautioned him not to travel after sundown through the wilderness of Ashdowne Forest. The rustic warned that the woods were infested by outlaws who would readily slit a traveler's throat for as little as a silver penny or two. Edmond shrugged off the well-meant advice. His humble attire was unlikely to tempt bandits seeking rich prey. Besides, if attacked, he was confident of being well able to defend himself against one or even two assailants.

The walk was exhilarating. A full moon bathed the columnar ancient oaks, elms and ash trees with a silver haze that transformed the forest into an apparent fairyland. Edmond idly speculated as to whether even the animals were enchanted because there was no sound of them stirring as could be expected on such a still night. The only noises were the crackle of dry leaves and twigs under his thick leather soles. He thrilled on recalling that in this very forest King Alfred more than a century ago had led his army to a celebrated victory over a host of Danish invaders. As if in a dream, he momentarily fancied that in the shimmering moonlight he beheld the struggling warriors and heard the clash of weapons, with a tall, blond leader urging on the English, exhorting his small band to greater effort whenever the surging Danes threatened to overwhelm it.

A shrill whistle shattered the illusion, as well as the silence of the silvan setting. Edmond was barely able to leap from the path, put his back to a huge tree trunk, and assume the ready position with the quarterstaff before three men emerged from the enfolding dense brush. He was surprised as well as relieved that they had not ambushed him, something they might have done easily.

"There you go, Arn, always spoiling the fun," grumbled the one in the middle, the tallest of the three, scowling at Edmond with a single eye, the other covered with a faded black patch. "You roused the forest to no account, and alarmed this young churl when we could've dealt with him with no trouble at all."

Arn was a slender youngster with a face disfigured by a livid scar extending from his left eyebrow to the base of his ear. He laughed coldly. "A little sport, Gurth, a healthy frolic. There'd be little enjoyment in knocking such a stout lad over the head before he knew what hit him. Let's have a little fun first and test his mettle. We'll settle with him quickly enough."

"You were ever the one for pleasure," Gurth growled. "It'll be your undoing one of these days." He turned to the third man, "What say you, Eanwere?"

Eanwere contributed a grunt of agreement.

The three outlaws, wielding quarterstaves, encircled the tree in preparation for rushing upon Edmond. He felt a twinge of apprehension, yet it was tempered with the exultation that had inspired him at Dover. He drew his dagger, measured the range, and flung it full force at Eanwere, who had the misfortune to be the nearest. The blade struck the outlaw in the belly, and he writhed screaming to the ground. Gurth and Arn were momentarily benumbed by the bold, unexpected blow, and Edmond tried to take advantage of their confusion. He rushed at them, wielding his huge staff as if it were a flail, landing several solid blows before his foes recovered heart and resumed the attack. Despite the concerted efforts of his assailants, Edmond skillfully parried their strokes, taking care that neither brigand got behind him as he kept his back to the tree.

Unfortunately for him, however, Arn's whistle had indeed awakened the forest. Almost before Edmond became aware of it, he was surrounded by a score of outlaws, who had silently emerged one by one from the dense wilderness. At their coming, Arn and Gurth retreated slightly, leaving Edmond, the tree at his back his only ally, gazing in despair at the band of enemies hemming him in. It was a bitter conviction that he was about to perish ignominiously, as an unfortunate traveler murdered for a paltry few coins rather than as a king at the head of an army with a regal crown encircling his brow.

An outlaw fitted an arrow to a bow, and aimed at Edmond's breast.

"Drop your staff and sword, churl," the archer demanded. "Now! Or you're a dead man." He drew the bowstring in preparation for carrying out the threat but a short, stout man stepped forward with upraised hand.

"Hold! Hold a bit, Ned!" he barked, and turned to Edmond. "Come, lad, be sensible. Yield, and I promise fair play. These lads will listen to me."

Edmond grimaced. He put no faith in the outlaw's word. Still, he had no choice, other than to die. If he surrendered and the outlaws spared him there might be a chance for escape later. He dropped the quarterstaff to the ground, then drew his father's old sword from its scabbard. On impulse, he drove the sword blade into the tree trunk with all his might. It penetrated far deeper than one might have expected and its handle vibrated for a few seconds before coming to a standstill.

The outlaws were caught off guard by Edmond's abrupt action. Arn reacted first, springing forward with the obvious intention of pulling the blade from the tree but the stout man, obviously the troop's leader, again interposed, waving him off.

"Let it be for now, Arn," he ordered. "By the looks of it, it's worn out, worth little if anything, and we'll respect the lad's gesture, foolish as it may have been. If Earl Eadred decides to keep this youth with us we can send him back to recover his sword. Let it rust there for now."

Dismissing the matter, he knelt down beside the unfortunate victim of Edmond's accurate dagger toss. "Dead, is he? That'll go against you, lad. Not that Eanwere the Mercian was of much account. All the same, we must stand up for one another." He got up and decided, "We might as well bury him here. He had no family, none we know of."

The one-eyed Gurth pulled the dagger from the dead man's body, and used it to begin to scoop out a shallow grave in the soft, yielding sod. Several comrades joined in to help, and before long Eanwere's corpse was hidden under a pile of dirt, heavy branches and a few large rocks. With that done, a ferret-faced individual stepped forward at the leader's beckoning, and mumbled a brief prayer, which revealed faint traces of monastic training.

"That should do it," the leader determined. "Let's return. Sound the horn, Ned."

Ned the archer raised a hunting horn to his lips and its deep clarion call pierced the chill night air of the dense forest. The sonorous blast of a distant horn replied almost immediately. With several men surrounding Edmond as a guard, the little band began to scramble through the tangled underbrush in the direction of the summoning horn, which sounded from time to time in answer to intermittent blasts by Ned.

Edmond estimated that they had covered a mile or so by the time the sound of the calling horn became so loud that he expected to see its source at any moment. To his amazement, when the band filed into a moonlit, grassy clearing, he beheld a boy, who could be barely more than ten years old, sitting cross-legged upon a tree stump and blowing the horn. The child looked for all the world like a snake-charmer. He wore a bright green tunic fringed with gold tassels, which glittered in the moonlight as if iridescent. A red velvet, fur-trimmed cap tilted jauntily on his head, and a richly embroidered baldric for his horn graced his shoulder. The instrument, though smaller than Ned's, was far more elaborate, its silver mountings chased with delicate patterns.

"I thought you'd never return, Oswald," the boy cried joyfully, jumping off his perch, and running to meet the troop. "But you bring a stranger! Is he a prisoner?"

"Aye, that he is, and a husky, lusty quarrelsome lad, too, Master Edward," smiled the outlaw leader. He looked around with a frown. "Where's Alvin?"

"Father sent me to relieve him. He said it was time that I became a man, that I began to learn a man's duties."

"Earl Eadred may have the right of it, Master Edward, and who am I to gainsay him—though you're a trifle young for such tasks. Now, however, we'll leave Gurth here so that you can return with us to the hall."

Oswald nodded to Gurth, who took up his post, then led the band along a narrow, well-beaten path leading out of the clearing. The boy skipped gaily along with the others until he caught up with Edmond. The silver ring on Edmond's finger, which glittered from time to time in the moonlight, attracted his attention.

"Show me the ring," he ordered peremptorily.

Edmond shrugged indifference though he was apprehensive about having to surrender the precious token, and extended his hand. The boy took a fleeting glance and sniffed disdainfully.

"It's pretty old, isn't it?" he commented. "All beat up. I wouldn't wear anything like that. You may keep it." He waved his hand magnanimously, and dropped back in line to prod Arn into giving him a blow-by-blow description of the prisoner's capture. On hearing of Edmond's fierce resistance against three men, and how he had killed Eanwere, the boy regarded him with new respect bordering on admiration.

The group finally emerged from the forest into a broad meadow. The bright moonlight revealed that the clearing extended about two miles in length and a mile in width. The field was so level and almost devoid of growth that it seemed as if a giant in need of a bed had uprooted all vegetation and smoothed the ground for comfort while leaving the surrounding verdant woodland to curtain it off from prying eyes.

Almost at the midpoint of the meadow, on the banks of a small, quick-flowing stream that bisected it, lay a cluster of buildings. The soft silvery moon glow contrasted sharply with the rude reddish-yellow glare of several campfires, but the light cast altogether was enough to reveal the crude log construction of the cabins surrounding a fair-sized hall like chicks clustering around a mother hen.

Despite the late hour, the sounds of talk, laughter and song, reached the advancing band, which soon plunged into a welcoming crowd of relieved and eager questioners, and a dozen or so joyous hounds that snapped and bayed their welcome.

Chapter Seven

An Outlaw Earl

Oswald detailed two men to guard Edmond by the entrance to the long hall before he and young Edward entered the building from whence came a deafening uproar of chatter, laughter and snatches of song, as well as the barking of dogs disputing the leavings of the feasting band of outlaws.

The guards permitted Edmond to seat himself on the ground by a fire because once off his feet he was less likely to attempt an act of desperation. Actually, he was not even thinking for the moment of trying to escape. He was tired, hungry and thus content to observe the feverish activity all around the encampment. An entire large wild boar was being turned on a spit over a nearby blaze, and about a dozen women were preparing side dishes for the feast. The savory aroma of cooking meat was a tantalizing reminder that he had not enjoyed a hot meal since before Osgood's death two days earlier. He became increasingly impatient to be summoned into the hall regardless of whatever fate was in store for him if first he could take a bite of barbecued pork and wash it down with ale.

As he hungrily ran his right thumb across his tongue he suddenly became aware of someone staring at him. He looked up almost in annoyance, but then smiled in amusement when he realized he was being inspected by a mere boy. The child was about ten years of age, if that, and large immensely sad brown eyes dominated his gaunt, high-cheeked face. A withered left arm hung at his side. Edmond thought it likely that the infirmity explained the lad's melancholy expression. In a cruel and unsympathetic age, a cripple was invariably the butt of countless indignities and insults inflicted on him endlessly by the thoughtless cruelty of more fortunate children.

It was obvious that here was someone who, while not a prisoner, was even more unhappily situated than he was. He beckoned to the youngster to approach, which he did timidly: "What's your name, boy?"

"Godfrid," the child replied hesitantly, as if alarmed that Edmond had spoken to him, and glancing apprehensively at the guards. They scowled but Edmond ignored them and reached out to reassure the youngster with a friendly pat on the back. Encouraged, the boy added almost in a whisper, while looking shyly at the ground, "They call me

Whitehand, though."

"Godfrid sounds much better to me," Edmond declared heartily. "Such a name has a noble ring to it, and I'm sure you'll measure up to it when you become a man." Godfrid rewarded him with a grateful smile.

Before they could converse further, Oswald hurried out of the hall and beckoned to the guards to escort Edmond into the building while he led the way. Even the indifferent lighting provided by a roaring fire in a huge hearth and a few rush torches scattered about the long hall did not entirely dim the brilliance of the scene. The walls were hung with the outlaws' colorful shields, each decorated with its owner's individual design, his spear leaning beside it. Bare wide oak planks, encrusted with the leavings of previous meals, were supported by trestles to form a continuous series of tables running virtually the entire length of the narrow chamber, with one end crossed by a small table perched on a platform, the whole arrangement taking the form of a letter "T". A middle-aged man, a young woman, and the boy Edward sat at the head table. Several dozen retainers, nearer the three Edmond took to be their master and his family, crowded crude benches placed on both sides of the boards extending the length of the hall.

The man sitting between Edward and the woman was a blonde-bearded giant in his late thirties or early forties. He grasped a large, lavishly decorated silver tankard with a huge left paw and wielded a sizable joint of meat in his right hand. He ate with enormous gusto, alternately gnawing the meat off the bone, then draining the ale horn with loud gulps. An attendant busily kept his platter full and horn filled to the brim. Edward sat to his right, valiantly trying to imitate the sottish imperfection of his elder's defective table manners, but youthful inexperience hampered his childish efforts. Edmond's impulse to burst out laughing died stillborn, however, when his attention turned to the girl sitting to the giant's left. She was so striking that he reluctantly admitted she might be a match in beauty even for Adele.

It was with pure delight that his eyes traced the delicate perfection of a face so regular in its features from her daintily curved nose to her bow-curved red lips and mirror-image gently convex cheeks as to seem the product of an artist's idealistic depiction. Her complexion was without the slightest blemish and her skin almost translucent. Beneath a golden tiara of artfully arranged silken blond hair pale blue eyes regarded him with what he imagined to be an inquisitive, perhaps even wistful, glance. A gold necklace embraced her snow-white, swan-like throat, and came to rest upon a bosom just beginning to bloom into the ripeness of mature femininity. Her flaxen, almost fragile-appearing beauty was set off admirably by a lustrous deep blue satin gown.

She gracefully turned her head to whisper something to the outlaw chief, and he responded with an imperative command for Oswald to bring Edmond toward the platform. The clamor in the great hall quickly died down. All strained to see and hear how their chief would deal with the prisoner, who ignored their stares and approached the platform without betraying a hint of apprehension.

Oswald halted Edmond within three feet of the head table, then informed his chief, "Earl Eadred, my lord, this is the man who killed Eanwere the Mercian."

Eadred sternly studied Edmond, his right hand still brandishing the joint of meat as if it were a mace. Edmond had deprived him of a follower on whom he had set no great value, but Eanwere's death was to be lamented if only because he might be hard to replace. The times were good and few able-bodied young men could be persuaded to leave peaceful pursuits for the uncertainties of banditry. He also felt an obligation to his followers to exact vengeance for any harm they might suffer in his service. Injury called for monetary compensation while death demanded death. In most cases he would have struck down a perpetrator without compunction, but in this instance he hesitated. If the prisoner had been old, weak, the decision would have been easy. But Edmond was young, strong and, from what he had been told, extremely handy with weapons.

"Your name?" Earl Eadred rasped.

"Thane Edmond."

"Churl Edmond, more likely, but it's all the same. You owe us a wergeld for murdering Eanwere the Mercian. That or your life."

"I owe nothing. I killed the nithing in self-defense."

"You dare call Eanwere a nithing, a wicked, faithless knave! Let me tell you, the man you murdered was one of my most loyal, able followers. You'll pay for him, one way or another." Eadred nodded to Oswald, who ordered the guards to search Edmond. After a cursory glance, they ignored the tarnished ring as worthless, and were content to confiscate his near-empty purse and battered old scabbard and toss them on the table. Eadred snorted at finding only three silver pence in the pouch and disgustedly shoved the decrepit scabbard aside. He looked menacingly at the prisoner.

"Well, lad, it looks like we'll have to settle for slitting your throat if we're to obtain just redress for the death of poor Eanwere. It'd be a sad waste, though." He paused to further consider how his followers might react to an alternative he had contemplated as soon as he had sized up Edmond. Why not have this strong, likely-looking lad replace Eanwere in his service? All said and done, it would be a definite gain. What if some in his band grumbled? Let them. He was their lord, after all.

"On the other hand," he began, gazing sternly around the hall to discourage objections, "maybe we'll have him work out his wergeld, that of a churl, not a thane such as he pretends to be. Bring him to me in the morning, Oswald." There was only a mild murmur of protest and Eadred instantly silenced it with an angry thump that rattled his table, then nodded to a gaily-clad individual seated nearby. "Come, good scop, give us a song to turn our minds from this sad business," he ordered the minstrel.

Edmond had remained silent during the entire mock trial, but now could no longer contain his indignation at being treated and insulted as if he were a serf. He sprang forward, seized the scabbard lying on the earl's table, and wielding it like a flail brought it down on the nearest guard's head. The man fell like a stone to the floor. Before the other guards were able to react, Edmond had cleared a space about himself, and had seized the fallen man's sword. He placed his back to a wall, resolved to sell his life dearly rather than to undergo further humiliation.

The hall was in an uproar. A dozen bandits seized the spears ranged along the walls and rushed to dispatch Edmond. Only Eadred retained his composure. He seemed more amused than alarmed as he raised his right hand to halt the impending attack on Edmond before his men could cut him down.

"Hold! Hold!" Eadred roared. "I like the lad's spirit, and it would be a pity to slaughter such a bold rascal." He contemplatively took a huge bite from his joint of meat, drowned it with ale, then continued, "As for you, churl or thane, whatever your station, I'll make a bargain with you. Tomorrow is a holiday with us, a day sat aside to make merry, a sort of fair. Oswald tells me you're handy with the quarterstaff. We'll see how good you really are. I'll give you a chance to earn your freedom though you're more likely to get a broken head. If you're better with that stick than I am, well, we'll let you depart without harm. I'll even return your miserably few pence, and that worthless scabbard. If I best you, you'll remain with us to take Eanwere's place in our band. I can't speak fairer words or offer you a more honest bargain. What say you to this?"

Edmond shrugged. He had no real choice. Besides, he longed to give this bandit chief—or earl if that's what he really was—a good beating, and he was confident of his skill with the quarterstaff. "I say yes."

"Good," Earl Eadred grinned wickedly, "and I promise to give you a cracked skull." He motioned to Oswald. "Get him something to eat. I don't want him fainting with hunger when I give him the thumping of his young life."

Oswald cleared a space at the long table for Edmond, provided him with a platter of meat and rough bread and a stoup of ale. He then kept careful watch on the prisoner while he made up for several days of near fasting.

All attention now turned to the minstrel, who took a prominent position near Eadred's table, then struck up his harp. As soon as he began a melodious chant with a pleasant baritone voice, an appreciative hush silenced the customary boisterousness of the outlaw band. All listened intently and with obvious pleasure to a lay of the north relating the heroic deeds of King Harold the Fairhaired of Norway. The excitement reached a crescendo and many of the company enthusiastically stamped their feet and pounded the tables when the minstrel reached the climax of his tale:

> *Against the hero's shield in vain*
> *The arrow-storm fierce pours its rein.*
> *The king stands on the blood-stained deck,*
> *Trampling on many a stout foe's neck;*
> *And high above the dinning stound*
> *Of helm and ax, and ringing sound*
> *Of blade and shield, and raven's cry,*
> *Is heard his shout of "Victory!"*

When the last notes of his lay died down, the minstrel paused to take a sip of ale as well as to drink in the crowd's applause. The assembly shouted and banged the boards clamoring for him to favor them with another song. Earl Eadred added his voice, as well as a hefty purse of silver pence, and the minstrel willingly obliged, continuing on and on. After a while, Edmond heard little of the words and accompanying music, becoming drowsy from the combination of heavy food, strong ale, and the physical and nervous strain of recent days. In his dreamy state, he found himself speculating as to whether the beautiful blond girl seated next to Earl Eadred was his wife, sister or daughter. Probably the last, he thought, because of her close resemblance to Edward. She was certainly too young to be the boy's mother, and her youth also made it unlikely she was the earl's sister. For some reason, the conclusion relieved him, but then he thought of Adele and smiled inwardly at the fickleness of his fancies.

Rousing himself from torpor, he asked Oswald if he could find a place for him to bed. The steward delegated two men to escort him to a ramshackle hut in which he was permitted to sink gratefully onto a pile of dirty straw, the distant, muffled sounds of the minstrel's voice and harp within the hall quickly lulling him to sleep.

Chapter Eight

Army of One

Edmond was astonished to discover the morning advanced when he finally awoke. He was alone in the hut, except for some insects which had emerged from the straw bedding to taste him. He quickly became aware of the shouts of children at play and the chatter of women at their household tasks drifting in through a half-open door.

He had slept fully clad except for his sandals and he strapped them on, got to his feet, brushed off the straw and voracious bugs, then stumbled through the surprisingly unguarded door into the open, blinking at the bright sunlight. It was a cloudless, temperate day, ever so welcome in early autumn, which enhanced the natural beauty of the forest setting. The dilapidated hut in which he had slept squatted on a hillock, distinctly separate from the rest of the small settlement, and so he could view unbroken the entire length and breadth of the immense clearing. He was momentarily puzzled by a persistent rhythm of dancing shafts of light at the northern verge of the meadow until he realized they were reflected from the sweeping scythes of reapers. Much nearer coursed the small but lively stream upon whose banks several women were scrubbing and rinsing laundry. His guards were also there, too busy chaffing with the women to keep close watch on their prisoner, not that there was much chance of Edmond escaping undetected. The hut lay between Eadred's long hall and the stream. Edmond would have to pass by the building to reach the rivulet, and it was inconceivable that he could do so without touching off a hue and cry.

He dismissed the notion of attempting to flee and turned his attention to a scene of hectic activity. Directly across the stream, several dozen men were setting up a row of crude benches fashioned of bare, newly-hewn planks. As soon as the stands went up, some women decorated them with a few bright-colored streamers and pennants. This then was to be the site of the festivities Eadred had mentioned.

To Edmond's left, upstream from the benches, several straw butts for the archery competition were already in place. Downstream, to his right, one space had been marked off for wrestling bouts and another for the play at quarterstaves. Edmond peered a little more intently at the latter because he had a personal stake in the layout of the ground. It appeared almost level, with no obvious advantage at any point of the terrain.

He strolled to the creek upstream from the laundry women to wash his face and hands, luxuriating in the cool, clean water. Refreshed, he removed his sandals on a whim to dangle his feet in the current. His guards glanced at him occasionally but seeing no cause for alarm continued their banter. He felt so relaxed that he was about to doze off again when he became aware of someone silently coming up behind him. He whirled about. It was Godfrid, the crippled boy he had met the previous evening. The child was too shy to say anything, but mirrored Edmond's smile.

"Sit down beside me, Godfrid," Edmond said, patting the ground. The boy plopped down and let his bare feet sink into the brook next to Edmond's. They were silent a while until Edmond finally asked, "Where are your parents, Godfrid?"

"My mother died last spring," Godfrid replied, fighting back a sob. "I never knew my father. I suppose he's dead, too."

"Who takes care of you?"

"Takes care?" Godfrid was bewildered. "No one, and I can fend for myself. I do errands for Earl Eadred, for Oswald, for whoever asks. I help in the fields. I seldom go hungry. I wouldn't mind it much but for this." He touched his withered left arm.

Edmond put a hand on the lad's right shoulder. "It's not as great a handicap as you might suppose, son," he said softly. "You've never heard of Olaf the One-Armed, the great Danish jarl? A great warrior. It's said he slew three men with one stroke of his great sword. One arm is all you need if you have a stout heart, and I venture that some day you'll make a fine soldier like Jarl Olaf."

"Do you think so!" Godfrid cried. "Could you teach me how to wield a sword and handle a spear?"

"To draw a bow, too," Edmond assured him. "Why not? If Olaf the One-Armed could slash and thrust with the best of them, you can learn to do as well. I could train you to become my shield-bearer. That is if you would want to go with me when I leave." He was surprised at his own impulsive offer but he did not have the heart to retract it. He felt sorry for the boy. He had always sympathized with the weak and unfortunate, and this crippled lad with his sad yet intelligent eyes surely faced a life of misery and contempt if he remained with Eadred's band. Besides, the lad might prove useful as an attendant.

"Do I want to go with you?" Godfrid shouted in joyful amazement. "Do you really mean it? I could ask for nothing better in the world. I'll be your page, your man-at-arms, your shield-bearer." He sprang to his feet and jumped about excitedly.

"My whole army," Edmond laughed. "But sit back down, my page, and tell me something about Earl Eadred's wife?'

"His wife?" Godfrid echoed in puzzlement. "But his lady died long ago, they say."

"Then who is the blonde girl who sat beside him in the hall last night?"

"That would be his daughter, the Lady Edith."

"His daughter!" Edmond felt strangely pleased at the discovery, but immediately wondered, almost guiltily, why he should be. He believed himself to be genuinely attracted to Adele and it seemed disloyal that any other woman should evoke such a reaction. Yes, he felt deeply about Adele. He chuckled inwardly at the memory of how confused and embarrassed she had been, how she had humbly begged his forgiveness for having been so pert with him. Yet why could he not stop thinking of this outlaw chief's daughter? Reminding himself that he had never even as much as exchanged a single word with her, he decided that he must be an absolute fool, and laughed at his fickle fancies. A huge hand falling heavily on his left shoulder startled him out of his reverie.

"You'll have need of this twig," rumbled a deep voice.

Edmond swung around to behold Gurth, the one-eyed giant, who was offering him the quarterstaff the outlaws had confiscated on his surrender. "I thought you'd be wanting your own stick after I heard about last night. I bear no grudges, lad, and I liked the way you handled yourself against me and Arn. You beat a pretty lively tune on our heads yesterday." He grinned as he gingerly touched the top of his head.

"You had it coming to you," Edmond reminded him, accepting the quarterstaff, which he was grateful to have in his grip again. He had never owned a better one.

"That I did," Gurth admitted, "and so did Arn and Eanwere, though as little as I cared for the Mercian, it's a sad matter that you killed the knave. We didn't intend to cut your throat, just your purse string. As we found later, it wasn't worth the effort, and surely not a man's life, no matter how worthless."

Gurth sighed, crossed himself, and heavily sank to the ground beside Edmond and Godfrid. The boy tried to jump up in alarm, but Gurth pulled him back down. "Nay, boy, stay put! I won't harm you."

Edmond shook his head. "I was merely defending myself."

"True, and that you did, too skillfully for Eanwere. But I didn't come to explain anything. Nor is it out of mere good will that I return your stick."

"Could there be a better reason?" Edmond bantered.

"More than one reason, that's for sure—two or three huge lumps on my head. When I felt how large they were this morning, I swore I must be revenged, though it pains me to have to leave it up to Earl Eadred. 'Comfort, Gurth,' I told myself, 'that boy will have a far sorer head tomorrow than you do now after the earl finishes with him.' A comforting thought to help ease my pain. I worry though that our master will dispose of you too quickly with just one solid whack on your hard head. I was wondering about how to make sure you got the beating you've earned when my eyes lighted on your quarterstaff. You handled it so well against me and Arn that I thought that if I return it you'd be able to hold off the thane a little longer and get a few good knocks on the head before he's through with you." A burst of laughter finished his explanation.

Edmond grinned. "I thank you for your concern, friend Gurth, but I'm not sure your master will have so easy a time. I warrant you he'll have some lumps and bruises of his own before we finish."

"Little chance of that," Gurth declared confidently. "There never was a better man with the staff than Thane Eadred, and I know what I'm talking about. Some say I'm not unskilled at the art yet when we've been at stick play the thane usually has landed two solid blows to my one. There are those who think it unfit for a man of his rank to use a churl's weapon but I agree when he says there's no shame in doing anything honorable if you do it well."

"I can't argue with that. Your master has the right of it. The staff is a noble wand. I love the stick play, best when I'm up against a man who knows what he's doing."

"Then this is your lucky day, even if you're sure to be overmatched," Gurth assured him. "If anyone knows stick play, it's Thane Eadred."

"You call your master, Thane Eadred. I thought he was an earl."

Gurth hesitated uncomfortably, looking around to see if anyone was within earshot. "He wishes he were, but he's a king's thane, or rather was before his trouble."

"He has lost the king's favor?"

"You might even say he never had it. Not this king's, that's certain. He's an outlaw by the king's order."

"When was he outlawed?"

"Since the time of King Cnut," Gurth replied, puzzled and uneasy, wondering what this questioning was leading to. Still, he saw no reason to be less than truthful. It was all common knowledge, though never to be mentioned in Eadred's presence.

"King Cnut?" Edmond was astonished. "He was one of Cnut's thanes then. But King Edward pardoned most of them, and took them into his fealty. Yet he will not pardon your master?"

"Now you're asking something I know nothing about."

"No matter. It's clear enough." It was to Edmond. Here was someone who had displeased King Edward beyond pardon. Such a man might well be willing to seize an opportunity to join in an effort to change rulers. It was something to keep in mind.

Despite the impending combat with Eadred, whether earl or outlawed thane, Edmond felt at peace with the world. It was pleasant to spend a lazy morning chatting with Gurth, who proudly outlined the program of festivities planned for the afternoon, and watching the boisterous, merry crowd streaming from every direction toward the stands and a few traders' booths set up nearby. Vendors soon were shrilly hawking their wares, and by noon the roar of the crowd became so loud that Edmond and Gurth could scarcely hear one another speak.

It was time to go. Edmond and Godfrid, accompanied by the guards who had kept an eye on him all morning, crossed a rickety bridge across the stream, heading for the area in which he was to battle Eadred. After wishing him good luck, Gurth returned to the great hall to attend his master.

Chapter Nine

Guest of Honor

Accompanied by guards, Edmond wandered with Godfrid trailing among a lane of tradesmen's booths, inspecting a surprising variety of items offered for sale. Among them, in addition to farm products, were ready-made tunics, hose and other articles of clothing, leather goods, inexpensive jewelry, metal mirrors, bone combs, religious articles, and agricultural and household tools and implements. Because Edmond's purse had been confiscated he and Godfrid could only look and admire. Not that Edmond wanted anything for himself, but he wished he were able to provide Godfrid with something better in the way of clothing than the rags he wore.

When a horn sounded the signal that it was nearly time for the organized portion of the festivities to commence, a growing crowd began to swarm toward the stands to secure the better vantage points. The guards urged Edmond to join the traffic flow, and by dint of rudely shoving aside all in their path, while ignoring heartfelt curses and dirty looks from the victims, led him toward the downstream end of the benches. The steward Oswald impatiently awaited their arrival.

"It's about time, Elmer," Oswald barked at one of the guards. "We're almost ready to begin. Turn your prisoner over to Gurth and Arn who are waiting near where Earl Eadred is expected to take his place."

Edmond whispered, "Godfrid, stay with me."

Oswald overheard, but shrugged indifference as the boy tagged along. Edmond and Godfrid followed Elmer to a bench that had been placed in front of the stands, facing a section of cushioned seats obviously meant for Eadred, his family, and his guests. Gurth and Arn stood by the bench, the former greeting the prisoner with a friendly nod, the latter with a scowl. Edmond was pleased to see that from this spot he would have a clear view of the archery contest.

As soon as the crowd filled the stands, the field was cleared, and Ned the archer stepped forward in full view of the entire assembly, which became hushed in expectation. He raised his hunting horn to his lips and sounded three quick blasts, the deep sounds reverberating from the stands and the enveloping forest. The third note had scarcely faded when the sweeter tones of a more highly pitched horn sounded reply and a magnificent troop of riders crossed the bridge from the direction of Eadred's long hall.

In the van, astride a bay palfrey, rode young Edward, blithely winding his silver-chased horn in answer to Ned's harmonious summons. His father Eadred came next, upon a ponderous Flemish warhorse, which despite its size and strength was sore put to bear its rider's enormous bulk. Beside the thane, astride a resplendently caparisoned prancing black stallion, rode a striking figure, a blond young man whose bristling golden mustaches adorned a haughtily handsome if unnaturally pallid face. The rider's cold gray eyes disdainfully swept the crowd as he approached the stands, then rested briefly on Edmond but with no sign of recognition. Edmond was momentarily puzzled. He had seen this man before but where? Dover! This arrogant horseman was the furious youth who had so stormily rushed out of the tavern after flinging a flagon at his Norman companion.

His garments all of black cloth fringed with silver, the young man controlled his noble stallion with the effortless assurance of a master horseman, as he rode silently and without changing his expression in sharp contrast to Thane Eadred, who smiled and waved acknowledgment of his people's enthusiastic welcome. As the little troop of riders approached the stands, the name of Eadred's companion swept like a rumor through the buzzing crowd.

"Sweyn Godwinson, may God preserve us," growled Gurth loudly enough so that Edmond could hear. "I wonder Thane Eadred trusts having such a villain near his side. He's a devil if there ever was one, a murdering villain who killed his own cousin, Beorn." He paused to spit. "Foul beast! Beware, friend Edmond, beware of that nithing!"

Surprised by Gurth's outburst of hatred tinged by dread, Edmond scrutinized Earl Sweyn with even greater interest. Everyone knew the story of how Sweyn had lured his trusting cousin Earl Beorn aboard a ship to have him strangled. What had made the murder an even more atrocious villainy than most was that it was done without apparent reason. As far as anyone knew, Beorn had never done anything to offend or cross Sweyn. The heinous crime had revolted and shocked even a people hardened and accustomed to treachery and murder. The popular outcry was so great that the king's council had outlawed Sweyn, declared him a "nithing," someone put beyond the pale of humanity. He had been stripped of his lands and title, and no one was to give him food or shelter under penalty of similar punishment.

It was only through the intervention of his powerful father Earl Godwin, as well as the almost inexplicable pleas of a saintly churchman, Bishop Ealdred, that Sweyn had regained his status and property. Yielding to their urging, King Edward had restored Sweyn's title and estates, though there was no way he could remove the blot on his reputation. Neither his peers nor the people were likely to ever trust him again, which might explain why he was consorting with the chief of an outlaw band in a remote forest district. He undoubtedly was seeking an ally. Edmond wondered if there could have been a connection between Sweyn's visit to Dover and the subsequent arrival of Count Eustace of Boulogne. The possibility was worth keeping in mind.

Edmond turned with relief from speculation about Sweyn to admiration of the Lady Edith, who looked even more beautiful than she had the previous night. Her flowing crimson velvet gown stood out even amidst a colorful company. She rode gracefully on a milk white palfrey, her confident horsemanship markedly contrasting with the laughable insecurity of her attendant, a plump, middle-aged woman who clung to a mule's saddle with the desperation of a drowning man clutching a piece of driftwood. Ignoring her companion's near-terror, Edith was chattering gaily, clearly in the highest spirits.

A score of young men wearing ring mail hauberks and gleaming helms, and bearing short lances and round shields, brought up the rear of the procession. They comprised Earl Sweyn's personal bodyguard. Edmond admired their fine bearing and the quality of their equipment and horses. He felt a twinge of envy. After all, he was entitled to an even larger following of companions. Was he not an atheling, a prince of the house of Wessex? What was Sweyn, when all was said and done, but nothing more than the son of a shepherd. Legend had it that tending flocks had been Earl Godwin's occupation before he had won the notice of a Danish jarl and begun to storm his way into King Cnut's favor and to subsequent elevation to unmatched power in England. The wheel would turn, Edmond swore, biting his lips and twisting King Alfred's ring on his finger as the procession of riders reached the stands. Thane Eadred, Earl Sweyn, Lady Edith, her companion, and young Edward took their places in the front row, with Sweyn's guards surrounding the area.

At a nod from Eadred, Ned raised his horn and blew three notes. When the final blast faded, Oswald stepped out front and center to address the crowd:

"Earl Eadred, our most gracious lord, bids you all to welcome his most noble guest, Earl Sweyn Godwinson, who honors us with his presence, and to join in this celebration to mark his visit. Furthermore, know you all that the good, noble and gracious Earl Sweyn has generously offered a hundred silver shillings and a place in his personal following to the archer who proves most skillful in today's competition."

The crowd roared appreciatively, and Oswald continued: "Let the archers who wish to contend for such a great and generous prize step forward."

More than a hundred men answered his call, among them Gurth, Arn and Ned. To Edmond's surprise, Gurth shouted an invitation to him to join in the competition, but he shook his head. The good-natured Gurth persisted all the same, and even offered the bow and quiver of one of the guards for the prisoner's use. Edmond, reflecting that if he made a good showing it might prove useful later on when the outlaws decided what to do with him, finally gave in to join the group of archers preparing for the tournament.

Twelve straw target butts had been set up. Each archer was allowed three flights in the first round. The two most accurate among each group of eight or nine men would gain the second round, and so on. The final round was to pit the most skilled pair for the championship.

Edmond tested the borrowed bow and while not of the best quality it was at least adequate, with good balance and tension. The well-fletched arrows in the quiver were unexceptionable. He was not used to the unfamiliar weapon, however, and his first shot was completely wide of the target, eliciting a derisive howl from the crowd. He flushed and bit his lips, then carefully fitted the second arrow to the string, sighted, drew and released. This shot struck the target only a few inches off center. His confidence enhanced, the third flight was a bull's-eye. It gained him the second round.

The competition was extremely spirited, with several excellent bowmen demonstrating their abilities. Most notable was the outstanding marksmanship of the surly Arn, all three of whose shots in the first round struck the heart of the target, the last piercing its exact center. The crowd wildly cheered his bull's-eye and Arn, for the first time, permitted himself a grimace, which apparently was as near as he could approximate a smile. His companion Gurth was neither as capable nor fortunate, and was quickly forced to retire from the competition, disgruntledly rubbing his tousled head of hair.

"A child's toy, not a fit weapon for a grown man," he muttered disdainfully, slamming his bow to the ground.

The two survivors of the first round each received a silver penny from Eadred, who handed it to Edmond without comment. Edmond wondered if it was an omen when to his surprise the well-worn coin turned out to be one minted by his grandfather, King Aethelred, but dismissed the thought.

For the second round, the cluster of targets was reduced to four, with two dozen men remaining in the competition. The two best bowmen from each group of six would advance to the third round, which was to be the penultimate.

By this time Edmond felt more confident of his ability to handle the borrowed bow with some chance of getting off an accurate shot. The first round, while brief, had given him the opportunity to gauge the quality and characteristics of the weapon. Before taking his place for the second round, he adjusted the string tension to his satisfaction, and shaped the fletching after selecting the best of the remaining arrows. His first shot this time split the center of the target just as Arn's had done to finish his first round. A few in the crowd responded with a cheer, though most remained silent as they understandably favored their own people. His next two shots were almost as accurate, but he might just as well have left the arrows in his quiver because the first shot had won the round for him. He received two silver pennies and again gave his winnings to Godfrid, who was jumping up and down with excitement.

Eight archers stayed in the running for Earl Sweyn's prize when the tournament entered the third round. In addition to Edmond, they were Arn, Ned, a red-haired yeoman, an elderly, pot-bellied tinker, and three of Sweyn's followers. Only two targets remained, with four men in each group of competitors. Edmond's rivals were the red-haired yeoman, the gray-haired tinker and one of Sweyn's men. The tinker was a jolly fellow who played up to the crowd with broad grimaces and exaggerated postures as he tested the wind direction and fumbled with his bow while fitting the arrow. His contortions sent the crowd into gales of laughter and much good-natured heckling.

"Stick to your pots and kettles, old pot-belly," shrilled a spectator, while others took up a chant: "Old pot-belly! Old pot-belly! Old pot-belly!"

The tinker complacently patted his portly paunch, and retorted with pretended outrage, "Go ahead, mock me, you miserable skeletons, but starving scarecrows like you are always jealous of a man of dignified appearance. I take good care of my belly and it takes excellent care of me. It's where my great skill as a bowman is conceived."

"Misconceived, you fat knave," someone shouted, touching off a roar of laughter to drown out the tinker's indignant retort.

Once the bantering died down, the tinker forced the crowd to give him his due. He was a truly formidable archer, with an accurate eye as well as silk-smooth technique in drawing the bow with ease and releasing the shaft without the slightest tremor. He registered a near bull's-eye in the first flight while the best both Edmond and the red-haired yeoman could do was come within a hand's length of the target's center while the fourth man was even farther off. Edmond however matched the tinker's skill on the second flight, both their arrows striking the very edge of the mark that indicated the heart of the straw butt, while this time the redhead and Sweyn's man were not much closer than on their first shots. On the third flight, Edmond struck the heart of the target for the second time that day. None of the other three could quite match his superb shot and the round was his, drawing a slight scattering of applause from the spectators, who cheered much more enthusiastically for the losers, particularly the tinker, whose lively, good-natured response to their earlier jeers had won their support.

Edmond pretended indifference to the crowd's reaction, but cast a furtive glance toward Lady Edith. He wondered if it was his imagination but he thought he detected a hint of interest and encouragement in her smile, and a slight nod of the head.

The second group of competitors, consisting of Arn, Ned, and the other pair of Sweyn's followers, was well-matched. All four bowmen struck the target within a finger's breadth of the bull's-eye on their first flights. On second effort, Arn and Ned again registered in the innermost area, but one of their rival's arrow landed a littler farther out and the other's shaft drifted to the outermost fringe. Arn secured the victory on the third flight, his arrow just perceptibly closer to the center than Ned's, while neither of the visitors could match their outstanding shots.

It all had come down to Edmond and Arn, much to the surprise of both. Edmond was astounded to have done so well, particularly with a borrowed weapon. He had never considered himself more than a competent archer. As for Arn, he had expected either Ned or someone of exceptional skill from among Earl Sweyn's men to give him the stiffest battle, not this captive youth.

Nevertheless, in spite of all expectations, the final decision contention was between Edmond and Arn, with one target left on the field. Each man was to have three flights, shooting alternately.

Edmond was granted the first shot. He tested the wind direction with a moist index finger, then carefully selected the best balanced and fletched arrow from his quiver. He flexed and adjusted his bow, making sure the string was drawn tight before placing it in the notch of his bolt. The crowd became hushed as he stepped up to the starting point, drew his bow, and watched intently as the arrow sped toward the target. It struck slightly to the left of center, a hand's breadth away, drawing some applause from the crowd. Apparently at least a minority of the spectators disliked the surly Arn, and was prepared to support even a stranger in preference to him.

Dissatisfied with his shot, Edmond glanced covertly toward Edith. She was smiling, and he thought he saw a slight nod of encouragement.

He was heartened when Arn's first effort was no better than his own, the arrow landing almost next to his. This was only the second time Arn had failed to reach the innermost circle of the target.

Edmond carefully chose another arrow, and decided to allow a little more for the breeze, which was blowing almost at right angles to the flight path. This time he struck the target almost dead center, kindling his supporters' applause, but Arn immediately matched the shot to evoke a much louder cheer from the spectators.

After the tumult died down, the judges examined the target and declared that the contestants were perfectly even. The final shot would decide the outcome of the match.

Edmond coolly stepped forward and selected the best of the few arrows left in his quiver though its fletching did not seem as fully-feathered as those he already had used. It would have to do, and perhaps he could compensate. As he stepped up to take his last shot, he again glanced toward Edith. This time there could be no doubt. She flashed a brilliant, encouraging smile. He light-heartedly drew the bow and let loose. A tremendous roar went up from the crowd. It was almost a perfect shot. The arrowhead had nicked the edge of the small center dot.

As Arn stepped up to take his turn, his scar seemed livid and stood out glaringly against his even more than usually pale face. Yet he revealed no outward emotion as he checked his bowstring, chose an arrow with the utmost care, fitted the notch to the string, and after a steady draw discharged the shot. The arrow just brushed the fletching of Edmond's, cutting through a feather before it transfixed the center dot. A perfect hit!

The magnitude of Arn's feat momentarily stunned the crowd, but the shocked silence quickly turned into an uproar far greater than excited by any previous shot of the contestants. Even those who disliked Arn could not withhold applause. Possibly for the first time in years he permitted himself a broad smile. He was keenly aware that his exploit would be celebrated in verse and song for years to come, even if the telling of it was lavishly embellished as time glossed over the more prosaic details.

By dint of shouting himself almost hoarse, and waving his arms about like a windmill, Oswald eventually succeeded in calming the turbulent crowd so that he could announce, with some hope of being heard, the judges' official confirmation of the winner.

"Arn Olafson, you have proved yourself the king of bowmen, and the undoubted champion of our competition," Oswald proclaimed. "Step forward to accept the prize you've so clearly won as the greatest archer in Ashdowne Weald, and almost surely of all England, from the hands of our gracious and generous guest, Earl Sweyn Godwinson."

Oswald solemnly escorted Arn to a position in front of the stands, where the master archer knelt down before Earl Sweyn. The earl's host, Thane Eadred, beamed with pride and gratification that one of his faithful followers had distinguished himself.

"Your skill is so great, and your aim so true that none can rightly envy your good fortune in deservedly capturing the prize we've pledged to award to the winner," Sweyn said as he handed Arn a purse containing the hundred silver shillings. "It would pleases me even more if I could turn your victory to my own profit as well. Your master, my good and most noble friend Earl Eadred, has graciously agreed that if you desire to enter my service he freely and gladly will release you from fealty to him."

Arn was astounded, but hesitated only momentarily. "I'll gladly become your man, and I'll serve you as faithfully and truly as I've ever done my good lord, Earl Eadred," he stammered, dazed by this deluge of good fortune. It was no small matter to transfer from the service of a minor nobleman of doubtful reputation who was forced to shelter himself in a wilderness to that of one of the great noblemen of the realm. Oswald had to nudge him before he realized that he was expected to kiss Earl Sweyn's extended right hand, and then follow the steward to take up his place among the visiting lord's bodyguards.

With the archery concluded, it was time for the competition in wrestling and tumbling in which several dozen young men participated. Edmond declined an invitation to try his strength, prudently deciding to husband his energy for the test at quarterstaves which was soon to follow. He was particularly impressed by Gurth's dexterity and technique. Despite his huge size, the outlaw was exceptionally agile, and with his great strength and superior skill disposed of a succession of adversaries with ridiculous ease to maintain his reputation as the greatest wrestler of Ashdowne Weald.

As he had to Arn, Earl Sweyn presented a heavy purse to Gurth, though he did not attempt to persuade him to enter his service. The visitor obviously was careful not to risk offending his host by luring away another of his best men.

After the completion of the wrestling and tumbling came the play at quarterstaves. Ned again sounded three blasts on his horn to summon the contestants, but Oswald immediately raised a restraining hand to turn back a dozen or so young men who rushed eagerly toward the space designated for the competition.

"There'll be time enough for you, good lads, to crack each other's heads," Oswald shouted. "First, make way for our noble lord, Earl Eadred, who has amiably consented to engage in the merriest of sports, a bout with the quarterstaff. He intends to teach this young man a lesson." He nodded toward Edmond. "Make room!"

Everyone fell back to leave Edmond alone in the area cleared for the quarterstaff competition. Eadred laid down his sword and dagger, removed his cloak, upper garment and jewelry, then strode out of the stands to confront his adversary in the cleared area. Gurth handed his master a long, thick quarterstaff which he hefted with confident ease.

Despite years of abundant living, the thane presented an imposing sight when stripped to the waist. His biceps and shoulder muscles bulged with promise of enormous strength. The circumference of his chest was a good match for the trunk of a century-old great oak. Yet there was more than a hint of blubber around his midriff, suggesting that he might find it difficult to maintain a strenuous pace for long. Not that the crowd imagined such a possibility. Edmond's trim and husky figure, while respectable by any standard, seemed to their prejudiced eyes almost puny in comparison to their master's.

The adversaries squared off directly in front of the section of the stands in which Earl Sweyn and Eadred's family were seated. Edmond glanced toward the Lady Edith and was surprised by what he thought to be a look of concern. He wondered if it was anxiety for her father or him, though he preferred the latter interpretation. Maybe she feared that her father would injure him seriously. His imagination was running wild, he realized, then flushed hotly even as he parried an exploratory swipe by Eadred. Why should Edith take an interest in what happened to him? They had never even spoken. He fended off another stroke from Eadred, admonishing himself to be more sensible. Still, he felt a touch of bitterness. Was he fated to be ever alone, a stranger in an unfriendly world?

The antagonists warily circled each other, like angrily alert hostile dogs confronted for the first time. The earliest quarterstaff strokes were tentative and exploratory, seeking an opening, a weakness, and were easily parried. The tempo quickly increased and Edmond soon became conscious of his adversary's immense strength, as the power of Eadred's blows at times almost turned his own stick against himself.

While Eadred concentrated on attempting to land a solid blow on Edmond's head, so as to make quick work of him, the latter decided his best tactic was to let the bigger man wear himself out by fending off his strokes and waiting for an opening. He knew his greatest advantage was superior agility, though he was hard-pressed to avoid several of Eadred's more deft attacks. But each time Eadred seemed about to break through Edmond's defense with an exceptionally hard stroke aimed at his head, the youth averted disaster at the last instant with a skillful parry. The furious assault began to slacken, and Edmond tried several feints at Eadred's massive legs. He discovered that his adversary was not easily tricked, and got a sharp, though fortunately glancing, rap on his own shins. Encouraged by the hit, Eadred redoubled his attempts to break through Edmond's defense of his head, but failed to land a blow. Thwarted, he shifted the thrust of his attack toward the upper body, finally scoring a sharp blow on the youth's side that almost made him lose his grip on his staff. Gasping for breath and in some pain, Edmond struggled to regain his balance and concentration. He was barely able to beat off a sustained attack on the same side before he recovered fully.

A rain of futile strokes left Eadred arm-weary, and he relaxed his guard for a moment. Edmond took immediate advantage of the opening, a glancing blow from his stick raising a huge welt on the thane's right hand.

"Well done, lad!" Eadred muttered through gritted teeth, then rallied to rain a series of blows aimed as before at Edmond's head. He was not entirely successful, but the heavy staff twice found Edmond's shoulders, staggering him. He retreated briefly to a defensive posture to shake off the pain before renewing the battle in earnest.

He did not wait long before rushing back at Eadred as soon as he sensed that the thane was tiring, and his reactions might be slowing. His instinct was correct. A skillful thrust found an opening and he landed a glancing blow on Eadred's head. A little more direct and it would have ended the contest. But Eadred recovered and parried two furious following strokes before a sweeping thrust grazed Edmond's head in turn, dazing him for an instant. Eadred sprang forward to follow up the advantage, but was able to merely tap Edmond on the right shoulder before the youth deftly danced out of range. The prolonged, vigorous battle began to turn in Edmond's favor as Eadred's parries slowed and his attacks seemed to lack their former force. He was obviously tiring. Edmond took full advantage of his superior agility to avoid Eadred's ponderous strokes and to land a series of light but smarting blows on the outlaw chief's upper torso and legs.

When Eadred, breathing heavily, fell back to regain his wind, and momentarily lowered his staff, Edmond realized the moment had come to risk all. He feinted toward the thane's injured, swollen right hand, and when Eadred lowered his staff to ward off the stroke, he changed direction and landed a solid rap on his opponent's head. The blow stunned the outlaw, who abruptly dropped his guard. Before he was able to recover, Edmond clouted him again, this time with all his considerable strength.

The astonished and dumbfounded crowd, stunned into awed silence, beheld Thane Eadred topple like a felled ox to the ground to sprawl headlong at Edmond's feet. A concerted groan, like a chorus of disbelief, broke the stillness. What had happened was unthinkable. No one ever had defeated Eadred at quarterstaves before, not even the massive Gurth. Yet this young stranger had conquered beyond dispute.

Chapter Ten

An Offer Rejected

The majority of spectators muttered and whispered to each other in unbelieving astonishment at their leader's misfortune. A few hotheads furiously demanded Edmond be cut down on the spot, but Oswald and several guards formed a protective circle around him. The steward was too canny to risk anticipating his unpredictable master's verdict.

Edmond ignored the commotion, leaning wearily on his quarterstaff and contemplating his fallen opponent with near sympathy. He knew what it was to have a sore head, and Eadred's battered pate was sure to throb for several days. His elation at the victory was muted because it might well lead to his undoing if Eadred decided to exact immediate, even fatal, revenge. He stole a furtive glance at Lady Edith as soon as Eadred regained his senses and painfully pulled himself up to a seated position on the ground. She was half standing, the palms of her small hands pressed together as if in prayer. She sighed relief as her father finally stumbled to his feet, then smiled as Eadred refused Oswald's support and stood unaided, though swaying unsteadily. Next to her, Sweyn looked suitably concerned, but Edmond fancied he detected a smirk of satisfaction on that arrogant face.

"Get away from me!" Eadred roared when Oswald approached again, evidently to help him walk back to his seat in the stands. "What do you think I am, a doddering old man?" Gingerly rubbing his head, he staggered to the benches, and threw himself heavily onto the bench next to Sweyn. "A well-aimed, well-struck blow," he muttered. "Let's hope it served to pound some sense back into my head. To think that I, Earl Eadred, should fall for such a simple trick." He took a long pull from a tankard of ale, wiped his mouth, then turned to Edmond. "You've earned your freedom, lad," he said heartily. "I didn't think you had it in you, more fool I, but you showed me your mettle today. A brave lad, that's certain. But did you have to crack my head?"

"You threatened to cut my throat yesterday," Edmond retorted.

"True enough, and I was tempted to do it, too," Eadred admitted. "I would've saved myself a terrible headache, but it would've been a sorry loss. I could use a brawny, deft fellow like you." He beckoned to Oswald. "Give the lad back his scabbard and whatever else we took from him."

Edmond strapped on the empty scabbard, a rueful reminder that his sword remained stuck in the tree trunk into which he had driven it in his fit of bravado, and tied his shrunken purse to his belt.

"I'll fill them both for you," a voice rang out. It was Sweyn. The earl beckoned to Edmond to approach and leaned forward to give him a friendly tap on the shoulder. "I'll put a new sword in your scabbard, and fatten your slender purse with silver. I can use a lad with your spirit. You'll have what I gave that good archer, Arn, a hundred silver shillings, if you become my man."

The crowd gasped amazement. It was a handsome, even superb offer. Putting aside the money, to become a member of Sweyn's guard was an honor some people might consider superior to being numbered among King Edward's housecarles. After all, the king was singularly devoid of martial qualities.

Edmond stared searchingly at Earl Sweyn, but discerned no mockery in that bland smile. The earl was making the offer in earnest. Not that it made a difference. He was not in the least tempted to agree to serve such a disreputable master. Still, he had to be careful to express his refusal without insulting the earl.

"I thank you, gracious lord, for your most noble and generous offer," he replied smoothly. "Next to the king, there's no one I would be more honored to serve than yourself. Yet as it is my ambition to serve only the king, and none else, I can't accept."

"You aim high," Sweyn remarked with a frown. "Well, good luck, friend."

He turned away to converse with Eadred, who had sworn to himself in wonder at Edmond's rejection of the earl's offer. Edith gasped her astonishment, then smilingly beckoned to Edmond to approach. Her brother Edward jumped up and down

"You go to serve the king then?" she asked.

"My lady, I serve the king every moment of my life," he replied earnestly. "I will do so until my last breath." The words came from the heart, though the king he meant was not the Edward who sat on the throne. There was no way, of course, she could guess that he meant himself.

Taken back by the fervor of his declaration, she whispered, "I wish you well, as does my father."

Edmond then nodded farewell and strode off, scarcely aware of Godfrid at his heels. To his relief, no one attempted to stop him. Eadred apparently was as good as his word, and held no grudge over his defeat.

He and Godfrid crossed the bridge and soon left the settlement a few hundred yards behind them. He intended to try to retrace the outlaws' route from the point at which they had taken him prisoner. He even hoped to regain his father's sword, though the tree into which he had driven it would be hard to find. For that matter, even if he did discover the tree, someone might have succeeded in extricating the weapon.

Lost in thought, and wordlessly plodding along with Godfrid silent at his side, he suddenly became aware of the thud of running heavy feet. He wondered if Eadred had changed his mind and was seeking to recapture him, but when he glanced back only a single man was following them. When he recognized Gurth, he could scarcely keep from laughing. The giant was not only red-faced because of his exertion but was so short of breath he was beginning to wheeze and stumble as he caught up to them.

"I've not run like this since I was a boy no older than Whitehand," Gurth gasped, thankful that Edmond and Godfrid had stopped for him. "Thane Eadred sent me to guide you back to where we found you."

Edmond wondered if that was Eadred's sole motive. But after a keen glance at Gurth, who was almost totally exhausted by his unwonted sprint, he upbraided himself for being so easily suspicious. If Eadred had meant to drag him back, he surely would have sent more than one man, or at least someone more subtle as well as a faster runner than this good-natured giant. He invited Gurth to fall in step with them as they resumed the walk.

He smiled at Gurth. "That's a kind thought. We might have trouble finding the place without help." After a pause, he continued, "You were right, honest Gurth. Your master is a fine hand with the quarterstaff. I've never met a better."

"That may be so, but you taught him a lesson, that's certain. I wouldn't have thought anyone could do that. He's as good as they come, and I've had many a knock on the head and shins to prove it, though no one else would dare challenge me. No, lad, you're as good as they come." He hesitated, apparently weighing his next words, then plunged on. "To tell the truth, I was doubly sorry to see you win because it meant that you'd probably be leaving us. I hoped Earl Eadred would be able to knock some good sense into you and then take you into his service. He's a bluff, impulsive man, but there's good in him. And he needs stout, brave young fellows like you to stand beside him."

Edmond intently scrutinized the outlaw's earnest face. Evidently, he was not such a simpleton as the undiscerning might take him for. "You must mean Earl Sweyn, if I'm not mistaken, Gurth. I'd sleep with an eye open at all times if such a one were my guest."

Gurth nodded. "You think as I do. I believe my lord hopes that if he joins hands with Sweyn it might help him regain the favor of King Edward—rather, the favor of someone much more powerful than even the king, if you know whom I mean."

"Earl Godwin?"

"I thought you a shrewd lad."

"But Sweyn's not the sort to give anything without expecting something in return."

"You're right. He expects Thane Eadred to assist him in some scheme. It's not clear just what he has in mind. And there's something else."

"What?"

"He yearns for Thane Eadred's daughter, the Lady Edith."

Edmond came to an abrupt halt. "He wants the Lady Edith?"

"Yes, that nithing, that scoundrel wants to marry our pretty lady," Gurth choked out as if the words were strangling him. "That son of Satan, that adulterous, murdering, faithless thief wants to take away the sweet child I dandled on my knees when she was no higher than your scabbard." He stomped his feet in anger.

Edmond mused, "You can hardly blame him. What man wouldn't admire such a beautiful woman?"

Gurth glanced sharply at him, but withheld further comment. He concentrated on retracing the route, and before sunset they were approaching the place where Edmond had first encountered the outlaws. They soon arrived at the huge tree trunk into which Edmond had thrust his sword. The battered old weapon was still there. Apparently no one had seen it, or if they had, they had scorned to bother with such an antiquated blade. It would have been no easy matter to retrieve it in any case. Despite Edmond's great strength, he was able to free it only with extraordinary effort. He was thankful to regain it, even if mainly in respect for his father's memory, and slid it back into the scabbard.

Gurth tugged at his mop of hair in embarrassment, shuffled his feet and then held out a firm hand to Edmond. "This is as far as I've been told to go, friend. I leave you, but I wish you good fortune. May you give more hard knocks than you get. You're a stout lad, that's certain."

Edmond wrung his huge paw, then continued with Godfrid on the path northward while Gurth plunged back into the brush to return to the outlaw camp.

Chapter Eleven

Edwy and Christina

After parting from Gurth, Edmond and Godfrid trudged along a few hundred yards in the gathering twilight before the boy broke the silence.

"Why do you wish to join King Edward's service, Master Edmond?"

Edmond glanced at him in surprise. "Did I say that I intend to serve King Edward?"

"Isn't that what you told Earl Sweyn?"

The youngster was quick-witted. Edmond was impressed by how much he picked up. He waggled a finger. "No, Godfrid, I didn't say that I was going to enter King Edward's service. What I said was that I was going to serve the king."

Godfrid's face screwed up in puzzlement. "Isn't that the same thing? I don't understand."

"Perhaps I'll explain it to you some day," Edmond halted to pick up a pebble and bounce it off a tree trunk. "Anyway, how would you like to hear a story?"

"About King Alfred's wanderings or Edmond Ironside's battles?" Godfrid skipped with excitement. "Or maybe about the saga of Beowulf or the poem about Maldon?"

"Well, those are good tales too, but no, I'll tell you another story, and I think it's a fine one. There may come a day when it might mean something special to you."

"Tell me! Tell me!"

"Well then, pay attention and I'll begin. It'll help pass the time on our journey. Many long years ago in the early days of King Cnut, a poor but noble Danish thane named Arnulf had a small holding of land near the town of Bosbury, which is far to the west, the place I come from. Arnulf had followed his lord, King Sweyn Forkbeard of Denmark, to England in hopes of winning enough plunder so that he could buy land at home. It happened, however, that during one of King Sweyn's raids Arnulf carried off a maid of Kent named Gunhilda, and he grew so fond of her that he willingly made her his hand-fast wife. After King Sweyn gave him a few hides of land, Arnulf decided to settle down. He was happy enough for a brief time but much to his grief Gunhilda died while giving birth to their first child, a daughter. Arnulf named the baby

Christina to mark his conversion to the true faith by his wife's persuasion.

"After King Edmond Ironside died and King Sweyn's son, Cnut, became ruler of all England, Arnulf was content to live out his life peacefully, rearing his daughter on his modest estate. He hung up his weapons and tilled his small holding with a few serfs.

"By the time Arnulf's hair turned gray, Christina had grown into a beautiful maiden, by far the fairest in the shire. Arnulf was proud of his daughter, but with old age approaching he worried about what would happen to her after his death. He would often urge Christina after she turned sixteen years of age to accept one of the many young thanes who clamored for her hand despite her meager dowry. She was so fond of her father, however, that she dreaded leaving him alone and rejected all suitors.

"One day as Christina drew water from a well near the cottage in which she and her father lived, a clear young voice rang out, 'Can you spare a cool drink for me, pretty one?'

"She spun about in surprise and alarm since neither Arnulf nor any of their serfs were home. Much to her relief, she beheld the friendly, handsome face of a broad-shouldered lad who had come up unnoticed along the road, not much more than a path, which ran past the cottage. She judged him to be someone of quality. His outer garments, while torn and mud-spattered, were too well-made for those of a villein or serf. She also noted that though smiling he was so weary that he could barely stand upright. She quickly handed him a dipper of water. He tossed it off at one gulp.

"'Thank you, sweetheart,' he said cheerily, then turned to continue along the path. He took only a single step before his knees buckled and he slumped to the ground.

"Alarmed, she ran to help him, but he waved her off and struggled back unaided to his feet. As he got up, his cloak fell open to reveal a torn tunic splattered with fresh blood. He protested at first, but she finally persuaded him to enter the cottage and lie down. She urged him to remain until her father returned. Arnulf, as was his custom, spent much of his time at an ale shop swapping tales with fellow old sea-dogs.

"Despite her inexperience as a nurse, she bandaged a shallow but long cut on the lad's chest, which on inspection proved less serious than one would have supposed from the quantity of blood staining his tunic. He fretted impatiently as she bound the wound, and tried to struggle to his feet the instant she finished.

"'I must leave,' he insisted. 'It won't be safe for you and your family if I'm found here.'

"He attempted to rise once more, but she succeeded by exerting all her strength to push him back down.

"With a rueful smile of resignation he whispered, 'Well, I suppose it wouldn't hurt to rest a bit before I leave. But at least stay by the door and warn me if any horsemen approach. They must not find me here or it'll be the worse for you.'

"He dozed off while she kept watch at the door, wondering just who the young man was and why and by whom he was being pursued. She was also about to doze when she thought she detected rising dust in the distance. She ran to gently tap the youth's shoulder. He awoke and instantly became alert when she reported what she had seen.

"'My enemies are near. They must not find me here or you'll come to harm.'

"'You can hide in the loft,' she suggested.

"'No, I must not be found here,' he insisted and shakily got to his feet. Yet the brief nap had clearly restored much of his strength and he walked firmly toward the door. He was about to leave the cottage when he noticed Arnulf's great bow above the hearth, where it had been hung idle for many years. Ignoring her protests, he took it down and carefully inspected it to determine whether it was still usable. Satisfied of its utility, he also took up a quiver of arrows from a corner into which Arnulf had tossed it long ago, and slung it over his shoulder.

"'I must not be found here,' he repeated as he left the cottage and continued a few dozen yards up the road before halting beside a large tree. Christina peeped out of the doorway to watch him, then heard a swelling clatter of approaching horse hooves from the direction in which she had seen the rising cloud of dust.

"'Back into the house and bolt the door,' the young man shouted, forcing a wan smile. Despite his injunction she kept the door slightly ajar to watch as he loosened the great sword in its scabbard hanging at his side and fitted an arrow to the ancient bow, then placed his back to the massive tree trunk.

"The wounded youth had scarcely prepared to defend himself before two mounted soldiers displaying emblems identifying them as King Cnut's housecarles swept around a bend in the road and thundered past Arnulf's cottage. Immediately on discovering their prey they dismounted, apparently intending to take him prisoner. But his bow string twanged a dirge and an arrow transfixed the chest of the foremost housecarle. Undeterred, his partner drew his sword and lunged forward to cut down the young man, who immediately dropped the bow and met the housecarle with his blade. He fell back before the soldier's fierce assault, but handled his sword adroitly enough to keep his foe from penetrating his guard.

"Sparks flew as steel struck steel, and the metallic clatter provided an almost musical accompaniment to the desperate battle to the death. As she watched in fascinated trepidation, Christina feared that the youth's earlier loss of blood would undo him. And the housecarle's superior brute strength almost enabled him to break through. He did succeed in flicking past the lad's guard to inflict a scratch on his thigh. The young man reeled as if faint with shock, but it was a ruse to encourage the housecarle to recklessness. Drawn in, the soldier tried to end the battle with one sweeping blow, but his agile opponent avoided the thrust and plunged his sword point under his foe's blade deep into his chest. The soldier leaned momentarily on his sword, spat a torrent of blood and then collapsed to his knees before slumping dead to the ground.

"Entirely spent, the conqueror fell in an unconscious heap beside his enemy's corpse. Horrified, Christina opened the door, intending to run to his aid, but became dizzy. She leaned for support against the doorway, her stomach quavering at the blood-spattered scene, then fainted and also sank to the ground.

"As fortune would have it, just then Arnulf returned home, coming around the bend of the road that shielded the site of the battle from view until the cottage was reached. He began to curse in alarm and fear when he saw his daughter lying by the threshold of the house and ran toward her as fast as advanced years permitted. He had pulled her into his arms when to his intense relief she opened her eyes.

"'I'm all right, father,' she cried. 'I'm not hurt. He's the one who needs your help.' She pointed toward the young man, who was just regaining consciousness though still outstretched on the ground by the tree up the road.

"'Help him? Who is he? Why should we help him?' Arnulf sputtered as he took in the entire scene, the two dead housecarles, their abandoned horses and the wounded young man who now was sitting up. 'He's a stranger, a Saxon by the look of him.'

"'I don't know him, I've never seen him before,' Christina admitted as her father helped her stand up, finally convinced she was unharmed. 'But we must help him. He's wounded.'

"'We'd better not have anything to do with him,' Arnulf protested. 'He has killed King Cnut's housecarles, and their comrades will soon be after him. He must be an outlaw. If we assist him we'll be accused of treason, of harboring a fugitive from the king's justice.'

"'We can hide him in the loft until he's well enough to leave,' Christina pleaded. 'We can't just stand by and let him bleed to death, or be hunted down like a wild beast. Please, father, we must help the poor wounded lad.'

"Arnulf never had been able to refuse Christina whatever she asked for that was within reason, and though this certainly did not fit that description, he yielded to her persistent pleas. He reluctantly agreed to examine the youth's wounds and help him into the house. He would decide later whether to hide him from potential pursuers.

"As an old campaigner, Arnulf had tended to many wounded men in his time and a brief inspection of the stranger's wounds convinced him there was no cause for alarm. 'He'll be well enough in a few days with a little rest, daughter,' he announced. 'I've forgotten many worse scratches than these. Come, help me get him indoors.'

"Arnulf lifted the wounded man by the arms while instructing Christina to take hold of his legs. Between them they succeeded in carrying him into the house and laying him onto a bed. Christina ran to fetch water and strips of cloth to attend to the wounds. Her father skillfully cleaned and bandaged the cuts, none of which were deep, then stepped back to admire his handiwork. Satisfied, he sat down at the rude table and looked expectantly at Christina, who wearily sank to an opposite chair, still shaking with excitement over the dreadful scene she had witnessed.

"'Well, daughter, calm down and tell me just what happened?'

"Christina poured out a breathless relation of what she had seen, placing particular emphasis on how defiantly, bravely and skillfully the youth had met his two foes. She was sure this aspect of the battle would appeal greatly to her father. Arnulf smiled and frowned alternately as he listened to her tale. To her great relief, he smiled broadly when she concluded her story, and rubbed his gnarled hands with pleasure.

"'It's good to know they still make such stalwart lads,' he declared. 'I would've been proud to sire such a son.' He grinned at Christina. 'I'd even welcome such a husband for a daughter.' Smiling broadly at her blush, he started for the door, explaining over his shoulder as he left the cottage, 'I'd better make sure no one discovers what has happened here. I'll do what I can to hide the evidence and clean up. Luckily for us, and for our young friend, none of our people were in the house or nearby.'

"He ruefully reflected that while the absence of his servants, whom he had given leave to attend a market day at Bosbury, made it less likely that anyone would discover what happened it also burdened him with the arduous task of concealing the evidence without assistance. He was not getting any younger, he sighed.

"He decided that rather than bury the housecarles on or near his property and risk attracting attention to the cottage, he would remove them as far as possible. He flung the bodies across the backs of their horses, which he led over a seldom-frequented path to a deep pond several miles away. Stripping the corpses, he dragged them down the banks of the small lake, weighted them down with rocks, and flung them into the water. He also threw in the garments and horse trappings.

After making sure everything sank out of sight, he drove off the horses in a direction opposite to that from which he had come.

"It began to rain as he trudged home after completing his grisly task. Though drenched by what quickly turned into a heavy downpour, he was grateful. The storm would wash away bloodstains and other traces of the combat that had taken place near his property. Only the wounded lad lying in the cottage remained as evidence of the fatal struggle that had taken two lives.

"Unaware of what was being done on his behalf, the youth slept until mid-morning of the following day. On opening his eyes, he was startled to behold the fierce-looking, grizzly-mustached old Dane sitting by the hearth languidly contemplating a simmering pot of stew whose savory aroma permeated the cottage. The young man tried to sit up, but a stab of pain reminded him of his wounds, and he sank back with a muffled groan.

"Arnulf glanced at the invalid, and called, 'He's awake, Christina!'

"His daughter darted into the room, clapped her hands in relief and placed a palm on the invalid's brow. His fever had subsided.

"'How do you feel?' she asked.

"'A little weak, but not all that bad,' he replied, flickering a wan smile. He again tried to sit up. Frowning, she pushed him back down.

"'Stay put!' she commanded. "I'll get you something to eat. You must rest until you get your strength back.'

"She would not permit him to grasp a spoon, insisting on feeding the stew to him as if he were an infant. He ate heartily, much to Arnulf's approval and amusement. 'You'll be on your feet in three days,' the old man predicted.

"His forecast was accurate. Youth, an excellent constitution and a pretty nurse were far more effective than any medication would have been, and by the fourth day the young man was back on his feet, if not quite ready to set out again on his travels. Although he was cheerful and polite enough, giving his name as Edwy, he was cautiously secretive, not revealing why the king's men had pursued him. He reassured Arnulf and Christina that it was unlikely that any other housecarles would search for him in the neighborhood. He was convinced that his two pursuers had come across him by accident without having had an opportunity to disclose his whereabouts to anyone else. He felt sure no one could possibly know he was in this part of England.

"Edwy's wounds were fully healed, and he had entirely regained his strength by the second week after his arrival. Inexplicably, while frequently insisting he had to leave soon, he lingered without quite knowing what kept him. Neither Arnulf nor Christina, for far different reasons, were eager for him to depart and whenever he spoke of going both were quick to supply him with cause to further delay his departure.

"He proved a politely attentive listener, and Arnulf took great pleasure in entertaining him during his convalescence with anecdotes of his colorful experiences as one of Sweyn Forkbeard's followers. The old man became increasingly fond of the lad, and began to think of him almost as a son. Much as the Dane loved Christina she was a female and could not properly appreciate his tales of wartime feats, some wholly true, others fancifully embellished, and a few entirely imaginary. Edwy listened with far greater understanding and empathy and enthusiastically enjoyed Arnulf's colorful accounts, even those that seemed wildly improbable.

"The old Dane did not permit himself to be troubled by the obvious warmth of the friendship developing between Edwy and Christina. Indeed, he appeared to encourage it, often leaving the young people for a time while he wandered off to the alehouse to visit with his old cronies. Besides, his servants, to whom he introduced Edmond as the son of an old friend, had returned and could keep an eye on them.

"Christina was soon struck by Edwy's essentially serious nature which contrasted so strongly with her customary gaiety and high spirits. Clearly, something was deeply troubling him. He was often moody and laconic. At other times, however, he responded merrily to her joyous approach to life, and they shared bouts of laughter as they idled away the time when she was not busy with household tasks. He made himself useful as soon as he regained his strength, contributing to his hosts' larder by hunting in the nearby forest. He seldom returned without at least a fat hare hanging from his belt or a deer slung over his shoulder. At other times they strolled in the fields and woods, Edwy carrying the basket as Christina filled it with berries, fruit and herbs.

"After several weeks of such pleasant dalliance, they arrived at an understanding that seemed to them as natural as that night should follow day. They asked for Arnulf's consent to their union. The old man was not caught off guard. He had expected, almost hoped, for such an outcome, though he concealed his delight behind a solemn mask. He was determined to learn more about Edwy before he accepted him as a husband for his beloved daughter. He asked them to sit down while he stood with his back to the hearth.

"'Before I give my consent and blessing, I have some questions,' he began. 'It's not that I don't like you, son, because I do. While I suppose my dear Christina might find a wealthier husband, or one more nobly-born, I'm certain she couldn't marry anyone more acceptable to me. Nor someone more courageous. You've proved yourself in my eyes. I say all this because it's comforting for an old man to know his grandsons will come of brave and worthy stock. There's nothing I despise more in this world than cowardice and dishonorable actions. Though I feel convinced you come of good family, Edwy, I've not heard you say so. I would be shirking my duty to my daughter if I permitted her to marry someone not at least equal to her in birth. I must know more about who her husband is, where he comes from, who his father is or was. You must reveal this to me, Edwy, before I can freely give my consent. I cannot ask less of you.'

"Edwy proudly looked Arnulf in the eye before speaking in measured tones: 'I can tell you only this, good Arnulf, and you must not press me further. My father's name was Ethelred, and no man in all England came of nobler stock. My blood is as good as that of Cnut, the one who calls himself king—nay, better'

"The extraordinary claim astounded Arnulf, but he was impressed by the gravity and earnestness of Edwy's words, and decided to take them at full value.

"'You need say no more, son. I once was as near to King Edmond Ironside as we are to each other now and I'll not deny you look as if you might be kin to him though I have only your word for it. It'll serve." He reached for Christina's right hand and joined it to Edwy's, solemnly declaring, 'Your children will be of noble and brave stock, my dear daughter, a thought that will comfort me all my remaining days.'

"A few days later Edwy and Christina were wed in a proper church ceremony rather than in the frequent hand-fast manner. They lived happily together for several years and, though their first three children were daughters, Arnulf comforted himself with the hope that their fourth would be a son. So it proved. But the price was heavy. Christina died shortly after giving birth to the boy and the little girls quickly followed her to the grave, falling victim to a sweating sickness that swept the country at the time. As grief-stricken as Arnulf and Edwy were, they took consolation in rearing the surviving boy together. Arnulf lived until his grandson was seven years old. In his final days he gloried in holding the child on his knees and entertaining him with the same tales of wild adventure with which he had amused Christina and Edwy.

"After Arnulf died, leaving his slender worldly goods and small estate to his son-in-law, Edwy remained in the cottage, managed his property, and persevered with the twin duties of acting as both father and mother to his son. He taught him to wield arms, and tutored him in all the skills as well as the codes of honor and duty, proper for a man of noble birth. He entrusted his schooling to the monks of a nearby abbey so that he would be able to read and write, as well as cast accounts. Edwy was determined to prepare the boy for whatever demands fortune might make of him.

"Edwy kept a great secret from his son until the end of his life. He did not tell him of his ancestry until almost his final breath. It was then that he revealed their descent from the royal House of Wessex. But he cautioned his son not to seek his heritage, being convinced that such a course was hopeless. He urged him—even extracted his pledge—to leave England and seek his fortune abroad. As an obedient son, the young man felt obliged to carry out his father's wishes. So when Edwy died, he left home to embark on a journey abroad."

When Edmond's voice trailed off at this point, Godfrid looked up expectantly, waiting for him to continue. The boy had listened raptly to every word of the long narration, though not always with complete understanding, and was eager to hear the end of the story. He was bewildered by what seemed to be its abrupt conclusion. After deciding Edmond had indeed broken off, he summoned up enough courage to ask some obvious questions.

"What's the name of Edwy's son? What became of him."

"His name?" Edmond echoed, wondering whether to reveal it even to this simple youngster. It could do no harm. With a careless toss of the head, he laughed, "You'll not believe this, Godfrid, but his name is Edmond, the same as mine. As for what's become of him, or is to become of him, who can tell?"

Chapter Twelve

Invitation to a Bride-Ale

N ot until far after sunset, when Edmond was convinced they were a safe distance from Eadred's outlaw band, did he halt to bed down for the night. He chose a secluded small clearing among the brush a few dozen feet off the beaten path from which it was well hidden. He and Godfrid wrapped themselves tightly in Edmond's heavy woolen cloak to keep out the night chill and make themselves as comfortable as possible on the mossy but hard ground.

Despite the late hour and the strenuous exertions of the day, Edmond was too agitated to fall asleep immediately. His mind churned with speculation as to the consequences of the skirmish in Dover and whether Earl Sweyn's visit to the outlaw band was somehow connected with it. Luckily, he was better informed about the politics of the day than most ordinary rural thanes were likely to be. Although Herefordshire was remote from the capital of Winchester and other centers of political matters, his father had closely followed reports of the major events of state. For reasons that had not become clear until his startling deathbed revelation, Edwy had always made it a point to discuss with Edmond the latest news from King Edward's court and other governmental affairs, as well as their significance. Shortly before his death, Edwy said he thought King Edward was seeking a pretext to diminish the power of his father-in-law, Earl Godwin, to whom he literally owed his throne.

"Behold the ingratitude of man, Edmond," Edwy pointed out. "Without Earl Godwin's support, Edward Ethelredson almost surely would still be living off the bounty of the Normans in Rouen instead of being in a position to parcel out our England to them. Yet he's seeking to discover a pretext, as well as to recruit the supporters he would need, to rid himself of Godwin and his brood of over-mighty sons."

When Edmond protested that the king could not be so ungrateful, Edwy muttered about the thick-headedness of youth before pressing the point.

"Surely, my son, you understand that this Edward, our king, is more Norman than English by education, training and habits. Not only was his mother Norman, but from early childhood on until he turned forty, Edward was an exile in Normandy. He grew up in a French court and values foreign ways of doing things, manners, customs and even amusements far more than those of our people. His most trusted friends are Norman and he keeps so many of them about him that it's disgraceful and insulting to our people. He made his sister's son, Ralph, earl of Herefordshire. His great friend, Robert of Jumieges, is now Archbishop of Canterbury. He has honored and enriched more Normans than I have the patience to name without losing my temper. Even more worrisome is that there are plenty of other hungry Norman wolves clamoring for their share. It's true that Earl Godwinson stands in their way, but if they can drive him from power they'll snap up many of the offices and estates remaining to our people."

Edwy's face became flushed with rage.

"Look you, son," he cried. "Not more than a half-day's ride from here one of those Norman dogs, Richard son of Scrob, is building a tower of stone such as no private Englishman ever has dared erect for fear of the king's displeasure and punishment. What can be its purpose other than to overawe those who live nearby? If our Lord Edward truly cared about his people would he allow such an instrument of oppression and defiance of the king's writ to be erected in his territories?" With a snort of disgust, Edwy stamped out of the cottage to regain his calm by taking a long walk.

If his father had been correct, as Edmond thought probable, King Edward and his Norman advisors might seize on the Dover incident as a pretext to undermine Earl Godwin. Count Eustace of Boulogne would surely complain to the king about how rudely he had been treated by the inhabitants, and demand redress. If Godwin attempted to protect Dover from punishment, the king could accuse him of being disloyal for supporting the townsfolk. He might be emboldened to recruit the earl's many enemies to unite against him in an effort to reduce his power or even drive him out of England. Edward could point to a precedent for action against Dover by citing a similar situation eleven years earlier when his predecessor, King Harthacnut, had pillaged and burned the town of Worcester for the murder of two of his housecarles who were collecting taxes.

There could be little doubt of Earl Godwin's reaction to any attempt to severely punish Dover, which lay in his earldom. The old man hated and despised the Normans and Frenchmen whom he knew to be well on their way to displacing him in the king's confidence and affection. As far as Godwin was concerned, the foreigners rendered Edward no service other than companionship, amusement and flattery yet they were gaining more influence with the king than the man to whom Edward owed his throne. Godwin has put the full weight of his power and wealth behind Edward's successful bid for the kingship after

Harthacnut's death nine years earlier. Godwin had bound the king even closer by making him his son-in-law through marriage to his daughter Edith.

Such considerations made it almost certain Godwin would oppose any effort by King Edward to chastise Dover as Harthacnut had punished Worcester. While Godwin had participated in the expedition against Worcester, he had argued against it before joining in to avoid a break with King Harthacnut. Even then he reportedly had mitigated the brutality of the housecarles' assault on the townsfolk. He probably would make an even firmer stand against disciplining Dover though it was likely to fail as well. The king and his Norman allies, with the possible support of the powerful Earl Siward of Northumbria, who was jealous of Godwin's influence in the south, might choose to make a major issue of the incident at Dover. If the dispute came to a head, however, Edmond vowed he would know with which side to cast his lot—that of Godwin and England.

He turned with relief from the tangled web of political intrigue and hatreds to what should have been a more pleasant topic, that of women, specifically Adele and Edith. He obviously knew little of Edith other than that she had seemed sympathetic to him during the archery tournament and his duel at quarterstaves with her father. He laughed at himself. He might have been imagining her interest in him. Yet somehow it vexed him to think of her becoming the bride of Earl Sweyn, whom he instinctively despised for his history of villainous conduct.

Well, what was Edith to him, after all? He should be far more concerned about Adele, though it was certain that Aegelsig would take good care of her. Not only had Aegelsig been Osgood's best friend, but their wives had been sisters, making Adele the armorer's niece. There surely was no cause for anxiety about Adele's financial welfare as she was the heiress of the richest man in Dover, and Osgood had chosen Aegelsig to be her guardian in the event of his death. What disturbed Edmond was the memory of how distraught Adele had been after her father's death, as if somehow she bore some of the blame for his murder. To judge by the way she looked at him at their last sad meeting, she even seemed to think him at fault for the tragedy. He was alarmed. Women had been known to enter convents on lesser pretexts than such a great calamity and he shuddered at the thought of her deserting the world. No, she could not do that. She had too great a passion for life. He recollected her full red lips, glossy black hair, ardent handclasp, and impish smile. How could such a one bury herself in the living tomb of a convent?

He reverted to Edith, but his opinion of her was far different, more detached, less emotional. Her fragile blonde beauty might have captivated his eyes, but his mind and heart remained untouched. How could it be otherwise when he and Edith had exchanged only two or three words. He knew little of her beyond what Gurth had told him, but still it was a pity to contemplate her being handed over to a suitor so notorious as Earl Sweyn.

Consideration of Sweyn swung his mind back to politics even if this time the usually prosaic subject was tinged with a touch of romance. In one of his many infamous actions, Sweyn five years earlier had seduced and carried off the beautiful Abbess Eadgifu of Leominster in violation of the laws of church and state. Perhaps to his credit, after they had lived together for a while, Sweyn sought to marry her, but the church was adamant in its rules for a woman who had consecrated herself to Christ. When it forbade the marriage, Sweyn flew into a violent rage and in frustration abandoned his earldom to seek his fortune abroad for three years. Eventually tired of wandering, he returned to England, but soon quarreled bitterly with his cousin Earl Beorn, who had taken over part of his estates during his absence. Sweyn lured the unsuspecting Beorn aboard one of his ships on the pretext of arriving at an accommodation, and once at sea had strangled him to death and thrown his body overboard.

When the atrocious crime became known not even Earl Godwin's stature and influence could save Sweyn from being outlawed and banished by the horrified and indignant king and council. It took Godwin months to obtain a pardon and permission to return to England for his son. Though Sweyn regained most of his estates, he sulked because Herefordshire remained in the hands of Earl Ralph, the king's French nephew. Edmond surmised that Sweyn's mysterious visit to Dover, overtures to Thane Eadred and wooing of Edith were part of a scheme to recover his lost lands.

"What does it all matter to me?" Edmond finally muttered disconsolately. "To the devil with Sweyn, Eadred, Godwin and all the rest," he decided, then fell asleep beside Godfrid, who had drifted off long before.

When they awoke in the morning, they washed the sleep away at a nearby brook, shared Edmond's remaining bread, cheese and ale, and resumed their journey. They paused only briefly at mid-day in a village where Edmond was able to buy enough food and drink to last them until they reached London.

They arrived at the outskirts of the city on the fourth day of their trek. Southwark lay directly before them. Godfrid never before had seen anything grander than Eadred's rude settlement and a few villages so he danced in excitement as they began to pass the substantial buildings scattered along Ermine Street. The highway ran northward toward a junction with Watling Street, another ancient Roman road. The high embankment was lined on both sides by the large timbered dwellings of the wealthy merchants who were transforming London into the foremost center of commerce in northwestern Europe. Spacious gardens with bountiful orchards surrounded the houses, many belonging to prosperous Danes who had quickly abandoned the lawless if profitable freebooting of their fathers to engage in lawful and even more advantageous commerce. Others were owned by rich Flemings and Germans who were making the most of the growing trade between England and their native towns. Intermingled with these were the mansions of England's greatest earls and thanes, maintained for their occasional visits to London. Many of the buildings rested on foundations sunk by the Roman and British founders of Southwark, a settlement which many centuries earlier had dwarfed the small Roman fort lying along the northern bank of the Thames River, the seed that was to grow into great London.

Edmond and Godfrid both were awed by their first glimpses of what already was acknowledged to be the principal city of England. Their route upon the metalled road raised high above the sometimes marshy ground unfolded one wonder after another, but none more imposing than a huge mansion whose magnificence dwarfed all the others. As they approached, they saw that its grounds were swarming with people bustling about dozens of tables laid in rows surrounding the main building. The din of music, talk and laughter, and the clatter of hundreds of dishes and tankards of ale swelled into an uproar as they came near the building.

"Welcome, travelers!" one of the merry-makers shouted to Edmond. "Come, join in the bride-ale. There's food and drink aplenty for all comers."

Edmond was tempted, but shook his head. He was eager to cross the river he knew to be nearby so that they would reach London before nightfall.

"Don't be foolish, lad! When ale is to be had for the mere asking one must drink it if only to please Earl Godwin."

The words rang out crisp, clear and commanding. Edmond spun about to discover a young man on horseback who had just come up behind him. The rider was tall, strongly-built, richly-dressed and of commanding appearance. His eyes, now green, now blue, examined Edmond and Godfrid with a penetrating yet friendly glance. A hooded peregrine falcon perched upon his leather-protected left wrist, its talons still moist with the blood of a victim that no doubt hung among the string of birds tossed over the shoulder of one of the two servants attending him.

"Nay, by the holy rood, nay!" the horseman swore good-naturedly as he swung out of the saddle to grasp Edmond's hand. "You must not pass by the hall of Earl Godwin without drinking in good fellowship to celebrate my brother Tostig's wedding day. Not while Harold Godwinson stands between you and the road. Every traveler, of whatever degree, is welcome, such is my father's command."

Edmond yielded to the young man's enthusiastic and obviously sincere invitation and with Godfrid tagging along followed Earl Harold through the throng of celebrants into his father's great hall. Even in the midst of the joyous revelry and deafening noise, he marveled at the quirk of fate that had brought him face to face with Harold Godwinson, who in ordinary circumstances probably would not have paid him the slightest attention, let alone personally invited him to sit at his great father's table.

Chapter Thirteen

The King's Summons

There was no mistaking Earl Godwin even among the most distinguished-looking of the dozens of high-ranking guests making merry within his great hall. He stood out like a wolf amidst a pack of hounds. England's most powerful magnate, a shrewd-eyed, red-faced, gray-haired formidable old man with a haughty and commanding air, occupied the high seat at the head of a series of tables spanning the length of the immense room. His ordinarily stern face was wreathed in smiles as he repeatedly raised an ale-horn to welcome the guests who had come to celebrate the wedding of his third son Tostig to the Lady Judith, a daughter of Godwin's foreign friend and ally, Count Baldwin of Flanders.

Count Baldwin sat at his host's right elbow, his flushed face suggesting that if he was remarkably quiet it was because he was too busy drinking to waste time in idle chatter. He kept his right arm familiarly around Tostig's shoulders as he whispered occasionally to the bridegroom. Tostig's oft-brooding narrow face shone with uncustomary warmth, his eyes from time meeting those of his bride, who sat joyfully beside him. At Earl Godwin's left was his wife Gytha, who divided her attention between beaming on Tostig, her favorite son, and frowning at several of his younger brothers, Leofwine, Gurth and Wulfnoth, because they were raising havoc with their loud revelry at the far end of the hall.

All heads swiveled and the commotion diminished slightly when Earl Harold entered the room with Edmond and Godfrid following at his heels.

"Ah, it's you at last, Harold," cried Earl Godwin, half-rising in his chair and waving his ale-horn in reproof. "You should have been here long since. What kept you, my son?"

"I beg your indulgence, my lord father, and especially yours, brother Tostig, and that of my dear sister-in-law." Harold bowed with a flourish. Judith flushed before mirroring Harold's warm smile, but Tostig scowled, then looked away.

"I was so caught up in the pleasures of falconry that I lost all perception of time and forgot this was the happy day of your wedding. I can now truly appreciate, brother Tostig, why you yourself are so fond of such fine sport. I assure you, however, I didn't intend to slight anyone. To prove my good will, here's to my new sister, the beautiful Judith, to my cherished brother Tostig, and to our noble kinsman, Count Baldwin." Harold seized a full tankard from the table and emptied it without pausing for breath.

Edmond fidgeted, so far forgetting himself as to tap his toes impatiently while standing at Harold's elbow through the earl's graceful apology. Harold swung around to discover the source of the repetitive noise. Catching Edmond in the act, he laughed boisterously.

"Well, good friend, you are poorly entertained by the sorriest of hosts," he barked. "Come. follow me, we can sit beside my good mother." Two places quickly emptied beside Gytha, Harold taking the seat next to her and inviting Edmond to occupy the other. "Quickly, quickly, something to eat and drink for my young guest," he ordered. A full platter and ale-horn were immediately set before Edmond who ate and drank heartily, making sure to share with Godfrid, who had shyly stationed himself behind his seat.

Earl Godwin glanced nonchalantly at Harold, but Edmond's appearance arrested his attention. His eyes narrowed as he examined the stranger thoughtfully, then relaxed to remark, "You must have a rare gift for falconry, Harold. I congratulate you on bringing back such a fine bird. He reminds me of someone but I can't for the life of me think of who it could be. You haven't introduced your companion."

"It's my day for being ill-mannered," Harold exclaimed, striking his forehead. "I haven't even asked my young friend his name."

"Edmond Edwysson, my lord. I'm a thane of Herefordshire and my father's lands were near the town of Bosbury."

Godwin shrugged almost imperceptibly as if to dismiss any vague concerns he might have had about the newcomer's resemblance to someone he had met at one time. Though unimpressed by Edmond's rank and origin, he remained polite. "Welcome to our bride-ale, Thane Edmond," he said heartily, hands spread to indicate the heavily-laden table. "Enjoy our hospitality, young man. We must usher Lady Judith into our family in fitting fashion. Come, let's eat and drink the tables bare!"

It was a remarkable goal in view of the seemingly inexhaustible supply of meat, bread, fruit and drink constantly being replenished by Godwin's household servants. Not wishing to embarrass their host or themselves by failing to meet the challenge, his guests endeavored mightily to live up to his expectations. They gorged themselves until the majority could no longer open a mouth because of sheer exhaustion. Godwin's lavish bounty ensured that the bride-ale of Tostig and Judith would never be forgotten, surpassing even that of King Edward and the Lady Edith Godwinson, the great earl's daughter, in the memory of those fortunate enough to have attended both celebrations.

Edmond would not permit his busy hands and mouth to divert him from also making the most of his eyes and ears. It was important to take advantage of the opportunity to learn what he could about Earl Godwin's powerful family. The sullen manner in which Tostig had greeted Harold Godwinson's arrival had not escaped him. Edmond also caught the whispers of some of those within earshot who speculated as to the whereabouts of Godwin's eldest son, Sweyn, and whether he was intentionally keeping away from his younger brother's wedding feast. Edmond discovered that Tostig was jealous of both Sweyn and of Harold, and not entirely without cause. It was worth keeping in mind this rift among Godwin's sons. He might need to exploit it some day.

The afternoon wore away quickly as it usually does on happy occasions such as wedding feasts, and it was almost twilight when the loud blast of an approaching horn cut through even the deafening clamor of the celebration. The crowd quieted expectantly, all eyes turning toward the entrance through which strode a dust-covered royal courier, who stumbled to his knees in exhaustion before the astonished Earl Godwin.

"I come from King Edward, great earl, from your lord the king," the courier gasped, thrusting a rolled-up and sealed document into Godwin's hands. The earl unsealed the parchment, glanced briefly at the message, and rose to his feet.

"Prepare my arms and horse! Summon the housecarles!" Godwin ordered his household steward, who had rushed to his side at the courier's arrival. "We set out for Gloucester at daybreak. You, Harold, will come with me. No, no, Tostig, this is your wedding day," he added, his manner softening as he turned to the bridegroom, who had exchanged unhappy glances with his bride but nevertheless leaped to his feet to await his father's orders. "No need for you to desert your pretty Judith. Neither is it a matter for you, Count Baldwin. The king commands our presence at council to discuss some skirmish or the other between his Norman pets and my good people of Dover. I'll know what to advise him."

Godwin paused with a frown. "But it would be well to have my eldest son, Sweyn, by my side. Where is he?" He pounded the table angrily, glaring at those nearest as if to extort a reply from them. "Full two weeks have passed since we last were honored with his ungrateful presence."

"You call me, father?" The reply was mild as the slender, graceful, yet sinister-looking Earl Sweyn appeared suddenly before Godwin. Those who had not seen Sweyn enter the hall across the threshold moments before he spoke were ready to swear that he had materialized out of thin air so stealthily had he approached his irate father. "You needn't shout, my good lord. I've heard you and I'm ready to obey your command to accompany you though I fear King Edward and his worthy friends would be best pleased if I were to keep away from them."

Angry though he was, Godwin could not repress a smile, and the rest of the company felt free to laugh. King Edward's hatred of his brother-in-law Sweyn was matched by the latter's contempt for the effeminate monarch. The outburst of hilarity was a good note on which to break up the bride-ale. Earl Godwin's retinue scattered quickly to prepare for setting out on the long march to Gloucester the next day.

Earl Harold put a hand on Edmond's shoulder. "You've a mind to come with us, my friend?"

Earl Sweyn overheard his brother and, recognizing Edmond at a glance, silkily interjected, "I wouldn't be surprised if he would. I suspect this young fellow knows more about the tumult at Dover than most of us are likely to."

When Edmond returned his insinuating wink without blinking, Sweyn added, "Come now, friend, admit I'm not far from right."

Edmond shrugged off the glib remark with a smile, careful to conceal his uneasiness. Sweyn clearly knew something about what had taken place at Dover, and his part in the battle. If it had been anyone other than Sweyn, Edmond might have dismissed the matter. But the earl's reputation for intrigue and double-dealing was notorious. He would not hesitate to reveal or conceal what he knew if either course furthered his interests. It was possible, however, that Edmond's own knowledge of Sweyn's visit to Dover and the outlaws of Ashdowne Forest might silence the earl. He might not want his father and brother Harold to know about them. Sweyn's indirect way of bringing up the subject, almost as if he meant to warn Edmond to keep quiet about his own adventures, gave this view some substance. All the same, it was annoying that Sweyn apparently knew of his part in the battle of Dover. Perhaps he had not left the town after the heated exchange with the Norman in the tavern witnessed by Edmond and Wiglaf. But where had he been during the clash between the Normans and the townsfolk?

Earl Harold wheeled about in surprise at Sweyn's remark, and glanced keenly at both his brother and Edmond. "You've met before?"

"Briefly, at some country fair," Sweyn replied guardedly, a glance warning Edmond not to elaborate. Edmond nodded, pleased to have his suspicion confirmed. Sweyn wanted to keep secret his visits to Dover and Ashdowne Forest.

Harold accepted his brother's curt answer, and again asked Edmond, "You'll come with us then?"

"Most willingly, my lord." Edmond was sincere. He was curious to see just how this matter of Dover would unfold. He was also anxious to visit the royal court at Gloucester. It would be an opportunity to learn more about the factions and rivalries swirling about hapless King Edward without arousing the least suspicion of himself. It was time to begin his political education.

"It's settled then," Harold said. "We'll leave at dawn as my father has ordered."

When they set out in the morning, Edmond was impressed at how quickly Earl Godwin had been able to assemble a formidable force. He found himself and Godfrid part of a long column of horsemen and foot soldiers that left Southwark shortly after dawn. Earl Godwin with two of his sons, Sweyn and Harold, accompanied by more than two hundred men, took the road across the breadth of England toward distant Gloucester. The troops were well equipped and disciplined, most of them veterans who had been among King Edward's housecarles. The king had pruned his guards a few years earlier to economize, and Godwin had been quick to enroll the best men into his private army.

Edmond rode armed like the others. Earl Harold had loaned him equipment out of his own stock except for the ancient sword Edmond kept by his side. While the borrowed hauberk, shield and battle-ax did not compare in quality to those Edmond had left in Dover they were far from despicable. Harold also had provided him with a horse and even a mule for Godfrid, who clung to its back proudly if precariously, weighed down by his master's shield.

As Southwark quickly receded behind the small army, Earl Sweyn struck a note of foreboding.

"Mischief may come of this, my lord father," Sweyn commented to Earl Godwin "The Normans may take advantage of any differences between you and our good king over how to deal with Dover to undermine your influence."

Godwin growled. "I don't fear the Normans, my son. I've always been able to handle them—Edward as well. My royal son-in-law has his sulky moods, even fits of temper, but he's a weak reed like his father, Ethelred. I'll know how to deal with him. He'll come around to our way of thinking."

Chapter Fourteen

King Edward the Confessor

T he rolling plateaus and bare limestone uplands of the Cotswolds
glowered ominously in the direction of Gloucester as Godwin's
troop neared its destination. Once the royal city came within
sight though, the slender, heaven-thrusting spires of the great minster
smiled in lofty defiance at nature's ruder architecture. Edmond felt as if
he were almost home. His native district around Bosbury lay only a
day's travel to the north.

In deference to his most powerful subject, King Edward emerged
into the courtyard of the royal hall to greet Earl Godwin and his sons.
Edmond gazed with unbounded curiosity upon the royal uncle whom
he had never seen before, and who was surely unaware of his nephew's
existence. The king was a handsome man of middle height whose rosy
cheeks contrasted oddly with the full white beard and abundant head of
hair encircling his face. His most noteworthy physical feature was his
hands, which were slender, white and femininely delicate. Flanking
Edward were the haughty, pale Robert of Jumieges, the Norman
archbishop of Canterbury, and Count Eustace of Boulogne, the king's
brother-in-law, who fortunately failed to recognize in Edmond his
antagonist on the streets of Dover.

Earl Godwin and his following accorded the king the full customary
honors due a monarch, but rancor was evident in the perfunctory
salutations given the archbishop and count, who returned such cold
courtesy with similar disdain.

King Edward chose to ignore the hostile atmosphere. "Your quick,
ready response to our summons pleases us, Lord Godwin. We hope it
signifies that you are in accord with us as to the punishment which must
be meted out to these insolent, rebellious townsmen of Dover."

Interpreting Godwin's silence as assent, Edward led the earl and his
sons into the presence chamber. Edmond heeded Harold's whisper to
remain at his side. The king seated himself upon a massive chair of state,
rested his chin upon those delicate hands, fingers intertwined as if in
prayer, and studied Godwin's grim yet respectful expression. "What say
you, my lord?"

Godwin set his lips firmly. "What are the charges against these good
townsmen?"

92

"What are the charges?" Edward echoed, frowning. "We detailed them to you in full in the summons we sent you, my lord. But let Count Eustace refresh your memory so that there'll be no confusion or misunderstanding." He leaned back in his chair, plucking nervously at his beard, and frowningly dropped all pretense of cordiality.

Count Eustace haughtily rattled off his interpretation of what had taken place at Dover. He represented that a polite request for suitable lodgings for himself—as only fitting for someone of his rank, who was also the guest and brother-in-law of the king—had been met by unprovoked violence. The townsfolk unexpectedly had set upon his entourage and murdered nineteen of his men while wounding many others. At this point in his relation, the count worked himself into such passionate indignation that he shrieked that Dover must be burned to the ground if justice was to be done. No lesser punishment would serve, he swore.

"You see, Earl Godwin," King Edward interjected, "these rascally burghers must be taught a lesson they and any like them will never forget. They've grown far too insolent and unruly. If you require more men, take as many of our housecarles as you need to harry Dover."

Edmond bit his lips to keep from interrupting Count Eustace's flagrantly distorted account of what had touched off the conflict. He wanted to shout it was all a preposterous lie. What about the Normans' insolent demands? And the murder of innocent Osgood? He was shocked by the king's attitude, though he should have expected it considering Edward's widely-known affection for his Norman courtiers. Yet he could scarcely believe the king would so readily side with strangers against his own loyal subjects. How could he so readily accept a foreign interloper's word against his people? Why did he not suspend judgment until the citizens of Dover had been given an opportunity to tell their side of the story? He was relieved to hear Earl Godwin speak up.

"Count Eustace's charges against my people of Dover are grave indeed, my lord king," Godwin began deliberately. "He demands harsh punishment, as he should if the accusations can be proved. Yet justice requires that an investigation precede any hasty action, that the people of Dover be called on to explain and justify—if they can—their actions. Let's not forget there is a law supreme over us all—king, earl, count and thane, as well as lesser folk. Or if not law, it's the custom of our people to let every man accused speak up in his own defense. Let us honor both law and custom, whichever best applies to this matter. We've heard Count Eustace's account of what happened in Dover and what caused the conflict. He has charged the townsfolk with a serious crime, of breaking the king's peace, neglecting the obligations of hospitality, and of having attacked him and his men without the least justification. But we haven't heard from the people of Dover. It's only right they should be called on to answer the count's accusations. Let's send for the town magistrates so that they can state their case before you and the council, lord king. Give them a chance to defend themselves. Let's discover whether they can explain and justify their actions and disprove Count Eustace's charges. If it is shown that they wronged Count Eustace and his men, as well as you, King Edward, then let us punish them severely. But never, never will I consent to take arms up against our people without first having heard what they have to say on their own behalf."

At Godwin's defiant conclusion the king leaned forward on the edge of his chair as if to spring upon his father-in-law.

Godwin raised a restraining hand, then continued. "I've a duty to the people of Dover, who look upon me as their lord, as well as to my king. The men of Dover are under my protection and will remain so until it's proved they no longer are deserving of it."

After that ringing declaration, Godwin bowed to King Edward, then stepped back to join his sons, Edmond, and several of his officers in a group which had drawn perceptibly apart from the king's assembled courtiers.

Edward's white hands clutched nervously at a golden cross embroidered upon a fold of his long gown near his left knee. The natural rosiness of his cheeks gave way to a deep flush of rage that made it seem as if he was on the verge of suffering a stroke. Archbishop Robert, stationed at the king's left, remained impassive though Edmond fancied that a flash of scorn flickered across his face during Godwin's defiant speech. Count Eustace gnawed angrily at his mustache, clearly hungering for an order by the king to let his men fall upon Godwin and his sons. Despite Edward's rage and frustration over Godwin's uncooperative stand, he was not prepared to go that far.

"You may leave us, my lord!" Edward's voice rose to a high pitch. "You may depart until we send for you again. We shall consider what you've said and render our decision. But you may be certain we won't forget your obstructive attitude."

Godwin politely inclined his grizzled head, spun about, and stalked out of the hall, followed by Sweyn, Harold, Edmond and the rest of his company. Edmond kept a firm grip on his sword hilt, expecting the king's men to fall upon them at any moment, but Godwin's group reached the courtyard without incident. As Godwin was helped onto his horse, he remarked, "Our good king has a fiery temper, but a weak will. His petulant fit will soon pass. He'll be more disposed to accept our advice after he has had time to consider how reasonable I've been in demanding that justice be done."

This time, however, the cunning old earl had misjudged his son-in-law, or rather had underestimated the influence of the king's advisers. They exerted more power over him than Godwin realized. Left to his own inclinations the king might have agreed with Godwin's stand, but he was surrounded by a coterie of Norman advisors and the earl's English enemies. They combined to poison his mind against Godwin, accusing him of undue ambition not only for himself but also for his sons, and of undermining the royal prerogatives and appropriating them to himself.

Count Eustace insistently repeated, embellished, and enlarged upon what he described as the insolence of the people of Dover. He characterized their harsh treatment of the king's brother-in-law as rebellion against the crown as well as disrespect for King Edward himself.

Archbishop Robert, the foremost churchman of England, was even more assiduous than the count to disparage Godwin. With all the cunning and force of his subtle and incisive mind, the archbishop of Canterbury diligently revived past calumnies to reinforce real or fancied injuries of the present. The archbishop's sharpest weapon was to remind Edward of the rumor that implicated Godwin in the brutal blinding and killing of the king's brother Alfred many years before when the ill-fated prince had come to England to seek support for his claim to the throne. No one doubted that King Harold Cnutson had a hand in the atrocious crime, but Godwin's complicity had never been established. The earl twice had stood trial on the charge of murdering Alfred and both times had won acquittal from a jury of his peers, not all of them his friends.

Archbishop Robert constantly reminded Edward that the murder of a brother must never be forgotten nor lightly forgiven. Edward groaned and tore his beard at the recollection of the horror and sorrow he had suffered when the news of Alfred's pitiful death reached him during his exile in Rouen.

"No one can deny that Earl Godwin helped you reclaim the throne, that he assured your election, but it was yours by birthright, my lord," the archbishop argued. "Then he had the temerity to exact a price for his assistance by forcing his daughter on you as your wife. Ever since he has acted more as your master rather than your subject. See how he defies you in this matter of Dover? Who is the king, the sovereign, the lord of England? Is it you, sire, or Earl Godwin, a lowly shepherd's son if what they say is true?"

With Edward's petulance and anger stoked by the archbishop as well by the count and other advisors, the king's weathervane mind became so hardened against Earl Godwin that he burned with impatience to have his most powerful subject dragged into his presence bound in chains.

Unaware of the depth of the hostility building up against him, Earl Godwin, established his entourage on an estate belonging to Earl Sweyn at Beverstone, a small community in the billowing folds of the Cotsworld to the southeast of Gloucester. Almost immediately, Sweyn vanished without informing anyone of his whereabouts. Godwin shut himself up to reflect in isolation upon what had taken place, plan his next move, and await what he confidently expected to be a more conciliatory attitude by the king.

Abandoned by his father and brother, Earl Harold insisted upon Edmond remaining constantly by his side. He was delighted to discover that his new friend was a competent chess player. The earl was passionately fond of the game, but none of the people around him were skillful foes. He rejoiced in finding a worthy opponent.

"By St. Swithin's beard, friend Edmond, that's a shrewd move," he exclaimed as they sat at the chess board a day after the confrontation with the king. "You've checkmated me. I see no way out for my king. I would to heaven we had King Edward in a similar situation."

"Your father believes him to be. He seems confident the king will come around to his way of thinking."

Harold shook his head. "With all respect, I'm afraid my father undervalues the influence his enemies have gained with the king." He opened the chess game by advancing his king's pawn two squares. "If I had my way, I'd round up his Norman friends and ship the lot back to Duke William. I'd begin with Archbishop Robert."

"Easy to say, hard to accomplish, rash boy!" exclaimed Earl Godwin, who suddenly appeared in the doorway. "When you're my age, you'll be more patient, my son." He put an arm fondly around Harold's shoulders. "But you're right, these foreigners have more influence with Edward than I thought possible. He has called for a meeting of the Witan, and not only to consider the matter of Dover but to sit in judgment on me."

Sighing, the old earl sank wearily onto a bench, his wrinkled countenance more deeply furrowed than ever. The king had become astonishingly intransigent to judge by the latest reports from the court in Gloucester. What Godfrid considered Edward's ingratitude was a bitter blow to the venerable kingmaker, who feared his arduous labor of many years was about to be undone.

After securing the throne for Edward following the death of King Harthacnut, Godwin had used his immense influence to exalt his own family, placing his large brood of sons in control of much of England. By marrying his daughter to the king, he even hoped to become grandfather to a future king. Unfortunately for the latter ambition, the union of Edward and the Lady Edith had been unproductive. The malicious accused Godwin's daughter of being barren. Others whispered that Edward refused to cohabit with a wife he disdained because he resented her father. Churchmen and the religiously inclined exalted Edward as a saintly celibate, who avoided the pleasures of the flesh as violation of the precepts of his faith. Godwin believed the bitter reality was that Edward was neither man nor woman, but of indeterminate sex lacking normal male instincts.

Harold became impatient with his father's protracted and meditative silence. "You say the king has called the Witan to sit in judgment upon you, my lord? On what grounds? What are you charged with and by whom?"

Godfrid smiled weakly. "Come, my son, surely you can't be so naive, so unknowing. For the death of the Atheling Alfred, of course."

Harold jumped to his feet. "For Alfred's death. I can't believe it."

"Yes, Alfred's death! By the devil's horns, yes!" Godwin groaned, banging his fist on the table so fiercely that the chessmen flew off in every direction.

"But you've been tried twice on that false, detestable accusation, my lord."

"And acquitted twice!" Godwin cried. "When Alfred came to England fifteen years ago I was among the foremost to welcome him, that's true. But I did so chiefly out of regard for his royal blood. I told him, with all respect, that I couldn't support any attempt by him to press his claim to the throne against those of the sons of my dread master, King Cnut. When King Harold Cnutson, demanded that I turn Alfred over to him, I had no choice but to obey. The king pledged Alfred would come to no harm, that he would be shipped back to Normandy. I was as horrified as anyone when those around the king blinded the atheling, and slaughtered his retinue. Soon after, Alfred died, whether of his wounds or because he was murdered, I don't know.

"As heaven is my witness, this was the extent of my involvement in Alfred's sad fate, yet Edward still holds his brother's death against me after all these years, and after all I've done on his behalf. If there be guilt in what I did, why I have paid for it long and bitterly. Now it seems I must continue to do so if my enemies prevail with the king."

Earl Godwin pulled himself laboriously to his feet and stomped around the room, swearing under his breath.

"What do you propose to do, my lord?" Harold asked at length, idly fingering a rook he had picked up off the floor.

"I've sent a courtier to the king. I demand an audience for myself, and for you and Sweyn so that I can refute these calumnies. I've even offered to renew my compurgation on the charge of slaying the Atheling Alfred." The last was uttered savagely, and the old man groaned, tormented by the indignity of even having to acknowledge such a base accusation. He sank to the bench, called for wine, and brooded in silence over his cup while Harold and Edmond somberly played another game of chess.

Godwin's messenger to the king at Gloucester was back by mid-afternoon.

"What does our gracious lord king have to say to my respectful and humble request?" Godwin demanded, his hopes raised by the speedy response from the court.

"King Edward instructed me to say that he will not see you, nor your sons, nor will he accept your compurgation. He demands that you appear immediately before the Witan to stand trial for the charges that have been made against you."

Godwin fell back as if struck by a bodily blow, and turned purple with rage. He could barely speak in his anger, forcing out his next words through gritted teeth.

"Return to Gloucester and inform the king that unless he surrenders Count Eustace to stand trial for his high-handed—nay, criminal—actions in Dover, I'll come and seize that misbegotten, over-proud Norman." Godwin slammed his fist on the table. "What's more, inform the king that I insist that he also deliver into my hands Richard Scrobson, who is violating the laws, customs and usage of our people by building a castle on our soil. I'll raze it to the ground and burn every timber. I'll rid our land of the Norman scourge and safeguard our time-honored liberties."

The messenger, tired as he was from having ridden to and from Gloucester that day, nevertheless turned to obey Godwin's orders when Harold intervened.

"Wait, Sebert, let Esegar or Sexwulf, noble thanes as devoted as yourself to our house, carry my father's words to the king. Get some rest. We may have another mission for you before the day is out."

Harold turned to Godwin. "If you intend to enforce your demands, my lord, you'll need far more men than the handful we have with us, fewer than two hundred or so. Besides, the king's people are more likely to agree to a compromise when faced with vastly superior forces."

"Compromise!" Godwin roared. "Who said anything about compromise? I intend to flay that arrogant Norman, Count Eustace—he's a bastard like his lord, Duke William." The outburst relieved his anger and he continued in more measured tones, "You're right, of course, Harold, we must arrive at some bargain with my dear son-in-law, King Edward. As you suggest, we'll need more men. We must rally the people of Wessex and East Anglia and the Mercians under your brother Sweyn to our support."

After a pause, Godwin snapped, "Where is Sweyn? Why is he never on hand when we need him?"

He cursed in exasperation at his elder son's unreliability, then looked suddenly and piercingly at Edmond, "With whom do you side, young man? Are you sworn to Earl Harold?"

"I'm sworn to no man," Edmond replied with stiff dignity. "However, if Earl Harold needs me, I'll stand by him of my own free will because I believe you have the right of this matter."

"I accept your offer, Thane Edmond," Harold said warmly, extending a hand to shake Edmond's. "I'd rather be served well by a man of his free will than indifferently by one sworn to me. I welcome your friendship and help."

"Well said, Harold!" Earl Godwin cried; his gloom lifted by this display of the warm-hearted trust of youth. "Keep Thane Edmond at your side and I trust you'll both deserve well of each other."

"We'll both get what we deserve if we stick together," Harold laughed, slapping Edmond's back. "Enough words. Now let's seal our compact with a deed, friend Edmond. If you will, find Thane Sebert and bid him to send messages to all of our loyal followers. They are to join us here fully armed as quickly as possible. There must be no delay."

While Edmond complied with Harold's request, he reflected on the importance and risk of casting his lot with the House of Godwin. The decision was not altogether impulsive. It had been dictated partly by his feeling of responsibility for what had happened in Dover. It would have been more judicious to stand aside and hope to profit from the turmoil of a struggle for supremacy between the king and Earl Godwin. Yet such a course would have been dishonorable, too jackal-like. Besides, what could he accomplish on his own, an unknown thane with no following? Now if Godwin prevailed he would gain status and influence, perhaps even a voice in the conduct of affairs. The gamble was worth the risk.

Before sunset, messengers set off in all directions from Beverstone to summon Godwin's great following from the vast districts of England under his family's control. The issue was about to be joined. It would soon become clear who were the real masters of England, Earl Godwin and his sons or King Edward and his minions.

Chapter Fifteen

Godwin and Leofric

Despite being apprehensively aware of Earl Godwin's immense resources and power, King Edward and his Norman advisors chose to challenge and try to bring him to account for defying the monarch's authority. The Normans convinced the usually indecisive Edward that this was a heaven-sent opportunity to rein in their over-mighty rival and his brood of overreaching sons. The king was sufficiently enraged by Godwin's demand that he surrender to trial his dear friend Count Eustace to dispatch couriers to Worcester, Coventry and York. They summoned the earls Ralph, Leofric and Siward from their capitals to a meeting of the Witan at Gloucester. Edward urged Godwin's peers to bring all the forces they could muster on such short notice.

Much to the king's relief and gratification, all three of the great earls obeyed the call. Ralph and Siward hated and resented even more than they feared Godwin. Leofric, while friendly to Godwin, was also loyal to the king and hoped to avert a civil war that might lead to virtual domination of England by the Normans.

During the interval before the Witan was to meet, Earl Harold put Edmond in charge of a dozen men posted to maintain watch over one of Gloucester's gates. He was under strict orders to merely observe and report any entry of troops into the town. On no account was he to skirmish with the king's men or those of his supporters.

Other than during the affray at Dover, it was a novel experience for Edmond to command armed men. He relished his modest authority almost as much as if he had been placed in charge of the entire body of royal housecarles. It was satisfying to make decisions and confront difficulties, slight as they were under the circumstances. It was almost as if he were a king, he reflected, touching the silver ring to his cheek. He laughed at himself, but without bitterness. For the moment he was content to be a buoyant cork on what might be a rising tide of fortune. Earl Harold's friendship was not to be despised. Young as he was, Godwin's son had proved himself as a commander both on land against Welsh border marauders and at sea against Danish pirates. One could learn much from Earl Harold about the art of war and how to handle men. The situation offered an excellent opportunity to establish a reputation that someday might help advance a claim to the throne. Edmond smiled at the grandiose thought, then excused himself with the reminder that the opportune encounter with Earl Harold in Southwark seemingly had turned his luck.

He found the vigil outside Gloucester tedious, especially since he was under orders to avoid all confrontation, but Godfrid's company helped alleviate the boredom. It was satisfying to teach the boy how to overcome the handicap of a shriveled left arm. Bright and agile, Godfrid proved adept at learning how to make the most of his right hand when Edmond drilled him on wielding a sword, casting a lance and drawing a bow. The last was most difficult, but Godfrid managed to accomplish it.

Edmond welcomed frequent visits by Earl Harold during his new found friend's rounds of checking all the outposts.

"Look, Thane Edmond!" Harold pointed at a body of troops entering Gloucester through the gate under surveillance. "By St. Dunstan's beard! There's a miracle! Earl Leofric must have found a scilling or two to spare from his endless building of churches and minsters that he could spend to clap helmets on his thick-headed Mercian lads."

The next arrival evoked even more pointed comment.

"St. Cuthbert, help me! It's Ralph the Timid himself! See what a fine show that Norman rascal makes! His uncle, royal Edward, should be pleased. But will Ralph stand up better to our good English swords than he did to those thieving Welshmen a couple of years ago?"

Far more respectful was Harold's comment on the third group to enter Gloucester by the same gate.

"Look sharp, Edmond! These are real soldiers. That old bear Siward probably sired half of them himself. Their horses can scarce carry them, they're such a lusty lot. They'll give our lads a merry tussle if it comes to swordplay."

Harold's outward display of frivolity and unconcern clearly masked his genuine anxiety over King Edward's accumulating power. Gloucester was fast becoming an armed camp, overflowing with royalist supporters. Harold estimated that Edward could field five or six thousand men. When he reported this to Earl Godwin, his father was alarmed. The old man had not thought the king would be able to assemble a force of such size so quickly. Of course, he had expected earls Ralph and Siward to support the king, the former as Edward's nephew as well as a Norman, the latter because he resented Godwin's influence eclipsing his own despite his domination of much of the north country. Nevertheless, Godwin had hoped Leofric for one would have remained neutral, or brought only a token handful of men. He was puzzled why his old friend had led so large a contingent. Was Leofric also turning against him?

Yet while Edward's allies had been extremely successful in assembling a formidable army, Godwin's also had been diligent. The Cotswolds about Beverstone were crowded with nearly as many men as the streets of Gloucester. The levies of Wessex, East Anglia and from Sweyn's share of Mercia were apparently willing to support Godwin even against their king, Edward Ethelredson.

Earl Godwin decided to strike soon after Harold reported the arrival of Earl Siward's men. Further delay might enable the king to attract even more support, rendering his power overwhelming. When Edmond was recalled to Beverstone by Harold, he found the headquarters in turmoil. The troops had struck their tents and were forming up for the march on Gloucester while Godwin held a final council of war with Harold and his other commanders.

"There can be no doubt, Lord Godwin, that we'll be attacked." Thane Sebert's voice rose to a high pitch in emphasis. "Our friends in Gloucester agree that Earl Siward and his Danes are urging the king to let them attack. So far only Earl Leofric's influence has restrained King Edward. The archbishop, Count Eustace and even Ralph the Timid oppose any settlement. It's certain the king will eventually give in and agree to move against us either late today or early tomorrow."

"Well then, shall we sit here and wait for them?" Godwin demanded, touching off a roar of nays. He grimly settled his gilded helmet on his gray hairs, then slapped his sword hilt. "Your reply is what I wanted to hear. We're agreed. Let's meet the enemy at the gates of Gloucester. We march within the hour."

A friendly arm descended on Edmond's shoulder as Earl Harold whispered, "I've been waiting for you, Thane Edmond. I want you by my side if there's swordplay. We may have need of your right arm. This will be no easy matter." He hesitated before continuing, "There's something else," then drew Edmond aside so none could overhear. "If I should fall—no, one must prepare for the worst even when ready to do one's best—remove this trinket from my neck." He fingered a massive gold chain supporting a jewel-encrusted cross. "Take it to my house at Nazeing and give it to the Lady Edith so she'll have remembrance of me." Edmond was uncertain whether Harold's eyes misted because the earl quickly looked away to conceal his emotion. There was an awkward pause, but Edmond needed no explanation. All of England knew how Harold had taken Edith Swan-neck, the celebrated beauty, in hand-fast, or common-law, marriage. Even though the mother of Harold's children, she was too low-born as the daughter of Earl Godwin's steward to share in the honors proper to a great nobleman's wife. Nevertheless, the fame of their mutual devotion was so widespread that minstrels sang its praise. Such fidelity was rare among a nobility that ordinarily shed concubines and common-law wives as if discarding worn boots or tattered tunics.

Harold broke into Edmond's respectful silence. "I ask this of you because it's an office for a brother or a friend, not a servant. In truth, I wouldn't readily entrust such a task to my brother Sweyn, nor even my father. But you, Thane Edmond, inspire confidence and I believe I can regard you as a good friend, even though we've known each other such a short time. Will you honor my request?"

"My lord, I'll do as you ask though I hope there'll be no need for such a sorry errand."

"Is there anything you'd like me to do for you in similar circumstances?"

"No, my lord, I'm alone in the world." Even as he spoke he thought of Adele. It was possible his statement was not entirely true, but why should he add to her burden of sorrow if indeed, as he flattered himself might be the case, she might grieve at his death.

Harold laughed. "Well then, I have the best of the bargain." He slapped Edmond on the shoulder as they rejoined the group around Earl Godwin, who was explaining his plans. The old earl turned to his son.

"We're ready, Harold, but we must march without Sweyn." Godwin's carefully level tone concealed the sorrow and anger he felt at his eldest and favorite son's inexplicable absence. To vanish at a time like this! Not a word, not a hint of Sweyn's whereabouts had come to his father since the young earl had disappeared on the day of the confrontation with King Edward. Almost as irascible as cunning, Godwin at other times might have raged openly against his son, but it was crucial not to reveal his concern and dismay lest some of the thanes among his supporters might be tempted by Sweyn's absence to desert his father's cause.

Harold sensed Godwin's suppressed agitation, and spoke gently to spare him. "If it can't be helped, we must march without Sweyn, my lord. King Edward's power grows by the moment. Rather than wait for Sweyn here while the king gathers more men, let's meet our enemies and decide all at one stroke. If Sweyn shows up at the last moment it'll be all the better, catching our enemies off guard. If he's absent, why all the more glory for those who are here. Let's march!"

What began as a murmur of assent by the thanes swelled into a mighty roar of defiance of the king. At Godwin's command, the thanes rushed out to mount their horses and take charge of their followers. As Edmond rode at Harold's side among the vanguard, he admired the confident and well-equipped East Anglian axmen who formed the bulk of the earl's contingent. The troops were distinctly eager for combat, chattering and laughing as they rushed out of their encampment.

Earl Godwin's army poured down the flanks of the Cotswolds with the irresistible force of a flooded mountain tributary rushing toward its confluence with a larger stream. Indeed, the broad Severn River twisted through the plain at the foot of the hills, its roiled waters flashing golden in the glow of a glittering sun. Barren wineyards clung to the rising ground all about, their rich, bloated fruit long since harvested from the clambering vines to yield their succulence beneath the bare feet of the rustic laborers. They produced a wine some compared favorably with those of France, though the Normans despised it as mere vinegar. Beyond the rapidly swelling Severn a seemingly unending range of uneven, ragged hills tumbled toward the eastern horizon until the peaks merged into the mist cloaking the rugged territory of the unconquered Welsh. As the army threaded toward Gloucester, Edmond noticed at intervals the crumbling relics of fortresses and camps reared in antiquity by the Britons and their conquerors, the Romans. Most imposing of all those hoary monuments was the sprawling hill fort of Ulcybury whose extensive ruins testified to the days when the savage Britons had shouted defiance of the Roman invaders before they yielded to the legionaries' superior tactics, discipline and weapons. After Ulcybury, the towering church spires of Gloucester eventually came into view.

A swelling murmur of anticipation ran through the army as the columns neared the winding walls protectively embracing Gloucester like a mother cradling her child. The hour of battle was at hand. Edmond's heart pounded, his pulse quickened and he could feel blood mount to his head. He tightened his grip on his horse's reins and looked eagerly toward the city walls whose walkways were blackened by the bobbing, helmeted heads of scurrying defenders preparing to resist attack.

A great shout went up from the East Anglians in the van when to everyone's astonishment the nearest city gate swung open. Earl Harold halted his men to prepare to confront the expected sally, but instead of an outpouring of a large force of defenders, a small band of horsemen emerged. It was led by a richly dressed elderly man who, despite his age, rode with easy grace. Without hesitation, the little troop made directly for Harold's contingent. The clamor and shouting with which the army had approached the city faded into near silence as Earl Godwin rode up to join Harold.

"It's Earl Leofric, my lord," Harold told his father. "What can the old fox want? The time for talk is over yet he must mean to parley."

"You're right, there's nothing left to discuss," snapped Godwin. "The king has chosen his course—war! Well, we're as prepared to settle our differences by force as he is, and I'll tell Leofric so."

Nevertheless, in contrast to his resolute words, Godwin was not sorry to seize on a chance to delay hostilities. Sweyn's inexplicable absence disturbed him more than he could admit even to himself. Despite his love for his eldest son, he was painfully aware of the young man's many faults, which did not include impetuosity. Sweyn was cold and calculating and Godwin suspected that his passion for intrigue and treachery might have led him into betraying his father by abandoning him on the eve of a battle so critical to his fortunes. He was almost grateful to delay testing his strength against that of the king until he could discover Sweyn's whereabouts. Accordingly, though he feigned reluctance, he rode forward to meet the approaching Earl Leofric. He was accompanied by Harold, Edmond and a score of soldiers, their numbers roughly equal to Leofric's entourage. When the bands closed to within a few paces, Godwin halted his troop, ordering only Harold and Edmond to join him in meeting Leofric. The old earl, noting Godwin's action, followed suit and advanced to meet his old friend with only his son Alfgar and a trusty thane at his side.

The grizzled earls, more often allies than foes in the past, approached so near that their horses snorted and shied off to avoid contact. They surveyed each other silently for a moment. Godwin noted his old friend had aged greatly since they last had met. Yet shrewdness still crinkled the corners of those ever-bright gray eyes.

Leofric spoke first. "How is my Lady Gytha?"

The unexpected question caught Godwin off-guard. He shot a glance at Leofric, who grinned. He responded by breaking into a hearty laugh. "My wife is well, praise God. And how does the Lady Godiva?"

"In the best of health, Earl Godwin, in the best of health." Leofric spread his hands and turned to his son Alfgar, a huge, red-faced warrior. "Do you see, my son, how well Earl Godwin and I know each other? Could such old friends be enemies? It would shame our declining years. If old age cannot boast of wisdom, where's the merit of it? No, Godwin, I tell you it would be a betrayal of true friendship and an affront to the blessed Lord for us to spill our people's blood." He lifted his eyes piously skyward.

"I bear you no grudge, friend Leofric," Godwin replied calmly. "It's King Edward and his Normans whose insults I resent. The king has wronged me! He has wronged me as a subject, as a friend, as his father-in-law. What's worse, he has sought to unjustly punish my good people of Dover for the sake of that ravenous pack of Norman curs who bay at his heels." Godwin spat the final words angrily, bitterness at being treated so unjustly almost swamping his friendly feelings for Leofric.

"Don't misunderstand me, Lord Godwin," Leofric said hastily. "I've nothing but sympathy for your position. Our Lord Edward has done you a great wrong, and I don't agree with him. I don't even want to or intend to speak of it. What troubles me greatly is the danger to you and our people. It would be a grievous matter if Englishman should fight Englishman and brother should slaughter brother in a quarrel stirred by foreigners. What would it benefit us to exhaust ourselves in civil war only to discover that the Normans have become our masters? If we are foolish enough to fight each other, I fear that would be the certain outcome."

Godwin spread his hands. "What would you have me do? I've been goaded beyond endurance by the king. What's more, among the foremost to spur him on is that ugly old bear, Siward. He has always been jealous of my influence and hungry for my ruin. You, good friend, may sympathize with me but do you imagine that devouring pack in Gloucester will let go if ever they seize me by the throat?'

"No, but you must not permit them to justify pushing matters so far. You know you couldn't expect our good king to dismiss Archbishop Robert and surrender Count Eustace to trial. It's unreasonable to demand something so damaging to his royal dignity. I believe, as I've told the king, that a compromise is possible. He has consented to go this far: both armies are to withdraw from Gloucester after an exchange of hostages, and a meeting of the Witan is to be delayed until Michaelmas in London. You must agree that this is a much more reasonable way to handle this sad business than plunge blindly into battle that can benefit no one and do irreparable harm to all."

Leofric's calm, reasoned tone was persuasive and Godwin grudgingly admitted that the Mercian's proposed compromise made good sense. Sweyn's absence tipped the scales. With his eldest son at his side, Godwin would have rejected all overtures of reconciliation and put his trust in the fortunes of war. As it was, he weighed Leofric's offer carefully. It offered a temporary solution without loss of face or honor.

"As ever, Lord Leofric, you are the most judicious of men. You've always had the coolest head of any of us. It would be shameful indeed to waste the good red blood of true-born Englishmen in a conflict that could benefit only enemies. Tell the king I welcome and accept his proposal. My sons and I will attend the meeting of the Witan in London."

Edmond noted that Earl Harold bit his lips on hearing his father's reply. He was clearly eager to decide the matter immediately. But Harold quickly concealed his disappointment, and on a signal from his father exchanged embraces with Alfgar at the same time as Godwin and Leofric saluted each other. The parley ended, Leofric's entourage returned to Gloucester to report to the king while Godwin led his band back to rejoin the main body of his army.

Neither Leofric nor Godwin was greeted with unmitigated joy. Both forces had been too highly keyed for the anticipated battle to relish the news that instead of combat a long, tedious march to London awaited them. Godwin's men had looked forward eagerly to sacking Gloucester, a town already renowned for its wealth. They were as sullen as a pack of hounds deprived of prey after cornering it. On the king's side, the Normans and Siward's Danes did not even trouble to conceal their disappointment at being thwarted from a chance to destroy the power of the House of Godwin. But they had no choice other than to accept King Edward's decision.

Ignoring the disappointment of the hotheads, the wiser among the king's advisors congratulated Earl Leofric, assuring him that his achievement as a peacemaker was equal to endowing a dozen minsters. Archbishop Robert averred that his labor for peace was pleasing to the eyes of God. The shrewd priest might have added it was also pleasing to the eyes of Archbishop Robert, who counted on the delay in confrontation as likely to split and disaffect Godwin's supporters, making his eventual fall all the more certain.

After the exchange of hostages was completed, Godwin's army turned eastward to begin the long, weary trek toward London.

Chapter Sixteen

Return to Dover

A few days after Earl Leofric's successful mediation outside the walls of Gloucester, two travelers dressed as humble tradesmen though well-armed, ostensibly for protection against outlaws on the roads, pulled up their horses on the outskirts of Dover. The shorter of the pair gazed eagerly toward the landmarks now engraved forever in his memory although he first had visited the town little more than a month earlier. The brief passage of time since he had arrived in Dover to seek Osgood's help now seemed almost a year—so many and varied had been the adventures that had followed. He shuddered on recalling Osgood's death, and wondered whether Adele still blamed him for his role in the events that led to her father's murder? Or did she now accept that neither of them was at fault for what had happened? Would she greet him with her earlier warmth, or would she be as cold and indifferent as she had seemed when they had parted?

Edmond's companion impatiently tapped him on the shoulder to rouse him from his reverie. "Your pardon, my lord," Edmond flushed. "I was thinking of things that happened the first time I was here. Shall we move on now?"

"Pleasant thoughts, I hope, Thane Edmond? By St. Dunstan's beard, I venture there's a girl in Dover." Earl Harold laughingly slapped Edmond's shoulder. "You may have a chance to visit her but not until we've completed our mission. We must catch my dear brother Sweyn off guard. He should be in the waterfront inn at this time, if we can rely on that Norman turncoat's word."

Harold had discovered Sweyn's whereabouts, still a mystery to Earl Godwin, from an informer the previous day. Acting on the knowledge, he and Edmond hastened directly to Dover while Godwin continued to hope his missing son would turn up at any time. Neither Sweyn nor any word of him had come even after Godwin had returned to his mansion outside London. The old earl was torn between fury at such apparent rank abandonment by his eldest son and fear that something might have happened to his favorite. After questioning all whom he suspected of knowing where Sweyn might be and extracting only unvarying professions of ignorance, Godwin retreated into the seclusion of his chambers. He refused to see anyone other than his sons Tostig and

Harold or his great friend and spiritual advisor, Bishop Stigand of Winchester. He spoke little even to them, morosely content to hear their suggestions without issuing the orders needed to implement the advice.

Partly as a result of its master's seeming indifference, the army Godwin had managed to keep almost intact during the long march from Gloucester dwindled quickly once it reached Southwark. The levies had enthusiastically heeded their lord's summons to Beverstone even if it was to confront their king. But after the early burst of enthusiasm wore off, qualms beset many. In addition, impatience over the delay in assembling the Witan combined with Godwin's apathy prompted many to slink off to the duties and comforts of home. So even as Harold and Tostig looked on in dismay, Godwin's army drained into the roads leading away from Southwark.

A few days before the Witan was to meet, Harold and Edmond were beguiling the leisurely hours at chess in the great hall of Godwin's mansion. Harold had just dismayed Edmond by capturing a rook when Thane Sebert interrupted.

"It's a Norman rascal, my lord. He insists he has important information fit only for your hearing." Sebert's voice sank to a whisper. "He claims to know Earl Sweyn's whereabouts."

"I'll hear what he has to say." Harold dismissed all in the hall with the exception of Edmond, then added, "Not that I trust such renegades, but sometimes they're useful. For a price, of course."

The Norman's appearance did not inspire confidence. A squat, sour-looking, middle-aged man-at-arms, his eyes darted nervously from Harold to Edmond and back, then fastened on Godwin's son, having decided the commanding figure seated at the chessboard was indeed the earl. Edmond realized he was vaguely familiar, but where and when had he seen him?

"Well, what's your business with us?" Harold demanded.

"It would be best if I spoke to you alone, my lord," the Norman replied, glancing meaningfully at Edmond.

"You can speak before both of us, or not at all," Harold snapped.

"If that's your wish, lord count, but it's a family matter, if you know what I mean, something about your brother, Earl Sweyn." The words came haltingly, as if the Norman was reluctant to confirm himself a traitor. When he spoke Sweyn's name, Edmond instantly recalled a scene in the inn at Dover. This was the man at whom Sweyn had angrily flung the tankard.

"What do you know of my dear, noble brother?"

"Only that I know where he is, where you can find him."

"And what's that to me? Why should I want to find him? Earl Sweyn doesn't have to answer to anyone, ask anyone's leave, least of all mine, before he decides to go somewhere." Harold's eyes narrowed as he glared threateningly at the Norman, who fidgeted nervously but held his ground.

"It's well known, my lord count, that Earl Sweyn has been strangely absent at a time his father and brothers might want him on hand." The Norman's effort at an ingratiating smile was more of a smirk. "It should be worth something to find him, and know who he's with."

Harold frowned and bit his lips. For a moment, Edmond thought he would strike the informer, but the earl restrained himself. Taking a purse from his belt, he flung it at the informer's feet. The Norman scrambled to pick it up, lofted it to estimate its content, then thrust it under his tunic with a sigh of satisfaction.

"You have your price, Judas. Speak up!"

"Dover, my lord! That's where he is."

"You're sure of that?"

"I saw him myself just yesterday," the Norman insisted. Edmond chuckled inwardly. No doubt of that, he thought. The scoundrel was probably dealing with Sweyn. But the man's next words showed he was mistaken. "He was conferring with one of Earl Ralph's most trusted men, his steward Rene."

Harold grimaced. He had feared as much but had hoped for a less damning explanation for Sweyn's disappearance. A love affair for instance. That would have been credible in the light of Sweyn's past, his amour with Eadgifu, the abbess of Leominster, having been just one of many less ungodly liaisons. Now the worst was confirmed. Sweyn was dealing, perhaps even in league, with his father's enemies. Not that such a betrayal was altogether surprising. Sweyn's predilection for treachery was notorious.

"Do you have any idea what they discussed?" Harold asked.

"I have it only second-hand, my lord, but I was told Earl Ralph urged Earl Sweyn to remain in hiding until after the meeting of the Witan. If he does so, Earl Ralph will add to the lands promised for not joining Earl Godwin at Gloucester."

Harold raised his right arm as if to strike the informer, thought better of it and expended his rage by scattering most of the chess pieces to the floor. Suppressing his anger, Harold contemptuously dismissed the alarmed, cowering Norman. As soon as the man was out of sight, he turned to Edmond. "Will you accompany me to Dover?"

"If it pleases you, Lord Harold." Edmond made no comment on what had just taken place. The wisest course in any quarrel between brothers was to avoid taking sides. When brothers made up, as they usually did, they would inevitably resent all outside interference or partisanship.

Such a neutral stance was all the easier because Harold was in too great a hurry to confront Sweyn to waste breath in chattering about him. He immediately told Godwin he was leaving to scour the Dover area for deserters and to recruit several thanes who while uneasy about the king's policies had been reluctant to come out openly against him. Godwin listlessly approved Harold's plan, his only comment being that he should not forget the meeting of the Witan at Westminster, now just four days off. The old earl seemed happy Harold would be gone, permitting him to remain wrapped in gloom without the annoyance of constant prodding to take action.

Disguised as merchants and without attendants, Edmond entrusting Godfrid to Sebert's care during his absence, he and Harold left Southwark under cover of darkness. They timed their journey so as to arrive within the outskirts of Dover mid-morning.

After the brief pause and conversation, they urged their horses to a canter and headed directly for the waterfront inn where Edmond first had seen Sweyn, hoping to surprise him. The informer had said Sweyn was meeting Earl Ralph's steward within its ramshackle walls. As soon as the inn came into view, Harold and Edmond spurred their mounts to a gallop, scattering poultry, swine and people in all directions as they stormed down the narrow street. They came to an abrupt halt in a cloud of dust, vaulted from their saddles and, after tossing the reins to a gawking stable boy, rushed into the building. They immediately beheld Sweyn sitting at a table with a swarthy stranger. As soon as Sweyn recognized his brother, he leaped to his feet but before he could draw his sword Harold's was pressed against his chest. Edmond similarly detained Sweyn's companion. Unable to resist, Sweyn and the Norman steward glared sullenly at their captors.

"Father has been asking for you," Harold began abruptly.

"He didn't send you to fetch me, that's certain," Sweyn snarled with rage.

"No, he doesn't know where you've been keeping yourself," Harold admitted, sheathing his sword to show his peaceful intent, then placing a restraining hand on his brother's shoulder. "But he misses you sorely. He thought at first you had taken a fancy to another abbess. It would horrify him, but he would understand, knowing you as he does. But what he doesn't understand is that at a time when he's beset by enemies and needs you desperately, you're not at his side."

Sweyn's mask of arrogant indifference was unbroken. He apparently believed Harold was unaware of his intrigues with Godwin's enemies. Sensing this, Harold was determined to dispel the illusion. "If he knew of your treachery, it would break his heart."

A physical blow could not have struck harder. Despite Sweyn's vicious and inconstant nature, he retained a tinge of affection and a great deal of respect for his father. Harold's words shook him. His expression wavered between remorse and impudence as he tried to brazen it out. "Treachery? I don't know what you're talking about, brother Harold."

"Do you dare deny it? Who's your friend? One of Earl Ralph's liegemen, if I'm not mistaken."

Edmond's prisoner made as if to speak, but a sword prick kept his mouth shut.

Sweyn studied the rush-strewn floor before replying, "I see you know a great deal. Or you think you do." He glanced at Edmond. "Perhaps I'm indebted to your friend for this unfortunate confrontation. We've met before, if I'm not mistaken. I seldom forget a friend, or an enemy for that matter." He spoke softly, as if in resignation though his eyes raked Edmond malevolently. "Since you know so much, there's no more to be said."

Sweyn did not intend to either confirm or deny Harold's suspicions. He would have disowned such a reaction furiously, but after his initial anger he was almost relieved by his brother's intervention He was tiring of the false game he was playing, not because of an outbreak of scruple, but rather since the possible advantages to be gained fell short of his ambitions. He had agreed to desert his father at Beverstone only after being assured by Earl Ralph and Archbishop Robert that they sought to merely lessen Godwin's grip on the king. In no way, they told him, did they aim at depriving him of his holdings or intend personal harm. Their only goal was a larger share in the direction of the nation's affairs. In return, they promised to restore the greater part of Sweyn's properties that remained alienated because of his former outlawry for the murder of his cousin, Earl Beorn. Blinded by land-hunger, Sweyn had been only too ready to believe their pledges and the truce agreed upon at Gloucester made it seem even more likely they would be honored.

The possibility of a peaceful compromise lured Sweyn out of his forest hiding place to a meeting at Dover with Earl Ralph's steward in an effort to hasten restoration of his confiscated estates. Yet, instead of confirming his master's agreement, the steward brought a new proposal. If Sweyn stayed away from the meeting of the Witan at Westminster, Earl Ralph was prepared to turn over to him his earldom of Herefordshire. Sweyn was tempted, but the magnitude of the offer aroused his suspicion. It made him wonder whether some deeper purpose than an attempt to redress the balance of power lay behind such intense efforts to divide him from his father. Nevertheless, he was prepared to bargain. He refused to abandon Godwin and told the Norman that while he was willing to help reduce his father's hold on King Edward he would not endanger him personally. He would use his influence to persuade Godwin to agree to punish Dover, but would go no further. As capricious and untrustworthy as Sweyn was, he retained a trace of loyalty to Godwin and would never go so far as to consciously assist his enemies to ruin the old man. He had told the steward as much, and he and the Norman for two days had sought some middle ground until Harold's startling interference had brought negotiations to an unexpected halt. As angered as he was, Sweyn eagerly seized on the opportunity to exit the cul-de-sac into which he had maneuvered himself.

Unaware as he was of Sweyn's inner turmoil, Harold merely sought to make the best of the awkward situation. "You'll return to Southwark with me, brother?" It was more command than question.

"It seems I have little choice." Sweyn could not resist a sneer, though sobered immediately by a reflection: "Does Father know anything of this?"

"He's puzzled, indeed grieved, by your unexplained absence. Nothing more."

Earl Ralph's steward, shocked into silence until now, could contain himself no longer. "What shall I tell my master, Earl Sweyn? Do you turn your back on him?"

Sweyn shrugged. "Does it matter? What is there to tell him? You see I no longer have freedom of action." He paused to consider. "Yet, tell him this: I expect him to fulfill his pledge to me as I fulfilled mine to him. For the rest, the matter is closed."

"You can be certain, my lord, he will fulfill his promise to you as you fulfill yours to him," the Norman sneered. "You may think the matter closed, Earl Sweyn, but I'll wager my master will consider it just begun." He looked at Harold. "Have I your leave to depart, my good lord?"

Harold nodded. The steward mockingly bowed to the little group and stamped out of the inn.

"There's an end to mischief," commented Harold.

"It's only the beginning," Sweyn growled. Edmond silently agreed.

Chapter Seventeen

Adele's Disappearance

Harold Godwinson was as relieved as pleased at finding Sweyn so quickly and persuading him to return to their father's side without a fuss. If Sweyn had balked it might have turned into a ticklish, possibly even bloody, affair inevitably damaging to the House of Godwin. Instead, Sweyn quietly, if sullenly, agreed to accompany Harold to Southwark to make his amends to Earl Godwin. Harold suspected his brother had reasons of his own for returning so tamely but thought it better not to pry into them. All had gone so well that Harold genially agreed to Edmond's request for leave to visit what he described as "an old friend" in Dover.

Edmond approached Aegelsig's house with an eager step but some apprehension. As before, the din of metal hammering metal, hiss of bellows and roar of an intense fire was overwhelming even at a considerable distance. As he hoped, his changed attire and the passage of time, brief as it was, shielded him from recognition by bypassers as the young man who had so boldly led the townsmen against the Normans. When he entered the armorer's shop, Master Aegelsig's broad back was to the entrance and he was too engrossed in labor to hear footsteps over the tremendous din.

"Good day to you, Master Aegelsig!" Edmond bellowed.

The startled armorer almost dropped the white-hot sword blade he was hammering and spun about to curse the intruder, whoever it might be. A colorful expletive strangled in his throat as he recognized Edmond and instead he barked joyfully, "Welcome, welcome, my good lord." Yet his broad smile instantly turned into a worried look as he added, "My lord, you don't know what danger you run into by returning. If you'll permit me to say so, you shouldn't have returned to Dover. King's men and Normans have been as thick as horse flies around here since that black day our good friend Osgood was murdered."

Edmond wrung the armorer's sweaty, horny hand. "Not all the bastards of Normandy could keep me from your hearth, good Master Aegelsig. I take such delight in marveling at your handiwork I can't keep away."

Aegelsig waggled a thick finger. "You don't fool me, young man. I suspect there's an even more attractive lure that brings you back."

Despite his attempt at levity he looked uncomfortable.

"Has anything happened… to her?" Edmond could no longer dissemble about his interest in Adele or anxiety for her welfare.

"No, no, the child is in good health, Thane Edmond, but she's no longer in our keeping, much as my wife and I wanted her to stay with us."

"She's not here with you!" Edmond exclaimed. "Where then can she be?"

"She has given herself to God, my lord. She has joined the good sisters in a convent."

"A convent!" Edmond stared at Aegelsig. Adele a nun? Unthinkable! Inconceivable! Incomprehensible! He could more readily believe she had run off with a Norman. After all, she was half-French herself. But to enter a convent? She was too much in love with the joy of living, the dream of adventure, the excitement of anticipating the future, to bury herself so irrevocably. How could it be? His mind in a whirl, he seized upon the comforting notion she had entered a convent only until the sorrow of losing her father diminished.

He hopefully suggested this to Aegelsig, but the armorer dejectedly shook his head. "No, my niece is a novice. She has sworn to dedicate herself to the service of God, to become a nun." Aegelsig looked as if he could not believe what he was saying. "It's true, my lord. She plans to take the vows."

Edmond's mind was in a whirl. He could see no reason for Aegelsig to deceive him about Adele's decision to renounce the world as being voluntary. It was true he probably would be able to claim all or much of Osgood's large fortune, which otherwise would go to Adele, if she entered a convent but Edmond dismissed the base thought that Aegelsig had forced his niece. He believed the armorer was honesty personified.

"Why would she do such a thing?" he finally permitted himself to wonder aloud.

"I've been asking myself the same thing over and over since she told me what she meant to do," Aegelsig replied. "My first thought was it was because of shock and grief at the death of her dear father. Then I suspected it might that she felt she was imposing on her aunt and myself, not realizing that since we have no children of our own we were only too happy to have her stay with us. She also might have felt out of place in our home, away from her beloved garden and familiar surroundings. Yet none of those reasons seemed enough to account for her behavior. Of course, there was that other matter." Aegelsig shook his head as if to dismiss the notion. "I think she was distressed at displeasing me in the matter of Master Heinrich of Bremen."

Edmond sucked in his breath. "Heinrich of Bremen?"

"Yes, a fine man. I asked her—merely by way of preparation, as Osgood's death would not permit a union until after a decent period of mourning—whether she would consider a marriage with Heinrich. He's an Easterling, a foreigner, that's true, but a good man for all that, and among the wealthiest and most respected of wool merchants."

Aegelsig scratched his head in puzzlement over his niece's cool reaction to his proposing such an excellent match. "It would have been equal in every way. True, Heinrich is nearer my age, but then a young girl needs an older, wiser hand to help settle her down. It isn't as if she didn't know the Easterling, who often dealt with Osgood and, being a widower, was very attentive to her whenever he visited their house. Besides, he could take over the business without a hitch. Most women would have jumped at such an offer. Not that Adele needs to do so. There are few richer heiresses in England, if any, no matter how high their station. Osgood knew his business. Heinrich couldn't do better, and neither could she. Yet she wouldn't even talk about it. When I first suggested the matter, she just stared at me, burst into tears and shut herself up in her room.

"The next day she told me, as cool as you please, that her father's death had decided her on a step she had been thinking about a long time—not that I believed her. She said she was determined to retire into a convent and donate all her worldly goods to the church." Aegelsig looked horrified at the thought. "As if I'd let her throw away everything my brother-in-law worked hard for because of a girlish whim. I've kept most of her fortune in trust for her though I wouldn't let her enter the convent without a lordly gift. I wanted the abbess to know she was no common girl." He sighed at the recollection. It was clear his years as a slave of the Arabs had made him skeptical about religion in general.

"Where is the convent?" Edmond asked. He had a vague notion of trying to change Adele's mind. It was not too late. As a novice, she could still withdraw.

"It's not for me to tell you. It was her wish—no, her demand—that I not reveal her whereabouts to—well, to anyone."

Aegelsig's embarrassment was obvious and it seemed useless to press him further. Edmond realized that if he was to find Adele it had to be by other means. He reluctantly changed the subject and listlessly agreed to again inspect the regal weapons Aegelsig had stored for him.

"Do you wish to take these with you, my lord?"

"No, save them against the day when I'll have more need of them. They're in the best of hands if I leave them with you, Master Aegelsig. I know you'll keep them safe for me no matter how long they remain here."

"That goes beyond saying, Thane Edmond. I'll keep them as bright and fit for use as they are now. The Good Lord willing, the day you'll demand them is not far off."

"Only the Good Lord knows," Edmond smiled wistfully. "We must be content to hope it comes soon, but I doubt it will." At the moment, his mind was far from thoughts of pursuing his heritage. After a little more desultory conversation, he let Aegelsig resume his work and left to return to the waterside inn.

The cool outside air felt doubly refreshing after the stifling heat of the armorer's workshop. He struggled to reorder his confused thoughts and turbulent emotions as he retraced his steps. He entertained a succession of wild schemes to discover Adele's whereabouts. He would methodically visit every convent in southeastern England. He would enlist Bishop Stigand's aid. He would interrogate all the women of Dover who might have known her. He would... He groaned in frustration, realizing the difficulties that lay in every and any direction he chose to take, their virtual impossibility in the present state of affairs. His duty was to remain at Earl Harold's side. Until the crisis with the king was resolved, it would be dishonorable to desert his friend. He was so wrapped up in thought that he lurched into someone who crossed his path just outside the inn.

"By the bones of St. Cuthbert! Look where you're going!" The angry roar came from a familiar voice and was followed by a ham-sized fist that Edmond was barely able to evade by ducking his head. An irate, moon-shaped red face glared at him for an instant, then melted into a broad smile as Wiglaf recognized his young friend.

"Always spoiling for a fight," Edmond laughed, his spirits greatly lifted by the unexpected meeting. "You would even knock down an old friend."

"Never you, Thane Edmond, never you," the sailor growled, wrapping his thick arms around Edmond in a bear hug and lifting him off his feet. "Ah, it's good to see you, my lord. But the devil take it! You shouldn't be here. Someone might recognize you. Quick! Let's duck into the inn to celebrate this lucky meeting. A good capon or two, a few generous horns of ale, and you can tell me what you've been up to since we parted. What say you to my suggestion?"

With arms still enfolding Edmond, Wiglaf lifted him over the threshold, virtually carrying him into the inn, totally ignoring laughing protests that he was perfectly willing to enter on his own. Edmond finally struggled free as they approached a table at which sat Harold and Sweyn. "I'd like nothing better than share a drink with you, good Wiglaf, but I'm with these two gentlemen and must await their pleasure."

Harold smiled approval of Edmond's discretion in avoiding names. It might be awkward if it became known that Godwin's sons had visited

Dover. Only the innkeeper had observed the earlier scene when Harold and Edmond had come upon Sweyn and the Norman steward. A warning and a few silver pennies had shut his mouth.

"Come, your friend may sit with us and welcome, too," Harold said heartily, indicating the bench opposite himself and Sweyn. He was not being merely polite. Wiglaf would provide added cover. Who would dream that a common sailor would be permitted to sit at table with two of England's greatest nobles.

Wiglaf was the last man to refuse an invitation to share meat or drink. He cannily accepted Edmond's explanation that Harold and Sweyn were old acquaintances met by chance on the way to Dover, though his quick wit told him otherwise. He speculated they were thanes out of favor with either King Edward or Earl Godwin, reason sufficient to disguise themselves. Well, it was no business of his and he happily gorged himself with a double share of a lavish meal, enlivened by affable conversation and ample liquid refreshment. Sweyn remained somber at first, but even his dour mood eventually yielded to the mellowing influence of wine.

More to keep the conversation moving than out of real curiosity, Harold asked Wiglaf, "How long have you known our good friend, Thane Edmond?"

"Four or five weeks, if I'm not out in my reckoning. We must have met a week or so before that bit of a scuffle between the good people of Dover and the Normans."

Harold's eyes narrowed, and he leaned forward with greater interest. "Ah, you know something of that?"

"A little, just a little, good friend." Wiglaf replied cautiously, uncertain whether it was prudent to continue the topic. "Just what I've heard, and who knows what really happened, though it's said the Normans took a beating they'll not soon forget."

"You can speak freely," Harold encouraged. "We're all friends and I've no more love for Normans than any good citizen of Dover, and you know how they feel. Quite the contrary, to speak plainly. If it were in my power, I'd hound them all out of England. So tell us what you know."

Wiglaf detected Edmond's almost imperceptible nod as did Sweyn, who chimed in, "Yes, my friend, tell us about it. We've heard much but it's not easy what to believe, what's true, what's false."

Wiglaf now thought he knew Harold's identity and suspected Sweyn's. He had heard of Harold's goodwill toward Dover though he was not sure of his brother's. Nevertheless, he resolved to speak freely and began to paint a colorful, if not strictly accurate, account of the battle. He took care to omit nothing that would display Edmond to good advantage, emphasizing his young friend's enterprise and bravery in leading the ill-equipped townsfolk's assault on their far better armed foe. Edmond flushed in embarrassment at Wiglaf's lavish praise.

Harold shook a playful finger at Edmond. "You never told me you took part in this affair. And such a big part, too."

Sweyn cut in dryly. "You should have asked me."

Harold stared in surprise at his brother. "You know something about this, don't you? Now that I think of it, you made some remark earlier that should have alerted me. You hinted at having met friend Edmond before. I should have guessed. You were in Dover all the while during this unhappy business?"

"It's possible."

"Come, brother, you were here, that's certain. While all this was going on, I'll wager. And you just sat by, watched the whole thing, and did nothing about it?"

"I judged it best to keep out of such a shabby affair. If I had interfered it might have made it seem more important than just another street brawl. What would our enemies have made of it? It was in our family's best interest to ignore the matter."

"You might as well admit you stayed out of it because there was nothing in it for you no matter how it turned out," Harold commented bluntly. He paused, wondering for an instant whether it had been injudicious to question Sweyn in Wiglaf's hearing, but a glance at the sailor's cheerful face reassured him. He could depend on Edmond's loyalty, and Wiglaf was obviously devoted to the young thane. All the same, there was little to gain by further pressing Sweyn to explain his behavior in Dover during the battle. He decided it was preferable to keep his brother in his present almost affable mood rather than risk irritating him. He turned to Edmond. "How did it happen that you, who had never been in Dover before, came to be involved in such a local affair, friend Edmond?"

Edmond was hesitant to talk about himself but did not want to offend Harold by ignoring his question. He related his adventures in Dover simply but was not entirely candid, avoiding the secret of his birth that brought him to the town as well as mention of Adele. While Harold listened intently, Sweyn appeared bored and Wiglaf limited himself to an occasional grunt of assent at Edmond's description of the fighting or the interjection of a compliment on his friend's behavior. When Edmond arrived at the point at which he left Master Lewin's ship at Pevensey, he broke off, promising to finish the story another time. Harold nodded indulgently but Sweyn's smirk reminded Edmond the earl had witnessed his bout at quarterstaves with Thane Eadred in Ashdowne Forest.

"You've done well, Thane Edmond," Harold approved. "By St. Dunstan's beard, I wish I'd been on hand to help you against that arrogant knave, Count Eustace." He stroked his chin thoughtfully before turning to Wiglaf. "You must know where to find your seaman friend if there's need. The ship's captain. What's his name?"

"Lewin, Master Lewin, if you please, my lord." Wiglaf touched his cap, embarrassed at having let it slip that he knew Harold's rank to be much higher than suggested by his plain garb.

"My lord! Well, if you'll have it so, my friend. I might have use for Master Lewin's services. Do you think he might be persuaded to sail to Bristol to await further orders? He won't regret it. Those for whom I'm authorized to speak are sure to pay well, or I'll hear of it. I've been told I might even advance a tidy little sum." Harold reached to his belt, unfastened a bulging purse and dangled it enticingly before Wiglaf who instantly turned cold sober.

"I can speak like a brother on Master Lewin's behalf, my lord. He returns tonight or early tomorrow from a quick venture across the Channel, if the Lord grants a stiff wind at his back. You can depend on my word that he'll sail for Bristol as soon as possible and as quickly as the good ship *Eldrytha* can carry him—and myself as well for I've been beached too long to suit a weathered old sailorman. There's work to be done and silver to be won, if I'm any judge."

"You're shrewd, my friend," Harold laughed approvingly, tossing the purse to Wiglaf, who caught it deftly, weighted it, then hid it underneath his tunic. "We'll have need of good men like yourself, that's certain. There'll be plenty of silver for those who deserve and earn it. Tell Master Lewin to wait in Bristol until he hears from me, no matter how long he has to anchor. It may be a few days, two or three weeks, perhaps even longer. But he must not stir until I send word."

"I'll tell him so, my lord," Wiglaf replied as soberly as if he had not emptied a cask of brew. "Master Lewin will not stir a step from the White Whale, a most excellent inn I've often honored with my custom." He broke off, then plunged boldly on. "But who shall I say commands our obedience?"

"Harold of Wessex!" the earl whispered. then stood up. "Come, brother Sweyn and friend Edmond, we've tarried long enough here. It occurs to me that if we detour slightly and visit Ashford on our way back to Southwark we might be able to persuade our double-dealing friend Thane Ethelric to join us."

Bidding goodbye to Wiglaf, who was to await Master Lewin's return, Harold, Sweyn and Edmond rode out of Dover toward Ashford. However, the attempt to recruit Ethelric, one of the wavering thanes who formerly had supported the House of Godwin, proved futile.

Ethelric was not at his estate. His steward informed Earl Harold he did not know where his master was or when he would return. Ethelric clearly had gone to ground to avoid committing himself. Nevertheless, the apparent defection failed to disturb Earl Godwin because it was overshadowed by joy at Sweyn's return when Harold and his companions arrived in Southwark. His father waved off Harold's attempt to explain his absence. Godwin was delighted to be able to sit down at the table with his eldest son and feast himself back into a confident mood.

With Sweyn at his side, Earl Godwin declared he feared no one and nothing, least of all his son-in-law King Edward and his Norman allies.

Chapter Eighteen

Fleeing the King's Wrath

The Witan convened at Michaelmas in King Edward's favorite palace of Westminster without Earl Godwin and his sons in attendance. Godwin prudently disregarded the summons to an assembly most of whose members he knew to be hostile to him. The mistrust was abundantly confirmed by the reports of each day's deliberations that reached the few supporters of the House of Godwin remaining at Southwark.

The magnitude of his enemies' first major success overwhelmed Godwin, though it did not surprise Harold who knew the extent of Sweyn's treacherous behavior and disloyalty to his family. Godwin's old friend and advisor Bishop Stigand of Winchester brought the news of the Witan's condemnation of the earl's eldest son.

"They've outlawed Earl Sweyn once again," Stigand gasped even before exchanging the customary civilities with Godwin. Disregarding his ecclesiastical dignity, the bishop had hastened from Westminster across the Thames to Southwark to report the Witan's action. He and Godwin had been friends for more than two decades, since they both were protégés of King Cnut. More than mutual regard prompted Stigand to rush to Godwin's side. The ambitious prelate was keenly aware that his chief hope for further advancement depended on retaining and cultivating his old friend's goodwill, and helping to keep him in power.

The outlawing of Sweyn shocked Godwin so deeply that he let his wine cup clatter to the floor as he leaped up from his seat at the head of the long table.

"What false charges are they making against my dear son?" he roared, infuriated by this renewed, unexpected attack upon his favorite. "Who's spreading lies about him? Fools! Traitors! Do they think I'll let them banish him again?" He sputtered into near incoherence as he sank back into his chair.

Edmond stole a glance at Sweyn. The young earl's customary pallor became almost fish-colored and beads of perspiration clung feebly to his blond mustache. Earl Harold bit his lips and drummed his knuckles upon the rough-hewn table top, hard put to conceal that his anger was directed not so much against their common enemies but at Sweyn. His brother's incredible folly and greed were damaging his family's ascendancy.

Stigand waited until Godwin settled down. After a stern glance at Sweyn, the bishop began by echoing Godwin's outburst. "The charge against Earl Sweyn? There's more than one, my lord. There's the old calumny about Earl Beorn. Another involving the Abbess of Leominster—which I pray is untrue it grieves me so. Then there's your son's in-lawing—it's charged it was brought about by bribery and coercion. There were other slanders, too, such as disloyalty to the king, false dealing with his advisors and the like, but it's plain to all that these are mere pretexts for undermining you and your sons."

"I don't have to stay and listen to such a pack of damnable lies," Sweyn shouted as he stormed out of the hall. He could no longer endure Bishop Stigand's litany of accusations and Harold's cold stare of disapproval. He realized they understood, even if his father refused to, that his double-dealing had sprung a trap set by their enemies. Obviously Earl Ralph and Archbishop Robert were convinced Sweyn's reconciliation with Harold signaled the failure of their effort to drive a wedge between him and his family. They decided that if he refused to further their cause he must be put out of the way. As Edmond had foreseen, Harold's success in averting an alliance between Sweyn and the Normans was not the end of mischief.

Bishop Stigand ignored Sweyn's angry exit and continued his report of the Witan's actions. Spurred on by the fierce eloquence of Godwin's old enemy Earl Siward, the assembly censured Godwin and Harold as if they were criminals rather than eminent noblemen. The Witan peremptorily summoned them to appear before it. The insulting language of the original order approached being an accusation of treason. Its harsh tone was modified only after Earl Leofric and Bishop Stigand succeeded in convincing King Edward that sending such an inflammatory message was unworthy of his dignity. Edward still might have ignored Stigand though his reverence for churchmen in general overcame his dislike of this one in particular. Yet he had great respect for Leofric, whose piety exceeded his own. Not only was the wording of the summons softened, but rather than insisting on an immediate appearance, the Witan granted a slight delay. "Nevertheless, it's still ruder than I would like it to be," Stigand sighed as he handed the document to Earl Godwin.

A cursory glance was enough to rekindle Godwin's rage. "Let them summon me until doom's day but even if they flay every sheep in the land for parchment I'll not appear without safeguard. I'm not such a fool as to thrust myself into the jaws of that pack of wolves. Ah, if I had but half the force we mustered at Beverstone!" He pounded the table in impotent anger.

"We'll demand more hostages as a pledge of good faith," Harold interrupted. "If you get a hearing before the Witan, my lord father, your eloquent, reasoned words will restore them to their senses. Our enemies have had the king's ear thus far, but he owes you a great deal—the very throne itself—and you can remind him of that debt."

"Gratitude? Not likely. Not my weak-kneed, mealy-mouthed son-in-law. Our good king is a wisp of straw in the wind just like his father, unhappy King Ethelred."

"Maybe so, but he must grant you a hearing, if only for appearance's sake," Harold insisted. "You might convince him it's in his best interest not to drive us too far, that it would be dangerous to antagonize us beyond repair." Harold then suggested that in addition to the lesser hostages yielded at Gloucester, Godwin should propose the exchange of a younger son for one of Earl Ralph's children. He emphasized it was vital for his father to plead his case before the Witan and win over the undecided. Their army had dwindled to such an extent they could not hope to maintain even a standoff with the king's forces.

Bishop Stigand carried Earl Godwin's request for an additional exchange of hostages back to Westminster. He told the Witan the earl would not appear before it without the additional guarantee of immunity. Rather than agree to the request, King Edward's advisors took Godwin's proposal to be a sign of weakness. They resolved to press him even harder by demanding that he release all of the king's thanes still under his command at Southwark, and permit them to rejoin the royal army at Westminster.

Harold laughed ruefully when Stigand brought back the rejection of his father's proposal and the new demand. "They mean to flay us of our very hides. St. Cuthbert help me! Returning the thanes will be no great loss, that's true. I doubt there are more than six or seven king's men still with us." His estimate was painfully near the mark. Yet few as they were, the king's thanes' presence at Southwark had suggested an accommodation was still possible. Their departure was sure to prompt others at Southwark who were not bound by close ties to the House of Godwin to leave as well. Godwin's force would be stripped to a few loyal followers. Nonetheless, convinced that obtaining a hearing before the Witan outweighed all other considerations, Godwin and Harold yielded the king's thanes without demur in the hope that compliance might satisfy the assembly.

They were quickly disabused. Stigand reported the king had changed his mind. He refused to consider an additional exchange of hostages. "He declared that despite his displeasure he would receive you and Earl Harold, but would not permit you to be accompanied to Westminster by more than a dozen men." Stigand's voice faltered, he was so disconcerted by Godwin's glare. It was obvious he had something even more unpleasant to reveal.

Godwin barked, "Well, what else did my son-in-law demand? Tell us the worst, if that's what it's to be."

Stigand sighed, crossed himself, wiped his brow, then resumed haltingly. "It passes belief. If I hadn't heard the words from the king's own lips I wouldn't credit he could say such a thing. It's almost too monstrous to repeat." The bishop groaned as if in anguish, but urged on by Godwin's compelling stare resumed his account. "He said—and most solemnly as if what he demanded was credible—that you could hope for pardon only if you restored to him his brother Alfred and his companions, safe and sound." Stigand almost choked on his final words and hastily seized a tumbler of wine and downed it as if to rinse away the foul taste of this astonishing message.

Earl Godwin shriveled into his chair. All the weight of his advancing years seemed to press in on him. His seamed, usually ruddy face turned into a death mask. It was as if for the first time he was fully aware that the king's hatred was all-devouring and that his coterie aimed at his utter destruction. To be mocked so cruelly by a callous renewal of the charge of a horrendous crime of which he had been acquitted many years earlier was incomprehensible. His enemies were seizing on the Dover affair as a convenient lever to topple him from power. The Witan had been summoned ostensibly to hold a free and impartial discussion of points in dispute between two parties, both of which supposedly enjoyed the equal trust and friendship of King Edward. The national assembly instead had been transformed into a tribunal to condemn and outlaw Godwin's eldest son without a hearing and to summon himself for judgment upon a crime of which he had been judged innocent. It was atrocious. He felt ill, drained of strength, so struck down he was unable to respond to the accusation. He sank into gloomy silence while Harold, mastering his outrage, spoke up for his father.

Harold chose his words carefully. "We'll ignore what the king said. My father has done him more than a little service, and King Edward knows it well. Earl Godwin deserves better of his lord than such idle, wanton mockery gathered from a dunghill of malevolent and groundless rumor. We can't and won't appear before the Witan unless and until we receive satisfactory hostages. We've obeyed and honored the king our master at all times and will always do so in all matters consistent with our honor, dignity and safety, but we won't attend the Witan with a smaller retinue than is customary for people of our station. You can take that message back to Westminster, my lord bishop Stigand."

Harold was under no illusion that his response would receive serious consideration from the king's camp but thought it best to make a conciliatory gesture. It might tempt the king to adopt a more moderate tone, at least to the extent of inviting Godwin to appear freely before the assembly without the threat of having to face wild accusations. Yet Harold was aware that such a reversal by the king, even if agreed to by his advisors, would be almost miraculous. Accordingly, as soon as Bishop Stigand left to take his message to the king and Witan, Harold pulled Edmond aside.

"Good friend Edmond, I fear we've been checkmated," he admitted. "We'll await the king's reply, but I doubt it'll be anything other than another refusal and even further insults, though none could be greater. If I'm right, we'll have to leave England for the time being. My father and our family will go to Bosham, where his ships lie. They'll find a haven with Count Baldwin across the water at Bruges. I don't propose to waste my time in Flanders, which is why I engaged Master Lewin's ship to await us at Bristol."

"Then we go to Ireland?" Edmond left no doubt he intended to accompany Harold.

"Ah, you'll go with me then? I'll never forget it, my friend." Harold wrung Edmond's hand. "King Dermod of Dublin is sure to grant us shelter. What's more, he'll help me to recruit men with whom I can make King Edward and his following repent of this intolerable insult to my good father." Harold bit his lips, but suppressed an angry outburst. "King Dermod's lands are infested with Danish pirates and he'd welcome any means of getting rid of the nithings. I'll enlist a few hundred in my service and they'll enable us to give our good king a taste of bloodletting before the year is out. I'll need several men of rank I can trust to lead them. You've assured me of at least one."

"Two, Lord Harold," corrected Thane Sebert, springing forward to kneel at Harold's feet. The earl lifted him upright and gratefully slapped him on the back.

Edmond's decision to throw in his lot with the House of Godwin was not taken lightly. Even if Godwin and his sons were overmatched at the moment by enemies, Edmond believed it was to his best interest to take their part. Though he had no obligation to Harold other than that of budding friendship—and that might wilt if the earl decided he had no further need of him—no attractive alternative suggested itself. He could hardly hope to turn to King Edward and his supporters, certainly not after the part he had played at Dover. Even if the king pardoned him, the Norman-dominated court was no place for a young Englishman of the lesser nobility. It was best either to go his own way or to join Harold. He chose the latter, having faith in the young earl's ability to regain his earldom and restore his family's fortunes. He liked Harold, whose uniformly confident and vigorous attitude inspired faith in his energy and ability.

The choice made, Edmond joined in the preparations for the flight to Bristol, which Harold preferred to regard as a tactical retreat. The earl assembled a tiny retinue of his most trusted followers, telling them only that they should be ready to depart Southwark at a moment's notice for a destination he would reveal later. Harold disclosed the full extent of his plans only to Earl Godwin, but to his surprise and disappointment the old man shook his head. "You're making a mistake, my son. There are better ways of coping with the king and his Normans than hiring foreign pirates to do our work. England is our land and it goes against my grain to loose those Danish robbers on her again as in the days of Sweyn Forkbeard and King Ethelred."

Despite his father's objections, which seemed strange considering Godwin's affiliation with the Danes in his younger days, Harold remained firm in his resolve. Godwin was too dispirited to persevere in trying to dissuade him from bringing another scourge of Danish marauders into England.

As for Sweyn, he remained secluded in his quarters after Stigand brought word of his renewed outlawry by the Witan. His mercurial temperament always had alternated between periods of ebullient self-confidence and bouts of deep despair, the latter mastering him on learning of his latest disgrace. The Witan's action shredded the cloak of self-deceit under which he habitually sheltered himself. He was deeply embarrassed at having been so readily manipulated by Archbishop Robert of Jumieges and Earl Ralph into deserting his family's cause when it now was obvious they had not intended to honor their part of a bad bargain. Their blandishments had lured him from his father's side at Beverstone at a pivotal moment when Godwin still retained the upper hand. Once that was accomplished, they had sought to keep out of the way even longer until the Witan could entirely undermine his father's power. Harold's intervention at Dover to persuade him to return to Southwark had come too late. The damage had been done to the family's interests. Desertion had so weakened the once formidable army assembled by the Godwinsons at Southwark that it was no longer effective.

Tormented by realization of how he had undermined his own position as well as that of his family, perhaps irreparably, Sweyn was plunged by self-pity and remorse into a melancholy lassitude. He appeared to take no interest in the plans for flight other than to agree to go with Godwin, his mother Gytha and youngest brothers to Bruges.

Harold assigned Edmond to help prepare the followers who were to accompany them to Bristol. Edmond performed his tasks cautiously to avoid further alarming the few troops still in Southwark. Harold decided to limit his retinue to Edmond, Godfrid, Thane Sebert and a half-dozen picked men from among his bodyguard.

The day before they were to leave, Godwin's household took the evening meal in an understandably restrained mood. The old earl was sunk in silence, barely touching his food and taking only an occasional sip of wine. Earl Harold, with Edmond at his right hand and Sebert to his left, was in a reminiscent frame of mind, describing his recent campaigns in Wales. Sweyn stared glumly into his ale horn, disregarding the rest of the company. His brother Tostig exchanged whispers with his bride Judith as if reluctant to violate the general constraint by speaking aloud. Lady Gytha kept her arms tightly wound around her youngest son, Wulfnoth, as if afraid of losing him. The atmosphere of gloom was broken only by infrequent bursts of merriment caused by horseplay between Godwin's fourth and fifth sons, Gurth and Leofwine, who could not repress their adolescent high spirits.

The murmur within the hall was suddenly broken by a great clatter of hooves in the courtyard outside. Bishop Stigand burst into the room. Even Godwin gasped aloud at the prelate's disheveled, agitated appearance. Stigand's face was streaked with dust and tears. He grasped the old earl's hand as he sank to his knees. "I did all I could, dear friend, but the king won't listen to me or Earl Leofric. He's determined to drive you out of the land. He has refused the hostages and safe conduct. Tomorrow, or even as we speak, the Witan will banish you." Stigand groaned and buried his face in his hands.

Godwin roused himself from his apathy, his weathered face suffused with blood and contorted with rage. With great effort he pulled himself to his feet with an agility astonishing for his years. He kicked over the high seat with a curse and shattered his wine goblet against the wall.

"To horse! To horse!" he roared, and stomped out of the hall with Stigand, family members and retainers streaming after him.

Chapter Nineteen

Fork in the Road

The leave-taking was melancholy, as to be expected, the members of Earl Godwin's family not knowing when and whether they would see each other again. As an old campaigner's wife, Lady Gytha was hardened to such partings from her husband and elder sons. She stoically accepted that Harold was heading for Bristol rather than Bruges, the destination of the majority. Her second son was almost thirty and, other than his duty to his father, was his own master. But when young Leofwine asked to be allowed to accompany Harold, Gytha's mother's heart betrayed her and she pleaded with Godwin to order the boy to remain with them. To her dismay, however, the old earl, delighted with Leofwine's spirit, readily consented.

"He is much too young, husband," Gytha protested, tears streaming. She desperately clutched their youngest son, Wulfnoth, as if afraid he too would be taken from her.

"Nonsense! I was no older when I left my father's cottage to guide Earl Ulf to safety and earned his respect and support," Godwin scoffed. Ignoring his wife's further protests, he turned to Harold. "It's up to you. Do you want the boy?"

Harold glanced hesitantly at Gytha, half-smiling as if to ask her forgiveness, then nodded. He assured his mother he would be doubly watchful to see to it that Leofwine came to no harm. The poignant scene concluded as final farewells were made, Godwin and his party spurred off toward the junction with the Old Stone Road that would lead them to Bosham where they would board ship for Bruges.

Shortly after Godwin's group disappeared around a distant bend in the road, a single rider appeared, coming from the same direction. The darkness concealed his identity until he reached the circle of light provided by torches to help Harold's little troop make its final preparations for departure. With sword in hand, Harold awaited the approaching horseman. A torch flared, illuminating the newcomer's face, and Harold exclaimed joyfully, "Sweyn! Then you'll come with us to Ireland, brother?"

Earl Sweyn shook his head. "No, Harold. I've returned to tell you something I didn't want to speak off in front of our parents. I didn't want to add to Mother's dismay at this brave lad's decision to go with you." He offered a hand to Leofwine, who had run up on hearing his eldest brother's voice. "I go on a pilgrimage to the Holy Land." He spoke slowly, as if to emphasize his determination and sincerity. "Mother will know soon enough. I'll tell her at Bruges." His voice trailed off and he slumped momentarily in the saddle, the fitful torchlight intermittently disclosing his grim and pale face.

"But why now, why a pilgrimage at this time when we need you?" Harold demanded, scuffing at the ground. "Come to Ireland and there'll be time enough to make such a gesture of piety after we have dealt with our enemies and restored our honor."

"No, it must be now or I'm lost forever. God knows I've done harm enough and deceived far too many and far too often to expect easy forgiveness. I've let passions and greed rule my heart and actions. The result has been havoc and hurt to those who are nearest to me in blood. This pilgrimage will set me aright, and if I don't perform it now it may be too late to save my eternal soul." He paused to check his emotion. "I've come to take my leave, dear brother, because I fear we may never meet again."

Leofwine's cheeks were wet with tears as he clung to Sweyn's trembling hands and Harold's eyes misted slightly He quickly regained control and barked, "What sad words are these, brother Sweyn. Not like you at all. Come, forget all this and be assured that next spring we'll feast joyfully again in our good father's hall."

Sweyn pulled erect in the saddle and spoke almost as if directed by an inner voice. "No, brother Harold, I know it can't be so. I'm certain we'll never meet again in this life. So let's take our farewell now. God be with you, Harold, and with you too, young Leofwine." He leaned forward to grip Harold's right hand with his own and stroked Leofwine's golden hair with his left hand.

"Why then, good brother," Harold declared, "if we do meet again—and so we shall, God willing—we'll laugh at this womanish dread. If not, then it's a most excellent and loving parting and such a one as is proper for the sons of the great Earl Godwin." He released Sweyn's hand and his elder brother, after a final stroke of Leofwine's hair, gripped the reins, spurred his mount, and quickly vanished into the darkness.

After a final lingering glance at Godwin's great mansion, and with spirits subdued by the emotional encounter with Sweyn, Harold's troop set out on its long journey westward. It was imperative to reach Bristol as quickly as possible. The king's faction might get wind of Harold's destination and attempt to intercept and arrest him.

Harold's apprehensions were justified. When the king's advisors learned he was not among Godwin's entourage bound for Bosham, they suspected he might head west and seek refuge and help in Ireland. The morning after the precipitate flight of Godwin and his sons from Southwark, the Witan declared them to be outlawed, and ordered that they leave England within five days or face arrest and trial. Despite the apparent period of grace, King Edward immediately dispatched Bishop Ealdred of Worcester, in whose diocese Bristol lay, with a strong force under orders to intercept and arrest Harold. Bishop Ealdred, however, had no liking either for his mission or the king's disregard of the five days of grace granted by the Witan. Accordingly, he made haste slowly in order to make sure he would not reach Bristol until the fugitives had a chance to put to sea.

Unaware though he was of the good bishop's lack of zeal, Harold drove his men relentlessly along the Roman highways and lesser roads leading to Bristol. With only brief pauses for food and rest for men and horses, the troop sped through or past London, Eton, Reading, Kennet, Avebury, Calne and Chippenham until it came within sight of Bristol.

As road-weary as he was, Edmond roused himself to look about carefully as the troop entered the seaport through the east gate. The guards, unaware of the Witan's actions, and recognizing their lord Sweyn's brother Harold, permitted the small group to pass unchallenged. Although Bristol had begun to grow to a respectable size as recently as the time of King Cnut three decades earlier, it was already among the principal commercial centers of England, flourishing especially in the wool trade. Situated on a peninsula at the confluence of the Frome and Avon rivers and bounded on three sides by those streams, its affluence benefited from proximity to the coastline of Ireland, much of which was controlled by the Danes, or Ostmen. Edmond had first heard of the town because of the slave trade, its second most important market. The good monk Eanric, who had taught him his letters as a child, had often thundered against the wicked traffic in human misery upon which so much of Bristol's prosperity was based.

After the little troop passed St. Peter's church, which lay directly inside the wall at the extreme fringe of the town, there was palpable evidence all around that Bristol's merchants prospered hugely from exporting human chattel as well as wool. The tradesmen's houses marched side by side, solidly built with timber frames filled in with boards or plastered clay. They were a single storey high with sharply pitched roofs protected by thatch or tiles. Behind most houses ran gardens reaching back to lanes crammed with the crudely-built cottages of the less fortunate.

Harold led his followers past another church and then reached the heart of the town, an extensive, crowded market place. Because Bristol squatted upon a hill from which an incline dipped sharply to the River Avon, Edmond from the market place was able to see dozens of ships pulled up to slips cut into the steep banks flanking the stream. Boats of assorted sizes lay side by side like so many suckling pigs jostling for a sow's teats. At first the bright colors of the handsomely decorated ship hulls riveted his attention, but he soon became aware of the dreary scenes in the market place.

Amidst the stalls and enclosures displaying vegetables, grains, farm and household implements, cattle, horses, wines, ale, fish and countless other commodities were located holding pens in which slaves were offered for sale. The purchasers, mostly Danes and other seafarers, exported them to Ireland, Iceland, Scandinavia and even as far as distant Constantinople. Men, women, children, young or old, healthy or ailing, stood, sat or sprawled in the corrals, tied together in groups of four, six or occasionally even more. Some were debtors who had been seized by creditors. Others were children sold by desperately poor parents. There were others who—in violation of the ineffective edicts of king after king—had been kidnapped by outlaws or vindictive enemies.

Many of the women appeared to be pregnant. Thane Sebert, noticing Edmond's astonishment, explained that the merchants often hired out the young girls as prostitutes until they conceived because then they fetched a higher price as offering the potential of two individuals for the price of one.

The majority of the slaves were silent and sullen, even totally apathetic, apparently resigned to their fate. A few, however, kept up a continual low wail until the overseers or their companions in misery bullied, cuffed or kicked them into a muffled whisper or total silence. A handful were even surprisingly jovial to the extent of exchanging jeers and taunts with the seamen, merchants, churls and soldiers swarming in the market place. Prospective purchasers often stopped to closely examine a muscular young man or buxom wench and exchange jests on the female's charms in great detail and vivid terms.

Earl Harold, after impassively viewing the scene, commented impatiently, "I see the port steward is careful to keep out of sight, unlike on my earlier visits when he was all smiles and bows. Not that I blame Master Sewin overly much for being discreet. One can't choose one's friends too carefully these days." He turned to Edmond. "We'll have to find our own way. Where did that sailor friend of yours say he'd wait for us?"

"A tavern called the White Whale, my lord."

An inquiry of a passerby produced directions. The ale house lay at the foot of the slope by the river, a stone's throw from a quay near which Edmond recognized the good ship *Eldrytha* bobbing restlessly in the murky waters of the stream. Edmond led the way into the tavern and when he asked for Master Wiglaf, the innkeeper smirked and jerked a greasy thumb toward a closed door at the rear of a long common hall. "The fat sailor and his little friend are in there, but I doubt you'd be welcome to knock. They've a woman with them and might resent an interruption." He added with a leer, "She's likely a slave picked up in the market for a few bits of silver so they might be happy to turn her over to you cheap after they're done with her."

"Enough, landlord!" Harold snapped, stemming the innkeeper's torrent of crude humor. "Bring us something to eat and drink. Let it be of your best." He led the way to a table and gestured for Leofwine to sit beside him with Edmond and Sebert facing the brothers. The six men-at-arms and Godfrid took a nearby table. "And host, tell those sailors as soon as they come out of that room that I want to see them. Immediately!"

Harold's imperious air quelled the innkeeper, who rushed off to fetch food and drink and was soon sullenly serving his guests without further comment. Harold and his companions were washing down their meal with drink by the time the door at the end of the hall finally creaked open and the huge form of Wiglaf emerged. On recognizing Earl Harold and Edmond, the sailor flushed like a boy caught with his hand in the pickle tub, but immediately regained his composure. He rolled up to the table with lurching gait to nod a greeting. "There's a lot to be said for getting away from home," he began, wiping the sweat from his face before adding, "though I'll not deny my Hilda her comforts." Harold was in no mood to exchange pleasantries. "Is the ship ready?" he demanded, glaring impatiently down the hall. "What's keeping Master Lewin? Is he in there?"

"Aye, my lord, and the *Eldrytha*'s ready to weigh anchor any time it pleases you. Master Lewin will be along presently. It's a toothsome lass and he's taking his time. He's not as young as I used to be." Harold's scowl stifled Wiglaf's incipient chuckle in his throat and alerted him that the earl was in no mood for foolery. "I'll fetch him immediately, my lord," he added hurriedly, but paused before carrying out his mission to ask, "It's not true, is it, that the Witan has banished you and your gracious father, Earl Godwin?"

Harold exchanged surprised glances with his companions. "Is that what's being said here?"

Wiglaf was uncomfortable. "Nothing but hearsay, I don't doubt, but there's been such talk. A few Norman dogs have been bragging to anyone fool enough to listen that Earl Ralph and Archbishop Robert have the king's ear and they'll drive Earl Godwin and his people out of England. Aye, and even turn the good, sweet Lady Edith out of the king's bed. That's if she's ever been truly in it to any good purpose, if you know my meaning." The last slipped out, Wiglaf's tongue running ahead of his good sense. He shuffled his feet nervously, worried he might have offended Harold, the queen's brother.

The earl refused to be upset by a common sailor's thoughtless and crude remark, dismayed as he was at the possibility that King Edward might have discarded his wife. It caught him off guard. He had not supposed the king might carry his displeasure with the House of Godwin to the extent of separating from Edith. "Is that what's said, that the king is displeased with the Lady of England?" he forced himself to ask Wiglaf.

"From what I've heard, the Norman rascals claim she has been sent to a convent."

In a fit of temper, Harold kicked over the table, his surprised companions leaping out of the way to avoid the flying food, drink and utensils. It was infuriating enough that King Edward was so spitefully venting his grievances against the House of Godwin, which had supported him loyally for decades, by banishing its male members. But it was unbelievable that the king should mistreat and discard his wife, a woman whose reputation for kindliness, modest behavior and godly piety was renowned throughout the land. That he should even contemplate such an insult merely because she was Godwin's daughter was beneath contempt. Harold would have preferred to disregard Wiglaf's words but the sailor's account accorded so well with the tone of the entire wretched affair that he could not deny that it was almost certainly true.

Mastering his rage, Harold made a characteristically rapid decision and told Edmond, "If what's being said is so, it might be best to change our plans. The Lady Edith needs to be reassured and advised. Even if she's immured in a convent she's bound to hear how matters are going at court from friends who remain near the king and the people who wish to have a foot in each camp. Such information might be valuable. You could do me a great service by carrying a message to my dear sister. Will you go to her?"

Edmond nodded. Everything considered, he had no pressing reason to go to Ireland, or anything to gain there. If he could serve Harold and himself equally well by remaining in England he was content to do so. Besides, by staying he was more likely to find an opportunity to discover Adele's whereabouts.

"Has anyone mentioned the name of the convent to which my sister may be sent?" Harold asked Wiglaf.

"Was it Wharton? No, that doesn't sound quite right. It was Whar—Wher—Whermere—no, Wherwell. Yes, that's it, Wherwell, the royal monastery."

"All the better. King Edward's sister is the abbess, and she's well disposed toward my dear sister. That's reassuring. It suggests they don't mean her any real harm." Harold turned to Edmond again. "Do you know where Wherwell is, my friend?"

"In the neighborhood of Winchester, if I'm not mistaken, my lord."

"Nearby, that's true. You know our situation and what we intend. Find some means of gaining access to my sister and tell her where we stand. She may be able to learn things that could be helpful to us." Harold paused to reflect. "But how will you pass it on to us? I have it! If you want to get a message to me, seek out Wulfstan the prior of Worcester, a most pious and excellent man who loves me as a son. I'll find means of communicating with him."

As Harold clapped Edmond encouragingly on the shoulder, his attention was diverted by footsteps approaching in the hall. It was Master Lewin. The *Eldrytha*'s captain could not have chosen a better time to appear before Harold without risking a tongue-lashing. Now that the earl had decided on a course of action, he was too impatient to get underway for Ireland to create a fuss. As luck would have it, however, Harold was forced to delay a bit longer. When Master Lewin stepped out of the inn to check the weather, he found the winds contrary and the sea extremely choppy. He advised Harold it would be unwise to set sail before the outlook became more favorable. Harold chafed but grudgingly deferred to Lewin's superior knowledge of seamanship. He called for the chessboard that was always in his baggage and sat down to play a game with Edmond who was not to depart for Wherwell until the others had left for Ireland.

Wiglaf and Lewin, not sorry for the delay because they were hungry and thirsty, sat down at a convivial table with the six soldiers of Harold's following and Godfrid.

Earl Harold found Edmond a skillful chess opponent and checkmated him only after a strenuous effort. "If you wield sword and battle-ax as well as you play chess, there'll be few to match you," he remarked before leaving the table to go outside and judge the weather conditions. On returning, he rubbed hands. "I'm no sailor, but by my reckoning the wind and sea are calm enough. We should be able to get underway shortly. Now to convince our seamen." He tapped the shoulder of Thane Sebert, who was playing at dice with young Leofwine, and ordered, "Fetch Master Lewin and his fat friend. The sooner we leave Bristol the better."

As soon as Lewin and Wiglaf came to the table, Harold snapped, "Whether the wind's good, bad, or has died down, we depart immediately." Lewin was about to suggest it was advisable to check the weather conditions first but thought better of it and accompanied Wiglaf to the back room to fetch their belongings. Harold instructed Sebert to lead the six troopers to the *Eldrytha*, then had parting words for Edmond. "I have faith in you, my friend, and don't doubt that you'll accomplish what I've asked of you. Rest assured, before next summer arrives I'll be back in England, worse luck to those who try to stop me. Until then, I hope to hear from you. Remember Wulfstan!" He spun on his heels and left the inn with Leofwine at his side.

Master Lewin and Wiglaf reappeared in the hall and paused momentarily on their way out of the inn.

"Take care of yourself, Thane Edmond," Lewin said heartily with a friendly nod.

As Wiglaf followed Lewin out the door, he also had a final word. "Aye, take good care, my lord," he rasped. "Put your trust in none but God and yourself." He put a hand to his head. "Ah, I've forgotten. What about the girl? Master Lewin and I paid good money for her. But we can't take her along." His perplexed look slowly spread into a mischievous grin. He began to laugh. "We'll leave her to you, Thane Edmond," he boomed "She's a bit shopworn, but a tasty little wench for all that." Ignoring Edmond's astonishment, he forced his great bulk through the doorway to follow Lewin and the rest of Earl Harold's retinue toward the *Eldrytha*. As Edmond watched from the doorway, his companions quickly boarded the little ship, which immediately weighed anchor and began to drift downriver. Edmond's last glimpse of Harold was of the earl standing at the *Eldrytha's* bow, gazing out to sea, his arm protectively around his brother Leofwine.

Edmond contemplatively reentered the inn, sat down and ordered a horn of ale. All had left now except Godfrid, who had fallen asleep on a nearby bench, no doubt having drunk far more than was good for him. Edmond sipped his drink languidly while reviewing the circumstances that had led to his present precarious situation. After the incident at Dover, he had set out to seek service with some great lord in order to learn more about the political scene. He had hoped a better understanding might help him decide whether or not it would be anything other than utter folly to plan a bid for the high place to which he had an incontestable claim by virtue of his ancestry. Instead, here he was, alone in a far western seaport, the trusted envoy of a fugitive earl to a deposed queen. He twisted the silver ring around his finger and brooded anew on the vagaries of fortune. "AELFRED MEC HEHT GEWYRCAN," he read for the hundredth, perhaps thousandth time. Drawing off the ring, he playfully tossed it into the air, deftly caught it, then slowly restored it to his finger. He wryly wondered whether good King Alfred would have bothered to commission a silversmith to waste time and skill if he had been able to foresee that the ring would descend to such a hapless heir. The innkeeper's importunity at his elbow

136

abruptly curtailed Edmond's melancholy musing. "The girl, sir? What am I to do about her? She's in that room, and I want her out."

Edmond stared in astonishment. "It's none of my business," he shrugged.

The innkeeper was insistent. "She belongs to you, sir. The sailor left her for you. I heard him tell you so."

"He was joking. Surely you don't think he meant it? What would I want with her? I have no use for a slave, least of all a woman?"

"That's all very well, sir, but what's it to do with me? All I know is the room's mine and there's someone sleeping in it who shouldn't be there. Shall I have her thrown out?"

Edmond was almost as amused as confused. After all, it was true Wiglaf had said he was leaving the girl to him even if the sailor meant it as a joke. But he had problems enough without being burdened with a slave. Nevertheless, he probably had to do something about the situation, if only to ease the innkeeper's mind and see the girl came to no harm. He would have a look, then free her. As he approached the door, a thought struck him. If left alone in Bristol, the center of the slave trade, she would be in danger of being abducted and sold again by some unscrupulous scoundrel. Energetically cursing Wiglaf under his breath for handing him such a dilemma, he entered the room.

The woman lay naked on the bed, her thin but not unshapely body spread across what was little more than a rickety cot covered with a sack of dirty straw. A wreath of luxuriant if unkempt and tangled blonde hair framed the fairly regular features of a not unattractive face. Not much more than a child, he realized, but still woman enough to apparently stir and satisfy a man's desire, judging by Wiglaf and Lewin. Her small yet rounded breasts rose and fell rhythmically as she breathed regularly in her sleep of exhaustion. Edmond felt the blood surge to his temples. To avoid awakening her, and uncertain of his intentions, he attempted to close the door softly but it creaked slightly.

She stirred at the sound and her eyes flicked open. Startled and confused at seeing a total stranger, she barely succeeded in stifling a scream but revealed how alarmed she was in her despairing, pitiful glance at the intruder. Edmond tried to reassure her with a smile, but she began to whimper on realizing she was totally uncovered. She clutched feverishly for a flimsy garment lying at the foot of the bed. Finally getting a firm grasp on it, she fumbled awkwardly in her anxiety to pull it quickly over her head. Succeeding after a frantic effort, she tugged at the fabric as if to stretch it so she could cover herself from head to foot. Her struggle, laughable under other circumstances, had an effect opposite to what she apparently intended for they inflamed him even more. Yielding to instinct, he slipped into the bed beside her.

Chapter Twenty

A Hand-Fast Marriage

E dmond's return to the isolated settlement in the depths of
Ashdowne Forest was voluntary, unlike his earlier visit as the
prisoner of Thane Eadred's outlaw band. The rude village that
formerly had been so forbidding might serve as a sanctuary from King
Edward's persecution of Earl Godwin's supporters. Edmond was
relieved after a long and hazardous flight across the breadth of England
to arrive safely with his two companions. As unprepossessing as was the
tiny hamlet sprawled along the banks of the small stream trickling
through the clearing it was a welcome sight. It looked almost attractive
despite its huddle of ramshackle buildings squatting under a gray dull
November sky and the surrounding faded verdure of the formerly lush
green fields and dense, concealing curtain of forest.

Edmond bestrode a sturdy Flemish horse from Earl Harold's stable,
while Godfrid and the girl left on his hands by Master Lewin and Wiglaf
clung to a swaybacked dapple mare of uncertain age. It was partly on the
girl's account Edmond decided to return to the outlaw encampment.
After what had passed between him and the girl, whose name was Helga,
he was reluctant to abandon her to her fate in Bristol, most likely
renewed slavery. He might readily find a husband for her from among
Thane Eadred's followers. Unmarried women were scarce in the village
and the outlaws were not likely to be particular about the girl's past.

The journey from Bristol to the shelter of Ashdowne Forest, whose
vast extent could easily hide an army, had been circuitous and
dangerous. On several occasions the fugitives barely eluded hostile
patrols scouring the countryside to hunt down partisans of the House of
Godwin. Not until they reached the shelter of the great weald did
Edmond feel entirely safe from pursuit.

The village was yet shrouded in morning mist as Edmond and his
companions approached the stream slashing through the clearing, but it
was already bustling with the laughter and chatter of women at
laundering. By Eadred's great hall a huge figure became alert to the
oncoming hoof beats and rose quickly from beside a smoldering fire.
Stretching his massive limbs, he turned toward the newcomers and
shaded his single eye to peer at them. Even at a distance Edmond and
Godfrid recognized the great bulk of Gurth and were immediately

identified as well.

"Earl Eadred will be delighted to see you again, Thane Edmond," Gurth bellowed as soon as he thought the visitors could hear him. "How he's longing to see you again, to repay you fully for that knock on the head." His laughter was infectious and Edmond joined in, the more sincerely as Gurth's hearty greeting made it clear he was welcome.

"I've no quarterstaff handy this time, friend Gurth," Edmond replied, swinging out of the saddle to grasp the outlaw's immense paw, then wincing at the pressure. "I've other business with your lord, and I hope he has forgiven and forgotten."

"Forgiven yes, forgotten not likely," Gurth responded, nodding a casual greeting to Godfrid but turning wide-eyed on noticing the slender girl clinging to the mare's mane in front of the lad. A sly grin spread as he continued. "But can it be that you've taken a wife since you left us? Now it's clear why you were so anxious to depart. You wanted to make sure no one carried off this little beauty." He ran an appreciative eye over Helga, who lowered hers in confusion and hesitated to dismount even after Godfrid slid off the mare's back to stand beside Edmond.

Edmond was amused. "No, my friend, I've no wife, nor am I likely to seek or get one soon. Helga has no husband, yet more's the pity for she's a worthy maid. Though I wouldn't be surprised if she could find one here readily enough."

"That's as may be, though no sure thing," Gurth replied doubtfully. "There's not much of her by the look of it and most of the lads prefer a little more meat on a maid whatever her looks. Still, she might do well in that direction if she's willing, even if she's a tiny, skinny wench because she's not ill-favored. It's a hard life here and a stout, hale woman is what's wanted among us." Despite his discouraging words, he reached out to help Helga off the mare. When she resisted feebly, he shook with laughter and swung her high off the horse as if she were a baby, then deposited her upright on the ground with surprising gentleness. She glared indignantly at him, flushed and readjusted the modest garment bought for her in Bristol. Clutching Godfrid's good right arm, she hid behind Edmond.

Gurth ushered the newcomers into the great hall where they found Thane Eadred still seated at breakfast, listlessly gnawing at a flat bread cake. The outlaw chief's eyes lit up as soon as he recognized Edmond. He thumped the table in delight.

"By the holy rood, a welcome sight!" he thundered. "Night after night, day by day for months since our last meeting I've dreamt of cracking open your skull. I've not forgotten our little sport, you can be sure. I still feel the lump you raised on my noggin." He laughed disarmingly and it was evident he bore his conqueror no malice. Inviting

Edmond to sit beside him, he gestured to his people to make room for Godfrid and Helga at the foot of the table. Above all, Thane Eadred respected a stalwart, skillful fighter and none more than someone who could match his skill with weapons of any sort. Paradoxically, Edmond had earned the outlaw chief's lasting friendship and unbounded admiration by mastering him at quarterstaves.

Talk soon turned to what was going on in the outside world. News drifted slowly and often in garbled form to Eadred's isolated village so he questioned Edmond eagerly about the doings of the Witan and the conflict between the king's supporters and those of Godwin and his sons. He was reluctant to believe rumors that the Witan had banished Godwin's people, and he knew nothing of subsequent events. Edmond confirmed that Godwin, Sweyn and Harold had left England. He did not trouble to hide his partiality for the House of Godwin, aware Eadred was in some way allied or beholden to Earl Sweyn. He surmised Sweyn had won over Eadred by pledging to reinstate him in the king's graces and confirming his claim to an earl's status. It was ironic, Edmond reflected, that instead of restoring Eadred's standing, Sweyn had succeeded only in being outlawed again himself.

"I've no doubt Earl Sweyn will return quickly to claim his rights and harry his enemies," Eadred declared confidently after recovering from the initial shock of Edmond's disclosures.

"One can't be sure," Edmond temporized, careful not to alarm Eadred unduly by abruptly disclosing it was unlikely Sweyn would ever come back. "He left England with his father, and no doubt will consult with Earl Godwin as to their next step."

Eadred lifted an eyebrow. "He'll do what he likes, no matter what his father says. Earl Sweyn is too proud to yield meekly. He'd never surrender his rights without putting up a fight. It's not like him at all. If I know him as I think I do, he'll stop at nothing to regain his lands. No man is more relentless and determined if crossed or challenged."

"All the same, I've heard it said he won't be back soon," Edmond replied. "There's talk he might go to the Holy Land. If he does, it might be years until England sees him again."

Eadred frowned. "If he adventures so far, if he goes to Jerusalem, what you say could well be true. From what I've been told, not many return from the Holy Land." His words trailed off as he collected his thoughts. "But where does this leave my affairs? I've been relying on Earl Sweyn's help and now it seems I can't be sure of it." Troubled, he looked at Edmond almost as if to appeal for sympathy. "My first thought when I saw you was that you brought a message from him."

"I come from Earl Harold, not Sweyn," Edmond disclosed, sensing the situation might present an opportunity to entice Eadred into Harold's camp. "He has sailed to Ireland to gather strength and return to claim what's his by right."

"I don't see that's my concern, or offers any help to me."

"It could mean a great deal, a chance to mend matters," Edmond fixed his gaze on Eadred to gauge his reaction. "Unlike his brother, he's not gone so far he can't return quickly. When he does, there'll be an army at his back."

"I've nothing to gain by that. My allegiance is to Earl Sweyn, not to his brother, who owes me nothing and, to tell the truth, hasn't ever looked kindly on me."

"Here's your chance to change that. Earl Harold is a reasonable man. What's more, a dependable friend and lord who'll stand by those who serve him well. Can you look for as much from the king and his people? Would they have equal regard for you if you served them?"

"Regard? They'd have my head if they could track me down, and would've had it long since if I hadn't given them the slip more than once."

"So you've no love for the king and his Norman friends?"

"Love?" Eadred spat. "God's mercy, the king's people have never done or attempted to do me other than harm. As for his Normans, I'd willingly help drive them out of England."

"Why not join those who aim to do just that?"

"It's not all that certain they'll succeed," Eadred scoffed. "From what you've told me, the lords Godwin and Harold have fled England in disgrace, as has my friend Earl Sweyn who may not return for years. The king and his friends have the upper hand and I'm not fool enough to risk my neck in such a doubtful cause."

"If Earl Harold returns with a great power of ships and men, would you join him?"

"It'll bear thinking about if there's enough to gain," Eadred admitted. "If there's a good chance of success, why then I'll listen to what Earl Harold has to offer."

"What if I were to pledge Earl Harold's word that once he's restored to good standing, he'll persuade the king to revoke your outlawing?"

"A promise is just that, only a promise, but it might go a long way toward tempting me to support the earl. Tempt, I say. There's also the matter of my father's lands, so wrongfully taken from me to be handed over to the king's Norman friends."

"First Earl Harold must regain King Edward's confidence."

"You mean, regain control of our inconstant, vacillating shadow of a monarch," Eadred gibed. "Then string up a few of the Norman dogs around him so as to leave no doubt who's in charge."

"If he can enlist enough men of good will in his cause, Earl Harold will achieve that and more. What's more, he won't be ungrateful."

Eadred was too cunning to commit himself irrevocably, so he temporized by replying, "When Harold Godwinson lands, as you say he will, and with a respectable force at his back, then I'll consider joining him. Until then, my men and I, few as we are, remain here."

"You'd have no reason to regret swearing fealty to Earl Harold," Edmond pressed. "Stand by and be ready when he lands, then hasten to his side. He'll welcome you, that's certain, and his gratitude won't be limited to empty words." The assurance was a gamble on Edmond's part since Harold had not specifically authorized him to recruit for his cause. Nevertheless the earl, with his fortunes at such an ebb, would welcome assistance from any direction and not cavil at honoring a pledge made in his name. If Eadred could be won over, any chance to do so must be pursued.

Feeling he could do no more in that direction for the moment, Edmond's attention turned to Helga. He was anxious to find a home for her. After what had passed between him and the girl, instinctive and fleeting as it was, he had been unwilling to callously abandon her to her fate in Bristol, where she was most likely to end up in the slave market again. His first thought had been to take her back to her hometown, a village in Mercia, but when he suggested it she lamented that outlaws had murdered her entire family before carrying her off. She had no one to return to. Under the circumstances, he hit upon the notion of taking her to Ashdowne Forest where there was a good chance of finding her a husband.

"I noticed when I was here before there weren't many unattached women among your folk," he explained to Thane Eadred. "Some of your lusty young churls must be eager for a good wife so I've brought along this pretty maid. What's more," he continued, reaching for the heavy purse provided by Harold which was hanging at his belt, "she'll not be without a generous dowry." He made a show of counting out a dozen pennies, flinging them one by one to the table so the bell-like chink of silver striking hardwood would resound throughout the hall.

Eadred watched in amused wonder as the coins piled up, then turned his attention to Helga, looking her up and down before guffawing. "Woman, you say? Two of her wouldn't make a proper woman. All skin and bones like a plucked chicken. Not that she's all that bad-looking, I'll admit, especially with the silver-lining enhancing her charms. That should make it easier and, come to think of it, I've just the man for her." He shot a huge index finger at Gurth. "Here, you one-eyed thief! It's time you were wed."

Grinning from ear to ear, Gurth responded, "I've already had a wife or two, my lord earl."

"Yes, but not your own, you big dolt."

Eadred beckoned to Helga who again tried to hide behind Edmond. He gripped her shoulders and encouraged her to approach the head of the table, which she did hesitantly and with downcast eyes. Scrutinizing her, Eadred muttered, "I've half a mind to keep you for myself." She shrank back in apprehension and he demanded, "What, I'm not good enough for the likes of you? A bit of gray hair maybe, but you'd find me hearty enough if needs be." He patted her blushing cheek. "You needn't worry, child. I'm not the man for you, but here's one who'll do even though the knave's half-blind. Gurth, my lad, I've wife for you, someone to keep you out of other men's hen coops."

Gurth was canny enough not to assent straightway, not that he had any great objection to his master's command. After all, Helga was comely though slightly built and there was little harm in a hand-fast marriage. It could easily be broken off if a woman became tiresome. There also was that little heap of silver coins to consider. He lodged only a mild protest. "I've always hoped, my lord earl, that when I took a wife she'd bring me a bit more than just the rags on her back."

Eadred took the hint. His huge right paw swept the dozen silver pence off the table and Gurth scurried to retrieve them from the floor. "That's a richer dowry than you deserve, you knave, or would be likely to gain with any other wench who'd be fool enough to have you," Eadred roared. "Her rags look fine as silk to you now, don't they?" He turned to Helga. "Take his hand, girl! That's the way. I now pronounce you man and wife." He pulled the bewildered, dazed girl into his arms, gave her a resounding smack of a kiss, then rejoined her hand to Gurth's. "Now off with the two of you! But mind, no tricks until you're bedded properly tonight." He pointed to the door and amidst great laughter the newlyweds left the hall, accompanied by a grinning old woman appointed as a chaperone by Eadred to make sure they obeyed his final instructions.

Amusing as had been this farce of a wedding it also was a relief to Edmond as he no longer felt responsible for Helga's well-being. She was in Gurth's care now, and he seemed a sound and good-natured if rough-hewn fellow who probably would make as good a husband as she was likely to find anywhere.

Preoccupied by the endeavors to win over Eadred for Earl Harold and to get Helga off his hands, Edmond at first disregarded the absence of the outlaw chieftain's daughter Edith. When it occurred to him that she was not in the hall he was careful not to ask Eadred about her. His host might read more into his making such an inquiry than that it was merely a polite gesture. Accordingly, he was kept in suspense until the evening meal when Edith followed her father into the hall, accompanied by the matron who had been with her at the festivities in honor of Earl

Sweyn's visit. She took her place at her father's right hand and gave Edmond a warm smile when he sat down at her left.

"Welcome, Edmond Edwysson," she said softly and he was strangely pleased that she greeted him by name. "My father is delighted that you've visited us again."

"The pleasure is all mine, I assure you, Lady Edith," he replied gallantly. She was even more attractive than he remembered. He experienced an inexplicable blend of enjoyment at seeing her again and unease over comparing her to Adele whose dark beauty contrasted so strongly with this girl's pale loveliness. As if to explain his return, he blurted, "I've brought a bride for your father's good man Gurth."

"Indeed!" she exclaimed. "I would never have suspected you of being a matchmaker."

"A successful and skillful one, daughter," Eadred interjected. "You should have seen what an ill-assorted pair Gurth and his bride make. You wouldn't believe how tiny she is, a starved looking little maid, and with him being such a huge, ill-favored ox." He laughingly described the "nuptials" he had presided over to his daughter.

Edith professed to be shocked and waggled a finger in mock indignation. "It sounds shameful. What would good Father Elmer say to such a disgraceful union, one not sanctioned and sanctified by our holy church? I hope you'll arrange a more lawful wedding for me, one blessed in the eyes of God, or I'll have none of it."

"It's not likely to be a concern of ours for some time," Eadred snapped. "Earl Sweyn has left England and none can be certain as to when he'll return to claim you as his bride."

Edith could not hide her surprise. Clutching at her breast, she demanded, "What do you mean, Father? Where's Earl Sweyn gone and why do you say no one knows when he'll come back?"

"Thane Edmond can tell you more about it than I can."

Edith listened intently while Edmond dutifully told what he knew of Sweyn's decision to journey to Jerusalem on pilgrimage. He noticed, however, she did not seem as downcast by the news as might be expected. It was obvious she was not as eager as her father for the alliance with Sweyn. Her sole comment after Edmond finished his relation was a pious hope that Sweyn would return safely from his long and hazardous journey.

Eadred's disappointment at Sweyn's departure was clearly much greater than that of his daughter. "I don't believe you hope for any such thing, foolish girl," he growled testily and demanded, "Tell me, friend Edmond, would any other maid of gentle blood in all England turn up her nose at the prospect of becoming the bride of a great lord such as Earl Sweyn?"

Edmond prudently confined himself to a noncommittal smile.

Edith eagerly changed the subject to ask Edmond about his experiences since his previous visit. When he mentioned his brief call to King Edward's court at Gloucester, she wondered what Edmond thought of some of the great men he had met and most particularly of Earl Harold.

"Is it true he has sworn he'll never leave Edith Swan-neck?" Edith inquired. "I've heard it said he has refused all others no matter how advantageous it might be for him to take a high-born bride."

"He looks on Edith Swan-neck as his true and loving wife in the eyes of God and man," Edmond replied.

"They're united only in a hand-fast marriage, like that of Gurth and the girl you brought," Edith said dismissively. "Such a union has no meaning to Christian folk, least of all to the high-born."

"Yet from what I've heard it's as sacred to Earl Harold as if Bishop Stigand had performed the ceremony."

Edith's eyes widened in disbelief. "Then does he truly love this woman, this low-born daughter of his father's steward, something I find hard to accept?" She tossed her head as if overcome by distaste at the mere discussion of a match so unequal.

"There can be no doubt of it," Edmond assured her.

"What about you, Thane Edmond, could a man of your gentle birth contemplate marrying a woman beneath your station?" She spoke as if to challenge him rather than to pose a question.

He thought wistfully of Adele and ruefully that Edith was unaware of how high-born he actually was before replying warmly, "If the woman is worthy in herself, I wouldn't hesitate. True worth is not entirely dependent on accident of birth."

"You mean you could prefer, let's say a merchant's daughter, to someone of noble birth such as myself?" Mischief sparkled in her light blue eyes.

"I didn't say that," he sidestepped.

"Yet you don't deny you might," she pressed.

"Prefer anyone to you, my lady? It would be difficult indeed if the choice was mine to make. Impossible, I believe. Fortunately, I'll never be put to the test." He played the gallant well, and she rewarded him with a brilliant smile, gratified with his response.

After leaving the hall, he wondered if her flirtatious mood had any deeper significance but dismissed the notion. He could mean nothing to her nor she to him. It was apparent she had no love for Earl Sweyn, perhaps even feared and detested the eldest son of Godwin. Nevertheless, her father's word was law and if Eadred insisted she wait for Earl Sweyn's return from pilgrimage she had no recourse other than to obey.

Chapter Twenty-One

The Bride of Christ

King Edward's forsaken wife Edith, the Lady of England, readily settled down to the restful and routine rhythm of a religious community during the first few weeks after her forced retirement to the convent of Wherwell. Earl Godwin's daughter long ago had resigned herself to her royal husband's indifference. His refusal to cohabit with her, whether because of religious scruples, apathy or physical impotence, deprived her of an outlet for her plentiful energy in the rearing of children. As a result, she turned her attention to spiritual concerns and works of charity. Her sweet and benevolent nature made her doubly welcome at the convent, where she was an honored guest rather than a member, and enhanced the regard in which she was held by the Abbess Elfrida, King Edward's sister. The abbess at first was disposed chiefly to pity her sister-in-law, so cruelly torn from her husband's side, as being the victim of a struggle for power. She soon came to admire and love her, and could not exert herself enough to tend to Edith's comfort and well-being. She became the queen's constant companion despite the severe demands made on her time by management of the large and prosperous establishment Wherwell was becoming under royal sponsorship.

As was their frequent habit, the two great ladies, attended by a sole novice who sat apart in a corner of the solarium and kept busy with needlework, were engaged in a lively discussion on a late afternoon. The topic was a lawsuit being pressed by the convent against a neighboring landowner. Abbess Elfrida, with a clarity of mind that set her apart from her frequently incoherent brother, was elegantly summing up the legal basis for the convent's case when a nun entered the room to claim her attention.

"What is it, Sister Eudocia?"

"Your pardon, my lady abbess, but the gatekeeper has informed me that a young man has arrived and seeks permission to speak to the Lady Edith. He insists his message is too urgent to be delayed until morning."

Elfrida frowned. It was past the usual hour for admitting visitors, and the convent was about to lock its gates for the night. Yet it would be almost cruel to delay any good news, if that's what it was, from reaching the queen. After all, King Edward had put no specific restrictions on his wife's right to communicate with relatives or friends. His sole instruction had been to keep Lady Edith from leaving the convent.

"Let him come to us," the abbess decided. "We'll receive him here."

Sister Eudocia ushered a broad-shouldered young man with a shock of coarse, close-cropped brown hair into the solarium. His garments, though travel-stained and hard-worn, were those of a man of rank. He approached the two women hesitantly, obviously uncertain as to which was the queen.

"I understand you've an urgent message for my good sister, the Lady of England," the abbess prompted with a reassuring smile. Edmond turned his attention to her companion and was struck by how strikingly the queen's features, though softened by femininity, resembled those of her brother Sweyn. "The Lady Edith grants you permission to speak. What have you to tell her?"

"The message I've been entrusted with is meant solely for my Lady of England's hearing," Edmond replied uncomfortably. "So I was instructed."

"Indeed! I don't know if I can permit that." The abbess glanced at her sister-in-law. The queen was too proud to plead but Elfrida recognized a silent appeal in her eyes. "Well, I suppose there's no harm in my leaving the room for a few moments." She swept out of the solarium after beckoning to the closely-hooded novice to abandon her needlework and follow her.

Queen Edith briefly studied Edmond before inquiring, "If we're not mistaken, you come from my brother Earl Harold?"

"Just so, gracious lady."

"You've been with him to Ireland? We've heard rumors he's gone there."

"I did not accompany the earl. I left him in Bristol after he charged me to attend you as soon and as quickly as possible."

"And?"

"I'm to accept any message you may wish to send him."

"Ah! Why should he expect that I would have one?"

"He trusts to your sisterly regard…"

"I also have a duty to my husband, to the lord of England!" Edith's eyes flashed. "That comes first, it overrides all other ties." Her imperious vehemence shocked Edmond. He was at a loss for words. Believing he was being dismissed and that there was no more to be said, he bowed as if to take his leave. She thrust out her right arm as a command to stay put.

"Forgive my rudeness." An eloquent smile pleaded her case. "I've been so confused and distressed that I can't think clearly. I do want you to convey a message to my good brother. Nevertheless, though no matter how unkind and unfair my dear husband King Edward may seem to have been to me, I can't in good conscience serve as a spy or informer against him. Not even on behalf of my family, my father and brothers. Moreover, to do so would betray Abbess Elfrida's kindness and her trust in me. Whatever my sister-in-law, or anyone else, may tell me concerning the affairs of this kingdom I must keep to myself. I hope Earl Harold understands and respects my decision. You'll convey what I've said to him?"

"I'll do my best, my lady." Edmond who had come prepared to sympathize with the queen now found himself admiring her. Her principled loyalty to her husband and sister-in-law could only make her situation even more difficult. Her stand made it impossible for her to help her family or exert greater influence on her estranged husband.

"It's all we can expect from you," she replied softly before a rap on the door interrupted their tête-à-tête. "Come in, come in," she cried and the abbess reentered, again accompanied by the novice. "It's well you've returned so soon, Elfrida dear! As you know, I've no secrets from you and I wish you to hear me inform this young man we've no messages to send my brother Harold that you can't hear as well."

"You needn't be concerned, my lady, I'm sure of that," the abbess replied, but put a cautionary finger to her lips. "Others may not be so trusting. We must be careful not to let anyone else hear of this young man's mission. I'm told a band of Earl Ralph's men-at-arms have just arrived in the village."

Edmond stiffened. Luckily he had left Godfrid at Ashdowne Forest as an attendant to Thane Eadred's son Edward during his mission to Wherwell. If it became necessary to elude Earl Ralph's troop it would be much easier to do so without being burdened by concern for the lad.

"We must not detain you much longer," Lady Edith said, but then asked as if in afterthought, "Did you see my brothers Harold and Leofwine embark safely on their way to Ireland?"

"I saw their ship get underway."

"You haven't heard from Earl Harold since?"

"No, my lady."

"You do have a way of getting a message to him?"

Edmond nodded.

"That's well. Then tell him this: We are safe, in good health and spirits, and the king has not acted as unkindly toward me as some may be saying. I've often yearned to retire to a convent so how could he harm me by fulfilling my wishes? And tell Harold…" she hesitated, "…that his sister begs him to spare our dear land and good people the blood-letting, bitterness and agonies of civil strife. Let him rather await the unfolding of God's design. Our people already have suffered far too much harm at the hands of invaders. They deserve more just and kindly treatment by their kinfolk, for no matter how high God has raised my father and brothers that's what they are in His eyes."

"My lady…" Edmond began but a regal gesture cut him off.

"No! We can guess what you mean to say. We don't wish to hear it. Let it be Harold who attempts to justify the ungodly deeds he may have in mind in his wrath and desire for vengeance. Don't you speak for him."

Edmond appeared to be so dismayed and confused by her passionate words that the queen yielded to a twinge of pity. "Come, young man, we didn't mean to be harsh. I'm not angry with you but furious at those who care not what havoc they wreak or how much pain and suffering they inflict on the innocent as long they can obtain vengeance on their enemies and gain their impious ends. Tell us, what's your name and rank?"

"I'm called Thane Edmond Edwysson."

"Well thane, if we judge rightly, you're tired, hungry and disappointed. We can do nothing about the last, but we can see to it that you have something to eat before you leave." Lady Edith beckoned to the novice, still ostensibly busy with her needle in the corner. "Adele, my dear. Please conduct Thane Edmond to the refectory."

A muffled, almost despairing cry emerged from the depths of the novice's hood, which she pulled even more tightly around her head. Edmond stared at the young woman and added to the queen and abbess's astonishment by exclaiming, "Adele!"

The novice slowly pulled back the hood to disclose a tear-streaked face. "Yes, you've found me, alas," she lamented. "Far better if you hadn't, if we had never met again."

Her reaction left him at a loss for a reply and they silently looked at one another until the abbess overcame her initial surprise to intervene. "What does this mean?" she demanded, not unkindly. "This requires an explanation."

Adele shook her head, unable to speak and left it up to Edmond to explain as best he could. He quickly related the story of how he first had met Adele as a guest in her father's house, of Osgood's murder by the Normans, and of her subsequent sheltering by her uncle before he lost track of her whereabouts. He was circumspect enough however to conceal the extent of his interest in the young girl and not to make too much of his part in the deadly skirmish between the townsfolk of Dover and the Normans. The queen and abbess listened intently to his story, exchanging occasional sympathetic looks.

When he concluded, the abbess glanced at the queen. "Well, what's to be done, if anything?"

Edmond boldly interrupted, "If you'll permit, my lady abbess, could I and this young woman have a word or two together?"

Abbess Elfrida frowned and glanced imploringly at the queen for help. Queen Edith read the urgency in Edmond's face and signaled consent. "We can't leave you two alone in this room," the abbess said, "but we'll retire a few paces and permit you to whisper to each other to your hearts' content." Suiting action to word, she took the Lady of England's arm and escorted her to a corner of the large room, leaving Adele and Edmond together.

Edmond spoke first. "Do you love me as you did in Dover?" He reached out to grasp her hands but she evaded him.

"What makes you think I ever regarded you as anything other than a friend?"

"Your eyes, if not your lips, gave me reason to think you felt more deeply."

"Oh, if they did, I regret it with all my heart." It was almost a cry of anguish. After a pause, she added, "Much has changed since then."

"Even that, how you feel about me?"

"Even that! Especially that!"

There was a note of finality in her tone that pained him. He realized that try as he might he could not penetrate the veil of sadness and reserve with which she protected herself. It was an insurmountable barrier shielding her thoughts and emotions. Nothing he could say would elicit anything from her lips other than denial and rejection.

Yet he tried again. "You're resolved to become a nun?" He had to force the words out of his lips.

"Nothing can turn me from my purpose." She emphasized every syllable.

"But why? Is it because of anything I have said or done?"

"I wish to become the bride of Christ. I want to serve God."

There was no answering that. He was forced to accept that there was no hope of persuading her to abandon the religious vocation on which she was bent. He suspected something other than youthful religious fervor or distaste for her uncle's desire to have her marry the Easterling merchant underlay her refusal to hear him out, to deny there was any link between them. Was it her awareness of his royal descent? Did she fear he would abandon her if it became politically expedient to make an advantageous alliance?

Hopeless as it seemed, he made a final effort. "Adele, if you're doing this to avoid yielding to your uncle's wish that you wed Heinrich of Bremen, there's another course open to you. If you'll have me, I'll ask your uncle for your hand for myself."

She threw her hands up in despair, a sob escaping. When she swayed, he reached out to steady her for fear she was about to faint, but she pulled away and almost hissed, "I'm sworn before God to become the bride of Christ, of none else."

He gave up. The mystery of her behavior was beyond his understanding. Was it possible she blamed their flirtation, if that's all it was to her, for her father's death? If so, it was difficult to believe she could make such a connection. He mastered his despair sufficiently enough to hoarsely whisper, "God grant you happiness, my Adele, my love."

He looked into her sad blue eyes lingeringly and longingly. He thought he read love but could not detect hope.

The queen and abbess decided they had left the young people together long enough.

"You'll bear in mind what I've instructed you to tell my brother Harold," the Lady of England reminded, adding, "I'll pray for him as I do for all those I hold dear."

Edmond deferentially inclined his head. Casting a final, wistful glance toward Adele, who was again bent over her needlework, he followed Sister Eudocia to the refectory.

After a hasty meal, he cautiously left the convent and soon was safely on the road leading out of Wherwell without encountering any of Earl Ralph's men. As dejected as he was, he might have welcomed an opportunity to vent his frustration on an enemy if duty had not required him to safely reach Worcester where he was to relay the queen's reply to Earl Harold's message to the saintly Prior Wulfstan.

Chapter Twenty-Two

Farewell to England

Edmond considered it a near-miracle to have reached Worcester without being intercepted by one of the king's or Earl Ralph's patrols. He was so shaken by the doubly unsuccessful outcome of his visit to the convent of Wherwell that he ignored even the most elementary precautions to avoid discovery. In haste to fulfill his mission to Prior Wulfstan, he kept to the main roads rather than use by-paths and made no attempt to evade the occasional small groups of travelers he met. Sunk in thought, he rode the entire way from Wherwell to Worcester as if in a dream. It might have been this obvious indifference of the lone horseman to his surroundings that kept him from being challenged. Equally likely, the king's men were so confident Godwin's supporters had fled England they discounted any chance of encountering one in the open.

Edmond almost found it in his heart to despair of the whole of womankind after his frustrating interviews with Adele and the Lady of England. He could understand neither the queen's equivocal reaction to her brother's message nor Adele's abrupt dismissal of his attempt to rekindle the warmth of their previous relationship. He had not dreamed of finding Adele in the convent and upon doing so certainly did not expect her to fly into his arms or exchange endearments, much less joyfully accept a marriage proposal. Yet he was hurt she had not greeted him more warmly, or hinted at even a spark of the affection displayed during their early days together in Dover. Instead, she had repulsed him in exchange for a life of stark austerity and unworldly dedication. It was a cruel blow though he was not sure whether he suffered more because of ardor for her or merely wounded vanity.

As for the queen! Here was rank ingratitude to her father Earl Godwin and her brothers, a mystifying, almost shameful betrayal of hallowed family bonds. He was prepared to sympathize with her as having been terribly wronged by her husband King Edward. But he was dismayed by her rejection of Earl Harold's request for assistance. Such disloyalty was incomprehensible. Not that he did not grudgingly admire her selfless devotion to her husband despite the disdain with which Edward treated her. Nevertheless, that did not excuse her abandonment of her family at a time when its need was great and its situation desperate. It was indefensible, he thought.

Thus distracted by turbulent thoughts and conflicting emotions, he entered Worcester and glumly approached the monastery that was the town's chief ornament. He requested permission to see the prior and was rebuffed by the gatekeeper until he overrode the dour monk's grumbling with the curt declaration, "I come from the Lady of England, Lady Edith." Aware of Wulfstan's regard for the queen, the monk hastened to inform the prior of Edmond's arrival. He returned quickly to usher Edmond into the superior's presence in the writing room to which Wulfstan often retired with his clerk Alvin to inspect the monastery's accounts, write sermons or pursue scholarship.

"If you come from the Lady of England, my son, you are doubly welcome," the prior greeted Edmond as he rose from a bench and beckoned the visitor to approach. "There are none I love and esteem more dearly than Earl Godwin's daughter and good King Edward's wife."

"You might think otherwise, good father, if you knew the nature of the message I bring from her."

"I will always think well of the Lady of England, my son." The prior's smile lost none of its gentle serenity. "It matters not what sort of word from Lady Edith. Whatever she says, it comes from a good heart, and better unfavorable news from such a one than glib, soothing and false pleasantries from those of lesser faith and uneasy conscience."

Edmond was bewildered by Wulfstan's earnest sincerity. Yet it was obvious that the prior was no complacent fool, unable to distinguish between honest conviction and mere stubborn folly on the part of the queen. Those penetrating black eyes that regarded him so intently revealed a keen intelligence.

"But what she says is unfavorable to Earl Harold's cause," protested Edmond.

"Even so, my son, if her judgment may be at fault in our opinion we can still be sure she is guided by a well-intentioned heart and that compensates for much."

As impressed as he was by the prior's calm reception of the admission he was bringing unfavorable news, Edmond could not avoid a shrug. It was all very well to be so objective, serene and even admiring when the matter did not affect one personally. The Lady Edith's refusal to assist her family in any way could not harm this priest yet it might prove fatal to Earl Harold's chances of regaining power. Without Harold's support, what would be his own prospects?

Prior Wulfstan ignored Edmond's gesture, signaled to his clerk to leave the room, and resumed. "I take it you're the Thane Edmond mentioned in Earl Harold's letter?" Without waiting for a reply, he ran on, voice now brisk and businesslike. "The earl's affairs prosper in Ireland, he tells me. By spring he should be able to return to England with a force that while not large enough to confront his enemies in open battle should enable him to harry communities near the coast. He hopes to stir up the common folk so they'll demand the king agree to his and Earl Godwin's return. He insists, however, he would welcome more information on what the king's people and his Norman friends intend."

Edmond spread his hands. "He'll get no help from the Lady of England. She instructed me to tell Earl Harold he must be patient, await God's will, and spare our people from the horrors of civil war."

Wulfstan's earnest look again melted into a serene, almost approving smile. "A fit queen for England, that woman. Perhaps she sees matters more clearly than any of us, most of all myself, a man of the church. It may be that if Harold remains patient God will see to it that his family eventually will be able to return without needless bloodletting." The prior paced the room briefly, then demanded, "What other word have you for Earl Harold?"

Edmond disclosed the possibility of recruiting the outlaw Thane Eadred to Harold's cause. Wulfstan chuckled when Edmond spoke of Eadred's unspoken proposal that Harold confirm the alliance by betrothal to his daughter Edith.

"Your outlaw friend sets great store by his services," he said dryly. "I doubt Earl Harold would value them so highly. We must let him decided how to answer Thane Eadred as best he can and still gain the few score churls that apparently would be the young woman's dowry."

During the next few days, while awaiting Earl Harold's reaction to the reports sent him by Wulfstan, Edmond spent much of his time in the prior's company. He grew to appreciate the churchman's candor and infectious good humor, and the prior found the youth's quick and receptive intelligence refreshing. They chatted freely during the twilight hours when it was the good prior's custom to walk in the monastery garden that was his special pride and pleasure. Edmond was struck by Wulfstan's comprehensive and penetrating knowledge of worldly affairs, something not readily found among those who lived behind cloistered walls. Once Wulfstan had sized up Edmond's acumen, he spoke freely to him of serious matters, taking obvious delight in discussing with a young man affairs he generally reserved for deliberation with mature intellects. To Edmond's astonishment, the prior's usually calm demeanor gave way to heated fervor after he discovered that the visitor had beheld the Bristol slave market.

With arms upraised as if to exhort the apple and plum trees in the monastery orchard that served in place of a congregation, Wulfstan cried out, "Men dare come to me and ask, 'Father, how is it that all our affairs go ill, that our crops do not prosper, that civil strife and ravaging pirates come among us?' They ask this of me and if I answer them truly they shake their heads, profess to believe, but go away unbelieving. It is not for them to give up their greed of gain, their striving for power and dominion, their enslavement of their fellow countrymen. As you have seen at Bristol, it is shameful to mention how many Christian people are being sold out of this country at all times. It is hateful to God!"

Wulfstan excitedly pressed his hands to his breast and tore at his vestments as if to expiate the sins of his people. "It is horrible to know what too many who commit the crime often do, that men club together and buy a woman as a joint purchase and practice foul sin with her, one by one, each after the other, most like dogs do who do not trouble about sin. And afterwards for a price they sell her out of the land, into the power of the enemy, God's creature and own purchase whom he redeemed at great cost."

Exhausted by his tirade, the prior sank to a bench, his lips closed but still quivering, the words resounding in Edmond's ears to fall like drops of hot molten lead on his heart long after their echoes died away. More than anything else, this outburst by Wulfstan drove away the despondency that had clouded Edmond's mind since the disappointments of Wherwell to replace it with a sense of utter disgust with himself that he felt powerless to dispel.

The next day, after a sleepless night left him convinced that renewed activity would be the sole tonic for his melancholy and self-hatred, Edmond pressed the prior to entrust him with a new assignment on Earl Harold's behalf.

Wulfstan's response was a question. "In what way are you bound to the House of Godwin, my son?"

The inquiry caught Edmond off guard. "Only by the friendship I bear for Earl Harold."

The prior put a friendly hand on Edmond's shoulder and looked penetratingly into his eyes. "There is no self-interest in your attachment?"

Edmond colored. "It would be false for me to deny that I hope to be rewarded. A land-poor, almost penniless thane like myself can aspire to benefit from the goodwill and favor of the great lord he serves. Earl Harold may compensate me generously once he regains his estates and the king's good will."

"Your words ring true, and I don't mean to doubt your sincerity, but if I'm not mistaken you're after something more," the prior replied thoughtfully. His eyes shifted to Edmond's hands. "That bit of silver on your finger intrigues me. It's a curious-looking ring, something out of the ordinary, if I'm not mistaken."

Startled, Edmond tried to hide his confusion. "This old, bent piece of tarnished silver?" he replied dismissively, twisting the ring on his finger to conceal the inscription. "A gift from a dear friend, otherwise I'd not wear it."

"An unusual friend, whoever gave it to you," Wulfstan remarked, his eyes burning into Edmond's as if to read his mind. "One doesn't give away a ring like that but wears it to his deathbed, and then only if he is worthy of such distinction." Wulfstan paused to gather breath, then leveled an index finger at Edmond and thundered, "If you wear it through fraud I charge you to remove it for you imperil your immortal soul."

Edmond turned pale but defiantly brought his hand to his lips and kissed the ring. "I swear to you, good father, that I wear this ring by God's grace and by the right conferred on me by the blood of my forefathers."

Deeply impressed by the young man's fervor and apparent sincerity, Wulfstan impetuously seized Edmond's right hand and with an iron grip forced him to reveal the inscription. "AELFRED MEC HEHT GEWYRCAN," Wulfstan read. He shook his head in amazement and sank back to his bench, lost in thought for a brief interval during which Edmond remained proudly silent.

Wulfstan finally spoke. "Are you aware this may be the long lost royal ring of Wessex? If it really is that hallowed circlet of silver, know that all the kings of England from the time of the great Alfred to Edmond Ironside of blessed memory have worn it."

"I am mindful of it, good father. This is that very ring, none other, I swear to you by all that I hold sacred."

"Take care, my son, heed what you're saying lest you imperil your soul. If you believe what you assert you must also be aware that this ring, which has been missing since the death of the unfortunate Edmond, belongs by right to his brother, our gracious lord, King Edward."

"I can't and won't acknowledge that," Edmond retorted defiantly to the prior's astonishment. "Rather, I deny it altogether. None has a better right to this ring than do I, good father." He was goaded beyond endurance by the prior's questioning, the intimation that he was attempting to perpetrate a fraud.

"Not even King Edward?" whispered Wulfstan in wonder.

"Not even he!"

Wulfstan stared at him in dismay. The kind-hearted prior was troubled. He was beginning to believe Edmond's avowal, yet still half-hoped the young man was misinformed, misguided or even blatantly lying, whatever his motive. He was appalled by the possibly dreadful consequences that might ensue if an obscure branch of the royal line of

156

Wessex were to press a claim, however faint, to the throne. England was already too torn by factionalism to withstand more inner turmoil without falling easy prey to some foreign power, as it had in the not-so-distant days of King Cnut and his sons. After a deep sigh, Wulfstan decided to probe further and requested Edmond to elaborate on his claim to Alfred's ring.

If ever a man could be trusted, Edmond sensed it was the prior so he decided to keep nothing back. He poured the entire story of his life and adventures up to the present, even repeating the secret of his royal birth revealed by his dying father. Somehow, the process of unburdening himself of what he had kept inward for so long lifted his spirits and revived his self-respect, sadly undermined by his conduct at Bristol and the frustration he had experienced at Wherwell. He was almost desperate for reassurance and guidance and was convinced this saintly yet worldly prior would offer sage counsel and would receive his secret in strictest confidence.

Wulfstan's apprehension grew as Edmond unfolded his tale. He understood at once that Edmond's mere existence, let alone his ambition, could seriously threaten the future tranquility of England. He might be a solitary youth without land, wealth, followers or family support, but his royal birth would attract malcontents who would eagerly attempt to use him as a pawn to further their own designs. Here was a Pandora's box to further bedevil a land already torn asunder by the bitter quarrel between the House of Godwin and King Edward's Normans.

The crisis would come when King Edward died. His rightful successor, whoever he might be, would have to confront this stray twig of the royal tree, if that is what Edmond truly was. Such a pretender would be sure to attract the dissidents and discontented of the kingdom to support his pretensions, however tenuous. Edmond's claim to royal descent, real or imagined, would provide the rebels with a stick with which to belabor, harass and possibly even unseat the new king, who must of necessity, given King Edward's lack of a son, come from lesser stock.

Of necessity? Wulfstan pondered the phrase. It gave him pause. He had secretly nursed a hope that England might accept in Earl Harold Godwinson a worthy successor to the throne long held by Alfred's line. He believed he detected the seeds of greatness in the young and forceful earl, the ability and strength of character needed to hold in check the conflicting forces threatening to split and weaken England until it fell supinely into the grasp of Normans, Danes or other foreign invaders. Edmond's existence and his putative claim reminded him of the dangers of an attempt at the throne by someone not of royal blood so long as members of the old dynasty could dispute it. There must be a safer, surer answer to England's dilemma.

There was! Until now he had never seriously considered the surviving son of King Edmond Ironside as an alternative to Earl Harold. The long absent, almost forgotten prince might be persuaded to return to his native land. What did it matter that he was foreign-reared, approaching middle-age and had been away from England for more than thirty years since being smuggled out of the country and sent to Hungary to escape King Cnut's fury? King Edward's situation before being placed on the throne had been similar as he had been reared and educated in Normandy before the people had accepted him upon Earl Godwin's urging. Edward might be persuaded to designate this son of his half-brother as successor. Not only was this prince's claim by blood to the throne indisputably stronger than Edmond's, but it was, strictly speaking, better than that of the king himself. Yes, Edward Edmondson must return to England. With the support of Earl Harold, the people would rally around him and help dispel the threat of foreign domination.

As for Edmond—Wulfstan studied the lad's strong, determined-looking features—he might still pose a danger. The fine points of legitimacy would not deter the restless and the rebellious. They might rally around this young man if a new, foreign-reared king stood in the way of their aspirations. Edmond must be persuaded to give up his divisive and ultimately hopeless quest and spare England further domestic strife, which might lead to eventual domination by the Normans.

The Normans! They were Wulfstan's greatest concern. Visiting churchmen spoke admiringly of the young Norman duke, William the Bastard. His cunning, strength, covetousness, ruthlessness and vaulting ambition were widely known. Wulfstan's acquaintances among the Norman clergy did not trouble to disguise their master's hopes of succeeding his cousin and good friend King Edward on the throne of rich England. If the country did not unite in its determination to serve no master, but of its own choosing, William would almost surely realize his aims. Wulfstan vowed this must never happen and, consequently, Edmond's existence must not further jeopardize England's future.

Wulfstan finally broke a lengthy silence that followed upon Edmond's account of his adventures and family history. The prior spoke slowly and chose his words carefully to make certain there would be no misunderstanding.

"If what you say is true, my son—and mind you, I neither can affirm nor deny its veracity—then I have the greatest compassion for your plight and sorrow for your father's woeful decision to take the course he did. Your misfortune is great, shorn as you are of rightful status. It is sad to contemplate our England riven by lawlessness and the greed and cruelty of foreigners because of the incapacity of such an inept ruler as Edward when an equally legitimate and possibly far stronger king may have been available.

"Worse yet—and this may be difficult for you to accept—I am convinced you can never hope to obtain your rightful heritage even if you truly are a descendant of the great Alfred, as you claim. As near as I can hope to judge on such brief acquaintance, you have a quick mind, as well as the robust health and physical strength that promise much in such a young man. You well may have the makings of the capable, strong ruler our people desire and need.

"Nevertheless, Edmond Edwysson, there's far more at stake here than the wronging of a single individual, as hateful as that is in the sight of God and right-minded men. Alas, there are few who think as I do and I can only hope that you are among them, but we must put the good of our people first regardless of other considerations. Even though you think you have a better right to the kingship than Edward Ethelredson it would be a calamity for England if you found support for your claim to the crown."

Wulfstan ignored Edmond's attempt to interrupt.

"Your claim won't succeed and would only embroil the land in further strife, of which God knows we have far too much already. You might gain support from some with a grudge against the king or his advisors, a few whose demands, just or unjust, have gone unsatisfied, and a handful of adventurers and malcontents. They'd pretend to act in your behalf but their sole interest would be to further their own affairs. As soon as they discovered they could achieve their aims better by abandoning you, or even delivering you to your enemies, they wouldn't hesitate for an instant.

"Even now our unhappy land is torn between factions supporting the king and his Norman friends, or Earl Godwin's family, or others who harbor grudges and grievances of all sorts. What's to come is even more dismaying. This civil strife is taking place when England is approaching what is sure to be its greatest trial, the day when that fierce bastard of Normandy, Duke William, claims our crown. We must unite against that threat. If our forces are split, we're surely lost. This is why I support Earl Harold, not because I crave influence for myself. I believe Harold Godwinson is best fitted to unite and govern England under King Edward who with a strong hand to guide him can be a force for good. Despite his weak and petty nature, the king at bottom means well.

"You're sure to ask, 'This is all to the good, but where does it leave me?' But even if I accept that you're the rightful heir to the crown, the nephew of Edmond Ironside, and regard Edward as an usurper, here's something for you to consider: Our king always has been chosen by the Witan. The assembly reserves the right to select from among the royal family the man generally considered fittest to rule by reasons of age, ability and temperament. It has not invariably chosen the son or nearest relative of a deceased king. It's possible that if they had known your father was alive and if he had presented himself before it at King Harthacnut's death they might have anointed him. At Earl Godwin's behest, they picked Edward and he took the crown with general consent and approval.

"As for the consideration of heredity, there's someone who has even better right to the kingship than you do. It's Edward, the son of Edmond Ironside, who was spirited out of the land to escape King Cnut's clutches more than thirty years ago, and lives in Hungary. Some seek to persuade him to return to England so that the rightful successor to King Edward will be at hand when needed.

"You see, my son," Wulfstan concluded, "not only the welfare of our people but the very grounds on which you base your claim are against your chances of succeeding in what at best would be a desperate adventure."

Edmond was dazed, almost befuddled by the torrent of words and arguments with which the prior had seemingly demolished his expectations, fragile as he knew them to be. He buried his head in his hands, trying to rally his thoughts. The prior looked at him compassionately, arms upraised over Edmond's head as if in benediction. He regretted having to crush the young man's hopes but it was necessary to do so for the good of England's people.

Edmond slowly raised his head. "What would you advise me to do, good father?"

"If you were another sort of man I'd suggest that you seek your consolation in the church. I doubt that you, being who and what you are, would find peace in such a vocation. Neither you nor the church would benefit. It seems to me the best course would be for you to return to Bosbury and meddle no longer in great affairs. If that doesn't suit you, as I believe will be the case given your nature, it would be best if you left England for good and sought your fortune elsewhere."

Edmond nodded. The prior's advice was probably sound, though neither course greatly attracted him, but he would at least be obeying his father's dying behest if he went abroad. There was nothing more to say. He bowed farewell to the prior, then took two steps toward the door before remembering there was something else to resolve.

"What about Earl Harold? What is he to think of this desertion by a friend who has promised to serve him until he returns to England?"

"I'll inform him you've been lost while in his service," replied Wulfstan. "Indeed, it'll be true enough," the prior added, looking piercingly at Edmond. "He must not be told more than that for no good can come of his knowing your secret. If by some chance you and he meet again, you have my promise to set matters aright if Earl Harold mistakenly believes you've been disloyal to him."

Edmond had to be satisfied with that. He again turned to leave, but Wulfstan caught his sleeve. "Kneel, my son. I wish to call the blessings of the Lord upon you. What you are about to do makes me wonder if you indeed are not of the very mold of Alfred."

Edmond knelt and the prior uttered a simple prayer, then made the sign of the cross over him.

At twilight, Edmond, head sunk upon chest, rode unseeing out of Worcester, heading briefly southward until he came to a fork in the road. One branch led southwest toward Bosbury and the prospect of a future much like that in which his father had nursed his shattered dreams in seclusion. The other branch led southeast to Ashdowne Forest where he could rejoin Godfrid, and ultimately toward Dover and the narrow sea that would carry him to another land to begin life anew.

Which route should he choose? Did it really make a difference? His bitter laugh startled the horse even as it relieved the rider's pent-up emotions. His spirits oddly lifted by the outburst, Edmond spurred the mount into a gallop and the beast made a choice for him, taking the fork in the road that led him toward Ashdowne Forest.

★　★　★　★　★

If the ancient gods and spirits of Ashdowne Forest whom the priests and monks had exorcised from the soul and soil of England knew what had become of Edith, the daughter of Eadred, and the humble lad Godfrid they kept the secret well. One day late in the year 1051 Edith disappeared from her father's forest-shrouded encampment, never to be seen again by family or servants. At the same time, the crippled orphan lad Godfrid also vanished, though far fewer took note and none seemed to care.

Her brother Edward had been the last to see Edith when he had volunteered to accompany her on her customary afternoon ride. She had pleaded a headache and promised to let him attend her later in the day when she felt better. But when he returned, she had gone off by herself without even her usual woman attendant.

When she had not returned by sunset, Thane Eadred became concerned. He led his band in a search of the vast forest surrounding the settlement but could find no trace of his daughter, her horse or anything else belonging to her. He kept up the search for several days before abandoning it in despair, concluding Edith had been carried off by an enemy who sooner or later would seek ransom. But none came forth as the days, weeks and months passed.

Some of his people, less God-fearing than they might have been, whispered that the great deity Odin had been so captivated by Edith's beauty that he had abducted her. Others with even more vivid imaginations went so far as to speculate that Odin's wife Freya, jealous of Edith's golden hair, had seized her to serve as a handmaiden and guard her from Odin's attentions.

There were those, more Christian, romantic or realistic, who recalled Earl Sweyn's visit to the encampment and speculated that the impetuous lord rather than remaining content to wait for Thane Eadred to bestow Edith's hand on him in marriage had kidnapped her as he had the abbess of Leominster. Others scoffed at the notion, insisting that Sweyn had fled England with his father, and would not be so foolhardy over a woman as to return secretly and risk capture by King Edward's men.

As for Godfrid's disappearance, it was dismissed as mere coincidence that he vanished at the same time as Edith. None supposed there was any connection, given the boy's humble status, nor was anyone in the least concerned. Such defections were commonplace, and that of a crippled orphan lad was hardly to be lamented as he was more apt to be a burden than an asset to the community.

As so often, common supposition was erroneous. The events were connected in a way no one could have imagined likely or even possible. On arriving in the vicinity of the outlaw settlement, Edmond persuaded a young churl gathering firewood in the forest to bear a message to Gurth. He asked his outlaw friend to bring Godfrid to him, appointing as a meeting place the clearing along the path where he first so memorably had encountered Gurth and his companions.

To Edmond's surprise, when Godfrid approached the rendezvous he was accompanied not by the massive Gurth but by a slightly-built companion who was leading a saddled mare by the reins. The stranger's face was concealed by a hood pulled forward as if to shield it from the setting sun.

"Where's my good friend, Gurth?" Edmond asked when Godfrid and the dismounted rider, who hung back, halted in the clearing. "I thought he'd bring you himself rather than sending someone else to conduct you to me. Who's your friend?"

"Gurth couldn't come, Master Edmond. He said he wished you Godspeed but couldn't leave just now because Thane Eadred needed him and his first duty was to his lord. He bade me to join you if I chose."

"Do you wish to, my boy?"

"More than anything else in the world," cried Godfrid.

"Well then, Godfrid, it'll be as I promised. You'll be my shield-bearer, my page, my attendant, my entire army. We'll seek our fortunes together. Say good-bye to your companion and we'll be off."

Edmond leaned down from the saddle to offer the boy a hand to help him swing onto the horse's back behind him but Godfrid held off while blurting, "My companion wishes to join us if it pleases you, Thane Edmond."

"Indeed! Well, there's no harm, I suppose, in taking another brave lad with us if he's willing to take the risk of going abroad and promises to serve me loyally. But he should speak for himself. What do you say to going with us, friend?"

"I'd like nothing better!" came the ringing reply in a female voice as Godfrid's companion threw back the hood.

Edmond stared benumbed with astonishment at the smiling face of Eadred's daughter Edith as he speechlessly watched her spring onto the mare at the same time that Godfrid perched behind him on his horse.

Chapter Twenty-Three

Constantine IX Monomachus

In the summer of the year 1052, the great city of Constantinople was the capital of an empire ruled by two monarchs, neither of whom wielded even half of the authority properly belonging to a single Supreme Autocrator, Basileus or Emperor as the distant successors of Constantine the Great were variously termed. Constantine IX Monomachus had ascended the throne of the Caesars by virtue of becoming the third and most fortunate husband of the elderly Empress Zoe. He was fortunate in that her convenient and not untimely death two years earlier had relieved him of the apprehension of sharing the fate of two previous spouses and innumerable lovers who had preceded the ancient nymphomaniac into a tomb. He shared his uneasy preeminence with the Empress Theodora, Zoe's younger sister and co-ruler, though often chafing at his inability to disencumber himself of her annoying presence.

As was the case with the symbols and trappings of the great Eastern Roman Empire, the troops usually attached to a single ruler were divided between the dual successors to the throne previously occupied by such worthies as Constantine I, Justinian the Great, Leo III and the Empress Theodora's uncle, Basil II Bulgarocrator. The larger part of the army, not unnaturally preferring the command of an experienced soldier, took orders and pay from Constantine IX Monomachus, who resided in the great complex of the Sacred Palace situated at the southeastern tip of the peninsula that held the capital of the world and overlooked the benignly blue Sea of Marmora. Theodora, with a smaller complement of soldiers though a greater share of popular support because she was born to the purple and was fabulously wealthy, resided in the Palace of the Blachernae at the northwestern extremity of Constantinople, adjacent to the walls erected by her predecessors to shield the metropolis from landward attack.

Constantine IX, though an amiable, easy-going and pleasure-loving aging libertine, was shrewd enough to be wary of the people's ill-concealed and well-founded suspicion that he sincerely wished their saintly "little mother" Theodora would quickly join her sister Zoe in the Imperial Cemetery by the Church of the Holy Apostles. Failing that, he would have been satisfied if she would return to the Convent of Petrica from which she had been so inconveniently rescued by popular clamor in middle age. Since neither eventuality seemed imminent, he took great pains to forestall overt demonstrations of popular affection for Theodora from being turned against himself. He spent lavishly to secure the loyalty, if not the love, of the imperial guard, including the Varangian corps of recruits from northern Europe whose fighting quality and fidelity, immune to political and religious influence, guaranteed his security.

By the emperor's command, the Varangian Guard was kept at the ready at all times. Accordingly, on a warm and sunny summer morning a detachment of these elite troops, brilliantly uniformed in embroidered jerkins and gilded helmets, and bearing the battle axes and light swords which were their traditional weapons, were drilling on the Strategion, or parade ground. The field lay at the foot of a hill from which could be seen the columns, towers and rooftops of the suburb of Galata across the waters of the Golden Horn to the north, and the Hippodrome, Church of Hagia Sophia and walls of the Sacred Palace to the south.

Toke the Dane, the pentekontarchus or lieutenant who commanded the detachment, supervised the exercises from a position directly below an equestrian statue of Constantine the Great poised upon a column overlooking the Strategion. He had just dismissed his unit when an orderly from the staff of the acolyte, or commander of the Varangians, claimed his attention.

"What is it, Mauropus?"

"Sir, the acolyte directs you to report to him immediately in the emperor's chambers of the Sacred Palace. You're to bring along the Saxon recently assigned to your unit."

"That would be Edmond Edwysson," Toke muttered, peering at the dismissed troopers scattering across the field, some bound for the barracks of the Mangana, the great military arsenal, others headed for their usual haunts in the city. "Did the acolyte say what he wanted of us?"

"I've told you all I know, sir."

"Ho, Edmond! Edmond Edwysson!" shouted Toke on spotting a stocky, broad-shouldered soldier stripping off his armor and handing it to a young attendant who adroitly shouldered the heavy equipment despite a crippled arm. Edmond spun about and immediately responded to Toke's summons.

Six months had passed since Edmond—or rather his horse—had decided upon leaving England. He was little changed outwardly other than that his shoulders were a little broader, his features sterner and his formerly almost fair complexion bronzed by the Mediterranean sun. The rage of soul that at first had threatened to embitter him had quickly yielded to the soothing effects of time and reason. His calm features, upright figure and brisk stride pleased Toke, an experienced officer who appreciated a good soldier when he saw one.

Toke repeated the acolyte's order. Edmond nodded and resumed his armor. Once fully equipped, he whispered an order to Godfrid who had grown considerably while training to be his attendant. The boy ran off to carry out his master's instructions.

The orderly Mauropus led the way to the Sacred Palace. The route from the Strategion took them past the Chalcoproteia or Brass Market with its teeming stalls. Leather-lunged peddlers shouted the virtues real or imaginary of the vast array of wares gathered from a world whose wealth and products poured into Constantinople through the Golden Horn, which could as aptly have been named the Horn of Plenty because all that was useful, rare, beautiful, serviceable or merely salable arrived at its wharves. Glassware, jewelry, silk, ivory, enamel, weapons, tools, rare victuals, in short anything man could manufacture, mine, grow or steal could be purchased at the hundreds of booths. Even now, after being in the city two months, Edmond marveled at the profusion of goods, the splendor of the buildings and the magnificence of the boulevards in this immense metropolis that far surpassed any town in England, even London.

Among the most impressive structures was the Basilica within whose marble-encrusted walls the Senate of Constantinople, long ago divested of real power, continued to practice the ancient if degenerated art of rhetoric. The great building's splendor was barely diminished by the erosion of centuries and the porch, supported by six immense columns each a work of art in itself, gave entry to a treasure trove of the artifacts of ancient Greece. Within the Basilica were the group of Muses from Helicon, the statue of Zeus from Dodona and that of Pallas from Lindos.

The Basilica occupied a site on the eastern side of the Forum of the Augustaion, the navel of the empire. On an eminence directly across the forum rose the spires and vast dome of Hagia Sophia, the latter's gold leaf glittering in the bright sun, diverting the attention of bypassers from the Milion, a fine pedestal on four arches that supported a four-faced statue of Janus looking toward all directions of the Roman world whose distances were measured from it. Edmond and his companions quickly passed the great bulk of the Hippodrome on their right to reach the massive bronze entrance gate of the Sacred Palace at the southern end of the Augustaion. Its huge doors were set into the great wall surrounding the palace that had been erected by the Emperor Nicephorus Phocas more than eighty years earlier to make it a virtually impregnable fortress. Not that the walls had served their intended purpose of protecting that aged usurper because on the very eve of their completion he was stabbed to death in his bedchamber by his successor John Tzimisces. The assassin had circumvented the barriers by landing from a boat on the palace grounds fronting the Sea of Marmora.

Seven distinct groups of palaces, each set in its own opulent garden amid pavilions, pergolas, fountains of rose-water and luxurious baths, lay within the circuit of the great wall. They included polo grounds and palaestras for other sports as well as museums, concert halls, beauty parlors, treasuries and erotically-decorated chambers whose sole purpose was to facilitate lovemaking. All these facilities comprised the immense palace complex, the whole shielded from the rest of Constantinople by its circumvallation, and fronting the translucent Sea of Marmora. The cobalt-blue waters were studded with numerous jewel-like imperial yachts ever-ready to waft the pleasure-loving emperor and his court across the water to villas, dance halls and hunting lodges scattered at random along the nearby coast of Asia.

Toke, Edmond and Mauropus stepped from the Augustaion into this crescent of power, pomp and pleasure through the gate leading into the Bronze Hall known as Chalce. They passed through a domed museum along a route flanked by two lifelike marble horses taken from the Temple of Diana at Ephesus. In a vestibule whose walls were clad in green, flame-colored, white and blue-veined marble and which was sprinkled with choice Greek statuary, were stationed the imperial guards, splendid in their golden helmets decked with scarlet plumes and wearing red cuirasses. Each man held upright a naked sword. On recognizing Pentekontarchus Toke Arnulfson, their officer permitted the little group to enter a hall from which opened the doors leading to inner apartments and the passages connecting this section with the palaces of the imperial compound. Here were posted the Varangians, most of them Norsemen from Russia who wore their hair long, with arms bare except for silver torques, and were clad in leather jerkins embroidered with red dragons to match their ruby earrings. Each gripped a massive double-headed battle-ax. At the end of the hall stood their commander, Acolyte Joseph Bryennius, whose dark eyes brightened on Toke's approach.

"You do well to report so promptly," barked Bryennius. "The emperor is not accustomed to waiting. This is the Englishman?" He studied Edmond, apparently pleased at what he saw, glanced at a note in his hand, then continued, "You're Thane Edmond Edwysson? Good! You'll accompany me into the august presence. The rest of you are free to return to your duties." He nodded to an attendant to swing open one of the great doors leading into an inner chamber, waved aside the black mutes who with unsheathed swords sprang forward to bar entry, and with Edmond at his heels led the way into the presence of the Emperor Constantine IX Monomachus.

Heavy silk curtains suspended on silver triangles that glided noiselessly along massive rods of the same metal shielded the presence chamber from the sun's bright glare, which nevertheless was reflected brilliantly by silver candelabra hanging from chains festooned along the marble walls. Vividly colored tapestries depicting hunting scenes lightened the solemnity of the elegant room whose deep carpets muffled the heavy steps of the acolyte and Edmond. The furniture was ornate if sparse. Low divans upholstered in brocade, a few ivory stools and several heavy silver tables were scattered about. At the far end of the great room a high throne was placed under a gold brocaded canopy but it was unoccupied, the richly yet simply robed emperor instead being seated on an ivory stool. Constantine's extreme pallor and the ravages of middle age had not deprived him entirely of vestiges of the handsome features that had captivated an empress to his great fortune. He seemed so lost in thought as to be ignoring the vehement exhortations of an elderly man, apparently an advisor.

On becoming aware of the approach of Acolyte Bryennius and Edmond, Constantine rose and waved his hand to stem the aged counselor's harangue.

Bryennius sank to his knees and prostrated himself before the basileus. Edmond, ignorant of court ceremony, bowed awkwardly after doffing his helmet. Constantine's frown immediately stifled horrified murmurs from those of his attendants who were appalled by Edmond's flagrant violation of protocol.

"Young man, you'd do well to read the Book of Ceremonies written by my revered predecessor Constantine Porphyrogenitus," the emperor commented, a smile flickering across his face. "It would help you avoid such blunders in the future. No matter, we haven't required your attendance because we need more courtiers." Edmond's grasp of Greek was rudimentary but he understood the emperor's smile and returned it.

"Acolyte, inform the Varangian we've sent for him because he is newly-arrived from his barbarous homeland and that may fit him exceptionally for a mission we've in mind," Constantine instructed Bryennius. He kept his eyes fixed on Edmond while Bryennius interpreted his words, then added, "Ask him why he came to our great city."

"I've been told great honor can be gained by serving your imperial highness well and loyally," replied Edmond.

Constantine laughingly shook his head. "It's flattering, indeed, as well as most gratifying, to hear that a favorable judgment of our magnanimity has reached even so distant a land as your island home,

Varangian. We know something of the love of adventure, as well as the rapacity, of your countrymen. Yet it's said many of your companions flee to us because they've been outlawed at home. Are you among them, Edmond Edwysson?"

"I come of my own free will, your imperial majesty."

Constantine stroked his chin as he added slyly, "No doubt it was of your own free will that you supported Earl Godwin who I'm told fled for his life to Baldwinesland because of his king's displeasure."

Edmond's surprise showed in his face. While he had thought it possible that the emperor might have heard of England, he had never imagined he would be kept informed of its political upheavals.

Constantine was delighted at the Englishman's astonishment. He had taken care to inform himself of the affairs of the distant, barbarous and insignificant island of Britain. It was gratifying that his diplomatic service was in such good order that he could be kept up to date even about the internal affairs of such a far off corner of the world as England. It was a pleasure to be able to impress someone who might prove useful in an affair of state. Encouraged, the emperor continued. "Then you admit you were of the party of this discredited Earl Godwin and his son... Harold, I believe is his name?"

"It's true, your imperial majesty, that I am a friend of Earl Harold and have great regard for him, but I didn't leave England because of that. I might have safely remained if I hadn't decided to seek my fortune elsewhere."

Constantine shrugged. "Have it your way. It makes no difference to us why you left England." He picked up a bronze mirror from a nearby table and studied his reflection briefly. "Who is the woman who accompanied you?"

Edmond was thunderstruck by the unexpected question. He was well aware of Constantine's reputation as a libertine. On second thought, however, he reasoned it was absurd to suppose the emperor would have gone to such great pains to interrogate a lowly Varangian trooper merely to deprive him of a woman. A single word of command and Constantine could easily have disposed of him by flinging him into prison or even by some more sinister action. He certainly would not have bothered to summon him into his august presence for a chat.

Edmond chose his words carefully, uncertain what lay behind Constantine's strange line of questioning. "Her name is Edith, imperial majesty, and she is the daughter of a nobleman of my country."

"Are you wed in the eyes of your church?"

"No, my lord, we are not wed in any sense."

Constantine looked at him quizzically, then chuckled. "I'll believe that, if you wish, Varangian. Strange, as I'm told she is considered attractive, if in a pallid fashion. I've never fancied fair-haired women myself, but tastes differ." He put down the mirror and stretched out at length on a divan. "Don't concern yourself. It's true we're partial to beautiful women but scarcely to ones we've never seen. Others may not be so fastidious. Take my advice and keep her out of sight."

Edmond inclined his head to signify the emperor's hint was as good as a command and outwardly appeared undisturbed. Nevertheless, he was concerned. He sensed danger, whether from Constantine or another quarter. He berated himself again for having let Edith talk him into allowing her to accompany Godfrid and him to Dover, then across the sea all the way to Constantinople. He had foreseen it would mean nothing but trouble from the moment she had thrown back the hood to reveal her identity. Yet he had been unable to resist her fervent pleas to accompany him.

"I must escape," she had protested earnestly and tearfully. "I can't bear to stay. My father demands I remain patient until Earl Sweyn returns from his pilgrimage because he has promised me to him. He insists Sweyn will fulfill the pledges he has made of land and honors in exchange for my hand when he regains King Edward's favor."

"You don't share your father's faith in Earl Sweyn's trustworthiness?"

"Not in the least, nor does it matter," she had cried. "I detest Sweyn Godwinson. I'd rather die unwed or a nun than ever become his wife, if that's what he truly intended. He is false, ungodly, and treacherous as all the world knows, except for my father who is blinded by his hopes of profiting from an alliance. I hate, no, I loathe Earl Sweyn."

She had continued in much the same vein during their ride to Dover, Edmond having ruefully concluded there was no alternative to permitting her to come along. To have forcibly returned her to Eadred would have resulted in a confrontation with the outlaw band from which he was unlikely to escape alive. Eadred would certainly have put the worst construction on Edith's attempt to flee with him. As for the question of how she had learned Godfrid was to join him at the rendezvous, that was easily answered. Gurth's hand-fast bride Helga, whom Edith had taken into her service, let slip some unguarded words that aroused her curiosity. Uncovering the details of Godfrid's planned departure with Edmond, Edith disguised herself and accompanied him, overriding the boy's feeble protests. No one took much notice of a pair of lads leaving the village, and certainly none suspected one of them was their lord's daughter Edith.

After arriving in Dover, Edmond with his companions—Edith still disguised as a boy—had taken ship for Caen in Normandy where they encountered a merchant traveling to Italy on business who for a price let them join his escort. The next, last and longest leg of the journey was by ship from Venice to Constantinople where Edmond was immediately enrolled in the Varangian Guard. The generous enlistment bonus enabled him to establish Edith in a small villa in the vicinity of the Church of St. George at the Mangana. Though Edith retained her male disguise whenever she left the house, she felt more comfortable in women's garments at home, and no doubt this had enabled an imperial spy, one of the swarm in Constantinople, to discover Edmond's tiny entourage did not consist of two boys as it appeared on the surface.

The emperor broke into Edmond's thoughts. "What do you know of Earl Sweyn, Edmond Edwysson?"

This question caught Edmond even more off guard than the earlier one about Edith. Constantine might have been the last person he would have expected to inquire about Earl Godwin's scapegrace son. It was surprising enough that he was even aware of Sweyn's existence, but it was extraordinary he would suspect a connection between the outlawed earl and the recent humble recruit to his guard. Could Sweyn be in Constantinople? It was possible. He might be passing through on his way back to England from his pilgrimage to Jerusalem. Whatever the case, Edmond had no reason to keep anything he knew to Sweyn's disadvantage from the emperor. There had never been any love lost between him and Earl Harold's unruly brother. So he freely related the story of Sweyn's violent past and frequent disgrace. When Edmond finished, Constantine rubbed his forehead reflectively, then dismissed his entourage with the exception of Acolyte Bryennius and the mute black guards lined like statues along the walls of the chamber, swords bared for immediate use at their master's command.

"What you tell us about this Earl Sweyn accords with what we've been told," said Constantine. "This man recently arrived in Constantinople and that's why we've summoned you to attend us."

"Forgive me, imperial majesty, but I don't understand what Earl Sweyn's coming has to do with me."

"We suspect this Sweyn, your countryman, has come at the behest of our beloved sister-in-law, the Empress Theodora. We deplore the unworthy thought, but she might seek to employ him in a scheme to endanger our freedom, if not our life. Of course, it being unlikely that you as a foreigner, a newcomer, are fully informed about certain events in Constantinople in our day it might be well to recount them.

"Some years ago, when our great, good and beloved consort, the sainted Empress Zoe —may she be happy in Christ's bosom as we are certain she is—was still at our side, another Northman, in character much like this Sweyn, sought to betray us to our enemies. He was a devil, that one, a huge, hulking Viking named Harald Hardraade. I'll never know how we let ourselves be so deluded as to appoint him to the command of our noble and usually loyal Varangians, but we made that mistake, almost ensuring our doom."

Constantine paused to shudder.

"Bold, perfidious, heartless and greedy he was—or still is, for we're told he has prospered since returning to his savage northern homeland. We don't want another such plague to bedevil us. We were fortunate to outwit him, and he was lucky to escape our vengeance, but we've never faced so great a threat. It may be that our revered sister Theodora, who is regrettably jealous of sharing power, believes this Earl Sweyn could prove another Hardraade she could use as a weapon against us. From what you've told me and I've learned elsewhere, Sweyn is just the sort of bold, unscrupulous and dangerous adventurer Theodora would employ to gain sole possession of the throne we've shared since her sister Zoe ascended to heaven."

Edmond heard Bryennius's interpretation of the emperor's explanation with growing wonder and agreement. It was conceivable that Sweyn, judging by the reckless ambition that had plunged him into so much trouble in the past, might eagerly embrace an opportunity to profit by joining in a scheme of the aged empress. There was virtually no limit to the gain that might be made from a successful conspiracy to remove Constantine. A portion of the ancient throne of Rome was even a dazzling possibility for the man who was able to satisfy Theodora's desire to dispose of her co-ruler. After all, of the two emperors who had preceded Constantine IX Monomachus one had been a valet and the other the son of a shipyard caulker. Sweyn's ancestry, even if barbarian by Roman standards, was immeasurably superior to theirs. But even without such lofty aspirations, Sweyn, given his nature, would certainly be tempted to join in a plot to overthrow the emperor if promised sufficient reward by the Empress Theodora.

While Bryennius finished interpreting his words, Constantine closely scrutinized Edmond's face to gauge his reaction. Satisfied that the Varangian shared his evaluation of Sweyn's character, the emperor took another tack.

"But we didn't summon you into our august presence to merely tell us what you know about Earl Sweyn. What we require of you is to help us remove the danger he poses to us. Yesterday, Earl Sweyn and his retinue of about thirty men were allowed to cross the Golden Horn and enter Constantinople. They represented themselves as pilgrims returning from the Holy Land who planned to board ship to take them to Italy. They're staying at the Red Lion in the Drungarius district. So far as we know, they've not attempted to communicate with Theodora's court at the Palace of the Blachernae."

Disregarding protocol, Edmond interrupted. "If your imperial majesty knows where they are and what their purpose is, why don't you just banish them from the city or arrest them?"

"It's scarcely that simple, Varangian," the emperor sighed. "First, we want to know more about Sweyn, his intentions and his connections. To act upon mere suspicion would be folly. It's no secret that many of the common people prefer Theodora to us. They revere that dried-up old bitch as their 'little mother'. If we act rashly by seizing some of her followers we might touch off a riot or even a greater disturbance. Our people are prone to express their dissatisfaction by taking to the streets.

"Additionally, now that we know what sort of man we're dealing with and have someone in our service who knows Sweyn it would be preferable to use more subtle methods to avert the threat."

Edmond was puzzled. "I still don't understand what you expect of me, my lord."

"Patience, Edmond Edwysson, I'm coming to that. If I send my guards to seize or kill Sweyn and his followers it might lead to the very situation we must avoid at all costs, a demonstration or uprising on Theodora's behalf. On the other hand, since you and Sweyn are acquainted with each other, a personal quarrel that lead to combat would divert all suspicion of our involvement and wouldn't arouse the mob. Such violent affairs are all too common in the streets of our city, greatly to our embarrassment and regret."

"But I have no quarrel with Earl Sweyn, though it's true we've never been on a friendly footing."

"Don't play the fool with me, Varangian!" Constantine snapped, then chuckled as if relishing the opportunity to again catch Edmond off guard by demonstrating the efficiency of his police who could uncover even a barbarian's private secrets. "We know that the woman who accompanied you here from England is or was betrothed to Earl Sweyn. Isn't that so?"

Edmond could only nod affirmatively and admiringly.

"What's more to be said?" demanded Constantine. "Here are perfect, plausible grounds for a street or tavern brawl between you. A sword cut or dagger thrust and it'll all be over. No chance of affairs of state entering into it. A trifling, commonplace incident that'll arouse no suspicion and the affair is closed. We'll have one enemy the less, the empress will be deprived of a formidable ally, and you'll have earned some claim to our gratitude. Could anything be simpler?"

Constantine slipped a heavy gold ring set with a huge ruby from his fingers and offered it to Edmond who accepted it with bowed head.

"In advance," the emperor explained, adding as if in afterthought. "Of course, it might be preferable to lure Earl Sweyn into one of our prisons for questioning before disposing of him. The acolyte can tell you which dungeon would be best. Do whatever is most convenient and

173

report to us when you've accomplished your task."

Constantine indicated the audience was ended. Edmond began to follow Acolyte Bryennius out of the hall when the emperor halted him with a parting caution.

"Remember, Varangian, if you fall into the hands of the city police we've never heard of you and will leave you to your fate. It's a pity the officer in command of the Drungarius Vigilia is in the Empress Theodora's service."

Chapter Twenty-Four

The Velvet Trap

The resplendent church and monastery of St. George of the Mangana built several years earlier by Constantine IX Monomachus to testify to his piety was situated in the Mangana district north of the imperial palace of that name, a short distance inland from the military arsenal whose craftsmen supplied Constantinople's armies with weapons and equipment. The religious establishment lay in a meadow surrounded by private residences and gardens extending northward toward the Kynegion, an amphitheater erected by the ancient Roman Emperor Septimius Severus and serving principally as a place of execution for state criminals.

The small villa rented by Edmond was in this district, noted for being cooled even during the hottest days of the summer by a brisk north wind that often swept down the Bosporus from the Black Sea. He frequently sat with Edith at sunset in a small garden from which they could look over the seaward wall and enjoy the kaleidoscopic display of color reflected from the waters of the Sea of Marmora and the Asian coast and mountains that lay beyond.

Shortly after Edmond returned from the Sacred Palace, his purse bulging with the emperor's gold and provided with a specious leave of absence countersigned by the acolyte, he escorted Edith into the garden to recount the day's adventure. The afternoon's events seemed like a dream and he himself could scarcely believe what he was telling her. She admitted to wondering why he was later than usual in returning from his duties because he had instructed Godfrid to tell her only that he would be delayed.

He ignored Acolyte Bryennius's parting admonition to secrecy. He trusted Edith implicitly and besides she knew no one in Constantinople other than himself, Godfrid and the three servants he had hired to attend her. She listened in silent wonder until he came to the emperor's disclosure that Earl Sweyn was in Constantinople.

"Earl Sweyn! Here! It's not possible," she cried out in alarm. He nodded, somehow pleased she was apprehensive, almost frightened. At times he could not help wondering if despite her frequent fervent protestations during the half-year since they had left England together she had not found the wayward son of Earl Godwin more attractive than she admitted or perhaps even realized.

He watched for her reaction to his reply, "I've the emperor's word for it," and was relieved she betrayed no hint of pleasure at Sweyn's presence in Constantinople.

"Go on, what else did the emperor tell you?" she urged, then wondered, "And why did he inform you, of all people, that Sweyn is here? What does he want of you, a recent recruit to his guard he had never met until today?"

Edmond resumed his story as Edith listened intently without interrupting until he explained what Constantine expected of him. She stared at him in consternation.

"Surely, you don't mean to murder Earl Sweyn in cold blood?" she gasped.

The ugliness of "murder" and "cold blood" startled him. He had not regarded the emperor's commission in such a light but rather as just another order by a commander he was sworn to obey. If it came to shedding blood in a fair fight, why that was all part of his duties. At a loss for an answer, he shrugged.

The offhand gesture aroused her even more. "I can't believe it, Thane Edmond. Your countryman Sweyn arrives in Constantinople and you calmly accept an assignment to assassinate him. I thought better of you."

"No one said anything about assassination," he protested. "If there's violence, Sweyn won't be caught off guard. I intend to challenge him openly. And it may never come to that. The basileus hinted he would prefer to have him imprisoned and questioned."

"Then what? Do you imagine he'll be allowed to leave a dungeon alive?"

"His ultimate fate is out of my hands."

"That doesn't excuse your part in this disgraceful scheme. No matter how you view it, you're under orders to murder Earl Sweyn. Worse, you seem eager to carry out your wretched task." She spit out the accusation indignantly.

Her vehement contempt shocked him. He had not allowed himself to consider his mission so closely. It seemed so straightforward. The emperor ordered him to deal with Sweyn one way or another, preferably by arranging for capture and imprisonment It was his duty to obey his instructions unquestioningly. What happened to Sweyn after he met with him was not his concern. Or so it had seemed to him before Edith's objections gave him pause. He was forced to admit that if the mantle of being an affair of state was stripped away, his assignment could be regarded simply as murder or abduction for hire.

He grimaced. "What would you have me do, disobey the emperor?"

"What can you do?" she replied in weary disgust. "You must carry out your task or risk sharing Sweyn's fate."

Edith's disapproval was distressing but he tried to overlook it as if their friendship was unclouded. Since they had left England he had exerted himself to be as circumspect with her as possible for a young man in close and constant contact with an attractive woman. Even though during their travels she had successfully passed herself off with her male attire and close-cropped hair as Godfrid's elder brother, he had been at times only too disturbingly aware of her sex. He had suppressed his natural urges and respected her chastity not only by exerting extreme willpower but constantly reminding himself of Prior Wulfstan's fiery denunciation of what he termed sinful traffic with women. For her part, she had been careful not to tempt him in any way, as if aware of his inward turmoil. He was grateful.

Edith broke a lengthy silence. "The emperor must have told you where Sweyn is staying."

"What?" It took a moment to collect his thoughts. "Oh, yes. An inn called the Red Lion in the Drungarius district."

"Is that far?"

"No, just a short distance." He glanced at her quizzically. "Were you thinking of visiting your former admirer?"

She did not appreciate his stab at humor. "Of course not. What do you take me for, a churl's wench?"

Her reaction amused him, yet his feeble jest stirred an idea. "Perhaps you should go and see him."

She looked at him in horror. "Are you suggesting I take part in some scheme?"

"A scheme? You're too quick to take offense."

"Forgive me if I'm wrong but I thought you're considering using me as bait to lure Earl Sweyn into a trap."

"It's not what I meant," he insisted lamely. "You're putting a wrong construction on what I said. What I meant was that if you met Sweyn first it might help to avert an unfortunate confrontation, or even a riot in the streets."

"You're not serious," she cried.

"You might be able to separate him from his men and make it possible for me to meet him alone." When she glared at him in angry disbelief, he protested, "Come, no need to look at me like that. I don't intend to murder Sweyn, merely arrest him."

"I can't believe you would use me like that," she protested, tears welling.

His temper aroused, he growled, "Need I remind you that our fortunes are linked. You're only safe in this turbulent, dangerous city as long as I can protect you. I can't do so without retaining the emperor's trust. Your welfare depends on mine."

"Oh, Edmond, Edmond, how could you forget yourself so?" she lamented. "Do you think I would have accompanied you to this strange, frightening, foreign land if I hadn't believed you to be a man of honor? I put my fate in your hands, my very soul, and now you want to use me as pawn to facilitate the cold-blooded murder of a fellow countryman. What next? Will you send me out on the streets as a prostitute?"

His slap tumbled her from the garden bench to the ground. He was instantly beside her, pulling her into his arms, begging forgiveness, wiping away the tears. She pushed him away and with solemn dignity resumed her place on the bench, her bruised cheek bearing the angry red imprint of his hand.

He struggled for words before finally retracting. "Forget what I've said. I'll find some other way of dealing with Sweyn. But with or without your help I must carry out the emperor's command. I've no choice. It's either my life and liberty or Sweyn's."

She replied listlessly, "I'll do what you ask. I'll go to Sweyn."

He glanced at her sharply, then replied after an inward struggle, "It would be best. I wish it weren't so, but it would make matters much easier."

She nodded, looking away from him.

"Well then, we must consider how to arrange a meeting between you and Sweyn. It must seem to happen purely by chance."

"Is there a church in the Drungarius district?"

"You might as well ask if there are flies on a horse?" he replied with a forced laugh, trying to lessen the tension. "There must be dozens." He snapped his fingers. "Yes, a chance meeting at services. An excellent idea. See, you're already helping. Let me think."

He had wandered through the Drungarius district several times and noted the location of its major landmarks, including the prominent churches. If memory served, the Church of the Precursor, a stone's throw from the Gate of the Drungarii, was an ideal site for an attempt to arrange a meeting with Earl Sweyn. It was frequented mainly by foreigners—mostly merchants and soldiers—and if Sweyn decided to attend a church this was his most likely choice.

"I have it," he told Edith. "Just the place."

She leaned toward him and even in the gathering twilight he could see the color mounting in her cheeks. He attributed it to growing excitement at embarking on an adventure.

"There's a small church near the Gate of the Drungarii, not far from the Red Lion. If Sweyn retains any of that religious fervor which he claims sent him on a pilgrimage to the Holy Land, it's almost certain he'll say his prayers there."

"I'll attend the candle-lighting service tomorrow." Her voice was steady enough but he sensed gathering emotion, and was vaguely troubled.

"You needn't go through with this," he insisted in a sudden burst of conscience.

"But I want to." She sounded almost eager and his disquietude increased even after she added reassuringly, "In spite of what I said earlier, I know how much I owe you, Thane Edmond, and that if you displease the emperor I will suffer as well. I know what this means to both of us."

He reached for her hands but she folded them on her lap before asking, "What do you want me to tell Sweyn?"

"Anything you like, but persuade him, invite him or plead with him to visit you here. He must come alone. Do you understand?"

"Fully!" She smiled wanly. "What if he isn't at services tomorrow?"

He shrugged. "We'll try again or we'll find some other way."

"What will you do if he agrees to come here?"

"Let me worry about that."

She glanced sharply at him, then got up and went into the house. Lost in thought, he gloomily watched the sun set before following her example.

Chapter Twenty-Five

The Trap Sprung

Edmond awaited Godfrid in the Via Drungarius, the street running between the city wall and the waters of the Golden Horn. He had posted the boy within sight of the Red Lion to report when Sweyn left the inn. Disguised in the commonplace garments of a dockworker, Edmond leaned idly against a pile of lumber and surveyed the crowd continually entering and leaving the city through the Drungarii Gate. He smiled wryly on reading the stern inscription over the gate admonishing passersby that "to remember death is profitable in life".

As the time approached for the gate to be closed for the night he became impatient and decided to wait only a little longer before re-entering the city. Then he saw Godfrid pushing toward him through the crowd.

"Well, Godfrid, have you seen our friend?"

"Yes. He left the inn a little while ago and I followed him until he entered the Church of the Precursor."

"I guessed right then!" Edmond exulted. "Was he alone?"

"No, Arn was with him."

"Arn? You mean the scar-faced archer who left Thane Eadred to join Earl Sweyn's service?"

"The same. I didn't dare follow too closely for fear he would recognize me. I saw them enter the church, then came to tell you as you ordered."

"You've done well, my boy." Edmond tugged thoughtfully at his chin. "I hadn't reckoned on Arn. A shrewd, dangerous knave. He may make things more difficult. No matter, we can't back off. We'll go to the Holy Well from which we can spot anyone entering or leaving the church."

He gestured to Godfrid to follow and shoved through the crowd that was hurrying to enter or leave the city before the gate closed. The Holy Well, a shrine whose waters were believed to have curative powers, lay only a few paces from the gate. A throng of those afflicted with ills, real or fancied, crowded around the well to drink or even wash in the water, making it easy for Edmond and Godfrid to linger without attracting undue attention. They impatiently waited for the services to conclude in the small chapel whose entrance was clearly visible from the shrine.

Within the Church of the Holy Precursor, Edith became so fascinated by the solemn ritual and rich pageantry of the Greek rite—so different yet akin to the impressive enough though less elaborate form of the Latin church to which she was accustomed—that she almost neglected her mission. It was by accident that in glancing around the room she was startled to recognize Earl Sweyn and Arn a few feet away. Sweyn, though gaunt, looked as handsome as ever. Indeed, the suffering and privations endured on his pilgrimage and the bronze tan acquired under the Mediterranean sun emphasized the startlingly intense gray eyes with which he was calmly surveying the crowd of worshippers. She wondered if he would recognize her but because she was seated in a dark recess of the church he probably could see only the dim outlines of her form. She however was able to study his face, highlighted as it was by the altar candles.

She was sunk in reverie through the rest of the service, recalling those now distant days when this fiery, haughty young earl so often had visited the outlaw encampment in Ashdowne Forest. When her father Eadred had promised her hand to Sweyn she had been torn between moods of exultation at becoming the chosen bride of such a high-born, spirited lord and near dread at the prospect of a union with a man of his reputation. Few women could have resisted being attracted to someone so handsome and possessing undeniable personal magnetism. Nevertheless, the many lurid stories of his colorful past, his treacheries to men and betrayals of women, were scarcely calculated to permit a girl to contemplate with equanimity being married to such a firebrand. Yet there was no denying his overwhelming charm, and it never had entirely lost its grip on her vivid imagination. Now that he was near, she felt it reviving with full force.

She had entered the church without any specific plan of action, even to being uncertain as to whether she hoped to find Sweyn or preferred not to encounter him. Now that she saw the earl, she decided to make sure he recognized her so they could talk. It was what Edmond had asked, and she would obey him that far. Accordingly, when the service ended, she almost ran to the door, followed by her maid Sybilla, then paused to let the girl adjust her cloak as Sweyn and Arn approached.

Edith turned full-face toward Sweyn. Lost in thought, he almost passed by before recognizing her.

"Edith! Lady Edith! Can it really be you?" He was thunderstruck and gaped at her as if she were an apparition. Her confirming smile erased all doubt. He sprang to her side.

"It can't be you, Earl Sweyn?" she feigned surprise.

"But here in Constantinople! It's incredible! How came you here?"

She almost laughed at seeing him nonplused for once, the questions tumbling from his lips, his face wreathed in wonder.

"I could ask you the same questions, my lord," she parried.

"Ah, Edith, Edith, it's been so long since we last met. Do you recall those happy days in Ashdowne Forest when we met under your father's roof?"

"How could I ever forget them, Earl Sweyn."

"Ah, but this is no place to speak of such things. What are you doing here, where are you staying, where could we talk and relive the memory of those brighter, happier days?"

"I would scarcely imagine you to be so fond of the past, my lord."

"Don't mock me, Edith. I've traveled much, seen a great deal, suffered some, and strange to say my experiences have made the past more dear to me than I ever could have expected." He was almost eloquent.

He has never been like this before, she thought, and marveled at the change, the unaccustomed warmth of his usually cold voice. "If you're free, my lord, you're welcome to visit me at my villa in the Mangana district."

"Gladly! Indeed, eagerly! But I know little of this infernal, huge city, this ant heap. How shall I find this place?"

"If it pleases you, you could accompany my litter."

"Splendid!" Sweyn agreed, then turned to his companion, who had been standing by in respectful silence. "Arn, you remember the Lady Edith, I'm sure."

"My lord, I served her father for years," Arn replied, tipping his cap to Edith.

"Well then, you know with whom I'll be. Go back to the Red Lion and keep our men together until I return. They mustn't leave the inn on any pretext."

"As you wish, my lord." Arn turned to obey but Edith caught him by the sleeve.

"No, wait. I've something to say to your master," she said. Looking about to see if anyone was observing them, she drew Sweyn aside and whispered to him. He began to listen intently, at first in astonishment, then frowning fiercely. He tried to question her but could not halt her flow of words. Giving up the attempt, he finally nodded in agreement, then barked an order to Arn, who left the church and set off hastily in the direction of the Red Lion inn.

On seeing Arn depart, Edmond smiled in satisfaction. Apparently Edith was playing her role well. He ordered Godfrid to discreetly follow Arn and keep an eye on the Red Lion. The boy was to report immediately if Sweyn's men came out of the inn. When Edith and

Sweyn left the church, she entered her litter and the earl and her maid accompanied her at a fast pace eastward, toward the Mangana district.

Edmond took a roundabout route to avoid the risk of detection. Edith knew what was expected of her once she and Sweyn reached the villa. A leisurely meal, wine spiced with a sleep-inducing drug, and the earl would be helpless. No need for a confrontation with the possibility of bloodshed or a riot in the streets, and the emperor's order would have been carried out. Sweyn could be conveyed to the imperial prison with no danger of causing a tumult.

Edmond stopped at a small tavern near the Kynegion and slowly nursed a tankard of rare ale imported especially for the Varangian Guard stationed at the nearby barracks. He had told Godfrid where he would be. Several of his Varangian comrades were on hand but they were too experienced to evince surprise at his getup as a dockworker. One wit remarked he should take care as to whose bed he was headed for lest he be turned into an eunuch by an irate husband. "Not that it's the worst thing that could happen to you," another guardsman chipped in. "It might fit you to become an imperial advisor." Edmond joined in the laughter.

It was very late by the time he decided to return to the villa. Sweyn should be safely drugged by now if Edith had been successful. He had not heard from Godfrid so there was nothing to fear from the earl's followers at the Red Lion. He left the tavern and the huge bulk of the Kynegion quickly faded into the darkness behind him as he entered the Mangana district.

Arriving at his destination, he nodded curtly to the sleepy and grumbling porter who let him in. All was quiet and the only light in the house came from the library. On entering the room he found Edith alone, reclining on a divan and sipping moodily from a goblet of sparkling Lesbian wine. He was disappointed and puzzled, having expected to see Sweyn in her company but there was no sign of the earl.

He was direct. "Where is he?"

"Here!" crackled a reply. Before Edmond could pull his dagger from its sheath at his belt, the drapery shielding a door behind him parted and Sweyn advanced threateningly, naked sword in hand. Edmond's arms fell to his side. Sweyn touched his throat with the sword point and hissed, "You remember Dover?"

Edmond nodded.

"I'm not as soft as you," Sweyn said icily. "I'm sorely tempted to spit you like a partridge here and now. But it might be best to keep you alive for a while." He relieved Edmond of his sword and dagger.

"Betrayed!" Edmond finally gasped, glancing at Edith whose eyes had been averted from the scene until his accusation caused her to glare sadly yet defiantly at him.

"Yes, betrayed, betrayed to someone whom you'd have betrayed by one you've betrayed." Her almost hysterical retort ended in a sob.

"I believed you to have greater regard for me," Edmond wondered. "That you were grateful for what I've done for you, that you might even feel some friendship, even affection, for me after what we've been through together."

"Affection? Why not say love?" she cried. "Do you know I might have learned to love you after we left Ashdowne Forest, but you didn't show the slightest interest in me as a woman. You kept your distance, you didn't follow up your advantage." She spoke almost contemplatively, then turned shrill. "Now I hate you, yes, hate you. Last night when you urged me to carry out this shameful scheme to trap your fellow Englishman, a man to whom I once was betrothed, I had to restrain myself from spitting at you. I vowed to turn your plot against you, to save Earl Sweyn from being caught in a snare, come what may, and I've done so, God forgive me." Her tears flowed, and she buried her head in her hands, overcome by conflicting emotions.

Sweyn and Edmond were silently amazed by Edith's outburst. The earl kept his sword at his side while his disarmed prisoner wondered feverishly of how he might extricate himself from his perilous situation. If he could delay Sweyn a little longer, stay in the room with him and Edith until Godfrid returned, it just might be possible to overcome the earl with the lad's help. He had instructed Godfrid to stay on guard at the Red Lion until the midnight vigilia made its rounds, then return to the villa. He glanced at the water clock, but it was still too early.

Sweyn intercepted his look at the clock. "We've plenty of time to deal with you," he sneered. "Why don't we sit down and wait a little longer in comfort."

Edith vacated the divan and took a chair opposite Sweyn and Edmond when they occupied it. From time to time she stole a glance at Edmond but he seemed oblivious to her. He was lost in thought. What did Sweyn mean there was plenty of time? Did he know of Godfrid's assignment to keep an eye on the Red Lion? But Edmond had not told Edith where the boy was. Sweyn might have guessed it. Edmond gritted his teeth and tried to get up but Sweyn raised his sword threateningly. He stayed put.

Edith was the first to break a long silence. "Why don't we leave now?"

"We'll wait a little longer," Sweyn replied. "I want our friend to enjoy my sword point at his throat as long as possible. It'll remind him of the uncomfortable time he and my dear brother Harold gave me at Dover." Sweyn's white teeth gleamed under his blond mustache.

"What'll you do with him?" The evident concern in Edith's voice surprised Edmond.

"Does it matter?" Sweyn replied almost flippantly.

"You don't mean to kill him?" she asked in alarm.

Sweyn grinned. "Why not? Didn't you say he meant to cut my throat if I resisted arrest? Should I be less generous?"

"There's no arguing with you men," she burst out and began to sob. "You're all the same. Blood-letting and killing, it's all you think about."

Strange woman, Edmond thought. He could swear that one moment she might revel in watching him being torn to pieces by a pack of ravenous dogs, the next she would throw herself in front of them as a sacrifice to save him. He gave up trying to solve the mystery of womanhood and concentrated on how to deal with Sweyn. If only Godfrid would arrive or he could catch the earl dropping his guard momentarily. He had to take even the most desperate of attempts or he was lost. He tensed for a leap to wrest the sword away from Sweyn but just as he had made up his mind for the attempt a loud din erupted at the entrance to the villa. The pounding quickly ceased and after a muffled exchange of gruff words, the gate swung open. The villa came alive with the heavy tread of armed men swarming through the halls and Arn's scarred face soon appeared at the library door. At a nod from Sweyn, he entered the room accompanied by four followers. On Sweyn's orders, two men pinioned Edmond's hands behind his back.

"Any trouble?" Sweyn asked Arn.

"More than we bargained for," Arn replied sourly. "I had two men set upon young Godfrid, but one was a fool. He shouted, and that brought the vigilia down on us. I lost a man in the scuffle before we were able to give them the slip."

"What happened to him?"

"Dead. Dagger thrust."

"Good. He can't be questioned. What about the boy?"

"I think he's dead, but we couldn't wait to check."

"The night watch know where you came from?"

"Not likely. They didn't see us leave the Red Lion. As for Winsige, there was nothing on his body to identify him as one of us."

"How many men did you bring?"

"Sixteen. Fifteen, now that Winsige, may God have mercy on his soul, is gone. I brought four with me and the others are waiting at the appointed place."

"You've done well." Sweyn commended, and turned to Edmond. "It's time to leave, my friend, Thane Edmond as you call yourself." He prodded the prisoner, who had been listening in despair at the conversation. Godfrid killed! This grieved him even more than the failure of his mission and betrayal by Edith. He had learned to love the lad who so devotedly and eagerly had attempted to carry out his orders. It was a heavy price to pay for his folly. If only he had kept his mouth shut before Edith. When would he learn never to trust a woman? King Edward's wife, the Lady of England, Adele, and now this woman—all three had betrayed him or failed to meet his expectations. He scowled at Edith but felt a twinge of compassion because she looked so forlorn. Steeling himself, he asked Sweyn, "What do you mean to do with me?"

"Do with you?"

Edith unexpectedly interjected, "Yes, what are you going to do with him?"

"I'll consider it later," Sweyn growled. "I'm not sure yet. He may prove of some use alive. We'll take him along."

At Sweyn's orders, one of his men shouldered a bundle of possessions Edith had prepared and the group began to file out of the room.

Arn frowned and pointed at Edmond. "What if he shouts and brings the vigilia down on us?"

"We'll make sure he can't," Sweyn replied and brought the pommel of his sword crashing down on the back of Edmond's head to render him unconscious. "Put him in the lady's litter," he added. "We'll have to carry him, but it won't be all that far."

Chapter Twenty-Six

Death in a Dungeon

As Edmond regained consciousness swirls of luminous disc-shaped objects seemed to dance before his eyes. A dull but insistent throb heightened the steady and deep pain in the back of his head. He sat up with difficulty, his vision beginning to clear after a time, and he realized the darting discs existed only in his fancy and that he was in total darkness. He attempted to stand and succeeded in getting only to his knees before giddily slumping back onto the damp stone floor, his headache even fiercer. An urge to vomit overcame him and he retched painfully until he again lost consciousness.

When he awoke his headache had diminished considerably. It was as dark as ever and he realized he must be in a windowless dungeon. He succeeded in another attempt to get to his feet and took a hesitant step before becoming aware of an impediment holding him back. Reaching down, he grasped a bulky leg iron encircling his right ankle. It was attached to a heavy chain that he traced to a massive metal ring driven into a wall.

Still weak and becoming giddy again, he sank to his knees and held his throbbing head trying to piece together what had happened. His last clear recollection was of starting to walk along the hall of the villa between two of Earl Sweyn's men. He could remember nothing after that, but was overcome by a flood of recollection of the preceding events. He groaned, remembering his betrayal by Edith and Arn's chilling report of Godfrid's death. Nausea overcame him once more and he vomited until he felt drained and collapsed prone to the floor.

Strange, vague shapes flitted through his mind. They began to meld into a fixed pattern and the interior of his father's cottage at Bosbury took shape. Once more, the dying old man whispered, "You were born to be a king, my son." His declaration reverberated as the image faded and Edmond again felt the dank stones on which he lay. He was racked by uncontrollable mocking laughter, shouting over and over, "Born to be a king!" until the reverberations of the echo chamber that was his dungeon cell brought him back to sober and somber reality.

It was unclear for how long he lay on the stones unable, almost unwilling, to move, alternating between uneasy sleep and feverish semi-consciousness. Once he thought he was back in the presence of the saintly Prior Wulfstan who stretched out his arms toward him and repeated his kindly yet cruel advice, "...the best course would be for you to return to Bosbury and meddle no longer in great affairs... it would be best if you left England and sought your fortune elsewhere."

Wulfstan's image faded and it seemed to Edmond he was sitting on a stone bench in a pretty little garden overlooking a view of the white foam of breakers surging against the cliffs of Dover. Adele sat silently beside him, her intensely blue eyes fixed longingly on the mist-shrouded eastern horizon as if trying to pierce the haze and see the far shore. With a well-remembered gesture, she gracefully smoothed her wind-blown glossy black hair. He sighed. If only he could be beside her again. If only...

"If only you had listened to me," he cried out. The sound of his voice shocked him from his torpor and he sat up. His head seemed clear for the first time since he had become conscious in his prison. He wiped the nauseating filth from his face and discovered that he was hungry and thirsty. It was a favorable sign, and he took heart.

He gingerly felt the lump on the back of his head. It was so tender that even the slight touch was painful, but when he brought his fingers to his nose he did not smell blood though the dampness of his hair had made him wonder whether he was wounded. He struggled to his feet and took a few exploratory steps. The chain with which he was tethered was long enough so he could reach each of the four walls of the dungeon. Having worked his way around the cell without discovering an opening he concluded it was either skillfully concealed or in the ceiling.

Exhausted by the effort of examining his prison, he sank back to the floor to sit with his back supported by a wall. Did they mean to leave him to starve to death? He struggled to avoid panic. He longed to shout for food and water and it took all of his willpower to remain silent. He explored the floor and discovered puddles of water collected in small depressions. As filthy as it was, he eagerly lapped it up until his thirst was assuaged.

He again dozed off and on for what seemed an interminable period but became immediately alert when a faint glow penetrated the darkness. He looked up to discover a rectangle of light in the ceiling. As dim as the light was, he had been in complete darkness for so long that he was forced to turn away for an instant before focusing again on the ceiling. As he had suspected, a trap door provided the only entry into the cell. He stared at it in rigid fascination.

The door was pulled up and the dim line of light became a bright flood, illuminating the entire space below, reflected by countless water droplets clinging to the walls. Edmond was blinded momentarily but then saw the sharply outlined form of a man leaning over the opening to peer down at him. Satisfied that the prisoner was alive and conscious, the man grunted as he threw down a rope ladder which fell at Edmond's feet. As the visitor descended with the agility of an acrobat, Edmond noticed the flash of bare metal in his hand. He was holding an unsheathed dagger. Fearful that the man intended to murder him, Edmond almost sprang to his feet and retreated to the farthest wall, prepared to resist to the death. The newcomer, however, merely glanced at him, placed a wooden bowl and an earthen cup on the floor, re-ascended the ladder and drawing it up slammed down the trap door to leave Edmond alone again in the darkness.

Fiercely hungry, he pounced on the bowl and cup, having carefully noted where the visitor had put them. He devoured the mealy, tasteless mixture in the bowl and gulped down the cheap vinegary wine in the cup. He dismissed a momentary dread the food and drink might be poisoned. If his captors meant to kill him, they could have done so while he was unconscious. For that matter, he could have been left to die of thirst or starvation. No, for some reason Sweyn, or whoever was keeping him prisoner, wanted him alive, at least for the time being.

The pattern of visits continued for what he took to be several days. The trap door would open at intervals, the silent jailer would descend the rope ladder, replace the cup and bowl, and re-ascend and close the door. Since Edmond could not distinguish night from day his sleeping hours were irregular and sometimes he awoke to find that the attendant had visited the dungeon while he was asleep.

He made one attempt to address the warder but since his Greek was poor and he did not imagine the man understood English he was not surprised when the sole response was an uncomprehending shake of the head.

After numerous repetitions he became so accustomed to the routine that he scarcely glanced up when the trap door was raised once again, light flooded his cell, and the now familiar figure of the warder descended the swaying ladder. But to Edmond's surprise this time the jailer was not alone. Following him down carefully came a companion wearing a heavy black mantle which swung open during his descent to reveal a glitteringly elaborate corselet of gilded steel. Obviously unused to such a difficult descent, once he reached the floor he paused to regain his breath before turning to Edmond. The newcomer's face was covered by a black velvet mask with slits for the mouth and eyes.

"Edmond Edwysson, do you know where you are and why you're here?" he demanded in stentorian tones and almost accent-free English.

Edmond remained silent, but was astonished by the man's command of English. Almost as surprising was a vague feeling he had heard the voice before, although that surely was incredible.

"You're in an oubliette of the Palace of the Blachernae," the interrogator continued, "and you're here because you're a threat to the state. You've betrayed your trust and your oath. Do you deny it, traitor?"

Edmond kept his lips tightly compressed.

"Speak! Confess! Or by Christ's blood we'll know how to make you admit to your crimes." The officer gripped the hilt of an ornate dagger at his belt, then roared, "You'll soon swear before the notaries you've plotted to entrap, attack and treacherously slay our good friend Earl Sweyn Godwinson or we'll not leave a bone unbroken, a muscle untorn, a fiber unmangled of your treacherous body."

Edmond paled in spite of himself. He was well aware of the dreadful ingenuity and expertise of the Byzantine torturers. The streets were full of human wrecks begging for alms. Cripples dreadfully contorted and mangled, the vestiges of men without hands legs, noses, ears, eyes or tongues were a common sight on the streets of Constantinople. Even a petty crime could cost the pathetic culprit a limb or a faculty.

"Ha! My words aren't without effect," the officer exulted, perceiving Edmond's slight shudder. "Come, speak! It'll go less hard with you if you confess, reveal your confederates and who put you up to your schemes and crimes."

"I've nothing to say."

"Christ Pantocrator!" the officer swore, reverting to Greek in his rage and thumping his steel corselet so hard with a fist that the rings on his bejeweled fingers drew sparks from the metal. "Let none say we haven't given you every opportunity to confess voluntarily. But since you defy us we've no choice but to put you to the question." He spun about and though obviously weighted down by his armor almost scampered up the rope ladder, the warder at his heels. The trap door fell and the dungeon was plunged back into darkness.

Edmond slumped to the floor with his back to the wall, listlessly picked at the vile food and drink, and sought to make sense of what had just taken place. Who was the inquisitor? Somehow he felt sure he had met the man before. But when? Where? And what was the connection between him and Sweyn? The nub of the matter, however, was why was he being left alive? It would have been a simple matter to dispose of him.

Wearying of unanswerable questions, he turned to scheming of an attempt to escape, though that was patently impossible. His only viable move was to try to overpower the turnkey on his next visit and somehow free himself of his chains. Disguised in the man's garments and armed with his dagger he could ascend the ladder into the room above. But what would that gain? He would have to pass through an enormous building and evade countless guards before he could hope to emerge from what he knew to be a vast catacomb of a prison, the Palace of the Blachernae. Yet there was something to be said for an escape attempt, foredoomed as it was. Dying in the effort was infinitely preferable to enduring the horrors of torture if he was put to the question and even surviving such an ordeal as a hopeless cripple.

The mere notion of an attempt to escape finally aroused him from the near torpor that had overcome him since finding himself in the oubliette. A feverish longing to act, come what may, seized him. He ran his hands along the iron band encircling his leg, then followed the length of chain to the ring embedded in the wall. Strange how sensitive his fingers were in the dark. He could feel every irregularity, each indentation, the slightest protuberance of metal. He discovered a link that was somewhat smaller, slighter than the others. He began to strike it against the heavy ring set in the wall until the sparks flew and the clangor resonated in the small chamber with an almost unbearable cacophony. He stubbornly maintained the effort despite the clangor until his fingers became numb and ears so dulled by the din that he might not be able to hear the warder return and lift the trap door. He labored on in constant anxiety the man might come back at any moment. But when there was no reaction to the din he was creating it confirmed his surmise he must be incarcerated in the nethermost depths of the vast prison. It seemed an eternity had passed in banging what he conceived to be the weakest link against the heavy ring before he began to feel he had made progress. On examining it with his benumbed fingers he found it was totally out of shape though still intact. He sank in weary despair back to the damp floor, racking his brain for another approach upon the warder's return.

Eventually the light again traced the rectangular pattern in the ceiling. The glow brought him to his feet, every muscle tensed. He pressed himself against a wall and carefully drew up the chain in his hands and formed a loop. He waited breathlessly as the trap door raised and the rope ladder tumbled to the floor. To his relief this time the jailer was alone.

The man descended slowly, balancing a tray one hand, clinging to the ladder with the other. He put the cup and bowl on the floor and looked for the empty ones which Edmond had been careful to place by the wall at his feet, near the fastening of the chain. The turnkey, dagger in hand, kept an eye on the prisoner and reached for the utensils. Edmond tensed and when the warder bent down for the dishes flung the looped chain over the man's shoulders. Though caught off guard and staggered by the weight of metal, the jailer nevertheless closed in on Edmond, dagger poised to strike. Edmond reeled at the shock of the blade cutting into his left shoulder and with all his enormous strength desperately pulled the heavy chain around his opponent's throat as if it were a necklace. The jailer's neck muscles bulged and the blood vessels in his face swelled in protest against the grinding chain. Edmond grunted with intense effort as the turnkey gasped for breath. Was the man's neck a pillar of marble? At last, the moans and gasps dwindled into a final whimper and the jailer sank with a clanking of iron to the floor. Edmond sprang on his prostrate body like a beggar on a brass coin in the street. Two blows with the links of the chain, and the man's blood and brains spurted from his crushed skull, staining the floor.

Driven by the desperate realization he had to staunch the flow of blood from his shoulder wound lest the loss so weaken him that all his effort would have been in vain, Edmond ripped feverishly at the jailer's garments. He tore the dagger from the man's already stiffening grip and cut strips from his tunic to make a rough bandage with which to bind his wound. He was relieved to discover only the point of the dagger had penetrated slightly and the cut was unlikely to bleed much longer.

He turned his attention to the chain. He inserted the dagger blade as far as possible into the link which he had hammered out of shape. He filed blade against what he supposed to be the weakest point. Progress was agonizingly slow but a scattering of iron particles began to drift to the floor as the notch deepened. A final desperate twist with all his strength overcame the stubborn metal and the link broke but so did the dagger blade. He was free of the portion of the chain attached to the wall.

Free! He laughed almost hysterically.

Free! With a length of iron chain upon his leg and the stump of a dagger his sole weapon.

Free! With blood from a wound in his shoulder soaking an improvised bandage.

Free! Trapped in the innermost recesses of a vast prison, scores of reinforced doors, endless corridors and hundreds of guards between him and the outside world.

Free! He sank to the floor in frustration.

He shocked himself out of his momentary despair by the realization that even if he could not hope to escape he must act immediately if he meant to die honorably in combat rather than perish ignominiously under torture. He searched the warder, took a pouch with a few coins, then stripped the body and dressed himself in the man's rags. He reached for the ladder and began to ascend. If it only would stop swaying. He was half-way up when he became dizzy. A brief rest, and he resumed his climb. He was almost at the top when he heard a door creak in the chamber above. He froze in apprehension, then reeled, almost falling off the ladder. He peered upward. A masked face appeared.

"Christ Pantocrator!" the officer muttered, staring in disbelief upon the bloody scene below. While Edmond watched with all the fascination of a fly observing an advancing spider, the officer drew his sword and hacked at the ladder. It gave way, hurtling with its despairing occupant onto the dank and blood-spattered dungeon floor.

Chapter Twenty-Seven

Second Chance

B rilliant sunlight dazzled Edmond when he awoke and it took a few moments before he was able to comfortably examine the room he found himself in. Somehow he had been transported from the dark, damp dungeon into a lavishly furnished chamber hung with elaborate tapestry, floored with jewel-like mosaics and fronting a carefully-tended and luxuriant formal garden. He pulled himself up on his elbows so he could inspect his surroundings more closely but strong hands firmly thrust him back down.

"Gently, gently, Varangian, you must not move yet." The voice was authoritative yet not unkind and Edmond beheld a black-bearded, black-eyed countenance keenly examining him as its possessor leaned over the bed. "You've lost a good deal of blood."

"Who are you? Where am I?" Edmond wondered in broken Greek.

"Master Stephen Chrysellius at your service and you're—well, I think it best to permit someone else to tell you just where you are." Chrysellius picked up a small bottle from an ivory inlaid table next to the bed and carefully transferred a golden liquid into a small goblet. He adroitly propped up Edmond's head and poured the bitter fluid down the young man's throat before he could protest. "I needn't add I'm a physician—and a most competent one, if I say so myself," Chrysellius smiled reassuringly.

"But... but the dungeon of Blachernae and now this?" Edmond sputtered, unable to comprehend the change. His last recollection was of the officer slashing the rope ladder and his frightening fall to the floor before he lost consciousness.

"Blachernae dungeon?" Chrysellius was puzzled. "It might be the bruise on the back of your head? Or a fever caused by the deep scratch on your shoulder." Mumbling, he bent over Edmond, intent on re-examining the patient.

"No need for that, my dear doctor," came a deep and singularly harmonious voice. "My companion and I can explain what should be revealed to the young man. Even the dungeon."

Unnoticed by Edmond, two men had entered the room while Chrysellius was tending to his patient. The one who spoke was apparently in his mid-thirties and wore an elaborate court costume denoting he was an imperial minister, a logothete. His piercingly brilliant black eyes swept the room from beneath a formidable brow above a hawk-like nose. High intellect was apparent in every line of his face as was the fact that he was proudly aware of his powers. Edmond was startled to recognize this remarkable individual's equally impressive companion. It was the masked officer who had threatened him in the oubliette and thwarted his attempt to escape.

"I thought the shock suffered when he was wounded in the shoulder might have temporarily deranged him, most learned master," Chrysellius explained as he sank to his knees and humbly touched his forehead to the floor.

"No need for ceremony," the logothete protested, frowning. "You may leave us alone with your patient, Master Chrysellius. You've done well."

As Chrysellius left the room, Edmond studied his visitors, not knowing what to expect from them though he hardly cared because he felt so weak.

The court official approached and examined Edmond's wound. "Just as Chrysellius predicted, my lord," he remarked to his military companion. "The Varangian should be fully fit for service again in ten days or so at the most."

The officer was pleased. "Well then, we might as well proceed with the questioning before we decided what to do with him."

The logothete pursed his lips and stared sternly at Edmond. "You killed a man in your foolish, hopeless attempt to elude justice," he growled. "Your life is already forfeit but we're inclined to be merciful if you'll admit your part in a detestable conspiracy against our Christ-loving Empress Theodora Porphyrogenita. Come, confess you were hired by that unbelieving usurper, Constantine Monomachus, to murder a loyal servant of our dear little mother, our beloved empress."

Bewildered by the accusations, Edmond looked bleakly at the inquisitor.

"Christ Pantocrator!" hissed the masked officer, leaning over the wounded man. "I warned you earlier, speak or we'll rip the words out of you—and your tongue into the bargain. What dirty business did that heathen Constantine Monomachus employ you to carry out?"

Edmond closed his eyes and compressed his lips even more firmly. To his amazement, he heard the officer's burst of laughter. "Well, didn't I tell you, good Psellus? You'll get nothing out of this one. You might as well question the sphinx."

"Patriarch Cerularius would have him singing to whatever tune he wanted to hear," Psellus replied dryly, yet with the hint of a smile. "My master, you're ever too kind and gentle, even to your most bitter and dangerous enemies. Another would have persuaded this young fellow to confess to any crime, no matter how abominable."

"Don't speak ill of our revered patriarch to me," the officer chided, unfastening his mask. "I mustn't listen to such discourtesy and disrespect to the leader of our church. Yet I suppose you're probably right. I imagine, given our position, neither he nor sister Theodora would've hesitated to put this young man to the torture."

Edmond gaped in disbelief as the officer's mask came off. The Emperor Constantine stood at his bedside. No wonder the voice had sounded so familiar.

The emperor's companion then was almost certainly the brilliant Constantine Psellus, the imperial minister whose immense reputation as a scholar had penetrated even into the barracks of the untutored, half-barbarian Varangian Guard. It was widely known that Constantine IX seldom took a step without consulting Psellus.

But what were the emperor and his most trusted advisor doing at a simple soldier's bedside? What had prompted Constantine IX to visit him in the oubliette? For that matter, who had imprisoned him in the dungeon in the first place? How and why had he been transferred into this luxurious setting? Edmond's brain spun, beset as he was by questions, but he forced himself to remain silent. It was not for a Varangian to question the supreme commander, the viceroy of God on earth.

Constantine IX drew up a stool and sat down beside the bed while Psellus remained standing. "We aren't surprised you're confused, wondering what this is all about," the emperor began in English to further astonish Edmond. "It's not often that a basileus carries on a campaign with a single soldier but occasionally it's necessary to do so. That's why we've gone to great pains to test your loyalty and fortitude. Much depends on the outcome of the affair we're concerned in and we must be certain you'll keep your mouth shut if you fall into enemy hands. What's more, there's some suspicion of treachery in the affair we assigned to you earlier. You botched it rather badly, didn't you?"

"My lord..." Edmond began but the emperor cut him short.

"No excuses. Just tell us what happened."

Edmond related the arrangements made to arrest or dispose of Sweyn and how his scheme had failed because of betrayal by a woman. He carried the story to the moment at which he had been struck down in the villa, admitting he remembered nothing after that until he regained consciousness in the dungeon.

"When you came to you assumed you were imprisoned in the Blachernae?" Constantine grinned, nodding to Psellus.

"What was I to think, your imperial majesty? I was convinced Earl

Sweyn had turned me over to the Empress Theodora's jailers to be put to the question."

Psellus steepled his fingers and bowed to the emperor. "Your highness has conducted this affair most skillfully."

"We had to find out just how far we could trust this young Varangian, and whether or not he had betrayed us," Constantine replied smugly. "I think we've managed to accomplish that with a bit of trickery." He neglected to add that he greatly preferred guile to violence. Psellus was well aware of this trait in the emperor's makeup, as he was of his character in general. Constantine was at heart a just and mild man, generally averse to brutality and torture, though on occasion he reluctantly had to employ extreme means to gain his ends. The emperor may have been dissolute and self-indulgent but he was essentially kindhearted.

He returned to Edmond. "We hope you understand that your failure to carry out your mission raised doubts of your loyalty as well as ability. That might have cost you even more dearly than it has so far, but we thought you might remain useful to us in this matter of Earl Sweyn. That's why you've been spared, even if it means we must disregard the unfortunate death of one of our loyal servants, the jailer you killed."

The emperor could not help from laughing at Edmond's obvious bewilderment. "Maybe we've put the chariot before the horses, as they say in the Hippodrome. You're ignorant of what happened after you were struck down by Earl Sweyn, or one of his men, and before you came to your senses in the dungeon. Come, Psellus, tell the lad."

The logothete bowed, cleared his throat, then spoke slowly in Greek so Edmond could follow the explanation. "The first report of the affair was a message from the night watch of a brawl near the inn of the Red Lion in the Drungarius district. Normally, I'd take no notice of such a trifling matter but recently I've been careful to check out any unusual disturbance, knowing how important it might be to your majesty's interests.

"I asked for a further report of this event and was told that by the time the vigilia arrived a wounded youth lay on the ground with his attackers fleeing. The vigilia attempted to detain one man, but he was killed during a scuffle. The others escaped. There's some question, however, of how zealous the vigilia was in trying to track down the offenders because the captain in the Drungarius district is a known sympathizer of the empress."

Worried about Godfrid, Edmond asked, "What about the wounded boy?"

Though annoyed by the interruption, Psellus replied, "I'm told he's expected to recover under the care of a physician assigned to your

Varangian unit."

Edmond sighed relief. Godfrid was alive after all.

Psellus resumed his narrative. "Fortunately, the adjacent Mangana vigilia is commanded by our good friend Bardas Pharnakos, a most loyal servant of our true basileus. On receiving a report that a furtive band of men had passed by the Kynegion, Pharnakos turned out his detachment and set out in pursuit. The vigilia followed the intruders to a villa near the Church of St. George the Martyr. After the barbarians—Pharnakos identified them as a troop of Danes and Englishmen—entered the villa, the commander ordered the building surrounded in preparation for an attack, then closed in. A brief struggle ensued in which two barbarians were killed before the rest escaped, though several were wounded. However, they were forced to abandon a litter in which an unconscious man was found.

"Pharnakos, no fool, immediately recognized this was no routine police matter and, suspecting political intrigue, ordered the unconscious man taken to the Sacred Palace. He reported the matter directly to me rather than going through the usual channels and I, of course, informed his sacred majesty. The emperor, in his wisdom..." and Psellus again bowed to Constantine, "...commanded that the prisoner be placed in the most remote oubliette of the Daphne. He wished to discover whether the man, whom he recognized as one of his Varangians, had betrayed his confidence."

The emperor stirred. "Christ Pantocrator! An unlucky decision for that poor warder," he grumbled, frowning at Edmond.

"I was desperate to escape even if I died in the attempt, your majesty."

"You deprived us of a loyal if humble servant," Constantine complained. "See that prayers are said and ample candles lit for the repose of his soul," he commanded Psellus, then returned to Edmond. "No doubt you wonder why we've transferred you from that dismal oubliette to such a dainty little chamber in the Daphne Palace?"

Edmond nodded.

"After we found you unconscious we wondered if it was all a sham and whether you had betrayed our trust. Yet it seemed a pity to waste someone with your background, your familiarity with Earl Sweyn, and with the potential to redeem your failure. We decided to confine you in the oubliette both as a test and to prevent anyone from learning about your connection with us. As soon as we satisfied ourselves as to your loyalty, we decided to move you into somewhat healthier quarters so you could recover quickly and be able to serve us yet in this affair."

The emperor's tortuous and somewhat ingenuous explanation failed to convince Edmond but he was in no position to dispute its truth.

"We see you understand even better than we imagined you would," Constantine smiled ironically. "Now to return to Earl Sweyn. He eluded our faithful Pharnakos and found his way to safety in the Blachernae Palace. He took your mistress Edith with him, presumably to serve as a handmaiden to our dear sister, the Empress Theodora. The woman, of course, is your concern, though from what we've been told she is worthy of becoming ours. Sweyn is another matter. We must get him out of the Blachernae dead or alive, do you understand!"

The emperor's voice rose to a high pitch as he continued, "An enemy so dangerous, potentially another Harald Hardraade, is too great a menace to tolerate. We've had too many revolts and conspiracies in our time. Hardraade, George Maniaces, Leo Tornicius, even Romanus Boilas, fool that he is, have kept us sleepless in the past. We grow old, we're tired, even ill much of the time. We don't have many years left and long to enjoy those few in peace and tranquility."

The great weight of Constantine IX Monomachus's weariness and concern both for his people's and own well-being momentarily stripped away the mask of pride, dignity and royal imperturbability that normally shielded his inner self from his subjects' view. As he spoke his hands trembled with emotion and Edmond felt a touch of compassion for this aging ruler, so mighty yet so precariously perched on a shaky throne. It was difficult nevertheless to keep from smiling at the mention of Romanus Boilas, the court buffoon. Could the emperor really be concerned about such a specter of a man? Boilas not long ago had become infatuated with the emperor's latest mistress, Princess Irene, a hostage from Alania, and had concocted a half-baked plot to murder Constantine in hopes of succeeding him on the throne as well as in the young woman's bed. He had approached the emperor dagger in hand but lost his nerve and dropped the weapon even before the guards could intervene. Unaccountably, Constantine, always quick to pardon and brave to the point of recklessness, not only forgave Boilas but permitted him to remain at court.

Maniaces and Tornicius had presented far more serious threats and come perilously close to abruptly terminating Constantine's reign. A decade earlier, Maniaces had raised a considerable force of rebels and was well on his way to defeating an imperial army in battle when he unexpectedly died in its final stages. His fortuitous demise almost certainly saved Constantine from being dethroned and probably blinded, if not executed, the common fate of deposed rulers. Nevertheless, it had been a disastrous day for the empire. A skillful general, Maniaces had been Constantinople's sole bulwark against the Norman adventurers ravaging the imperial territory in Italy, and they conquered most of it after his death.

Tornicius, a disgruntled nobleman and formerly one of Constantine's boon companions, carried his revolt to the walls of Constantinople. Only a desperate defense by the imperial bodyguard, assisted by Constantine's hastily recruited civilian supporters, had driven off the attackers. Tornicius was eventually brought in chains before the emperor who characteristically regretted having him blinded and sent into exile.

Since the attempt by Tornicius to dethrone him five years earlier, the emperor had enjoyed relative peace at home, if not on the frontiers, which were constantly threatened by foreign enemies—the most formidable being the Persians and Normans. He remained on constant alert for any indication of a domestic rebellion and was determined to stamp out the slightest threat.

"There may be other ways of dealing with Earl Sweyn," Constantine explained to Edmond, "but it occurred to us that availing ourselves of your mutual hostility would blunt suspicion of political involvement and minimize the danger of disturbances. An investigation would disclose that you and your countryman are old enemies. It helps that your woman has deserted you for him. Another reason for deadly hostility."

Edmond choked back his doubts about the emperor's plan and the involved exposition. It would not do to cross Constantine, who looked so pleased with himself. But how on earth was he expected to accomplish anything in his present condition? Constantine caught his perplexed expression. "Of course, we'll have to delay until you've fully recovered," he hastened to reassure Edmond. "When you're pronounced fit come to us for further orders. Master Chrysellius will attend to you until then."

Edmond's recuperation under Chrysellius's care took two more weeks. Chrysellius proved not only a skillful physician but also an entertaining companion. He kept abreast of the latest court gossip and though Edmond knew few courtiers other than by name he enjoyed the physician's lively accounts of the scandalous goings-on.

"Rumor has it that Irene of Alania is entertaining Romanus Boilas in private again, if you catch my meaning," Chrysellius murmured while examining Edmond's shoulder wound. "Excellent, excellent, no need for this anymore," he decided, stripping off the bandage. "It may be true. The blessed basileus has been unwell lately and in any case is no longer a young buck. An ardent young woman might understandably feel neglected and seek comfort elsewhere."

"The emperor ill? He seemed well enough when he visited me."

"He has his good days and his bad as do most of us," Chrysellius philosophized. "It's the gout again, most aggravated this time. His left foot is dreadfully swollen. He has been confined to bed for three days now. Takes it remarkably well, never complains, unlike most of my patients." He examined Edmond's tongue, then gave him an encouraging pat on the shoulder. "Before I forget, I'm to inform you that Constantine Psellus grants you permission to exercise in the gallery. It'll be good medicine. Walk about as much as you like and flex your arm, in moderation at first. You may also use the garden. You'll be as sound as Igor the charioteer in a few more days, my friend."

Edmond happily took advantage of his new freedom to move about. He frequently strolled the long gallery and was lost in admiration of the luxuriant yet carefully ordered beauty of the garden to the south of the Daphne Palace. Exquisite sculptures splashed rose-scented water into onyx basins and kaleidoscopic tropical fish imported from lands beyond even fabled India darted about in pink marble ponds. Deer of species unfamiliar to him and resplendent peacocks wandered the pathways, unafraid of his presence. The deer, so small and docile unlike their relatives in England, turned his thoughts homeward.

It had been a while since he had allowed himself to speculate about affairs in his native land. The fateful interview with Prior Wulfstan had convinced him not to concern himself with England's politics, especially the struggle between the factions of King Edward and Earl Godwin. After leaving with Edith and Godfrid he had made it a point to concentrate on seeking his fortune in Constantinople. Even when his Varangian companions from England chattered about affairs at home he avoided joining in the conversation. But Earl Sweyn's surprising and unexpected arrival in Constantinople had brought the apparently dead past back to life.

He realized now that in a recess of his mind he still longed to return someday to England. He could not explain it, but there it was. If he did go back, he swore it would not be to pursue the inordinate dream that had possessed him before he left. Prior Wulfstan had convinced him of its futility. He would retire to some remote part of the country, possibly near Bosbury, with whatever wealth he brought back from Constantinople. He would shun politics, stay away from Earl Harold, Earl Godwin, King Edward and the rest. He had alienated all, and only prudence and good fortune would enable him to live out his days secure from hostility.

If he was to achieve this modest ambition, he must successfully carry out the emperor's plans. Failure might be fatal. Sweyn must be captured or dealt with in another way or his own fate was sealed. Constantine Monomachus was generous in rewarding success but might be intolerant of failure.

There was a lesser but equally real danger. If Earl Godwin, who doted on his eldest son, ever learned of Edmond's role in disposing of

Sweyn he would become a mortal enemy, as might some of Sweyn's brothers. Yet it was a long way from Constantinople to England and if Sweyn and his band never came back, the secret of what had happened would die with them. As for Earl Harold, he might not be all that sorry to learn of his brother's misfortune, much as he might choose to lament it for public show.

Then there was Edith. Edmond was more deeply wounded by her betrayal than he could ever have imagined he would be. For the first time he became aware of the depth of his attachment to this young woman, something he had resisted since she had joined in the flight from England. Their platonic relationship had been made easier because she had never displayed any outward affection for him. During all those months together they had been careful not to transgress the bounds of an innocent relationship. It was not as if he had lost something he had possessed. Yet he now regarded her behavior in a different light, wondering whether her frequent protestations of dislike of Sweyn resulted from an effort to resist his attractions. If that was the case, Edith had not so much betrayed him as she had finally yielded to Sweyn's fascination. Even then, however, he could not exonerate her from base ingratitude to someone who had protected and provided for her during their hazardous journey from Dover to Constantinople and afterwards.

He wondered if Adele would have behaved otherwise than Edith or were all women the same, unpredictable and untrustworthy. Would Adele have been as selfless and true as he would like to think her? Or was that pure fantasy? Did it really matter? She was lost to him forever, buried alive in a convent. Now Edith also was gone and he comforted himself that he really did not care what happened to her. Let her wed Sweyn, or worse, or perhaps serve as a handmaiden to the Empress Theodora. If Sweyn would not have her, the old lady would be able to provide her with a high-ranking husband, especially if the match was sweetened with a suitable dowry.

Lost in such thoughts, Edmond absent-mindedly twisted the silver ring around his finger. The involuntary action made him reflect ruefully how unworthily he was conducting himself for a descendant of King Alfred, immersing himself in base treachery and tawdry ambitions. He steeled himself with the justification of being sworn to serve and defend the emperor faithfully.

He was never alone in his strolls through the gallery and garden, being invariably accompanied by two Scholarian guards, the elite of the imperial army. They neither spoke to him nor permitted anyone encountered to do so as he discovered upon attempting once or twice to strike up a conversation with a passerby.

The emperor's illness was troubling. If Constantine died he would be left in limbo, an embarrassment to all. The rabble in the streets would probably clamor for restoring Theodora to sole power. With her consent, Sweyn would lose no time in ridding himself of an enemy. Even if the emperor recovered—and Chrysellius insisted he was in no great danger—Edmond's position would be insecure. Sweyn was unlikely to relax or relent in his efforts to dispose of a dangerous foe.

Edmond agonized over a plan of action. Perhaps as soon as he was fully recovered he could emerge from his gilded cage, elude Theodora's guards in the Blachernae, and confront Sweyn directly. Yet even if he got that far against enormous odds, what then? Sweyn might prefer not to settle the matter personally but to rely on his followers to deal with the threat. Edmond threw up his hands. He was caught between Scylla and Charybdis, he smiled ruefully, referring to his sketchy acquaintance with Homer's works, which to the people of Constantinople were as familiar as the Christian gospels to the clergy.

With his wound healed, he became increasingly weary not only of his fruitless meditations but of the surroundings which had become so familiar they had lost all charm despite their splendor. He began to wonder if he had been forgotten after several days passed without visitors other than Chrysellius, who pronounced him fully recovered. Thus he was overjoyed when Psellus finally entered his room.

"You look extraordinarily fit, Varangian," the minister remarked, black eyes appraising Edmond's sturdy frame. "It's well. We can't afford to wait much longer. The basileus wants to see you. He's impatient, indisposed though he is, to bring this matter of Earl Sweyn to a satisfactory conclusion. Come, we have an audience with him."

Preceded by Psellus and accompanied by the ever-present Scholarian guards, Edmond was led to the emperor's Corian apartments. In the past Constantine had resided in the Pearl apartments nearer the sea each summer, but he had been unwell so often in recent years that now he preferred the warmer winter quarters at all times. During the short walk from the Daphne Palace to the Triconchus where the Corian apartments were located, Edmond noticed that the guard posts were heavily manned. There were no Varangians but only Scholarians and Hicanati, or "Immortals" as the latter were called. The other elite guard unit, the Excubitors, had been apportioned to the Empress Theodora at the Blachernae.

The anteroom to Constantine's bedchamber was swarming with courtiers, military men, ministers, clerics and palace officials who suspended a deafening buzz of conversation and respectfully drew aside to open a path for Psellus's small contingent, bowing or saluting the great minister as befitted their social station or government office. Psellus obviously stood high in the emperor's favor. The chatter resumed and grew in volume once Psellus and Edmond passed along the colonnade of green marble and red onyx toward the bedchamber. At a nod from Psellus, the doors swung open to admit only the minister and his companion into Constantine's presence before slamming shut again.

The emperor lay sprawled on a huge bed in the middle of the elaborately furnished room, glumly contemplating the ceiling, an azure heaven dominated by a shiny green cross surrounded by golden constellations of stars. Four gilded imperial eagles, wings outspread and framed in green marble, decorated the room's corners. Mosaics depicting colorful flowerbeds ran along the lower border of each wall. As a reminder that Basil I, the formidable founder of the Macedonian dynasty, had built the palace, a mosaic highlighted by a contrasting background of glittering gold depicted the emperor and his family. Basil I, his wife Eudocia and their sons and daughters each held a holy book in one hand and made the sign of the cross with the other. They gazed down almost benignly on the emperor's successor, his visitors and a small knot of attendants effacing themselves at a respectful distance from the bed, alert for any request of the ruler. His attention, however, was diverted by the approach of Psellus and Edmond.

Constantine's sickly pallor was emphasized by the multicolored splendor of his surroundings but his voice was strong as he began, "Welcome, young man. You observe how fate has reversed our situations." He motioned to a slave who rushed to help him sit up. "It hasn't been all that long since I visited you in sickbed and now it's my turn to suffer."

"Your Christ-loving majesty will soon be leading your armies against the enemies of the Romans," Edmond murmured, slightly embarrassed by his lame attempt to observe the convention of flattery and hyperbole demanded by court etiquette.

"The young foreigner is quick to learn our ways, eh Psellus," the emperor laughed. "The fact is, I'm feeling somewhat better than I have for some time. But enough of pleasantry. Let's attend to more important matters."

"I await your sacred majesty's heaven-inspired orders," bowed Psellus.

"You've informed us that our agents are certain Earl Sweyn is in the Blachernae," Constantine began. "Obviously, we have to either enter that labyrinth of our enemies and drag him out or find a way to lure him into emerging on his own. He's unlikely to do the latter unless he sees a chance of doing mischief on behalf of our dear sister Theodora. We can't afford to wait. Our best course, my faithful Psellus, may be to go after him into the Blachernae."

Psellus frowned, hesitating to question the emperor's judgment but plunged on. "Your imperial majesty knows just how difficult, perhaps even impossible, that may be, not to mention the danger of setting off street riots. There may be a better way of achieving our objectives, if I might be so bold to suggest."

The emperor nodded and Psellus continued. "Someone in the inn of the Red Lion is communicating with the people in the Blachernae. We keep close watch on the inn and it's certain none of Sweyn's men remain in that den which always has been a hangout for troublemakers. Whether it's a patron, the innkeeper, a serving wench or stable boy, someone in there is in our enemies' pay. If we can uncover that person it would help us get our Englishman into the Blachernae with a minimum of difficulty."

Constantine and Edmond stared at the minister, the emperor being the first to confess his puzzlement. "What are you driving at, Psellus?"

"It's likely Earl Sweyn is eager for news from England," the minister replied. "He must want to know how his father and brothers are faring. What better way to take advantage of that than to have an English sailor, newly arrived on a Venetian ship which touched at an English port, seek a room at the Red Lion?"

"What English sailor?" Constantine wondered, then smiled his understanding, "You mean..."

Psellus tapped Edmond on the shoulder. "Yes, our young Varangian here, my lord. If I may remind you, none of Sweyn's men remain at the Red Lion, and if Thane Edmond enters disguised as a sailor none would know him. Whoever at the inn is communicating with the Blachernae is sure to report that a stranger recently come from England has arrived. As soon as Sweyn learns of it, he's bound to arrange for the go-between at the inn to send the newcomer to the Blachernae to pump him about matters at home. I can't conceive he'd take the risk of going to the inn himself, knowing we're on the lookout for him."

Edmond admired Psellus's ingenuity. The scheme just might work and if it did would solve the difficulty of getting at Sweyn. Of course, there was still the problem of just how to deal with Sweyn and escape from the Blachernae afterwards. He cautioned himself—one step at a time. It was enough for now to envision himself in the role of an English sailor. He thought wistfully, almost fondly, of Wiglaf, then returned to the situation at hand. Chances were none of Sweyn's men other than Arn would recognize him and, if luck held, he might not run into the archer before meeting the earl.

"Well, Varangian?" Constantine broke impatiently into Edmond's thoughts. "What do you think of Master Psellus's proposed stratagem?"

"It's masterly, your majesty."

Constantine smiled indulgently. "If you're mocking our good servant

Psellus, we pardon you. Masterly, you say, when you know as well as we're sure he does that it's a harebrained scheme at best. We could wish for something better, but this will have to do and it might even succeed. There must be no slipups this time or none of us will have anything to laugh about, least of all you, my young soldier."

Psellus added, "It'll be worth your utmost effort even if your life were not at stake. If you succeed, his majesty is prepared to reward you handsomely. Few of your countrymen have ever been promoted to the rank of kometes as commanders of a tagmata of the Varangian Guard. Moreover, the sum of fifty pounds of gold will be yours, payable wherever you wish, even in London if you chose to return to your homeland."

Edmond was both dazzled and astonished. "Paid in England," he stammered. "How can that be?"

Constantine and Psellus smiled indulgently at the Varangian's obvious ignorance of the banknote system long established throughout the empire and wherever imperial agents were found. The minister explained, "You'll be given a note signed by the logothete of the treasury and a Lombard banker in London will readily pay over to you the specified sum. Of course, if you'd prefer, you could follow Harald Hardraade's example and take the gold with you, but it would be much riskier."

Edmond joined in the laughter, his heart jumping nevertheless. Here was a chance to gain at one stroke a handsome fortune, greater than he ever could have hoped for. He would be among the wealthiest thanes in England if he did succeed in returning. Fifty pounds of gold was a staggering sum even in Constantinople, representing more than a year's pay for a strategus—a high-ranking general.

"You know what we expect of you," the emperor summed up the conference. "Psellus will make the necessary arrangements. Our police will be instructed not to interfere with you in any way." Constantine sank back onto the bed, stifling a moan caused by a surge of pain in his swollen foot.

Edmond hesitated when Psellus signaled him to join in respectfully backing out of the imperial presence.

"Is there something else, young man?" the emperor growled impatiently. "You have your orders, isn't that enough?"

"Your pardon, my lord, if I violate protocol by being so impertinent as to ask your majesty a question, but I've been puzzled ever since a masked officer in the dungeon spoke to me."

"What's bothering you?" Constantine asked more calmly.

"I'm amazed to find your majesty so fluent in the language of my people."

Constantine chuckled despite his discomfort.

"Some thirty years ago, for reasons of health—my revered predecessor, Basil II of hallowed memory, would have made us ill indeed—we considered it prudent to travel abroad. We spent some time in London where rather than entirely idle away the long winter we took pains to master the harsh, barbaric language."

Astonished by the revelation, Edmond followed Psellus out of the imperial bedchamber. So Constantine IX Monomachus, now the most powerful of monarchs, once had been a lonely exile in a strange and distant land. Who could have suspected then that London, at the far ends of the world, harbored a future emperor of the Romans? Was it possible that some day it would be remembered that Constantinople had similarly been refuge for a destined king of England?

Chapter Twenty-Eight

Inn of the Red Lion

Isaac Antiochus idly drummed knuckles on a counter top while glumly surveying his domain. It was the heart of the evening and yet the Red Lion, normally packed at that time, was almost deserted. Unlike the usual joyous—or quarrelsome—din, a modest hum of conversation among a few patrons further depressed his customarily buoyant spirits.

Isaac had prospered hugely since arriving in Constantinople from Antioch three decades earlier with a tiny inheritance clinking mournfully in the sorry excuse for a money pouch tied around his slender waist. Now he had no cause for complaint in either respect, both purse and waist being vastly expanded. Under his shrewd stewardship the Red Lion, a dreadfully rundown haunt in his predecessor's day, had become the favored hangout of seamen and foreigners in the Drungarius district. It could even be said to have gained an international reputation, attracting visitors to Constantinople from all over the world, as well as the horde of mercenaries in the imperial armed forces.

Nevertheless, Isaac was troubled, wondering whether the inn's attraction to such a diverse clientele might not lead to his undoing. Trade had declined markedly since the arrival of a barbarian nobleman with his retinue a few weeks earlier. Where were they from? Some obscure dunghill of the world, an island called Britain, he was told. Their stay at the Red Lion was brief, only a few days before they left hastily one night, but business had been slack after their departure. He was mystified as to why. The vigilia had not raided his place and there had been no riots other than a minor scuffle in the streets from which the barbarians fled. He had heard that one of them had been killed and a boy wounded.

He contemplatively swabbed the counter. There was nothing he could put his finger on to account for the drastic fall-off of trade. He sighed, comforting himself with the memory of his daily morning visit to the strongbox at the foot of his bed. It had been a delight to raise the lid and count the plump sacks of coins stacked within. Let people talk about how stingy the Empress Theodora was but he knew better. Every call her bursar, John Zingarious, made to the Red Lion confirmed her generosity. Zingarious assured him there was more to come if he kept his eyes and ears open. Isaac rubbed his hands together. Another payment or two and he could buy a tenement near the Mese he was keeping his eyes on. The income from rents would enable him to abandon this cutthroat business. He might even turn the inn over to his son-in-law John, not that he had much confidence in that layabout's business acumen.

Isaac's musings ended abruptly when a sailor entered the inn, walking steadily if with a rolling gait. The seaman evidently had not visited many of the numerous taverns in the district before coming to the Red Lion. He probably still had most of his pay, Isaac thought with pleasure as the newcomer dropped heavily onto a chair.

"Something to wet my parched throat," the sailor rasped, thumping the table to bring Isaac to life.

"I'll attend to the captain myself," the innkeeper told a serving wench who had flounced to greet the customer.

"Captain?" the sailor barked in amusement, his accent and the cut of his clothes making it plain he was a barbarian, most likely either a Dane or Englishman.

"What can I bring you, master?" Isaac hummed ingratiatingly.

"By the holy rood! Good brown ale, if you have it, and that quickly," the sailor boomed. "If not, I'll settle for good wine. None of your rotgut, if you please."

Isaac bowed and scurried off, quickly reappearing with a huge tumbler brimming with English ale. It was a costly import but profitable to stock. It was amazing how much of it these English and Scandinavian seamen and soldiers could consume at single sitting.

"Aye, that's the best swill I've swallowed in many a day," the sailor sighed contentedly, wiping his mouth with the back of his hand after draining the tumbler at one protracted gulp. "It's been a long and dry voyage from England."

"You come directly from England?" Isaac asked as he set down a second tumbler. Zingarious had told him to watch especially for travelers from that island, wherever it was. This sailor might bring him closer to that coveted tenement.

"Three months out of London town, if you can believe it," the seaman boasted. "I wouldn't think it possible if someone told me the voyage could be so swift. But here I am to prove it. The winds and currents were favorable from London to Rhegium, and our luck held up the rest of the way. No trouble with Moors, Arabs, Normans, or pirates." He hungrily tore a drumstick from the capon Isaac had placed before him.

"You'll be going back soon, I suppose," remarked Isaac, lingering by the table, reluctant to let the conversation drop.

"Returning? It depends. I'm not all that sure. I'd just as soon remain here as go anywhere else." The seaman cut himself a thick slice of bread. "I'm told you can make money here. I'm no captain, as you called me, but I'm a master seaman and know enough to get a ship from here to there. I met one of your nation in London who assured me that the imperial navy needs experienced sailors and pays good money."

Isaac nodded encouragement. Everyone knew there was a desperate shortage of men for the military, few citizens of the empire being willing to serve. The recruiters no doubt went as far afield as Britain in their search for manpower. He knew little of such matters but ventured, "Do you have a letter from the one you met in London to someone in the naval administration?"

The sailor was shamefaced. "Lost it at Rhegium. Lucky to hang onto my purse, not that there's much left in it. Damn the knave who stole most of my belongings. I hope the dog roasts in hell!"

"Sadly, there's evil everywhere," Isaac breathed sympathetically. "You may be in luck though. A customer who comes in here often happens to be a clerk to the logothete of the dromos, the admiralty. If you like, I'll introduce you to him the next time he drops in. He's sure to know something about getting into the navy."

"I'd be grateful for your help," boomed the sailor cheerfully. "To tell the truth, I wasn't expecting to find much of a welcome in Constantinople, but you're a good fellow to take such an interest in a total stranger. I can't imagine what you'd gain by helping me."

"Another good customer, that's what. You'd be dropping in often. By the way, what's your name, friend?"

"Wiglaf, Wiglaf Edmondsson," Edmond improvised, inwardly begging pardon of his companion of Dover days. Not that Wiglaf, wherever he might be, was likely to dispute or resent the borrowing of his name in Constantinople.

"Isaac of Antiochus." The innkeeper extended a hand, delighted by the virtual certainty that Zingarious would be interested in the sailor, who seemed a simple soul. He would immediately inform the imperial bursar of the new arrival from England. In the meantime, he must make sure to keep the seaman in sight. "You'll be staying tonight?"

Edmond nodded. So far, so good. He suspected this overly-solicitous landlord might be the agent communicating with the Blachernae. If he was, he might lead him in some way to Earl Sweyn.

"I'll summon my wench to light the way to your room," Isaac smirked meaningfully. Why let slip an opportunity to pick up a little change in the usual way as well as the reward he expected from Zingarious?

"No, no, I'm tired and all I want is to sink into a soft bed." Edmond suppressed a smile at the host's obvious disappointment. It might have been more sailorlike as well as enjoyable to take a girl to his room but he must be careful. He was not about to trust any woman, not after being betrayed by Edith.

Somewhat forlorn, Isaac lit the way himself, laboriously climbing the steep stairs to a third floor chamber. He rejected a temptation to have his serving men roll the sailor. Normally a lowborn foreigner such as this would be easy prey but it was more profitable to preserve him for Zingarious. He set a tumbler of ale and an oil lamp on a small table before bidding his guest good night.

As soon as the door shut behind Isaac, Edmond searched every corner of the room as well as under the dirty, straw-covered bed. Satisfied he was alone, he secured the door and lay down.

So far his scheme had been successful. The innkeeper had accepted his pretense of being a sailor newly come from England. If Isaac was the go-between he suspected him of being, he was well on his way to entering the Blachernae. Even if the innkeeper was not the agent, several patrons in the tavern had overheard their conversation and one of them might well be an imperial spy. Chances were Sweyn would soon learn of the sailor's arrival. It had been a good evening's work, Edmond told himself, though the goal was to thrust himself into the lion's den. He ran a hand along an inside leg to touch a concealed short dagger. It was comforting to have it handy.

He purposely dawdled in his room the next morning. Once or twice someone rapped on the door but he gruffly demanded to be left alone to sleep late. It was almost noon before he heard the innkeeper's voice. "Master Wiglaf! Open up! I must speak to you right away."

Edmond dressed hurriedly, then threw open the door. "You have good news for me, Master Isaac?"

"Good news, indeed," Isaac puffed importantly. "The very man I was telling you about last night is downstairs. You know, the clerk to the logothete of the dromos. Wonder of wonders, it turns out that he, too, is from England, though he left long since. He'd like you to join him at his table. He's eager for news from your homeland."

Isaac hoped his story sounded plausible, and while telling it fingered a newly-acquired purse dangling from his belt. Zingarious had been generous in his delight at hearing of the sailor's arrival. He had immediately assigned the man downstairs to accompany Isaac back to the Red Lion.

The main hall of the inn was almost deserted except for a scattering of idlers as it was too late for breakfast and too early for a mid-day meal. On entering, Edmond glanced around the room. It would not do if the man Isaac referred to as a clerk of the admiralty turned out to be Arn or—what was less likely—Sweyn himself. His concern vanished when Isaac indicated someone with his back to them who was too stocky to be either of his enemies. The man swung around on hearing Edmond's footsteps. He was a total stranger and obviously not a native of Constantinople, judging by his light skin, blond hair and the straight nose jutting over thin lips.

"Pull up a chair, friend, sit down and share a stoup of good home-brewed ale and something tasty to break your fast, Master Wiglaf." The genial, deep-throated greeting came in English, spiced with a touch of northern accent as the man offered his hand to Edmond. "Don't be surprised. My friend Isaac Antiochus told me your name. I'm Ivor Ulfsson, and I hail from York."

Edmond piled hungrily into a late breakfast while engaging in lively small talk with Ivor.

"Like yourself, Master Wiglaf, I decided some ten years ago that Constantinople was the place to seek my fortune. You know what they say up north about Miklegaard—that's what they call this city—that the streets are paved with gold and jewels and so on. I know better now, but all the same I've managed to make a good living at the naval office, and there are pleasures to be found here one doesn't even dream of back home."

Ivor's smooth chatter amused Edmond, who returned his smile with a grin. What a liar the fellow was. He would willingly wager a year's stay atop one of the countless columns in the city against a clipped obol that Ivor did not even know the location of the office of the logothete of the dromos.

"How long since you left England, Master Wiglaf?"

"Scarce three months?"

"Such a quick voyage! One would think it scarcely possible. Then you must know something of the latest happenings in our homeland, isn't that so?"

"I've always tried to keep up with goings-on," Edmond said noncommittally, determined not to say too much and so ruin his chances of being taken to the Blachernae. He attempted to change the subject. "Isaac Antiochus suggested you might be able to help me with your master."

"My master?" Ivor faltered before recalling his supposed role. "You mean the logothete, of course. I'm ashamed to admit it, and I wish it were otherwise, but I don't have all that much influence with my superiors. I'm merely a humble clerk. Still, I suppose I could help you apply for employment. I do know the ropes, and a proper application can make all the difference."

"I'd be grateful, I promise you." Edmond was increasingly convinced

Ivor was one of Sweyn's men, fortunately not one who knew him. It was time to stop fencing and get to the point. "You didn't mention your master's name. Could it be he's the son of someone named Godwin?"

Ivor replied smoothly without a change of expression, "A strange question. A common name in England but hardly so here. The logothete is Constantine, and I'm not sure, but I believer he's the son of one Michael."

"I must be mistaken then," Edmond replied slowly, staring directly at Ivor. "For some reason I supposed your master's mother might be named Gytha, the wife of someone named Godwin."

Ivor jumped up as if to leave, then thought better of it and sank back onto his chair. "I see you're in the mood to tease me, Master Wiglaf," he chuckled. "No harm intended, I suppose, so I'll go along with your strange humor. What if you were right, which I don't admit in the slightest, what then?" His eyes narrowed. "Your whimsy might even lead you into dangerous territory."

"You alarm me. All I meant is that it's a pity you don't know the man I'm thinking of, the son of Godwin and Gytha, because I've got important news for him." After looking around the room to see whether anyone was watching, Edmond tapped his tunic meaningfully. Ivor heard a slight crackle, as of parchment sewn into the lining.

Ivor made a decision, leaning across the table to whisper, "Strange how your mind plays tricks sometimes. I'd forgotten I once did meet someone who claimed Godwin and Gytha for parents. I don't understand though that anyone would come here all the way from England under the impression this person might be found here in Constantinople. He would be more likely to think him a pilgrim in Jerusalem."

Edmond sensed Ivor was about to yield and sought to remove his last suspicions. "God's will, no doubt, or merely a lucky guess. I thought it best to seek him here before continuing to the Holy Land."

Ivor took a deep breath, gazed intently at Edmond as if to read his mind before breaking into a reluctant smile. "You've landed in fortune's lap. My master is indeed in Constantinople, and I'm willing to take your letter to him if you'll give it to me."

Edmond shook his head. "I certainly would like to entrust it to an honest man like yourself. I wouldn't hesitate to do so for a moment if it wasn't that I have strict orders to personally put it in Earl Sweyn's hands."

If Ivor Ulfsson was startled by Edmond's bold use of Sweyn's name it was not apparent. He studied him momentarily before shrugging his shoulders as if to reassure himself there could be no harm in taking Edmond into the Palace of the Blachernae. One man, a common sailor, was hardly a match for Sweyn's band, let alone a detachment of the imperial guards.

"You were sent by Earl Godwin?" It was almost a statement rather than a question.

"Let's just say I've been entrusted with a message to his son," Edmond temporized, "with orders not to let it out of my hands until I can deliver it. You'll help me carry out my mission?"

"In good time, Master Wiglaf," Ivor replied. "What's the hurry?" It had occurred to him that Edmond might not be alone and he decided to play for time so he could discover whether the sailor had associates. He called for another round of drinks and a set of dice, remarking placidly, "Anyway, it's best to wait for nightfall. There are people in the streets who might make trouble for us if they recognize me."

Much to his disgust and discomfort, Edmond was forced to while away the day in idle chatter and desultory play at dice. Ivor Ulfsson was no fool. The Anglo-Dane repulsed all attempts to turn the conversation to Sweyn. While he appeared to believe Edmond's claims to be an ordinary sailor named Wiglaf and a messenger from Earl Godwin, Ivor was careful not to anticipate Sweyn's attitude toward the newcomer.

The last traces of twilight melted into darkness before Ivor pushed away from the table. "Come, it's time to be going," he told Edmond, fastening his cloak and leading the way out of the Red Lion.

A smile played around Isaac Antiochus's lips as the English sailor followed Zingarious's man out of the brightly-lit inn and vanished into the dark streets. Another such guest and that tenement on the Mese would be his.

Chapter Twenty-Nine

The Prison of Anthemius

A panorama of the vast imperial city spread out behind Edmond and Ivor Ulfsson as they headed for the Blachernae Palace. The seven rolling hills of "New Rome" were outlined imperfectly by the faint light of oil lamps and torches flickering in hundreds of palaces, mansions, monasteries, churches and other public buildings. On the right was the undulating surface of the Golden Horn, curving sharply northward beyond the bridge of the Blachernae until it met the gently-flowing sweet waters of Europe which gave it life. Ahead loomed the sprawling Blachernae complex, embraced protectively by an extension of the enormous landwalls which for seven centuries had maintained the integrity of Constantinople against the furious assaults of Goths, Bulgars, Russians, Arabs and other barbarian nations. Ivor led Edmond toward a rectangular tower which fronted the northernmost portion of the palace. No light shone from the few narrow slits cut high up on the walls, and there was no sign of life within.

Ivor made directly for an enormous metal-reinforced wooden door which interrupted the otherwise unbroken conformity of the stone tower's ground floor. The old structure had been long deserted and its notoriety as the "Prison of Anthemius" was far in its future. Ivor rapped forcefully until the huge door creaked open. Edmond was barely able to make out two people far back from the doorway in the shadows of what was clearly a large chamber. He put his right hand on the dagger sheath at his waist as he followed Ivor past the dark-hooded man who had opened the door and slammed it shut behind them. As they entered, one of the two figures in the background approached, the other hanging back.

"Is this the sailor recently arrived from England?" The voice was Sweyn's. There could be no mistaking the commanding, arrogant tone.

"Yes, my lord," Ivor replied respectfully. "This is the man who claims to bear a message to you from Earl Godwin. He refuses to hand it to me, insisting he was charged by your father to deliver it to you personally."

"You'll understand our reason for not lighting a torch even if I'd prefer to see your face, my friend," Sweyn explained, almost apologetically. "It wouldn't do to have anyone know of our meeting. That's why we chose this usually deserted place." He moved a step closer and Edmond, while holding his ground to avoid rousing suspicion, gathered his cloak's hood more tightly over his head. The action was almost superfluous. It was so dark that even with Sweyn virtually next to him he could barely distinguish his familiar features. Stab and run? He dismissed the impulse as despicable. He was prepared to lure Sweyn into a trap and seize him, or even kill him in the event of combat, but not to murder him outright. Even the notion of assassination was repugnant.

"Well, sailor, where's the letter you've brought from Earl Godwin?" Sweyn demanded impatiently. "You'll be well rewarded, I promise you on my honor."

Edmond assumed a hoarse whisper to lessen the chance of Sweyn recognizing his voice. "It's sewn into my tunic, my lord."

Sweyn snorted. "Well then, man, slit the garment open and hand me the letter. Surely, you have a knife. If you don't, here's my dagger."

Edmond was startled at Sweyn's offer of a weapon. It was as if fate was intervening to tempt him to a crime that went against his grain. He rejected the notion as well as Sweyn's dagger, using his own to slash the tunic, and fished out the letter to hand it to the earl.

Sweyn contemplated the parchment for a moment. "I'll read it at my leisure," he decided. "This is no place for a light." He was struck by a thought. "Tell me, sailor friend, how fares my lord father? Does he remain at Bruges?"

"No, my lord, he has returned to England," Edmond replied, uncomfortably noting that Sweyn's companion, who on his arrival had been waiting with the earl at a distance, was now much closer, having approached during the conversation.

"Earl Godwin is home again!" Sweyn shouted his surprise. "Then he must be back in royal favor. I would never have dreamed he'd be able to return so quickly though I never doubted he'd do so eventually. He always said King Edward couldn't long do without him."

"Your father is master of his broad lands once more and, one might say, of all England," Edmond declared, having decided that the greater the lie the more convincing it would be. He even elaborated. "The great earl landed at Pevensey at Eastertide with a strong force and many of the most influential thanes rushed to his side. Norman exactions and arrogance aroused so much hatred and discontent that most people longed to have them expelled from England. The nearer Earl Godwin approached Southwark, the greater his army grew. In alarm, King Edward restored him to his offices and lands after pardoning him and agreeing to dismiss most of his own Norman advisors."

"It sounds too good to be true," Sweyn interrupted in amazement. "I can't believe such a transformation could take place so quickly or that

King Edward would so readily forgive my father and keep him at his side."

Neither could Edmond, but he pressed on with his tall story. "He did so, my lord, I assure you. The great earl is back at his rightful place as King Edward's most trusted counselor. He is consulted on all of the king's decisions. The only thing wanting to complete his satisfaction is having you, his eldest son, with him again."

Edmond never had suspected he had such a talent for invention. The scope of his imagination staggered him. He had no idea what actually was taking place in England. The last he had heard, and for all he knew was still the case, was that Earl Godwin was disconsolately biding his time at Bruges while his sons Harold and Leofwine were raiding the west coast of England.

"Where's my beloved brother, Harold?" Sweyn asked, as if reading Edmond's mind. His disapproving, even hostile tone made it clear he not only disliked his brother but hoped for news of some misfortune.

"He returned to England at the same time as your father and is reinstated in rank and property," Edmond replied, then embroidered his account even more to play on Sweyn's jealous antagonism toward Harold. "He also has been granted Earl Ralph's former lands."

"He's been given Ralph's domains!" Sweyn growled, biting his lips. Edmond was thankful his smile went unseen. His elation was short-lived. He had failed to notice Sweyn's companion had edged even closer.

A whisper by a familiar female voice froze his blood. "I thought it might be you, Edmond. Now I'm sure."

To his surprise, Edith said nothing else before again receding into the shadows. He drew his dagger again as a precaution but Sweyn was too preoccupied with the unwelcome report of Harold obtaining the lands he considered rightfully his to hear Edith's whisper. "You're prepared to return to England?" Sweyn said at last, more as a command than a question. "I'll have a message for you to take to my father."

Edmond thought it best to play out the game. "If it's your wish, my lord."

"It is. I'd return with you but I must attend to matters here before I can leave Constantinople. When I've had a chance to consider what my father has to say, I'll write a reply. Ivor Ulfsson will hand it to you. He'll also give you money for your trouble. You understand?"

Far better than you realize, Edmond thought. Nevertheless, he replied, "Not quite, my lord."

"By Thor's thunderbolt, what's unclear, man?"

Edmond gambled. It was now or never. Edith might warn Sweyn at any moment—he was surprised she had not already done so—and if she revealed his identity he was doomed. He would never leave alive. Ivor

Ulfsson and the gatekeeper—whom he suspected to be the archer Arn—were at the door nearby and if summoned would be on him in an instant. Gripping the handle of his dagger, he took a step toward Sweyn. "I must speak with you further, my lord," he whispered, glancing at Edith, still a few steps away. Her continued silence puzzled him.

"What else is left to say?" Sweyn grumbled in irritation. "Your reward will be generous, I promise."

"Your father considered some things best unwritten and relied on me to fill you in by word of mouth." Edmond again looked at Edith, who had moved a little nearer but halted when Sweyn gripped him by the shoulder.

"Well, that's another matter," the earl decided. "Come, we don't want to be overheard." He signaled Edith to stay put and led Edmond into a corner of the huge chamber. "What was it that my father preferred not to write down?"

Edmond stealthily drew the dagger from beneath his cloak and moved closer. The earl stiffened with shock and alarm when the cold steel point of the blade touched his neck.

"Summon help and I'll slit your throat," Edmond whispered fiercely.

Despite the blade at his neck, Sweyn thrust his face almost into Edmond's in an attempt to discover his identity. Fortunately for the earl, Edmond anticipated the reaction and pulled back the dagger slightly.

"Ah, it's my young friend, brother Harold's companion in Dover," Sweyn murmured. "I should have guessed as much from what Edith told me. Your voice seemed familiar but I mistook you for one of my father's men."

"I relied on that."

"What do you want of me? Or do you mean to murder me now?"

"Dismiss your men and come with me."

"Do you think I'm fool enough trust you?"

"If you don't accompany me without resisting, I'll do what I must."

"Where do you intend to take me?"

"You'll know when we get there."

"Deliver me to my enemies? Before I accompany you like a sheep led to slaughter I'll see you rot in hell, hired assassin."

Edmond hesitated, unable to bring himself to cut down someone without a weapon in his hand. His indecision was costly. Sweyn flung his mantle over Edmond's dagger hand and charged into him. Knocked off balance, Edmond struggled to disentangle the blade as Sweyn fell back to draw his sword, at the same time shouting for help. Arn and Ivor ran to their leader's assistance. Edmond dropped the cloak barely in time to evade Sweyn's first sword thrust, then plunged into the darkest part of the chamber. He blindly ran a few paces before stumbling through a doorway leading to a spiral staircase. He bounded up the steep steps, followed closely by Sweyn, who fortunately for his adversary was unable to wield his sword in the confined space.

On reaching the top of the stairway, Edmond entered a faintly illuminated passageway. The corridor was lit by moonlight filtering through the window slits of rooms between it and the tower wall. He had put a little distance between himself and the pursuers but they were probably familiar with the layout of the tower and sooner or later would corner him. He decided it was best to stand and fight. He at least could sell his life dearly. He darted into a room but before he could slam a heavy door, Sweyn plunged in after him, sword extended.

Sweyn was breathing heavily, winded by the pursuit up the steep staircase and along the passageway. Nevertheless, rather than pausing to recover, he immediately sought to make short work of Edmond with a sweeping two-handed sword stroke his agile foe was barely able to evade. The attempt leaving Sweyn off balance with his chest exposed, Edmond grimly decided it was no longer time for scruples. He closed in before Sweyn could raise his heavy sword again and plunged the dagger point into his breast. The earl fell with a dying groan as Edward seized the sword from his failing grip. By the time Arn and Ivor Ulfsson arrived, Sweyn was dead and Edmond prepared to resist their assault. Luck favored him. Entering the room with a rush, Ivor tripped over Sweyn's prostrate body and sprawled headlong onto the floor. Edmond immediately skewered him with a thrust and extricated the sword in time to parry a blow by Arn. A brief flurry of swordplay ended when the archer decided he was at an extreme disadvantage against a nobleman in such a confrontation. He retreated to the doorway, then turned and fled pell-mell in the direction from which he had come, almost tumbling down the stairway in his haste to summon help. Edmond rushed out of the room after him, but halted abruptly when to his astonishment he discovered Edith huddled on the corridor floor.

"Sweyn, where's Sweyn?" she stammered, looking up in fearful recognition.

"On your feet!" he urged, reaching to pull her up. "He's in there dead," he added, waving his bloodied sword in the direction of the room where he had left Sweyn's corpse. "Now you're free to rejoin me." He pulled harder but she frantically resisted his efforts to make her stand up.

"Join you? Never!" she spat at him. When he let go of her hand, she surprised him by springing to her feet and attempting to claw at his face. He angrily shoved her back down to the floor. She began to sob violently, curling up. He was at a loss as to his next move. There was no time to waste. Arn would return at any moment with Sweyn's other followers. Any chance of escape would be gone. He made another desperate attempt to pull Edith to her feet.

"Leave me, assassin!" she shrieked and pummeled his arms. She glared, eyes red-rimmed and tear-filled. "Go with you? Never! I'd rather die than submit to Sweyn's murderer." Suddenly, to his surprise, she seemed to yield to his tugging and scrambled to her feet. But instead of following him along the passageway she disappeared into the room in which the bodies of Sweyn and Ivor lay in a pool of blood. He rushed in after her and was appalled to find her clasping Sweyn's corpse, weeping uncontrollably.

He gave up the attempt to drag her away on hearing the approaching clatter of boots and shouts. Arn was returning up the steps with reinforcements. There was no time to lose. He had to abandon Edith and flee. He ran down the passage in the opposite direction. To his relief, he reached another staircase, this one spiraling upward to the tower's third level. It led to another corridor, identical to the one on the floor below. He rushed into the first cell he came to and peered through a wall slit. A full moon now bathed the ground far below in a soft, gentle light. A careful inspection revealed that no one appeared to be guarding the approaches to the tower. All of his pursuers evidently were in the structure. He could hear the faint sounds of shouts, heavy steps and the clatter of weapons on the level immediately below. Arn was undoubtedly having every room searched and his men had not yet discovered the stairway leading further up. On reflection, Edmond realized why his foes had not taken the precaution of surrounding the tower. The only way to exit was through the single doorway on the ground floor. The window slits were too narrow for anyone to pass through.

He ran back into the passage and sprinted to the far end where he found another staircase. This one was short and in a moment he emerged onto the roof. His momentary elation waned when he examined the outer walls of the tower. It was well built, the stones so smoothly and precisely fitted together that he could not discover even the slightest footholds by which to risk an attempt to descend to the ground, perilous as it would be. His only hope, at best slight, was a solitary tree near the south side of the tower. An almost bare branch extended to within a couple of paces of the wall. He just might be able to reach it with a desperate leap. If he missed, the fall from such a great height surely would prove fatal but death was certain if his pursuers caught up with him. He could hear them on the level just below and they would reach the roof at any moment. Steeling his nerves, he carefully gauged the distance to the tree branch. It looked sturdy enough yet might break under the impact of his leap and weight. He smiled grimly. There was no alternative. He dropped the sword to the ground, noting where it landed, then launched himself into the air.

He sighed with relief as the limb bent without breaking under his weight and he was able to hang on until it stopped shaking. Holding his breath, he swung arm over arm along its length until he reached the trunk, then scampered down, careless about skinning his hands and ripping his clothes until he reached the ground.

The growing hubbub far above alerted him that Sweyn's men had reached the roof. Frustrated on discovering that he had eluded them by descending to the ground, they rained curses and threats. Thankfully, they apparently had no missile weapons other than hand axes, useless at such a distance. A few were hurled without effect and he was not about to remain a stationary target. Recovering Sweyn's sword and making sure he still had his dagger, he set off at a run toward the Palace of the Hebdomon.

By the time Sweyn's men reached the ground and resumed their pursuit, Edmond's head start was a half-mile or more. No one could possibly overtake him before he reached the safety of the Hebdomon. The palace guards were loyal to Constantine Monomachus and under orders to admit him at any hour of the day or night.

He ran without exulting in his escape, however, burdened by the memory of Edith's great grief at Sweyn's death and her harsh rejection of himself. He realized for the first time that her attachment to the dead earl had been far deeper than he had ever suspected or perhaps even she had realized.

He clutched at a flicker of hope in her puzzling behavior. She had recognized his voice during the conversation with Sweyn but had not betrayed him.

Chapter Thirty

A Marriage Proposal

The most noble and learned Michael Constantine Psellus, secretary and vestarch to the Basileus Constantine IX Monomachus, humbly requested an audience of Theodora Porphyrogenita three weeks after Earl Sweyn's death and Edmond's escape. The aged spinster in whose brittle imperial veins trickled the sole surviving blood of the great Macedonian dynasty knew Psellus well. Indeed, she frequently consulted the great scholar on literary and artistic questions. On this occasion, however, she awaited the favorite of her co-ruler and brother-in-law with impatient curiosity because evidently he was coming on a political mission.

The empress occupied a modest set of apartments comprising only a small fragment of the sprawling Blachernae Palace that her successors were to greatly embellish and occupy in preference to Constantine IX's more sumptuous abode. She shunned all but mandatory display and pageantry, a taste which might have left her open to damaging accusations of parsimony had not her popularity with the common people been unassailable.

The empress had been surprised upon being informed by a court official of Psellus's intention to visit her though the news was couched as protocol demanded in the form of a humble request to be granted an audience with her most sacred majesty.

"What do you suppose Vestarch Psellus wants of us?" Theodora asked the Patriarch Michael Cerularius who was paying one of his frequent side-entry calls to confer with the empress about joint interests.

Cerularius contemplatively stroked his gray-flecked beard before replying to the tall, thin yet unbent old woman whose brisk stride in pacing the room belied her more than seventy years. "If I weren't aware of our friend's polite and tortuous subtlety, I'd suspect him of being eager to crow over us in this unfortunate affair of that barbarian, Earl Sweyn."

"We're well aware of the high regard Master Psellus has for himself, not that it's entirely unwarranted, but as you say it's unlikely he'd dare boast of having made fools of us."

Theodora halted her nervous pacing to look at a stout, middle-aged clergyman standing deferentially at the patriarch's left. "Reverend

Bishop Alexius Spondylus, what's your opinion?"

"He'll make either a demand or a veiled threat." Spondylus, the patriarch's secretary and closest advisor, hesitated before overcoming a reluctance to be more specific for fear of offending Theodora. "I beg your indulgence, great empress, for venturing on such a distasteful topic but Psellus may ask that the young Englishwoman you've taken under your divine protection be transferred to the great palace."

"That wouldn't surprise me greatly," Theodora rasped. "That would be just like something that old goat, my brother-in-law, would have the temerity to request. Well, he won't have Edith. I've become fond of the girl, wild flower and barbarian as she may be. Given time in court among my women, with a bit of tutoring to refine the rough edges, she might make a suitable bride for one of our noblemen, say Maurice Hyrtacenus. Let that old satyr Constantine content himself with his Alanian slut."

"Your indignation and horror is justified, most sacred majesty," placated Cerularius, "but I can't conceive of Psellus undertaking such a disgraceful commission. He's far too clever and circumspect to risk offending you with such a scandalous request. Besides, the emperor has been unwell and friend Michael loves his university, books and creature comforts too well to risk losing them if Nicephorus Bryennius replaces our divine Basileus Constantine, may God grant him many more years."

"If I may be permitted to add, it's rumored Bryennius is displeased with Psellus," interjected Spondylus. "Our fiery general reportedly sulks in his Macedonian theme because Psellus failed to persuade Constantine to grant him the rank of Caesar."

"This botched affair of the barbarian noble's death may strengthen Bryennius's position," suggested Cerularius. "The basileus may look more favorably on adopting him as heir after what's happened. He's convinced this Earl Sweyn was involved in a plot to stir up the populace against him and that your sacred majesty's agents were behind it."

Theodora sighed. "If only my sainted sister Zoe for once had been content to remain a widow after that foolish fop, the caulker, met his end."

She frowned on recalling the least adroit and most unpopular among Zoe's husbands, the Emperor Michael V Calaphates who eventually had been dethroned and blinded by a mob infuriated by his tyranny. A onetime humble shipyard caulker, he was wafted to high office by his uncle Michael IV, Zoe's second husband. Upon the latter's death, the ever susceptible empress became so enchanted by the former laborer's good looks and superficial charm as to marry him. He repaid such imprudent devotion by driving her out of Constantinople before the people rose to her defense and his doom.

Theodora's usual good humor was restored in wry contemplation of the incredible twist of fortune that elevated a semi-literate caulker to imperial power. She motioned to Cerularius and Spondylus to accompany her into the audience chamber where she would officially receive Michael Psellus, her brother-in-law's envoy.

The empress seated herself upon an ornate gold and jewel-studded throne placed on a high dais. Cerularius and Spondylus positioned themselves to the right of the throne and the commander of the Excubitors, her guards, was on the left. Court officers bearing ceremonial rods, swords and the rhompeia, or heavy axes, formed an inner circle around the throne. Stationed nearby were Theodora's personal bodyguards who kept their eyes respectfully fixed on the floor. The rest of her attendants included ladies-in-waiting, lesser court officials and those senators and nobles courageous or careless enough to risk annoying Constantine IX.

Upon the chamberlain's ringing proclamation that the most noble and high dignitary Michael Constantine Psellus, secretary and vestarch to the Sacred Majesty of the Basileus Constantine, wished to pay his respects to the Basilea Theodora Porphyrogenita, attention swung toward the great hall's entrance. Upon a nod by the empress, the huge bronze door slowly pivoted open.

Vestarch Psellus, clad as simply yet fashionably as his position permitted, led a small entourage toward the high throne. At his heels strode a powerfully-built young man whose martial attire came close to violating the strict code of court ceremonial. He was clad in magnificently gilded armor. A scarlet cloak swung from his shoulders in rhythm with every firm step he took. The insignia of a kometes, the commander of a tagmata of the Varangian Guard, glittered on his steel cuirass.

Edmond's entrance set the court abuzz, making him self-consciously aware of the stir made by his appearance. He suspected his splendid attire and equipment was more suitable for someone of a far higher rank, perhaps even a Caesar or designated heir to the throne. The choice had not been his but that of the emperor who had ordered he be outfitted in trappings nearly equal to his own. Constantine was highly pleased with and impressed by Edmond for putting Sweyn out of the way. The emperor's favor even benefited Godfrid, fully recovered from his wounds, who proudly followed his master, resplendently clad as befitting the squire of an officer high in imperial favor.

Edmond sank to one knee and bowed his head perfunctorily while Psellus and his Byzantine entourage genuflected as protocol required on approaching the empress. The Englishman could not bring himself to touch his forehead to the carpet despite the courtiers' indignant murmurs. Theodora, too shrewd to create a furor even over such a serious matter as court ceremonial, ignored Edmond's offense to warmly receive Psellus.

"We are pleased to see you once more, most noble and learned Vestarch," she breathed graciously, extending a bejeweled wrinkled hand for him to kiss.

"As always, it's a great honor and an unmatched pleasure to be permitted into the presence of your most sacred majesty," Psellus replied humbly. "On this occasion, our delight in being graced by your benevolence is enhanced beyond our ability to express it by beholding in your company such a distinguished servant of God as the most holy of men, our revered Patriarch Michael Cerularius." He inclined his head toward Cerularius while darting a scornful glance at Spondylus, whom he despised.

The patriarch returned a benevolent smile while Spondylus gritted his teeth.

"I must confess, I'm somewhat mystified," the empress began playfully. "I know the pagan gods are mere devilish myths as our religion holds, but you seem to be accompanied by the very semblance of the warlike Mars."

Edmond flushed on grasping the gist of Theodora's attempted witticism as Psellus smilingly put a hand on his shoulder.

"Your sacred majesty is pleased to jest, and I must admit that if Mars did exist—which no true Christian believes—he couldn't have chosen a more appropriate form in which to appear before your greatness. But this young man is the Kometes Edmond Edwysson, a gallant Varangian who has done my gracious master no small service."

"We're only too well aware of it," Theodora snapped. "No doubt he comes to solicit a reward from us." Her sharp response set off a buzz among her attendants, many of whom craned necks for a better look at Edmond. They were astonished at his temerity in daring to show his face before her. Many knew of his role in blunting the alleged attempt of her agents to undermine her brother-in-law's power.

Theodora's frown silenced the crowd before she looked inquiringly at Psellus to demand an explanation.

"Your majesty, the Basileus Constantine commanded the kometes to accompany me in order to permit him to marvel at the brilliance of your court and behold your sacred self," Psellus said deferentially. "As for reward, I suppose one might consider what he longs for in that light. However, his petition must await the request duty requires me to make on behalf of my imperial master."

"Our beloved brother-in-law has no need ever to ask anything of us," replied Theodora with a hint of sarcasm. "He has only to decide what he wishes and we have no choice other than to yield it to him."

Psellus's smile was undiminished. "He prefers to appeal to your well-known generosity and sisterly regard. It has come to his attention that a dozen or more recently arrived young Englishmen and Danes have found refuge—heaven knows from what danger—under the roof of your palace. His imperial majesty would prefer to have them enrolled among the Varangians. With your assent and cooperation, of course."

"It's our understanding that enlistment in the Varangians is voluntary," Theodora observed mildly.

"That ordinarily would be the case. But my master, on learning these men have been deprived by some misfortune of their former leader, has magnanimously decided to put them under his special protection."

Theodora appealed silently to Cerularius. An almost imperceptible nod advised consent. After a first flush of indignation at Psellus's effrontery, the patriarch realized the emperor was offering a gracefully convenient way of shedding an embarrassment. With Sweyn dead, his followers were useless to Theodora's faction.

Theodora grudgingly ordered a court official to see to it that Sweyn's band of cutthroats was put at the emperor's disposal, then turned back to Psellus. "You suggested your young companion may make a request of us. We're not certain he has done us any great service, nevertheless we're disposed to hear his petition."

"His supplication concerns the Lady Edith, the young Saxon woman your majesty has so kindly sheltered in your court."

The empress angrily leaned forward and lifted a quivering right hand. "No further! That's enough! We'll not discuss her. We've taken her under our protection. We'll chose a husband for the girl, she'll marry him, and that's that."

Psellus pretended to be taken aback by the imperial outburst. He was much too suave a diplomat and courtier to admit to understanding Theodora's angry reaction. The vestarch was only too aware of Constantine Monomachus's weakness for women. Turning his palms up in mock astonishment, he protested, "But that's just what I've come to speak about. The basileus has authorized me to consult your majesty on the question of a suitable husband for the Despina Edith."

It was Theodora's turn to be surprised. "Indeed? My brother-in-law has someone suitable in mind? I wasn't aware he took interest in such matters."

"Usually, and rightly, he leaves all such decisions to your superior judgment. This time, however, he fears you might overlook an appropriate husband for the young woman. He believes the Kometes Edmond Edwysson to be an excellent candidate. He hopes your majesty will agree, approve and consent."

Theodora hid her astonishment beneath a practiced veneer of imperial detachment. Her attendants were less guarded, chattering their surprise. Amidst the stir, a few young women tittered readiness to take Edith's place if given the chance. Edmond flushed in embarrassment as he anxiously scanned the crowded room hoping to catch a glimpse of Edith. He failed to find her even among the flock of ladies-in-waiting. Absorbed in his scrutiny, he missed the prolonged look, gradually softening from outright hostility to grudging appreciation, darted at him by the keen-eyed old empress.

Theodora's gaze swung back to Psellus. "It's unlikely we could choose a handsomer consort for our ward," she admitted almost mildly, "and we've been informed the kometes is a capable and resourceful soldier, no doubt a worthy recruit to the Varangian Guard. We've heard of his recent remarkable exploit."

The recall of Sweyn's death renewed her irritation. Her manner became harsh again. "Unfortunately, we've also learned of his unscrupulous behavior, much to our injury and displeasure. We don't deny we'd prefer the Despina Edith be united to someone we favor yet in deference to our dear brother-in-law's request we'll permit her to decide for herself. Let her choose. What could be fairer?"

Though annoyed, Psellus bowed as if to acknowledge the justice and wisdom of the empress's decision while she gave orders to have Edith brought to her side.

Edmond saw Edith emerge from a far corner of the room where she had been hidden among the crowd. Her cool Nordic bearing was set off admirably by the way she was dressed. The deep wine color of her flowing silk gown, cut in the latest fashion, emphasized her delicately pale complexion, only a hint of color tingeing her cheeks. The crowd buzzed in appreciation of her beauty as it parted to permit her to reach the throne. On arriving before the empress, she sank deferentially to her knees and Theodora affectionately placed a hand on her flowing blond tresses.

"Dear child, no doubt you've heard what has been taking place," Theodora began gently. "We don't intend to force you to agree to anything against your will. Speak freely and without fear. Are you agreeable to marrying your young countryman, the Kometes Edmond."

"Never!"

Edith's ringing reply touched off an uproar, the courtiers being shocked, even scandalized by the blunt refusal.

Edmond was thunderstruck by Edith's defiance. He had nursed a spark of hope for a change of heart in the woman he had been forced to abandon while she wept over the man he had killed. During the three weeks since Sweyn's death and his flight from the tower he had almost convinced himself she would forgive him. After all, she had no one else to turn to now that Sweyn was gone. They had shared a great deal, perhaps even affection, at least on the part of one or the other during their time together. If she would just consider calmly and rationally what had taken place she would realize the breach between them was more her fault than his. Even setting aside such considerations, it did not seem possible she would prefer for a husband some foreigner whose customs and language were so different from her own.

At a kindly word from Theodora, Edith rose from her knees and the empress clasped her hands in hers. "Have no fear, my dear. While our brother-in-law has left us little say in most things, we'll have our way in this matter." She turned to Psellus. "You have your answer, no mistake about that. Let it content your master, as it does us."

Before Psellus could reply, Edmond intervened boldly. "Your majesty, if you would grant me one other request."

The courtiers held their breath at this enormous breach of etiquette but rather than taking umbrage the empress responded, almost as if amused. "Indeed! What do you ask of us?"

"I'd like to speak privately to the Lady Edith."

Theodora shot an inquisitive glance at Edmond as if to read his mind before making up hers, then said softly to Edith, "It's up to you, my dear?"

Edith replied faintly, "If he wishes and you consent, I'll speak with him. But my mind's made up. Nothing he can say will change anything."

Theodora beckoned to two ladies-in-waiting. "Anna and Maria, please accompany the Despina Edith to a side chamber and permit this young man to speak to her in your presence. But on no account leave them alone together."

The three women led the way as Edmond, accompanied only by Godfrid, followed into a small room next to the audience hall. Edith's companions retired to the far side of the room, keeping eyes fixed on Edith and Edmond. Each hesitated to speak first, though not for fear of being overheard because they were sure their companions knew no English.

A mixture of remorse and pity stirred Edmond as he studied her wan, accusing yet lovely face. How much danger, trouble and sorrow he had exposed her to in allowing her to accompany him from England. He was still unsure as to the depth of his affection for her. Maybe she served only as a balm for the deep wound left by Adele's rejection of his heartfelt and sincere devotion.

Edith read his look of pity and smiled faintly. "No, you needn't feel sorry for me. I believe I'll be happier here than I've ever been in my life."

"Then you were unhappy with me?"

"Not always," she admitted, reaching out as if to touch his arm before thinking better of it. "There have been times... but it does no good to speak of such matters."

"Yes, Edith, let's speak of our happier days together," he cried. "They can return if you wish." Surprised by his fervor, he paused before taking another tack. "Come, if you don't want me, I'll accompany you back to England where you're more likely to be happy."

"No, Edmond, no. We're too deeply divided now. I couldn't spend a moment alone with you without remembering what you did to Earl Sweyn." Her eyes flooded and she looked away. "I mustn't speak of that. I might become too angry to control myself. It's best to forget the past and to make the best of whatever the future holds for me here."

"You don't regret leaving Ashdowne Forest then?" he asked unexpectedly.

She bristled with indignation. "How could you ask such a question? You know how happy I was to leave with you." She realized he was teasing when he smiled broadly. She refused to be placated. "How can you laugh at me after all that's happened?" She clasped her hands as if in prayer. "Oh, Edmond, how I wish that you and Sweyn had not been such bitter enemies. You might have accomplished a great deal together." Carried away by enthusiasm, she gripped his arm for an instant and he thrilled at the touch. "For the sake of what has passed between us, I must try not to condemn you for killing him. But it's best we never see each other again. The empress has been kind to me and I'm resigned to accepting whatever she intends for my future."

She was right, of course. It was best for her to remain in Constantinople. She was in the empress's favor, no small thing, and was assured of a splendid marriage to a man of good family and wealth. Such a prospect was undoubtedly preferable to union with some obscure rustic nobleman of England.

In resigned acceptance, Edmond reached for Edith's hands and she did not try to withhold them. "I don't know when, if ever, I shall return home. It may be many years hence as I've good reason to avoid both King Edward's men and those of Earl Harold. But when I do return, I'll visit Ashdowne Forest and think of you and the time we spent there together."

She gazed at him, then as if frightened by her thoughts hastily withdrew her hands from his grasp. "Where are you bound now, Edmond?"

"I've been assigned to a frontier outpost in the land of Bulgaria to the north. It seems a people called the Petchenegs have violated a truce and there'll be a punitive campaign in the spring."

She shook her head sadly. "Oh, Edmond, at moments I feel drawn to you, but I've never felt able to trust my feelings because I don't understand you. One moment you're so hard, so purposeful, so merciless, the next you are thoughtful, kind even gentle. I've never known anyone so changeable, so unpredictable. What moves you and what do you want of life?"

"A kingdom, dear Edith," he laughed hollowly, drawing such a strange look from her that he fumbled at his cloak to hide his confusion.

"Kingdom indeed!" she scoffed, then added seriously, "I'll pray to God that you find whatever it is you seek." She impulsively seized his right hand and kissed it. The surprising action rooted him to the spot in shock while she darted out of the room and her companions hurried after.

He was lost in reflection until Godfrid attracted his attention. "Master Psellus sends word it's time to leave, Thane Edmond."

"I come," he replied hoarsely, staring blankly at the doorway through which Edith had vanished. He convulsively twisted the silver ring around his finger. "I go."

He forced himself to follow Godfrid back to the reception hall, muttering almost as if in despair, "I must always come and go.

"Good-bye, dear Edith. Good-bye forever!"

Chapter Thirty-One

Suicide Mission

The Strategus Nicephorus Bryennius stomped out of the headquarters building of the great fortress of Silistria and laboriously ascended a spiral staircase to a walkway atop its massive outer walls. Reaching an observation post, he stared gloomily at the dreary, desolate waste skirting the far bank of the broad and muddy Danube River. He angrily crumpled the dispatch handed to him earlier by a young officer who followed a few deferential steps behind to patiently await the commanding general's pleasure.

Bryennius was not caught off guard by this latest report of a raid into Roman territory by the barbarian Petchenegs inhabiting the lands to the northeast of the river. It had been a harsh winter of 1055-56, and the nomads must have suffered great losses to their cattle herds. Now that an unusually mild spring was at hand, it was inevitable they should endeavor to make good by plunder the depredations of nature. Fear of reprisals did not deter them even though Bryennius had repeatedly punished them in the past, most notably by destroying a great horde of invaders at Chariopolis in 1050. He placed no faith in the treaty of peace for thirty years exacted from their leaders after his victory.

Yet it was not the barbarian threat that troubled Bryennius as he paced along the top of the wall. He was irritated far more by a recent imperial order to remain indefinitely at this remote frontier post. He had hoped to return soon to Constantinople so he could cultivate his relations with Empress Theodora. Some years before he had nursed great expectations of being nominated by Constantine IX as his heir in preference to the emperor's own nephew, Theodore Monomachus. But Constantine had died two years earlier without having named a successor. With her co-ruler buried, Theodora's loyal supporters among the populace and military were able to strengthen her grip on sole power. Bryennius's enemies persuaded her to banish the general and confiscate his vast estates. He was forced to hide in disgrace for a year until it became apparent even to Theodora that a deteriorating military situation required her to recall him as the empire's most experienced and ablest general. Theodora grudgingly restored his offices and property, and sent him to defend Roman Bulgaria from depredations by its neighbors. With Theodora now in her mid-seventies—or even older,

Bryennius suspected—it was unbearable for a man of his noble birth and prestige, a potential successor to the throne, to be kept distant from the seat of power when it might fall vacant at any moment. He was only too familiar with the universal conviction that "whoever rules Constantinople rules the empire".

His musings were interrupted by the officer at his elbow. "Your excellency, the Kometes Edwysson has reported to receive your orders."

"Ah, what did you say?" Bryennius responded. "Well, let's return to my office." As he and his aide descended the steps to ground level, Bryennius smoothed out the crumpled dispatch and scanned it again though he knew its brief contents by heart.

Near New Arcadiopolis? That was the grandiosely named hamlet twenty or so miles downstream, near the point at which the Danube jogged sharply northward. A band of two or three hundred Petchenegs had crossed the river during the night, apparently careful to keep their distance from the castella protecting New Arcadiopolis. It was likely they were headed for the district around the Haemus Mountains to the south. They had not raided that area for years and might be counting on the lowland villages' renewed prosperity since their last descent. Bryennius pursed his lips, vowing he would teach the barbarians a lesson, then was struck by an idea. By the time he sat down in the headquarters office, he had formulated a new plan. He smiled in satisfaction when Kometes Edwysson reported in obedience to his summons.

Bryennius scrutinized Edmond sharply. Other than a tiny scar upon his right cheek, Edmond's physical appearance had changed little during four years of active duty. He still looked somewhat boyish if visibly more somber than in the past. The most marked change was in the way he bore himself, with far greater self-assurance and the air of a veteran officer used to command. The general was impressed by this model soldier of the empire.

"Kometes, you know the Petchenegs are back at their usual tricks."

"So I've been informed, Your Excellency."

Bryennius pulled himself to his feet and looked out a window, gazing at the muddy Danube, rendered turbulent by a quick spring thaw. The mudflats, ordinarily in sight at this point in the river, were submerged by the rising waters. Several naval craft were huddled at the foot of the fortress walls on the riverside.

Bryennius spun around. "Edwysson, I've studied your record. You've earned an excellent reputation. Your intrepid conduct during the storming of the walls of Pernik during the Bulgar uprising was a feat worthy of Digenes Akritas."

Edmond flushed at the pairing of his name with that of the legendary

Byzantine hero because of his recent exploit of being the first man over the wall in the storming of a barbarian stronghold. He bowed slightly to acknowledge the compliment.

"But you're undoubtedly aware I didn't summon you in order to discuss your exploits, worthy as they've been. I desire to give you an opportunity to further distinguish yourself in the service of our beloved Empress Theodora." Bryennius resumed his chair and beckoned to Edmond to move closer. "It's not easy for a foreigner, even a Varangian of noble descent, to win promotion, especially to high command, but there have been exceptions." An ingratiating smile suggested Edmond might join the select few.

Bryennius then leant forward, cupping chin in hand. "I'll be frank. The forces under my command in this Paristrian Theme are pitifully inadequate. I'd be hard put to scrape together enough men to form a turma. Imagine! The Strategus Nicephorus Bryennius, who has commanded as many as fifty thousand, would find it difficult to assemble five thousand." As persuasive as Bryennius' bitter tone sounded, Edmond knew better though he could not have guessed the reason for the general's dissimulation. Bryennius could certainly field a thematic army of fifteen thousand to twenty thousand men. Whatever the reason for the deception, it was no concern of his so he nodded sympathetically. After the pause to emphasize his alleged plight, the strategus resumed. "As you can understand, we're strapped for troops and have few to spare for special duty. That's why we've called for you. Basil Skleros recommends you as the ideal officer to command a small detachment for a difficult assignment against these pestilent Petchenegs. I've done my best to scrape up a pentarchy of infantry and two of trapezitae for the mission."

Edmond's force then was to comprise one hundred foot soldiers and two hundred cavalry, hardly a formidable command. It might suffice, however, to block the raiding Petcheneg band's advance, force it back across the river, and watch for similar incursions.

Edmond assumed that would be his mission until Bryennius explained further.

"I know what you're thinking, kometes," he smiled. "I suppose you've familiarized yourself with our manuals of warfare, such as the Strategion and Tactica. Their advice on how to pursue and destroy such marauding bands is admirable. But that's not the sort of task I've in mind for you. Something more striking is needed. Your assignment is to cross the river and teach the entire Petcheneg people a lesson they won't forget soon. There are said to be at least four or five encampments within four days' journey of the Danube. You must find, attack and destroy. Kill and burn! No prisoners! I expect your return in ten or twelve days. Any questions?"

Edmond was appalled and perplexed by Bryennius's orders. An occasional punitive raid into Petcheneg territory was salutary, even essential to keep the barbarians in check. They were customarily executed by swift cavalry units unaccompanied by slower infantry or carried out by a far larger combined force than the one entrusted to him. Skillful horsemen, the Petchenegs could gallop away from a small unit of heavy infantry or encircle it and harry it to destruction with practiced archery. The order by Bryennius to penetrate so deep into the barbarians' territory with a limited force risked its total annihilation. Edmond realized he was being sent on a suicide mission.

But why? He suspected that rather than wishing to drive off or destroy the small band of Petchenegs who had crossed the river, Bryennius sought to create a major confrontation. If he gave the Petchenegs an opportunity to wipe out the three hundred men under Edmond's command, the resulting alarm in Constantinople would provide a pretext to concentrate his forces from the entire Paristrian Theme. He also could call for reinforcements to be sent from other parts of the empire. With a large army under his command, he would be prepared for the moment when the throne of the Caesars became vacant. That time could not be far off. It was even possible that he might not wait for Theodora's death but would march on Constantinople in an attempt to seize the crown. Edmond hid his thoughts when answering Bryennius' inquiry as to whether he had any questions. "No, my lord Strategus, I understand you perfectly."

Bryennius glanced at him quizzically but could read nothing into the kometes' impassive face. He slapped hands together in satisfaction. "Then there's no more to be said. Quartermaster Skleros will see to it that you're adequately supplied, and I'll arrange for the naval drungarius, Manuel Angelos, to transport your force across the river tonight. But I want to see you again before you set out."

Edmond saluted and turned to leave, the thought flashing through his mind that Bryennius might intend to give him a message to carry to hell. Once across the river and deep in Petcheneg country, he and his troops would have little chance of returning alive. He shrugged. No use complaining. It was all part of a soldier's life. He would attempt to carry out Bryennius's orders and do his best to avoid a disaster.

If he had been clairvoyant, he might have felt a twinge of sympathy for Bryennius who as it turned out was nearer to misfortune than he was. A few months after sending Edmond across the Danube, Bryennius marched on Constantinople upon hearing of Theodora's death. His attempt to seize power failed and he was blinded at the orders of the new emperor, Michael Stratiocus, an aged general the empress on her

234

deathbed chose to be her successor.

Edmond returned to the barracks in a somber mood. He was under orders to lead several hundred fine soldiers to almost certain destruction. Nevertheless, he summoned his five lieutenants, the pentekontarchai, and ordered them to prepare the troops to set out at nightfall. He next went to the arsenal to requisition supplies.

"A sticky job," Drungarius Skleros remarked after delegating to a subordinate the task of issuing equipment and provisions to Edmond's troops. "I can't say I envy you even if I did recommended you to the strategus as the best man for it. I suppose you know your cavalry will be Magyars?"

"I thought I was to get two trapezitae of regulars."

"It comes to the same thing, two hundred light horsemen, much more mobile than the heavy cavalry. A match anytime for the Petchenegs. Bela the Short's band."

Skleros was probably right. The Magyars were less disciplined than the heavily-armored Byzantine cataphracts but far more mobile and better suited for skirmishing in open country. They might even be trusted now that they were converted to Christianity, which separated them even further from the pagan Petchenegs.

The final preparations for the expedition were the loading of supplies adequate for two weeks into the carts and the transfer of a medical officer and two assistants to the little army. This done, Edmond returned to quarters where he found Godfrid laying out his equipment for the expedition. "Pack only my field kit," he ordered as he threw himself on the bed for a brief rest. "Bundle up my other personal effects separately."

Godfrid was startled. Now approaching seventeen, he had grown into a tall, sturdy youth who handled himself so adeptly few people at first glance were aware of his shriveled arm. He looked questioningly at his master.

"You're going to take some things to England for me," Edmond explained.

Godfrid in amazement dropped a pair of Edmond's finest boots and gaped at him. "We're returning to England?"

"You. You're leaving first, and I'll follow in a few days. You know I hate to let you out of my sight lest you get in trouble but I think it best we travel separately."

It took effort to appear cheerful. He was resigned to accepting fate's decree for himself but saw no reason to waste Godfrid's life in a hopeless situation. He had often permitted the lad to accompany him in minor skirmishes as his shield-bearer and Godfrid had acquitted himself well. This was another matter. The Petchenegs were unlikely to burden themselves with a crippled prisoner though they might hold officers for ransom or spare some sturdier captives as slaves. The notion of being held for ransom almost amused him. Who would bother to retrieve him from the Petchenegs? Certainly not Strategus Bryennius or one of Empress Theodora's advisors who probably had not forgotten his role in Sweyn's death. As for Psellus, the learned scholar cum politician was said to be sheltering in a monastery, riding out the storm while his enemies held power. Ransom was inconceivable. No matter, but if he could not hope to survive he at least would make certain Godfrid did by sending him to England with one of the merchants stopping off at Silistria on their northwestward journey home.

"But Thane Edmond, who'll attend you, who'll take care of your weapons and armor if I leave?" Godfrid almost wailed.

Edmond patted the lad's back. "You and I are soldiers, Godfrid. We obey orders without question. Do you remember when we left Ashdowne Forest? You swore to serve me. I've not forgotten and nothing has changed between us since. Trust me. I'm doing what's best for us both."

He emptied the better part of the contents of his purse upon the bed. "Take this. It'll be enough not only to pay for your trip home but keep you until I return. When you arrive at Dover, ask for Master Aegelsig, the armorer. If the good man is still alive, he'll keep you for my sake. If not, no doubt you'll find other employment. You've become a handy lad, old enough to take care of yourself."

Godfrid disconsolately scooped up the coins, accepted several items Edmond told him to take to England, and added them to his few belongings. He made no further protest but an occasional tear betrayed his dismay.

Bela the Magyar entered Edmond's quarters at twilight. He was a short, bandy-legged soldier who walked as if he had been lowered from his saddle to the ground without being given a chance to unbend his legs. He bore scars from innumerable skirmishes, some on behalf of his current Byzantine employers, many against them before they had enrolled his band on the imperial payroll.

He saluted Edmond by raising a hand over his head. "My men are ready to move out at your orders, kometes," he reported in fractured Greek made even less intelligible by his harsh Magyar accent.

"Your scouts have reconnoitered the far bank?"

"There's nothing human alive on the other side of the river within ten miles," Bela asserted confidently. His tone implied that if there had been, it was no longer the case.

"That's well. We can cross unopposed. Be prepared to move out when it's completely dark."

Godfrid helped Edmond buckle on his armor, handed him his sword and dagger, then placed his field equipment into a baggage cart.

Edmond reached out his right hand to the lad who had so faithfully served him for five years. "Cheer up, Godfrid," he comforted. "We're soldiers, you and I. We part only to meet again." His tone exuded conviction, but he felt none.

Godfrid could only nod, too choked up to speak, gripping his master's hand as if he did not intend to ever let go. He finally stumbled back into the barracks, there to privately give full vent to his feelings.

Edmond strode to the parade ground to inspect his troops, including the hundred Thracian veterans who had served him well for two years. His first command, a banda of Varangians, long since had been recalled to Constantinople. The Thracians, if not equal in fighting spirit to the fierce Varangian axmen, were not to be despised. Most had seen a decade or more of service against the Petchenegs and Bulgars. Their equipment was excellent and morale high. Armed with spears and swords, they wore heavy ring mail coats over leather tunics, far better protected than the Magyars in formation behind them who relied on their swift ponies and agility. Those were mostly small, swarthy men upon shaggy mounts, armed with lances and bows. It was a pity, Edmond reflected, to waste such a fine body of men on so hopeless an expedition. It was little consolation that the Petchenegs were unlikely to get off cheaply before destroying them.

After completing the inspection, he made sure the number of non-combatants accompanying his troops was held to a maximum of under two hundred, including cart drivers. This gave him a total command of about five hundred people. Quite a little army, he reflected with more sorrow than pride as he and Bela reported to Bryennius for final instructions.

The strategus peered dreamily at them, nervously lacing his fingers.

"You're probably not aware of it, but some eighty years ago the Basileus John Zimisces of blessed memory forced Grand Duke Sviatoslav of Kiev to abandon this very fortification, then considered pursuing him across the great river."

Edmond's knowledge of Byzantine history was sketchy at best but he nodded anyway, wondering what this lecture was leading up to.

Bryennius continued, "He probably would have taken his army across had not more pressing matters elsewhere required his immediate attention. But who's to say such an expedition is impracticable. Though Kiev is far beyond the Petcheneg's territory, exploring the route toward it might be worthwhile to determine just how difficult it would be to reach that great and reputedly wealthy city." Bryenniius smiled at Edmond's obvious astonishment and paused to let his words sink in.

Edmond was torn between skepticism and reluctant admiration. It was just possible that Bryennius was contemplating some Caesarian expedition to the northeast in order to raise his prestige in the empire. After all, the great Julius had won Rome by conquering Gaul and Bryennius might hope to prevail in Constantinople by seizing Kiev. It seemed an outrageously far-fetched scheme, but perhaps Julius Caesar's subordinates had thought the same of his venture.

"This will give you something to think about on your march," Bryennius resumed. "We can discuss it in more detail when you return. You have your orders. Carry them out in the Roman way and I'm certain you'll accomplish your mission." He waved dismissal.

On leaving the strategus, Edmond concentrated his thoughts on the task at hand rather than speculating about Bryennius's alleged ambition and sincerity. As soon as it became dark, his little army of five hundred men, horses, equipment and baggage was loaded on a flotilla of naval boats and transported across the Danube, broad yet shallow at this point. It landed on a firm section of the far bank which for miles in either direction was mostly swampy. Edmond ordered his men to immediately move away from the embankment to higher ground to avoid the hazard of baggage carts sinking into the sticky black mud. Guides picked a safe route through the mudflats to lead the troops to a line of grass-covered hills on one of which Edmond established a marching camp.

The night was half over by the time Edmond, after inspecting the hastily thrown-up camp, approached his tent. He was too worked up to go to sleep immediately and lingered outside with his executive officer, Pentekontarchus John Lakanodrakon. The young scion of a family of rich landowners in the Adrianople district, was fond of philosophy and history. He could quote with ease both Plato and the two Plinies, more often than not to the annoyance of his less well-educated friends. Edmond, however, enjoyed his conversation, hungering as he did for information, no matter the source. Since Lakanodrakon's arrival in his command a year earlier, he had spent many enjoyable hours with his erudite subordinate.

Almost inevitably near the broad Danube, their thoughts turned to Marcus Aurelius, the revered emperor-philosopher who had campaigned in this very region almost nine hundred years earlier.

"It may have been near this very place the emperor wrote the greater part of his Meditations," Lakanodrakon surmised, gazing mistily at the stars which had shifted position only slightly in the nine centuries since Marcus Aurelius's day.

"I've been told he wrote something about accepting one's fate without lamentation because we could in no way change the course of our lives." remarked Edmond, whose formal education had included little history and less philosophy.

"I suppose you could interpret the Stoic philosophy in some such rough way," his companion replied, hard put to keep from laughing at his commander's ignorance. But then the kometes was little more than a barbarian if undoubtedly a fine fellow. As if in afterthought, Lakanodrakon added, "More to the point, kometes, is the Stoic view that the ideal person is the wise man who suppresses his emotions and governs the world through self-control."

"Governs the world through self-control," Edmond slowly repeated the phrase, trying to absorb a difficult idea heard for the first time. It was fascinating, perhaps even the key to the lifelong quest imposed on him by descent from the royal line of Wessex. Possibly it even implied he could not hope to govern anyone, let alone the English people, until he learned to control himself. "I'm intrigued by how you've phrased this concept," he remarked to his companion. "It reveals a great deal and perhaps someday I may grasp its deeper meaning. For the present, I must be content with the way I understand it. We're best off accepting our fate because it's sure to be upon us soon."

After that cryptic remark, he told Lakanodrakon good night and went to bed.

Chapter Thirty-Two

Campaign of Terror

The frequent flare-up of smoldering campfires outlined the ring of wagons surrounding the encampment in which the Petchenegs slept, serenely unaware of imminent danger. Under cover of darkness, Edmond led his force to within a few hundred feet of the settlement deep in the barbarians' territory. Not even the nomads' cattle were conscious of the nearby enemy because the little army approached from downwind.

The kometes held a council of war on a slight eminence that hunched like a wart upon the mostly level grassland. Bela the Magyar quietly explained the layout of the area surrounding the settlement to the assembled officers. The scouts had swept a huge arc of territory in advance of the northeastward route of Edmond's little army. The Magyars took care not to permit the Petchenegs guarding the outlying herds suspect their proximity. When the scouts discovered the settlement, Edmond ordered a forced march in order to press a night attack.

When Bela finished, Edmond made sure his officers had no questions before he added, "I see you gentlemen understand the situation. I propose we split the cavalry into two bodies, one to attack from north, the other from the higher ground to the west. Pentekontarchus Vatatzes, you will stay back with your infantry to protect against an attempt to raid our baggage. The rest will move into position for the assault."

He signaled Bela to remain behind when the other officers dispersed so he could caution, "It's imperative your men cut down the sentries before they can raise the alarm. There must be no warning."

"Only a few guard the cattle," Bela shrugged. "My men have marked their positions. The enemy suspects nothing, not this far from the Danube."

"I hope you're right. If that's the case, we've got an excellent chance of success without losing many men. All that's needed now is to coordinate the assault. Watch for a torch to be lit here, then move in."

Bela acknowledged his understanding, then hobbled off to join his horsemen with the awkward, bowlegged gait of someone unused to being afoot.

Edmond stared toward the dancing darts of red-yellow-blue flames scattered throughout the Petcheneg compound. He was hardened to the sight, sound and smell of blood, death and destruction after four years of frontier duty but what lay ahead gave him pause. Few other than the occasional pious Byzantine missionary amongst the pagans gave second thought to the incessant bloodshed and atrocities. He reminded himself that, given the chance, the Petchenegs would have no qualms about slaughtering his men. The certainty fortified his resolve to be ruthless. Not a single barbarian—of whatever sex or age—must be allowed to survive. If just one individual escaped to spread the alarm a Petcheneg horde would swoop down on his troops long before his heavy infantry could retrace the four-day march from Silistria. It was surprising enough that they had penetrated so deep into Petcheneg territory without having been detected.

He had no doubt of the success of the night assault. Judging by the extent of the encampment, it held no more than three or four hundred fighting men. The advantages of surprise, darkness and the overwhelming superiority in combat at close quarters of his Thracian heavy infantry would make the Petchenegs easy victims, especially as they were unused to hand-to-hand fighting on foot. He struggled to overcome qualms about making sure there were no survivors, reminding himself of the Emperor Basil II, nicknamed Bulgarocrator (Slayer of the Bulgars). The ruthless basileus had ordered the blinding of fifteen thousand prisoners taken in battle, leaving one eye to a single captive so he could lead his sightless comrades back to their homeland. Edmond steeled himself to look upon the Petchenegs just as Basil II had on the Bulgars, vermin to be exterminated without mercy.

When Pentekontarchus Lakanodrakon reported all units in position, Edmond inspected each one. He was pleased at how fit his men looked, remarkably so considering their near-forced march of four days. Their equipment also was in good order. He rejected the notion of having them smear their armor with mud to minimize reflection. The heavily-clouded sky made that unnecessary. It could not have been darker. He contented himself with impressing on his officers the advantage of spreading out their units so the encampment would be stormed on a wide front.

He returned to the hillock where he had held council and waited until Bela's Magyar cavalry wheeled into position. On being satisfied all was ready, he had a torch lit as the signal for the launching of the attack. With sword bared, he led the infantry at a slow trot toward the encampment. At first only the occasional clash of shield against armor sounded above the dull, almost rhythmic tread of the heavy boots of the one hundred and fifty men. That was soon reinforced by the drumming of horse hooves as the Magyars converged on the encampment from several directions. Soon the bewildered and half-asleep Petchenegs were stumbling out of their tents only to be met by the war cries of the Magyars and their leveled spears.

Within moments the formerly peaceful quiet of the night changed into a scene of hellish horror as Edmond's horsemen and infantry spread death and destruction. Riders bearing blazing torches swooped on the wagons and hide tents to set them afire. Half of the defenders were soon dead or wounded, the rest screaming in terror or shouting in frustration and despair as the merciless massacre raged. In the confusion, however, a few dozen defenders succeeded in gathering into a body to offer more determined resistance.

Warriors, old men, women and children crumpled in bloody heaps outside the tents, speared by the horsemen or cut down by the infantry's swords. Many perished inside the burning tents, their screams mercifully muffled by asphyxiating smoke before flames enveloped them. Edmond sat impassively on horseback, watching the slaughter without taking part, though splattered by blood, some of which outlined in red the delicate tracery of his gilded cuirass.

The smoke, flames, heat and all-pervading stench of burning flesh and hides were overpowering. At times the infantrymen found it difficult to distinguish the Magyar horsemen from the few-armed Petcheneg survivors being driven toward them from other sections of the settlement. More through luck than design, the Petchenegs who had been able to come together despite the Thracian infantry's furious onslaught were reinforced by others fleeing the Magyars. The united group was able to form a circle upon a small patch of higher ground. This eye of the holocaust quickly became the main target of a renewed assault by the Thracians. Edmond diverted the Magyars to the vital task of encircling the encampment in order to cut down anyone attempting to escape.

He finally decided to join in the assault by his infantry. Wielding his broadsword with both hands, he beat down the feeble defense of a Petcheneg armed with only a light lance. He sheared off the unfortunate man's right arm at the shoulder as neatly as if he had struck with a cleaver. The nomad gaped grotesquely at him, then fell in a heap, blood gushing from his body, his arm lying several feet away.

The kometes stepped back now that he had done his duty by taking part in the attack, planted his sword in the dirt, and leaned on the pommel as he surveyed the final stages of the conflict. Fewer than twenty Petchenegs, some wounded, remained on their feet but fought on, knowing they could expect no quarter. The destruction in the village was almost total, though now and then a Roman would discover someone still alive, often feigning death. They were immediately

242

dispatched whether man, woman or child. Occasionally a survivor would leap up and sprint toward the outskirts of the settlement only to meet death at a Magyar's hands. Even as Edmond rested on his sword, a boy darted past him, screaming in terror as he fled from a pursuing Thracian. When the lad tripped on a corpse lying in his path, the pursuer caught up and swept off his head with a single sword stroke. The body staggered a few more steps while the severed head struck the ground to bounce at Edmond's feet.

The last Petcheneg died at dawn, his body crowning a heap of mangled corpses in the middle of the camp. Some burned-out tents continued to smolder, augmenting the acrid stench of blood and scorched human flesh hanging heavily in the morning mist.

Surrounded by his officers, Edmond reclined wearily upon a grassy knoll that was moist with morning dew and viewed the widespread desolation more with sadness than satisfaction. The first part of his distasteful mission was a success. When reports of this bloody massacre spread, they should strike terror into the hearts of the entire Petcheneg nation. The nomads inhabiting the vast area from the Danube to the Don had been forcefully reminded there was no escaping the avenging long arm of the Byzantine Empire. Superstitious as the barbarians were, they might even believe their pagan gods had deserted them to favor the Romans. It might be a long time before raiders again dared cross the Danube in violation of the treaty pressed on them by Strategus Nicephorus Bryennius. Yet Edmond considered it important to drive the lesson home even more forcefully by destroying at least one more camp before retiring to Silistria.

While he rested, most of his troops were engaged in stripping the barbarian corpses of valuables. They tore precious metal rings and heavy gold armbands from the men and assorted jewelry from the women. Great heaps of other loot such as weapons, hides and valuable fabrics piled up in the baggage carts. Lakanodrakon brought Edmond the most impressive item of all the plunder, a jewel-encrusted skull formed into a ceremonial drinking cup. Edmond balanced it in his right hand and examined it carefully, wondering if it was the relic of one of his precursors, another Byzantine commander who had similarly penetrated deep into Petcheneg territory only to meet a grisly end.

A few choice head of cattle were slaughtered to restock the supply of provisions and the rest of a large herd were stampeded because to drive them to Silistria would slow the return march unacceptably.

The casualty list surprised and relieved Edmond who had expected far greater losses. The butcher's bill was astonishingly short considering how fiercely the barbarians had resisted. Twelve Thracians and seven Magyars had been killed and fewer than two score men over-all wounded. Most of the injured would be able to continue on the march. Those in serious condition were entrusted to a group of non-combatants whom he instructed to return to Silistria and report his initial success to Bryennius.

At mid-morning he called for an end to the looting, and ordered the laying out of a proper marching camp. His men fed and housed, Edmond retired to his tent to catch up on sleep the rest of the day. He intended to set out that night for the next Petcheneg hamlet. Bela's scouts reported it was less than two days' march to the northeast.

By the time he awoke it was dark and he noted with hungry satisfaction that a portable table had been laid out. He invited Lakanodrakon to join him for the meal.

"Tell me, John, do you think Marcus Aurelius would have been able to justify what we've done?" Edmond asked as he washed down a spartan repast with a refreshing light wine. "Would he have maintained that the Petchenegs we've slaughtered were fated to die as they have?"

Surprised at the question, Lakanodrakon replied hesitantly, "How else could anyone explain what's taken place? Yet it's possible such carnage, justified and necessary or not, might have dismayed him. Even savages can be objects of pity and compassion."

"Believe me, my friend, such a bloody undertaking sickens me as well. I would have preferred to take prisoners, but the risk was too great. Even if we had been able to allow ourselves to let any of them surrender, I'm not sure it would have been a great mercy to enslave these freeborn barbarians. What did Marcus Aurelius write about slavery?"

"I'm not certain, but I believe he considered slavery a crime against the brotherhood of man."

"Not unlike someone I knew in my homeland," Edmond said, recalling Wulfstan's impassioned words. How fiercely the prior had denounced the slave market at Bristol.

"For my part, whether it's right or wrong, I don't know how we could manage our households or cultivate our land without using slaves," Lakanodrakon remarked. "As it is, we're short of help on my family's estates and much of our property is suffering from neglect."

"You won't solve your family's problems on this campaign, that's for sure," Edmond replied dryly. "Our orders are to spare no one, take no prisoners, spread havoc and fear. We've carried them out so far, and I plan to do so until we withdraw. We'll give these barbarians a lesson they'll remember for a long time."

The campaign of unbounded savagery resumed when Edmond's forces reached the second Petcheneg compound less than two days later. It was at the farthest point from Silistria to which Edmond was permitted to advance by Bryennius' instructions. Upon its destruction, he intended to begin the return to the great fortress on the Danube.

The second attack followed the course of the first, and was similarly bloody and successful, though slightly marred by the possible survival of at least one Petcheneg. The nomad had lashed himself to the underbelly of a horse and his flight was not discovered until he got well free of the burning encampment. According to Bela's pursuing Magyars, they wounded him but he eluded them on an exceptionally swift pony. Edmond was not unduly troubled. The fugitive might not matter, especially if he had been seriously wounded. He would probably die before he reaching help. Besides, the army was ready to begin its retreat to safe territory.

At first all went well, but on the third day of the return march a Magyar scout, his pony covered with foam, galloped up to Bela who was in the vanguard with Edmond. The Magyar chief heard the trooper's report with growing concern, then told Edmond, "He says he spotted a small band of Petchenegs a half-day's ride to the north."

"Any signs of a large body?"

"He saw a large cloud of dust at a distance but dared not venture in that direction for fear he might be intercepted and unable to return to us with the report."

Edmond's mind was already racing on how to prepare for the possibility of a major force of Petchenegs descending on his little army. He dared not speed up the withdrawal, having pushed his troops close to the pace of a forced march for two days. He could not afford to exhaust them when they were still only halfway to Silistria, the return route being longer than the outward path. He had swung wide to the east to avoid retracing his steps and thus enabling the nomads to locate his whereabouts more readily. He wished he knew the strength of the Petcheneg force. If it was small, there was little cause for concern. A small band might harass his men but could not overcome them. On the other hand, a force numbering a thousand or more might cut off all hope of escape.

The first intimation that the Petchenegs were in hot pursuit came early the next day when advance parties began to cut down the Magyar scouts one by one until Edmond was forced to recall the survivors and assign Bela to protect the rear with half his horsemen. His sturdy Thracian infantrymen, though wearied by the rugged pace of what now was a forced march, kept ranks tolerably well. Seasoned veterans, they were keenly aware that to fall behind was to perish. But they were overmatched in this sort of warfare and only the cavalry shield provided by the Magyars kept them from being quickly decimated by the Petcheneg archers.

By mid-afternoon the situation was alarming. A Magyar from Bela's rearguard reported a large party of Petchenegs was closing in from the southwest, racing to block the direct line of retreat. He estimated that they numbered between five hundred and a thousand horsemen. Shortly later, two other large groups of Petchenegs converged from east and west on the retreating Roman force.

Edmond took care to appear confident despite the almost hopeless position as he discussed the terrain with his officers after halting his troops for a brief rest and a meal. It would not do to let on that he had almost given up hope. The expedition was taking almost exactly the turn he had anticipated from the start. He was deep in enemy territory without a reasonable chance of extricating his force. It was still too far from Silistria to expect help from the garrison even if Strategus Bryennius were willing to risk most of his command to give it. The Petchenegs, as nearly as he could judge from scattered reports, numbered at least three thousand horsemen. The only course left for his little army of less than five hundred was to fight to the last and die honorably.

At least, Edmond thought ruefully, the topography of the area they were in favored his resolution to resist to the end. His men had entered a hilly area, leaving behind the level plain where they provided easy targets for enemy archers. The irregular terrain made matters more difficult for the Petcheneg horsemen, though they would inevitably prevail through sheer weight of numbers.

Edmond called a war council. The officers agreed to mass their men on a sharply crowned hill. Its northern slope was defensible with minimal manpower and effort because the rise was too steep for horsemen to ascend. That would be the rear. The southern incline was much gentler and thus more vulnerable. The major part of the Roman force would have to be stationed to confront attack from this direction. Edmond immediately set the men to throwing up a makeshift barrier of logs, stones, debris and earthworks, there not being enough time to lay out a military camp in the regulation way. Fortunately, a creek wound through the defensible area. As for food, the remaining baggage carts contained supplies for three or four days, more than enough, he reflected grimly. It was unlikely any rations would be needed after that.

Chiefly to buoy his men's spirits rather than with any expectation of success, Edmond dispatched a Magyar courier to Silistria. Even if the messenger did slip through the net the Petchenegs were drawing, it remained probable that Bryennius would still prefer to write off a few hundred men as a means of advancing his scheme to assemble a large army for a possible coup d'etat.

Edmond decided to issue weapons to the previously unarmed cart drivers, tent bearers, and other non-combatants. The Petchenegs would not spare them. They would have to fight and die with the troops and might take a few more barbarians to hell. Edmond stationed these untrained men at the more easily defensible rear.

By twilight more and more Petchenegs, distinguished by their customary tall hats, appeared within sight astride their sturdy little long-maned ponies. At first, they arrived in twos and threes, but soon the dust raised by thousands of hooves swirled on every side of the Roman camp. When it became dark, the glare of hundreds of campfires dotted the surrounding area, visible evidence of the enemy's overwhelming numbers.

"How long will it be before a relief force from Silistria can reach us?" asked Lakanodrakon as he joined Edmond in surveying the scene from the hilltop.

"Four days at the least if our courier gets through," Edmond replied, wondering whether Lakanodrakon and the other officers realized the hopelessness of the situation. None other than himself suspected Bryennius was committed to sacrificing them to further his political ambitions. To the strategus, this small force might be of more use dead than alive. Edmond was reluctant to voice his conjecture to Lakanodrakon, but his subordinate's shrug at his reply made it evident he knew how desperate matters were.

"We may share the fate of Quinctilius Varus," Lakanodrakon remarked stolidly, drawing on a historical analogy that Edmond, despite his limited knowledge of the Roman past, could understand. A thousand years had passed since the Augustan commander Varus had led three Roman legions into an ambush laid by German tribes and had perished with thousands of his men.

"No doubt another Germanicus Caesar will someday find our bleached bones," he replied facetiously, referring to the imperial general who years after Varus's death discovered the site of one of the greatest defeats ever suffered by Roman arms. He stifled an impulse to laugh when he thought of Empress Theodora wringing hands and imploring, "Give me back my legions," as her distant predecessor Augustus had done upon learning of Varus having lost life and army. No one in the Palace of the Blachernae was likely to shed a single tear for Kometes Edmond Edwysson and his men as Augustus had done on the Palatine Hill in Rome for Varus and his troops. Not even Edith, he thought, with pangs of regret and remorse.

He gazed in fascination at the hundreds of tongues of flames licking so eagerly at the black body of the night before he followed Lakanodrakon's example and lay down for a brief rest to prepare for whatever the dawn and fate would bring.

Chapter Thirty-Three

Annihilation!

Edmond gained the highest point of the hill occupied by his troops so he could survey the surrounding plain swarming with Petchenegs. The silence of the night was now broken at dawn by the rumble of wagons, clatter of weapons, snorts and neighs of horses and war cries of the nomads preparing for an attack on the Roman force.

Despite vigorous protest by the Magyars who were accustomed to fighting on horseback, Edmond persuaded Bela to have them dismount and take up positions on the flanks of the Thracian spearmen crouching behind a makeshift barrier thrown up during the night. The Magyar archers would exact a heavy toll if the Petchenegs attempted a frontal, uphill assault. The cart drivers, baggage handlers, and other civilians guarding the steepest face of the hill at the rear had an easier assignment. It was inconceivable that the Petchenegs could ride up so steep a slope. Furthermore, even if they left their saddles to climb the precipitous incline, they were not at their best in hand-to-hand combat on foot.

"There must be more than five or six thousand now," remarked Simon Vatatzes, the slender, dark-featured, energetic infantry pentekontarchus.

"More than enough to bundle us all to heaven or hell before Strategus Bryennius can send a relief force," Lakanodrakon observed, glancing out of the corner of an eye toward Edmond whose expression remained unchanged. He was not about to divulge the sad truth that it was hopeless to expect help from Silistria.

"We can easily hold them off for two or three days," Vatatzes commented optimistically. "I've fought these barbarians before. They're fine skirmishers and harass a column of infantry like gadflies, but lack the stomach for a headlong assault, especially against a position so strong as ours. We should be able to beat them off several times. They'll back off when they've had enough of it."

Edmond paid little attention to the discussion between his officers. He was intent on observing the Petcheneg bands as they wheeled into formation on the plain below. While he watched, a small cluster of nomads on a knoll began to disperse, riding off by twos and threes in different directions. These were undoubtedly leaders rejoining their units after having concerted a plan of attack. As was Petcheneg custom, the chiefs would first whip their men into a frenzy with fiery speeches before leading them into action. When the assault began it was a straightforward charge uphill with no attempt at subtle tactics. The Petcheneg leaders apparently were so confident of their vast superiority in numbers as to believe they could prevail in one massive attempt.

At a signal from their chiefs, the horsemen in their thousands spurred their shaggy ponies into a gallop toward the most gentle slope of the hill defended by Edmond's troops. The barbarians sped across the plain like a flight of vultures swooping from the sky onto carrion, the drumbeat of hooves pounding the hard-baked earth rising to a crescendo as they approached the defenders.

As the great surge of wildly shouting horsemen bore down on them, the Thracians braced for the assault and the Magyars loosed a flight of arrows high into the air, the missiles tracing a parabola before descending on the packed mass of attackers and wreaking havoc among men and animals. The surviving Petcheneg horsemen wheeled about, released an answering swarm of shafts, then retired pell-mell downhill. The casualties on both sides and among riders and mounts were numerous, with the agonized screams of wounded horses almost drowning out the moans of men.

Among the dead was Pentekontarchus Vatatzes who fell with an arrow through his mouth. Lakanodrakon stifled a sob of grief and bent down to kiss his dead friend's forehead before obeying Edmond's orders to check on whether the enemy was attempting to scale the heights at their rear. To Edmond's relief, the Petchenegs at the foot of the steep northern side of the hill were still milling about on horseback, obviously uncertain as to how to proceed. Their hesitation gave him time to inspect the damage done by the attack against the frontal barrier before the Petchenegs regrouped for another charge. More than two score of his men were dead and a similar number wounded, many so seriously they were unfit for further service. The expedition's sole physician and his two helpers were hard-pressed to attend to all the injured.

Edmond gritted his teeth before deciding on an unpleasant but possibly useful action, ordering Lakanodrakon, "Have the men throw the bodies of the dead, ours as well as those of the barbarians, onto the barricade." An even more unpalatable order went to Bela. "Your men must slaughter their horses. They'll do more good obstructing the enemy's attack than serving as targets for their archers."

The Magyar chief's lower lip sagged in disbelief. "You mean all of them?"

"No exceptions," Edmond insisted. "They'll not only reinforce the barrier, but the smell of their blood will spook the enemies' ponies. If we survive this battle, we'll have no need of these horses. We'll be able to capture those of the enemy, and there are sure to be enough for all of your men."

Bela protested a little longer but yielded after being thoroughly convinced Edmond was adamant. The kometes was well aware that the Magyars out of the saddle were like sailors on land but the situation was too desperate not to clutch at any advantage, no matter how slight. At this stage in the battle, available horses might encourage attempts at desertion or treachery. He was determined to render either impossible. He looked on impassively as the Magyars wailed, cursed and tore at their hair after Bela transmitted the order. Fortunately, their chief's hold over them was strong and they reluctantly slaughtered the animals though tears diluted the blood.

By the time the Petchenegs were ready for a second charge, the barrier was raised to a more imposing height, built up with the corpses of animals and men. This time the attackers massed in two ranks, one behind the other, at the foot of the hill. The first wave thundered up the slope and absorbed a devastating hail of arrows from the Magyars before the survivors again executed a wheeling motion while discharging a Parthian shot as they retreated. The casualties on both sides were heavy, though Edmond's men suffered fewer losses than the first time because his men now knew what to expect.

On this occasion, however, there was little time to recover from the shock because the second wave of Petchenegs came immediately after the first had regained the bottom of the hill. The nomads crouched in the saddle, lances poised, and attempted to crash through the barricade of rocks, timber, human bodies and horseflesh like surf sweeping over a beach. The Magyar archers took a fearful toll before the barbarians jumped off their horses and began to climb over the obstacle to engage the defenders in hand-to-hand combat.

Edmond drove into the press, wielding his heavy sword with both hands, hewing down one after another of the lightly-armored attackers pouring in their hundreds over the barricade. He challenged a dark-skinned youth whose fragile sword soon snapped under the impact of his heavy blade which then carved into the Petcheneg's flank. Next came a much-scarred veteran who surprised by skillfully thrusting, parrying and feinting for what seemed an infinity before exposing himself to a fatal dagger thrust.

Arm-weary, Edmond fell back from the fray to take stock. The fighting raged fiercely all around and atop the barricade, but his heavy infantry was holding firm and the Petcheneg advance was stalled. He wondered why the enemy did not send another wave against and over the barricade to turn the tide. Perhaps poor Vatatzes had sized up the barbarians correctly in suggesting they lacked the determination to persevere against a resolute resistance. More likely, he decided, their chiefs no longer sought to overwhelm his force with one massive attack but now counted on wearing it down in several stages.

Lakanodrakon, unscratched though fatigued, ran up to Edmond. "Kometes, the Magyars on our right flank are being forced back and need support."

After making sure the left flank and center were holding, Edmond led a couple of dozen Thracians to the assistance of Bela's Magyars. Fewer than twenty of them remained on their feet of the more than fifty originally assigned to guard the infantry's right flank. Bela was urging his men on, his arms spattered with blood, obviously not his own judging by his energy. The Petchenegs had pushed his men a few paces back from the barricade and were slowly forcing them toward the center in an attempt to turn the defenders' flank.

As Edmond charged into battle with his handful of reinforcements, Bela stumbled over a rock and sprawled heavily to the ground. He was momentarily stunned and a Petcheneg leaped to straddle his body and poised his lance for the death thrust. Before he could strike, Edmond hurtled at him and with a sweep of his sword half-severed the barbarian's head. As the Petcheneg's body rolled away, Edmond reached down to help Bela scramble to his feet. The Magyar chief swayed uncertainly before regaining his balance and breath, then in a silently eloquent gesture gripped Edmond's right hand.

Edmond and Bela charged back into the fight but the Petchenegs had had enough for the time being. A horn sounded recall and they retreated over the barricade and scrambled back downhill on foot or horseback. Edmond drew grim satisfaction in noting that many saddles were empty, their former occupants fallen in the fierce combat.

The lull in the fighting enabled Edmond to confer with his officers and assess the situation. Only Vatatzes among those of rank had been killed, but the common soldiers, both Thracian and Magyar, had suffered grievously. More than one hundred and fifty of the fewer than five hundred men under his command at the start of the battle were either dead or severely wounded. Of the remaining three hundred or so, a third were cart drivers, tent bearers, cooks, and other civilians of marginal use in battle. Most of them were posted at the most defensible position, the rear of the hill with its steep slope.

Alexander Condylus, the veteran pentekontarchus in charge of this heterogeneous rear guard, had been summoned to the conference. Edmond asked him, "Has there been any sign of the Petchenegs preparing to attack your position?"

"Not so far. But they've picketed their horses and it wouldn't surprise me if they eventually try to come up the hill, even if it's sure to be hard going. I've kept my men busy throwing up obstacles and stockpiling rocks and logs to hurl down at them if they attack. They may eventually overcome us, but we'll make it hot for them."

Edmond slapped Condylus's back in encouragement and sent him to his post. He had no men to spare as reinforcements for that quarter. It was more important to make sure all was in order—as much as possible under the circumstances—on the main line of defense. He again ordered the corpses of both friend and foe dumped on the barricade. Despite sightless eyes and stiffened limbs, those victims of battle could serve a final tour of duty as ramparts defensive.

It was mid-afternoon when the Petchenegs began to mass again on the plain below the Roman defensive line on the hill. Edmond and his officers watched the enemy re-form ranks with the fascination of a fly observing a spider moving in for the kill.

"No flights of arrows this time," Lakanodrakon remarked. "They'll rely mostly on lances to try and force a breach in our ranks even if some climb over the barricades as they did before. There are far more of them this time. They apparently hope to overwhelm us with their numbers."

Edmond nodded agreement before remarking in an almost jocular tone, "You haven't mentioned the relief force from Silistria this time, my friend. Have you given up on it?"

Lakanodrakon grimaced. "Now Kometes Edwysson, please spare me. You know I didn't really believe it would arrive in time to save us. For that matter, I've doubted all along that Strategus Bryennius would attempt to come to our assistance, though I considered it impolitic to say so. Not that I blame him. It would be imprudent for a general to waste more good men in a hopeless cause."

"Wasn't this entire expedition ill-advised, even foolish and hopeless from the very beginning?" Edmond demanded, unable to restrain his bitterness any longer.

Lakanodrakon struck his forehead with his left palm. "I never expected to hear you admit that, kometes, though I thought so all along even if I considered it best to keep my mouth shut. It was worse than madness, even idiotic, to wander about so deep in hostile territory with such a small force." He was shocked by his own forthrightness into grinning sheepishly. "No use questioning the strategus's orders at this point. It's too late. Obviously, Bryennius gambled and so far as he's concerned we're no great loss."

Edmond could not resist a gibe. "That doesn't sound like something the spirit of Marcus Aurelius would say as he stalked the Dacian plain. Where's the stoic now?"

Lakanodrakon took it well. "I admit that while I may not be as good a Christian as I should be, Jesus help me, I'm not a great follower of the stoic school either. Yet I see my fate written on the ground with hoofprints." He pointed to the Petchenegs massing below and lapsed into silence.

A messenger from Condylus reported that the enemy had begun to climb up the precipitous northern hillside. Edmond hastened to check on their progress, but decided Condylus's rag-tag assortment of camp servants and followers would have to take care of itself. He contented himself with a glance at the hundreds of barbarians struggling up the incline, then advised the unsoldierly defenders, "Remember, these savages never spare a male captive. They must not reach the top of this hill. The best way to make sure they don't is to save your arrows and spears until they're so near and exhausted that you can reach out and twist their mustaches. Then have at them!"

Despite his encouraging words, he was under no misconception that the position would hold for long. It was certain the Petchenegs, wearied or not by their arduous climb, would quickly overwhelm Condylus's handful of untrained men. He gave the pentekontarchus a firm handshake, then returned to the main position.

Lakanodrakon greeted him by silently indicating the Petchenegs on the plain who by now had formed up several ranks deep. Even as he looked, a horn sounded and the nomads began a slow trot up the incline

Edmond grimly fastened his helmet's chinstrap, then sword in hand took up his position beside the standard bearer at the center of a pitifully thin line of Thracians behind the barricade. He was resigned to dying in battle under the symbol of an alien empire, yet one that honored him more than his native land ever would have been likely to do. He glanced up at the golden eagle badge above his head. The dragon of Wessex might be more fitting for a descendant of the House of Cerdic, but none in this foreign land would recognize the emblem of a distant island's royal line. It was just as well. When the eagle fell, as it certainly would, the dragon would remain unsullied by defeat.

The Petcheneg onrush gained momentum, sweeping toward and over the barricade. Horse hooves trampled and churned the tree branches, rocks, mud and corpses into a crimson slush in the frenzied assault. The Magyar bowmen took a heavy initial toll of the enemy, but soon were overwhelmed by the nomad lancers who rode over their corpses to split the last line of defense, herding the surviving Thracian infantrymen into bitterly resisting small pockets.

Edmond saw Bela felled by a blow on the head as the Petchenegs broke through the right flank of the defense. He soon could no longer distinguish the pattern of battle, only isolated incidents. The flaunted eagle standard nearby inevitably attracted the enemy's greatest efforts toward his position. With Lakanodrakon to his right and Demetrios, a sturdy Thracian non-commissioned officer, at his left, he fought on savagely, cutting down one assailant after another, slashing through light armor, flesh, bone, limbs and skulls with his great hacking sword. The superb armor given him by Constantine IX preserved him time and again from being seriously wounded despite suffering several minor cuts and bruises. During a brief respite gained by the fury of his resistance that forced his assailants to fall back to regroup, he was horrified to hear the triumphant shouts of the enemy approaching from the rear of the hill. They had succeeded in climbing the steep incline and overcoming Condylus and his men.

There was no time to regret the collapse of the rearguard because the Petchenegs, heartened by their success, resumed the onslaught on the few remaining defenders. A piercing war cry gave the signal and a youth wrapped in the ornate caftan of a khan, commander of one of the eight major hordes into which the Petcheneg nation was organized under their Great Khan, led his elite guard against the small band of Romans surrounding the dragon standard. All around, other Petchenegs were hunting down and killing the few surviving Thracians and Magyars not clustered around Edmond. The young khan charged toward the standard with lance poised and succeeded in piercing Lakanodrakon's throat, strangling in blood a quip the pentekontarchus was about to make to Edmond. Demetrios died next after breaking his sword on a foe's ribs and leaving himself open to a dagger stab by another Petcheneg.

The rest of Edmond's men also soon fell until he unaccountably alone remained on his feet, blood racing through his veins, his mind reeling into fantasy with fatigue. He felt as if he were dreaming while recalling Byrnthoth's defiance at Malden, Beowulf's battle against the giant Grendel, and of his own father Edwy's and royal uncle Edmond Ironside's feats at Assandun. He was following in their noble footsteps, sword in hand, prepared to die in combat, a warrior to his final breath. Such had been the fate of many of his ancestors of Cerdic's line. This was how Edmond, son of Edwy, descendant of the great Alfred, should yield up his life.

He laughed aloud, almost like a madman, as he confronted the beardless khan who had dismounted to claim the honor of personally cutting down the Roman commander, with his men falling back to let him fulfill his ambition. The laughter enraged the lad who thought he was being mocked. He abandoned all prudence to press an attack so furious that Edmond was hard put to keep him at bay. The khan's impetuosity was costly, Edmond's sword point penetrating the gorgeous, bejeweled caftan into his antagonist's side. At their leader's fall, his men gasped in horror, then rushed en masse at Edmond.

His sword hummed a bloody melody that reverberated in his consciousness like an accompaniment to his dying father's phrase, "Born to be a king... born to be a king... born to be a king..." as the sweeping steel cut down one assailant after another. The barbarians again fell back to gape in fear, wonder and even reluctant admiration approaching veneration, at this berserk Roman officer.

He proudly threw back his head to defiantly return their gaze despite being so weary he gladly would have clung to the standard pole still planted firmly in the earth at his back. He suddenly felt dizzy and began to imagine he was surrounded not by Petchenegs but by Norman men at arms. Yes, there were the casques, shirts of chain mail and kite-shaped shields. The Normans surrounded Edmond, king of the English, basileus of Britain, descendant of a race that among its most valiant sons numbered Alfred and Edmond Ironside. Here he stood, Edmond, the last defender of England against foreigners bent upon the rapine and subjugation of his people and land.

As the Petchenegs closed in to finish him off, Edmond pitched forward, reaching with his left hand in vain for the support of the standard pole, his right stubbornly clutching the sword hilt. He fell headlong to the ground, and the gold eagle emblem of empire clattered on top of him before rolling away into the blood-soaked mud surrounding his body and those of his fallen soldiers.

Chapter Thirty-Four

Prisoner of the Petchenegs

Edmond stirred fitfully before awaking with a start. He shook his head to clear his mind before laboriously raising himself on his elbows to survey his surroundings. Moonlight streamed in through a slight opening to dimly illuminate a tent too roughly made to be of Byzantine manufacture. He was too surprised to find himself alive to trouble further about that. His last memory was of the Petchenegs rushing at him in fury as he reached to support himself by clutching the eagle standard. Whatever the reason, they had spared his life. He tried to stretch his limbs only to be overcome by lassitude. He felt no great pain though his sore muscles protested at the effort. If he was wounded, it was slightly. He examined himself thoroughly and detected only a few scratches and bruises, none serious. He was almost unscathed and felt remarkably well considering the events of the last few days even if he was terribly thirsty and hungry.

He staggered to his feet and limped to the tent entrance. Pulling aside the flap, he peered out only to be confronted at once by two armed Petchenegs who scrambled up from beside a campfire. They threatened him wordlessly, lances poised in an indisputable command not to emerge from the tent. He retreated hastily, grateful to collapse back onto a pile of skins that served as his bed.

He was mystified at having survived. He could recall nothing of the final moments beside the eagle standard other than the Petcheneg onrush after he cut down their young leader. What had followed? He must have collapsed from exhaustion since he had not been wounded. On discovering he was still alive the barbarians possibly decided to reserve him for sacrifice to their gods. Better to have fallen in battle. If that was their plan, he would show his executioners that a soldier of New Rome, a descendant of King Alfred, could die bravely, even if he met a fate like that of the third century Emperor Valerian whose Persian captors flayed, stuffed and exhibited his body.

Despite such sobering thoughts, Edmond dozed fitfully until he was again awakened by the increased sound of activity outside his tent and brilliant sunlight pouring through the entrance. The Petcheneg encampment was bustling shortly after sunrise. The creaking of wagon wheels, lowing of cattle, neighing of horses and shouts, laughter and chatter of the nomads in their harsh-sounding language was almost deafening. Edmond now felt much better when he sat up despite extreme thirst and hunger. Did they intend to starve him to death?

The thought had hardly flashed through his mind when a woman entered the tent to provide a reassuring answer. She brought a wooden bowl and a horn and shuffled hesitantly toward him until spurred on by the guttural command of a guard at her heels. As she handed Edmond the bowl and horn he was struck by how singularly unattractive she was. He judged her to be not much more than twenty years of age but her dull black eyes, thick lips, high and projecting cheekbones and weathered skin were not redeemed by the slightest hint of feminine charm. What was he thinking of? He gazed with distaste at the bowl's contents, a sort of gruel of millet, the national dish of the Petchenegs. Never mind, he was hungry and thirsty enough to eat and drink anything. Raising the bowl to his lips, he let the tasteless concoction drain into his mouth, then scooped out the remnant with his fingers. The hornful of what he judged a kind of mead tasted much better, a sourish yet not unpleasant liquid. As he ate and drank he was conscious of the woman's sad eyes fixed on his face. She knelt beside his bed during his entire meal, patiently waiting until he finished, then took bowl and horn and scurried out of the tent.

He was left to his thoughts until about midday when a guard entered the tent and indicated with his lance that the prisoner was to accompany him. He obeyed, blinking at first in the bright sunlight as he followed the guard until they reached a group of about a dozen middle-aged and elderly Petchenegs seated in a semi-circle as if they were a panel of judges prepared to conduct a trial. He judged them to be the elders of the horde.

His attention was immediately riveted on the most impressive figure among those awaiting him, a middle-aged man clad in a elaborately embroidered caftan who sat in the middle. He was clearly the leader, perhaps the chief khan of this horde of Petchenegs.

As Edmond came to a halt, he was surprised to see Bela the Short standing before the Petchenegs. He had witnessed the Magyar being cut down during the battle, yet here he was alive, though bandaged and bedraggled. Somehow, Bela also had survived without a debilitating wound, judging by his erect stance and alert appearance.

"It's good to see you, kometes," the Magyar welcomed, almost jauntily. "I never thought I'd have that pleasure again, Your Excellency."

"Nor did I expect ever to meet you in this life, or any other for that matter, friend Bela," Edmond gasped. "I saw the enemy swarm all over you and thought they killed you. Yet here you are, and not all that much worse for the wear by the look of it."

257

"I'm just as surprised as you are, Excellency, to be able to greet you again," Bela grinned. "We should both be carrion for crows by now. Whether we're all that lucky to survive may be another matter. All that I'm sure of is that when I regained consciousness after being knocked over the head is that I heard Khan Sogra order his men not to spear you where you lay. And that though you killed his favorite son."

A guard's impatient gesture halted the conversation. The Petcheneg headman, black-bearded and mustachioed like most of his people, spoke to Bela, who understood the language. The Magyar translated for Edmond.

"Khan Sogra commands me to inform you that he has fought in almost as many battles and raids as the number of herds of horses and cattle he owns yet he never has met a foe he esteems more highly than he does you, kometes. He is conscious of the great honor and renown he has gained by overcoming one so valiant and resolute in the face of insurmountable odds."

Edmond inclined his head to acknowledge the compliment.

"Khan Sogra considered it unfitting, even dishonorable, to slay so brave an enemy while he lay unconscious and defenseless even after he had taken the life of his eldest son, the treasure and hope of his declining years. He mercifully delayed, deciding your fate after the emotions of battle had time to wane. He wished to be just, not vindictive, in recognition of the respect one commander owes to another. With the consent of his council, he has decided to offer you the opportunity to regain your freedom in exchange for a ransom appropriate to your rank."

Edmond maintained a straight face despite an overwhelming urge to laugh. Ransom indeed! Who would pay to free him, Nicephorus Bryennius or Empress Theodora? One was as unlikely as the other. He replied with solemn dignity, "Tell the great khan that much as I appreciate his proposal, no one will offer to pay a ransom for an insignificant officer, a humble Varangian such as myself. I'm just a plain soldier who possesses nothing more of value other than the armor and weapons he carries into battle."

The khan frowned at the reply. His councilors' scoffing expressions made it clear they did not believe Edmond's claim. Everyone knew the streets of Constantinople were paved with gold and silver. Even children's toys were carved of ivory and set with precious stones A poor Byzantine commander? This was not to be believed. They chattered angrily until the khan barked an order to the guards, then stalked off with the others trailing after. The guards ushered Edmond back to his tent, but not alone as Bela was ordered to accompany him.

Once inside the tent, the Magyar sank wearily to the floor, Edmond perching on the bed. Edmond spoke first. "I thought you were killed, my friend. I saw you fall when the enemy overwhelmed your position."

"I did go down under a heap of the bastards, one of whom landed a blow on my head, raising a helluva goose egg." Bela indicated an unsightly black and blue lump near his right ear. "The next thing I knew when I came to, I was under a heap of bodies, with the Petchenegs killing the wounded and stripping the dead above me. I kept quiet until I saw the khan approach, then yelled out my name and rank and offered to pay a ransom. Khan Sogra kept his men from slitting my throat so that he could question me.

"Fortunately for me, the khan has had dealings with one of my uncles in Hungary who treated him well. He thought it might be advantageous to spare my life. My poor men were not so lucky. Any of the wounded who made a sound or were seen to move had their throats cut."

Bela buried his face in his hands to hide his emotion. Most of his men had served under him for years, and some had been friends or followers since he had been a stripling. He regained control to add with a sigh, "Not one of my men survives."

"You and I may well be the only ones of my entire command left alive," Edmond mused. "More than five hundred men dead, yet here we are, the two of us, somewhat battered but not all that badly hurt. Almost miraculous, wouldn't you say?"

Bela nodded assent before dozing off while Edmond contemplated the inexplicable and desperate circumstances in which he found himself. Or was it destiny? His survival, while not assured for much longer, already was remarkable given the situation and the customary reluctance of the Petchenegs to burden themselves with prisoners. It was tempting to speculate he had been spared by God to fulfill the role his father had foreseen for him. The thought was attractive, but he rejected it out of hand. What a fool he was. It was shameful to continually grasp at such straws of hope. Only a madman would dream of a crown while virtually condemned to death, a captive in Petcheneg hands and unlikely to survive even as such much longer. With no ransom forthcoming, Khan Sogra, despite his professions of admiration, was almost sure to order his execution. Well, better die than live a slave to these barbarians.

He became aware of Bela being awake and studying him as if in sympathy with his thoughts, not that he could possibly understand them.

"No need to feel shame or regret, kometes," the Magyar reminded gently. "No man could have conducted himself better under the circumstances than you did. The khan has testified to that." He rubbed his chin, then looked sheepishly at Edmond as if in embarrassment. "Kometes, I heard what you said about a ransom, but you needn't be concerned. Rest easy, it's assured. Remember, I owe you my life."

"I don't understand."

"Remember, kometes, if it hadn't been for you I would have been killed before the enemy's final attack. You saved me when the Petchenegs overran our positions the first time and that tall fellow's lance knocked me down. I haven't forgotten." Bela cleared his throat before continuing. "My family is wealthy and powerful. My uncle sits at King Andras's right hand in council at Esztergom. It would be a small matter, but one conferring great honor, for my kinfolk to provide the ransom for you as well as me. Have no fear, they won't stint. The sum will be worthy of you."

Edmond could not reply immediately. The offer was so unexpected, and he thought unmerited, that he was stunned. He had done nothing for Bela he would not have done for any soldier under his command. If he had saved the Magyar's life it was in the line of duty, nothing more. Now it turned out that in rescuing Bela he might have redeemed himself. He masked emotion with a gruff response. "Your offer is generous, my friend, but consider further before you commit yourself that I have no means of repaying you in the foreseeable future. I told Khan Sogra the truth. My only treasure is my equipment. You'll have my gratitude if you secure my ransom, but other than that I can offer you only lasting friendship."

"That's repayment enough," Bela cried, grasping Edmond's hand and pumping it vigorously. "If you reject my family's help or say any more about it, I'll consider it an insult, a sign of disdain."

The next morning Edmond and Bela were again escorted to appear before Khan Sogra and his council.

"Kometes, much as we respect you as a valiant enemy it's not our custom to trifle with important matters," the khan began. "I demand an immediate answer as to whether you're able to offer or secure a ransom. If your reply is unsatisfactory, we've no recourse other than to exact punishment for your actions against our nation. You've had an opportunity to consider a means of securing a ransom appropriate to your rank and station. Have you discovered one?"

"I haven't searched, great khan, but I've found," Edmond replied. "My good friend Bela has pledged himself to provide the amount required for my release."

Khan Sogra blinked his black eyes in surprise and tugged at his mustache before barking a question at Bela. The Magyar replied unhesitatingly, apparently to the khan's satisfaction.

"You're as fortunate as brave, Kometes Edwysson, and we trust our mutual friend Bela unreservedly," said the khan. "My council and I deliberated long on whether to impale you or offer you up for ransom. The angry spirits of the hundreds of our people slaughtered on your orders cried out for vengeance and the stake was shaped and hardened for your impalement. Yet as we considered your fate, the sword with which you slew so many more of our warriors in combat lay on the ground before us. It was a reminder of the respect and admiration we should have for so valiant an enemy so we decided to offer you an opportunity to repurchase your liberty."

Edmond looked the khan in the eye. "I did only what any Roman commander would do, carry out his orders to the best of his ability."

"May our gods protect us from another such as you," the khan entreated with a skyward glance. "Not that we're likely to come up against an equal in the future. When the ransom is turned over to us, you'll be free to depart." He gravely inclined his head in a gesture of respect, then ordered the guards to return Edmond and Bela to their prison.

The following morning the Wolf Horde's tents were struck and packed into the wagons in preparation for moving on from the site of battle to a fresh grazing area. Men, women and children joined in loading their possessions since it was the custom of the Petchenegs to travel as families, even to confront an enemy. When all was ready, Khan Sogra gave a signal and the heavy wagons and herds began to lumber across the plain, following a generally northwestward course.

Edmond and Bela rode ponies, much to the Magyar's relief. They were closely guarded though escape would have been almost impossible, surrounded as they were by the Petcheneg horde. Edmond cast a sad, lingering last look at the receding hill on which so many of his friends and soldiers had died. No doubt Nicephorus Bryennius would use the loss of the expedition to bolster his request for reinforcements from an alarmed Constantinople as part of his plan to march on the capital. On the other hand, if the strategus had been sincere in suggesting that Edmond's mission was to explore the possibility of a thrust toward Kiev, it had proved only that five hundred or so imperial soldiers were no match for several thousand Petchenegs.

Edmond dismissed the conjecture. After all, what did Bryennius's motives matter to him at this point. He was unlikely to soon learn about the eventual repercussions of the debacle. He shrugged. What a pity it all was though. Lakanodrakon, Vatatzes, Demetrius, Condylus, all dead, all lost in a futile mission, good soldiers, good men, sacrificed for nothing other perhaps than a general's wild ambition. What of your philosophy, Lakanodrakon, how little did it benefit you when you choked on your own blood?

The Petcheneg horde pressed steadily on for several days in search of prime grazing land. Meanwhile, Khan Sogra had dispatched envoys to Esztergom in Hungary to convey the demand for ransom to Bela's relatives. King Andras's capital lay far beyond the Carpathian Mountains to the west and it would be several weeks before an answer could arrive, favorable or otherwise.

Edmond scrutinized the country they passed through with interest. Few of the people native to the area before the arrival of the Petchenegs remained in the lowlands of Dacia. Scattered throughout were isolated small villages whose residents tilled the soil, and yielded a sizable portion of their harvests as tribute to the Petchenegs. They bore their burdens patiently as they had for centuries during which they were abused, oppressed and occasionally massacred by their present masters and their predecessors.

Savage horsemen from time immemorial had invaded the area and seized crops, cattle, wealth and even sons and daughters. Many of the indigenous population fled into the hills and mountains to the south and west. The highlands were populated by the descendants of generations of refugees and preserved a language derived from Latin. It was an inheritance from mighty Rome which once had adorned the land with great country villas, palaces, fortifications and magnificent public works. Huns, Bulgars, Avars, Magyars, Petchenegs and other nomad peoples, many long forgotten, had poured in successive waves across the plains from out of the fertile breeding ground between the great Dnieper and Volga rivers. Some such as the Magyars and the Avars before them had penetrated the passes of the Carpathians and Transylvanian Alps to pour into the great plateau of ancient Dacia and the vast plain beyond to the west, the Nagy Alfold, as the Magyars called it. Some tribes even extended their dominion past the Danube into the land to the west named Pannonia by the Romans. Only the Avars, before they were crushed by Emperor Charlemagne, and the Magyars succeeded in controlling the area for any length of time. Thus between the hammer of the Magyars on the west and the anvil of the Petchenegs to the east the native peoples of this fruitful land were ground into sullen submission or forced to eke out a pitiful if free existence in the valleys of the great mountain ranges.

Edmond and Bela were mostly left alone as the Wolf Horde made its way. The Petcheneg guards seldom interrupted their conversations, neither desiring friendship with the prisoners nor daring to harm them because they were under the khan's protection. Edmond described life in Constantinople and even in England to Bela whom he discovered to be intelligently curious. The Magyar was greatly amused by Edmond's descriptions of the intrigues and clashes in both the Byzantine and English courts.

"It's much the same among our people in Hungary," Bela commented. "Since our great King Stephen died in my grandfather's time we've suffered a great deal from wars, both civil and foreign. King Andras must lie awake at nights worrying whether the German emperor will descend on Esztergom to take advantage of our quarrels and disunity as he did five years ago. It's rumored Emperor Henry is unwell, may he rot in hell, so we may be spared. All the same, King Andras, the queen, his brother Bela, his nephews and many of the great lords are at odds with one another. My uncle, Nador Imre—I suppose you could compare his office of nador to that of the grand logothete in Constantinople—has all he can do to keep his head firmly on his shoulders."

"England is just as disunited," admitted Edmond. "And matters may get even worse if anything happens to King Edward because he has no son to succeed him. A vacant throne invites conflict."

"No doubt of that," Bela agreed, then struck his forehead. "Your mention of English affairs reminds me of something I've almost forgotten. Some years ago when I was in Esztergom an English prince was among the king's guests at court."

"Was it Edward the Atheling?"

"I think Edward was the man's name, but what do you mean by atheling?"

"It's a title given a prince of royal descent."

"I was told that he and a brother who died young fled England some thirty or so years ago and eventually found sanctuary at our court."

"No doubt they feared King Cnut," Edmond explained. "With good reason, as they are the sons of his rival, King Edmond Ironside."

So his first cousin was still alive, waiting patiently in Esztergom for an opportune time to return to England and claim a throne to which—in the eyes of many—he had a better right than the present king. Superior to his own, Edmond acknowledged, since the atheling was the son of Edmond Ironside, his own father's elder brother. How strange the mutations of fate? Even adversity had its benefits. Being a prisoner of the Petchenegs was balanced by an opportunity to meet cousin Edward in Esztergom. Perhaps he could persuade the atheling to return to England and secure the king's support as his heir.

Bela broke in on his speculation. "You should see Esztergom. A perfect fortress city atop a hill overlooking the juncture of the Danube and Hron rivers. They say there's no church outside Constantinople to equal the one built by our King Stephen. To think that some sacrilegious dogs tried to burn it down." He spat in disgust, overcome with the indignation of a faithful Christian who loathed his numerous pagan countrymen.

"I thought all your people were true believers?"

"Most are, but some merely pretended to accept the faith until after

King Stephen died. Since Andras became king after Samuel Bela was deposed, he has spent much time and treasure in efforts to suppress those who've reverted to paganism."

Such discussions eased the monotony of a four-day-long trek that ended when the horde reached the banks of a shallow stream bisecting a broad, grassy plain. There was ample grazing for the Petchenegs' herds as well as the prospect of abundant game in nearby wooded areas. The customary circle of wagons shielding a village of tents sprang up quickly. Edmond and Bela shared a tent pitched next to that of Khan Sogra in the center of the encampment.

It was only now that Edmond encountered an unusually hospitable Petcheneg custom. As he and Bela prepared to settle down for the night, the flap covering the entrance to the tent parted and he was astounded to see two women shuffle in. He recognized one as the slave who had served him his first meal after his capture. As ugly as he had thought her then, she now seemed almost attractive when compared to her somewhat older, gap-toothed and even more weather-beaten companion. He drew back almost in consternation when the younger woman lay down on the skins next to him and the other snuggled down beside Bela.

The Magyar chuckled at Edmond's bewildered reaction even as he reached out to embrace his new companion. "These Petchenegs are hospitable folk. It's their custom to share their women with guests. Since we're prisoners, I didn't think they would extend such generosity to us, but evidently Khan Sogra doesn't want anyone to believe him lacking in good manners." After the explanation, Bela moved to the farthest part of the tent with his woman and though darkness cast a veil over what followed it could not muffle the sounds.

Edmond's companion pressed and flexed her warm body against his and instinct swiftly took over. Prior Wulfstan's denunciations of unlawful coupling were no safeguard in such a tempting situation and he yielded with little resistance to nature's demands. It had been long since he had lain with a woman and he had almost forgotten the pleasure of doing so.

During the rest of his captivity, each time he slept with his temporary concubine, he marveled anew at the extraordinary custom of these nomads who as a courtesy to guests even provided for their sexual needs. He shamefacedly admitted that while it was a pleasurable arrangement it was unpardonably at odds with the teachings of the church. How thunderously Prior Wulfstan would condemn him if he knew of such backsliding. Nevertheless…

Chapter Thirty-Five

Freedom and Frustration

Two troops of horsemen cantered into the Petcheneg encampment and rode directly to the large tent beside which fluttered the wolf tail streamer of Khan Sogra's horde to signify that its chieftain was in occupancy. The body of riders in the lead was greeted enthusiastically by the khan's followers as kinsmen from another of the nation's hordes. It was escorting the smaller group, a delegation from Hungary, through Petcheneg territory. The foreigners were outfitted in west European fashion, though with picturesque touches favored by the flamboyant Magyars who still clung to some customs of their nomad forebears.

On hearing the uproar, Edmond and Bela came out of their tent in time to see the band of Magyars pull up in front of the khan's quarters. Bela whispered, "I know at least one of them. Unless my eyes are playing tricks, there's Janos, my father's steward."

Several of the Magyars, including the one Bela recognized as Janos who appeared to be in his mid-forties, were immediately escorted into the khan's tent. Bela and Edmond attempted to follow, but Petcheneg guards blocked their way. They would have to await Khan Sogra's pleasure before being allowed to enter.

The summons came quickly, one of the khan's aides soon coming out to usher Edmond and Bela into his chief's presence. The sumptuous interior was dazzling, the tent being furnished in barbaric splendor. Heavy carpeting covered the earthen floor, silk hangings partitioned the space into private areas, and portable furniture made of rare woods lay all about. Khan Sogra, his council and the Magyar envoys faced each other seated cross-legged on stuffed cushions arranged in two crescents. The khan beckoned Edmond and Bela into the oval area separating his council from the Magyars, then addressed Janos who apparently led the envoys and spoke the Petcheneg language.

"Examine our prisoners, distinguished visitor, and satisfy yourself that they have been well treated and have come to no harm at our hands since we captured them in battle," urged Sogra. "We've given them no cause to complain of our hospitality. Do you recognize either one?"

"Great khan of the Wolf Horde, I rejoice to behold my Lord Bela, and am delighted to see that he looks so well," Janos responded with a deferential bow from the waist in Bela's direction. "Lord Bela is the valiant and beloved son of my illustrious master, Count Kalman, and the nephew of King Andras's most trusted advisor, the great Nador Imre, the wise and all-victorious, whose fame has spread to all corners of the earth and whose very name strikes fear in the hearts of our enemies."

"Yes, yes, we've heard all about the great Nador Imre, and are suitably impressed," Sogra replied impatiently, irritated by Janos's pomposity. "What about his companion, the Roman kometes? Do you know him?"

"I don't recognize him, great khan, though if he is a friend and companion to Lord Bela, as it appears, he must be a soldier worthy of our respect."

"That he is, I agree, because I've learned to esteem him for the manner in which he conducted himself in battle against us. It's no matter whether you recognize him or not. All we require is the payment of an appropriate ransom for him and your master's son, Lord Bela."

"I'm empowered to negotiate the terms of a ransom for both, great khan. First, however, with your permission, I'd like to speak in private with Lord Bela."

"I've no objection," the khan shrugged.

Janos struggled to his feet and drew Bela aside, out of the Petchenegs' hearing in case they understood the Magyar tongue. "Your uncle Nador Imre, in his infinite grace and discretion, has entrusted me with full power to deal with this matter as I judge best. There's no question, of course, about providing your ransom, but it seems unusual to me that you should concern yourself about the welfare of this Greek officer, a stranger and foreigner."

"Greek officer! Stranger!" Bela barked. "By heaven, he's no Greek but a Varangian of noble blood from England." His face reddened as he demanded, "Since when is my judgment open to question by my father's servant?"

Janos defended himself. "Dispute your decision, Lord Bela? I'd never dare take such a liberty. Yet it's my duty is to look out for your family's interests. Nador Imre and your good father Count Kalman instructed me to make certain the Petchenegs weren't trying to cheat them out of an additional ransom under false pretenses. How were we to know you took an interest in your companion's welfare, that the Petchenegs weren't scheming to rob your family, knowing as they do of its wealth and influence?"

"That's wrong, wrong on all counts," Bela huffed. "I'll not have anyone question my decisions, not my father, not my uncle, much as I respect them, and certainly not you. Nador Imre and my father have interfered in my affairs far too long and too often. I took service with the

Romans to escape their meddling. If it continues after I regain my liberty, I'll return to Constantinople where I'm valued more highly than among my own people."

"Calm yourself, my lord," Janos purred. "You'll have your way in all things if you can just learn to be patient. Your uncle and father have instructed me to assure you they'll give you free rein in the future. All they desire is that after this misfortune you'll return to where you belong, your native land."

"About time they treated me as an equal," Bela growled. "If they really do so, I'll remain in Hungary. We'll see. For the present, carry out your assignment and arrange a suitable ransom with these Petcheneg thieves—for the both of us—so Kometes Edmond and I are free to accompany you back to Esztergom."

"It shall be done," Janos assured, signaling one of his men to hand over a small but heavy and elaborately decorated wooden casket. He opened the lid, carefully checked the contents, then laid the box at Khan Sogra's feet.

"Great khan of the Wolf Horde, Janos, the steward of Lord Kalman, offers you the ransom your people have requested to secure the release of Lord Bela and his comrade, Kometes Edmond, and assure their safe return to the land of the Magyars. The amount in this chest is in accordance with what is suitable to their rank and dignity, I humbly request that you judge for yourself, Lord Sogra."

At a nod from the khan, a servant produced a set of scales and methodically weighed out the gold and silver contents of the casket. When the total value of the precious metals was announced, the khan consulted his council. Obtaining their approval, he solemnly proclaimed, "On behalf of the Petcheneg nation we accept the payment you offer though no amount, however great, can adequately compensate for these men's unprovoked attacks on our people. Our ancient traditions and customs permit us to demand a suitable ransom in exchange for the forfeited lives of captured enemies. This is the path we've chosen because Lord Bela and Kometes Edmond have earned our respect as valiant warriors. I decree they are to be released to leave with you, Steward Janos, whenever you choose to depart."

"I thank you, Khan Sogra, on behalf of my master Count Kalman, his excellency Nador Imre, and Lord Bela," Janos responded politely. "I now defer to Lord Bela's orders in all matters, among them when we are to set out for Esztergom."

As the Magyars and Edmond began to leave the tent, Bela tarried for a parting word with Khan Sogra. "I'm grateful for your generous treatment, my lord khan. If you ever decide to visit Esztergom or inspect my estate near Buda, I'll be delighted to afford you similar hospitality."

"I don't doubt it," Khan Sogra laughed, twirling the points of his mustache. "I may not keep you waiting long, Lord Bela. I've often longed to tour Hungary with the Wolf Horde to avail ourselves of your people's hospitality. Preferably, of course, accompanied by as many of our Petcheneg kinsmen as possible to make sure we're treated with all the respect due to a people who drove the Magyars out of their former lands."

"You'd be well advised to bring all of your people if you can," Bela replied grimly. "No matter how many Petchenegs come to Hungary, we'll give them a warm welcome, in fact we'll invite them to stay forever. We've land enough to give each of them a plot sufficient to cover his bones."

The khan was amused rather than offended by Bela's stiff warning not to attempt an incursion into Magyar territory, and gestured a polite if cool farewell.

Edmond breathed easier once he and his Magyar companions rode clear of the vast Petcheneg encampment. The nomads were notorious for being faithless. Treachery was always a hazard in dealing with them. This time, however, Khan Sogra kept his word and no one interfered with the departure of the small band led by Bela and Janos. Few even took notice of their going, though Edmond caught sight of at least one Petcheneg who did, her familiar homely face peering out of the entrance to the tent that he and Bela had occupied. She looked wistful and Edmond felt a twinge of regret before laughing it off. How unattractive she was, yet the custom was pleasant. He was tempted to wave back at her until a glance at Bela dissuaded him. The Magyar was staring straight ahead, lost in thought. He was obviously concerned only with what lay before not behind them. Edmond admitted that was probably for the best.

Days of hard riding took them through a kaleidoscopic landscape. The lowlands soon changed into hill country overshadowed by the still distant yet forbidding summits of the Carpathian Mountains. It helped that the weather remained mild because the rugged terrain with its steep declivities and countless intersecting streams might otherwise have been almost impassable. The approach toward Hungary from the southeast was the most difficult since the Carpathians and Transylvanian Alps resembled a massive rampart protecting the inhabitants of the Transylvanian plateau. Only steep canyons slashed through the antediluvian rock by rushing streams afforded ready ingress to this fortress land fashioned by the forces of nature. The most famous of these portals was the Iron Gate, far to the southwest, through which the Danube knifed on its long and rambling course to the Black Sea. Rather than this route, Bela's band followed a more direct one, choosing a somewhat difficult path through mountain valleys and across the plateau. The area was dangerous even if it was under the nominal rule of King Andras because there was always the risk of ambush by one of many fugitive bands lurking in the mountains. Among them were renegade Magyars who had reverted to the paganism of their ancestors and would give short shrift to those loyal to the Christian king.

Fortunately for Bela and his troop, they escaped all such hazards. They occasionally came upon villages that thrived in the fertile soil of the Banat despite sporadic raids by the Petchenegs and another nation of nomads, the Cumans. They were relieved, however, when they reached the first of the many military outposts established half a century earlier by Stephen, the Apostolic king of Hungary, and maintained by his latest successor, Andras. They finally were able to rest in safety and even replace their worn-out horses before continuing.

The fortlet was situated on the south bank of the Maros River which flowed westward after collecting the chill waters of several swift-flowing mountain tributaries It eventually entered the broader Tisza which wound its way from the north through the flat Nagy Alfold before emptying into the Danube.

Bela followed the Maros for a considerable distance before inexplicably turning southward again until they reached the ruins of a vast fortified town straddling a broad hill. Halting, he remarked to Edmond, "Here's something worth seeing, especially for a soldier of New Rome. It's an instructive, even sobering sight."

"What do you mean?"

"This is all that remains of what once was known as Ulpia Trajanus or, as the Dacians called it, Sarmigetusa," explained Bela, disclosing historical knowledge beyond what Edmond at one time would have credited him with possessing. By now he had learned not to underestimate the Magyar, who added, "This was the capital of the ancient Dacians before they were conquered by the Emperor Trajan who transformed it into a great Roman city."

Bela led his troop at a slow pace past the majestic ruins and into what must have been the city center, or forum, to judge by the skeletal remains of huge public buildings and temples whose fallen massive pillars and pedestals enclosed a plaza. The visitors startled small animals sheltering in the debris and Edmond fancied he even spied a human form scurrying out of sight. Perhaps a few pitiful descendants of the wealthy and powerful Romans who had ruled this once great city kept company with ancestral ghosts.

He felt a blend of awe and melancholy at this vivid testimony to the mutability of human affairs. The immense reach of former Roman power impressed him more than ever. Though these ruins were similar, if on a smaller scale, to many he had come across throughout Thrace, he had not been aware Roman rule had extended so far to the north. The vast ruins of Ulpia Trajana were telling evidence of Rome's extensive power. Perhaps Nicephorus Bryennius had not overstated his ambition. If Sarmigetusa, why not Kiev, as Bryennius had intimated was his goal? Edmond reined in speculation by reminding himself that the ancient Romans had been a different breed from the current claimants to the name.

A badly corroded bronze tablet caught his eye. He halted to examine it. The inscription was almost illegible and his Latin weak but he could make out three or four letters which he guessed to be part of the name "Traianus". "When you built this forum, great Trajan," he mused, "could you imagine it would collapse into this heap of debris, a dismal reminder of your power, conquests and glory?" He tore himself away from contemplating the awe-inspiring scene to rejoin his companions who were about to bed down for the night in the ruins of a temple.

The following morning the troop quickly left Sarmigetusa far behind as Bela retraced the detour to the ruined capital of Roman Dacia, then struck out directly for his homeland. The character of the terrain changed gradually but markedly. At first the Maros flowed downhill but the slopes became more gentle and before long the travelers entered a broad plain so level that its horizon was unbroken by anything loftier than a man's head. The rich, tall grass exuded a sweet scent. Edmond did not have to be told they had reached the Nagy Alfold, the great grazing ground of the land of the Magyars. Large herds of cattle and horses browsed on the lush vegetation and shuffled up to water holes under the watchful eyes of Magyar herdsmen. Every so often they entered large villages laid out in a generous rectangular pattern. The small box-like houses were roofed with thatch like those of England, if different in detail. The once nomadic Magyars had settled down over two centuries yet the configuration of their towns took form from their ancestors' tent encampments.

The travelers could relax their vigilance because they had reached a region firmly under the control of King Andras after a period of near anarchy resulting from the depredations of the Holy Roman Emperor Henry III. Andras had restored order in all of the forty-eight banats, or counties, into which King Stephen had divided the land of the Magyars. The great magnates and lesser nobility chafed at and sometimes openly resisted royal authority yet knew that without its help they could not hold off the Germans, Petchenegs and Cumans, or Byzantine adventurers who threatened their lands.

Bela explained all this to Edmond as they journeyed westward along the Maros, then to the north on the east bank of a larger river, the Tisza.

They followed it upstream to a ford, crossed it, then continued directly westward until they arrived at an even broader stream flowing south. Edmond was dumbfounded when Bela insisted this was the same great waterway they had crossed at far distant Silistria when they began their ill-fated incursion into Petcheneg territory. They followed the left, or east, bank upstream for two days until Bela drew rein to call attention to the other side where towering wooded heights were crowned by a partly ruined yet still formidable fortress.

"There's Buda," he said. "Legend has it that the Romans of old erected the first castle on those cliffs and now our king holds it. A small village at its foot is growing rapidly and I wouldn't be surprised if someday it might become almost as populous as Esztergom."

Bela's estate was in the vicinity, and he was tempted to visit it, but Janos impressed on him that his first duty was to report to his uncle and father at Esztergom. Nador Imre and Count Kalman were undoubtedly anxious to learn whether the mission to ransom him from the Petchenegs had succeeded.

Bela gave in, and they resumed their journey. A day after they left Buda behind, the river bent sharply to the west, not far from Esztergom, which was situated on its south bank near its confluence with a tributary, the Hron. Edmond's first glimpse of the Hungarian capital was of a church tower on a hill overlooking the town.

"Our great King Stephen was born in Esztergom," Bela said as they prepared to cross the river. "He was crowned here some fifty years ago. The crown came all the way from Rome, sent with the blessing of Pope Silvester II."

Edmond listened politely to Bela's explanation of how King Stephen had encouraged the conversion of the Magyars to Christianity, and had organized his government on the Frankish model.

"A strong, vigorous king can do much to improve his people's lot," Edmond remarked. "It's what's lacking in my homeland. England needs such a king, torn as it is by conflict among the nobility and by the intrigues of foreigners. From what you've told me, King Stephen set a fine example, one from which Atheling Edward may have benefited during his stay in Esztergom. If he has, he might prove England's savior. I wonder if your father's steward, Janos, knows whether the atheling spends much time in King Andras's court?"

Bela asked Janos, who lifted his eyebrows in astonishment and shook his head vigorously before replying. His reaction dashed Edmond's hopes even before Bela translated the steward's words.

"Janos says he thought it was generally known that your Prince Edward left Esztergom years ago. All that Janos remembers about the atheling, as you call him, is that it was rumored he had been invited to the German emperor's court at Aix la Chappelle, wherever that is, so he left Hungary. Some say the emperor was so pleased with him that he gave him one of his daughters to wed."

If Edmond had not been so disappointed at hearing that the atheling was no longer at Esztergom, he could have laughed at how all of his designs without exception were doomed to frustration. During the long trek to Esztergom he had built up hopes of meeting the atheling at King Andras's court. It would have been an opportunity to discover whether the prince was worthy of support as a man of character with the strength, vigor and will to save England from the Norman threat.

He soon came to terms with his disappointment, and took new heart in reflecting that the setback might be only temporary. His best course probably was to continue on to Aix la Chappelle as quickly as possible, and seek out the atheling if he was still in the emperor's court. Besides, the imperial capital was close to Bruges from where he could readily return to England whenever he chose to do so.

Yet despite the attempt to console himself for this latest reverse, he was downcast enough to be impatient to leave Esztergom even before he entered the town in company with Bela.

Chapter Thirty-Six

Edward the Atheling

A stocky, plainly dressed traveler on horseback paused to wipe perspiration from his brow and squint at the nearby towers of Aachen toward which he had ridden for weeks. It was unseasonably warm and dry for autumn so the dirt road was dusty. Edmond took a long pull from a leathern wine flask and sympathetically patted the faithful, sturdy little pony that had carried him from Esztergom in Hungary through much of Bohemia and Germany. On reaching Koln, he had crossed Rhine and continued to Aachen, the city called Aix la Chappelle by the French and Aquisgranum by its Roman founders who had been the first to test the healing properties of its mineral springs.

"I know, I know you need a drink too," he muttered into his pony's twitching ear as he patted its mane. "Patience! We'll soon reach our destination, and I'll allow you the honor of drinking from the imperial troughs."

It would be none too soon. He had despaired several times of his chances of coming this far safely. All southern Germany was in an uproar with authority slipping from an ailing emperor's hands. Five years earlier, Henry III had been all-powerful from the shores of the North Sea southward to beyond the walls of Rome, from Flanders to Transylvania in the southeast. Now the emperor was beset by a host of enemies who mocked his claim to be their overlord. Robber barons and bandits infested the roads to render travel almost suicidal for anyone without a large armed escort. Edmond twice had been set upon by outlaws and once by a robber baron demanding a fee for the privilege of being permitted to pass the roadside stone shack he chose to call a castle. Fortunately, his swift Magyar pony had been more than a match for the bandits' lumbering farm horses and the robber baron collected only a painful sword cut from his intended victim.

Edmond was able to relax his guard on nearing Aachen since the emperor's men controlled the few miles of road between his capital and Koln. He had hoped to find the imperial court at Koln but Henry III, in search of relief from a painful ailment, had transferred to Aachen to take advantage of its springs' medicinal properties.

He gently spurred the pony as he prepared to enter Aachen. It was comforting to hear the jingle of gold and silver in the fat purse pressed on him by Bela when he left Esztergom. A rare good fellow, that Bela! Not only had the Magyar royally entertained him in his uncle Nador Imre's palatial mansion, but had given him his best horse and had his equipment repaired, all the while begging him to stay in Hungary. Their parting had been emotional, knowing they were unlikely to meet again.

Edmond passed into Aachen by the gate known as the Ponttor, trotting across the bridge without challenge. The mid-afternoon traffic was light as the peasants who came to market in the morning to peddle their produce were not yet ready to leave the city. An old man-at-arms in pitted, rust-stained armor was the lone guard at the gate, mute testimony that the emperor's rule was still respected in the immediate vicinity of his court. The veteran hardly glanced at Edmond before waving him in.

Despite having been the capital of Emperor Charlemagne, Aachen was not about to awe anyone who had beheld the wonders of Constantinople. Nevertheless, an impressive dignity clung to the old public buildings towering over the mostly ramshackle dwellings bordering the crooked, narrow streets of the small city. Edmond glanced about with interest heightened by the universal fame of the legendary ruler. Even in England's West Country itinerant minstrels and scops continued to celebrate Charlemagne's wisdom, magnanimity, power and conquests. Who had not heard of his nephew Roland, the paladin of old who had fought to the death rather than yield to the Saracens? Edmond was impressed most by the great cathedral with its towering spires. It lay near the vast imperial palace. After a rest, he intended to visit both buildings the following day.

He halted at the first inn he came across, and wolfed down a cheap but hearty meal before surprising the innkeeper by demanding a private room rather than being content to bed down in the common hall. The host at first demurred, unable to conceive that this ordinary-looking foreigner could afford such luxury, but a silver penny set his mind to rest. Edmond wanted to sleep undisturbed with the security afforded by being able to lock or block a door.

It was not until he awoke the next day and discovered the sun already at its zenith that he realized how tired he had been. He no longer needed to disguise his rank so he carefully drew out the splendid Byzantine armor concealed in a sack all the way from Hungary. The cuirass glittered almost as brightly as it had when presented to him by Constantine IX. The armorer who had repaired it at Esztergom knew his trade. Only the closest inspection could reveal the slight traces of the dents and scratches left as memorials of numerous skirmishes and battles, the last and most deadly upon that blood-drenched hill in

Petcheneg territory.

The astonished innkeeper was almost overcome by servility when Edmond, wearing his resplendent armor, emerged from the room he had entered the previous night as an apparently nondescript traveler. Edmond stopped his flow of abject apology and timid inquiry with the clink of a large coin. The sight sent the host rushing to the kitchen to make sure the great lord's meal was suitable to his station. He soon placed a mutton pie, sweet pastry and mellow beer before Edmond.

"I couldn't dine better in Constantinople," Edmond remarked, flipping the landlord another coin as he leaned back with a full stomach. "You must entertain many visitors of quality to be able to serve such a fine meal."

"Few enough, my lord, not as many as we'd like," sighed the host. "Our good emperor's table is long and his bounty knows no limits. Many of noble birth take advantage of his generous hospitality and we humble landlords suffer. Now and then some great lord, mostly a foreigner or someone in disgrace with his majesty, honors us by dining here and we do our best to make him comfortable."

"Do you receive many visitors from England?"

"Not as many as formerly, though one or two drop in now and then. There were more some years ago when King Edward sent an army to serve with Emperor Henry. Those coming to Aachen nowadays are mostly visitors to the English prince at the court."

"Have there been any lately?"

"None have stopped at my inn, I'm sorry to say. I've heard there's an English bishop at court." The landlord sighed with a wry expression before continuing. "Oh, these are sad times. Our good emperor is ill and only last week was taken by litter to Badfeld, or Bodfeld, or some such little town." He crossed himself as if to suggest it was unlikely Henry III would return alive to Aachen.

"Did all the court accompany him?"

"No, many of his people remain here. Of course, all I know of what's going on is what I hear from kitchen scullions and the common soldiers who drop in for their beer. They say there's little hope for the poor emperor. More's the pity because his son is a puling boy, not more than six or seven years old." The host pulled a long face as he wrung his dirty apron to demonstrate the depth of his concern.

Edmond left the innkeeper to his sorrows and walked into the courtyard. He accepted his pony's reins from a stableboy, swung into the saddle, and rode through Aachen intent on exploring the sights. He was amused by the obvious admiration of those he met. Accustomed as they were to nobles of the highest rank visiting Henry III's court, the citizens of Aachen gawked at the resplendently appareled figure riding so casually toward the imperial palace.

Edmond's route took him past the cathedral which was similar to many of the churches of Constantinople. It was like a Romanesque edifice in Ravenna, Italy, which had been so admired by Charlemagne that he had built a near replica. Though severely damaged during the Norman invasions, the building had been fully restored by Emperor Otto III some seventy years before Edmond saw it.

Entrusting his pony to a street urchin, Edmond entered the cathedral. It was deserted and he was at leisure to explore its splendors. He could easily imagine himself back in Constantinople within this great basilica decorated so sumptuously and with such consummate artistry. Dwarfed by towering and ornate columns, he gazed up in admiration at the glittering and colorful mosaic depicting Christ and the twenty-four elders that fronted the gallery. He was equally impressed by a huge marble structure at floor level situated directly beneath the apex of the great dome. He approached and reverently read the name "Carolus Magne" incised into the stone. The tomb of Charlemagne! Beside it was placed a large ornate chair, the emperor's throne.

He knelt, overcome by feeling a bond of kinship with the monarch and statesman who had ruled wisely and justly over so many lands and peoples. He also was suffused with pride on reflecting that Charlemagne's blood as well as Alfred's ran in his veins. The seed of Cerdic and Pepin the Short had been blended by more than one marriage among their descendants.

Such grandiose thoughts! He laughed at himself. What did such illustrious ancestry matter to someone in his friendless, lonely position? It would be more beneficial to his cousin Atheling Edward whose lineage was similar. The justice of the atheling's claim to the succession was undeniable even if King Edward procrastinated about confirming his nephew's right. Whether the atheling measured up to his heritage was another matter. What Edmond had heard of him in Esztergom, where Atheling Edward had resided for years, was disquieting. He was described as dull in understanding and sluggish in disposition. That assessment might be discounted as the opinion of foreigners who did not understand English reserve. Nevertheless, it was disturbing that the atheling had never returned to his native land to claim his birthright. His failure to make the attempt suggested indolence, perhaps even timidity or cowardice.

The English bishop mentioned by the innkeeper as a visitor to the imperial court could be King Edward's intermediary with the atheling. The king might have agreed to get in touch with his nephew in an attempt to persuade him to return to England. It was possible some of the king's English advisors had suggested the atheling would be a useful counterpoise to Duke William of Normandy's pretensions. If so, all might yet turn out well. William the Bastard could not seriously contest the claims of someone so logically and rightfully the obvious successor to the throne.

Speculation was idle, Edmond finally concluded. He must size up Atheling Edward in person rather than rely on others' opinions before taking a stand. The bishop might be helpful, but it would be best to confront Edward directly. With that in mind, he proceeded from the cathedral to the enormous palace, built like the great church by Charlemagne, virtually destroyed by the Normans, and restored by Otto III.

"I come to pay my respects to Atheling Edward," he informed the guards at the palace gate. "Thane Edmond of Bosbury, a kometes of the Varangian Guard of Her Most Sacred Christ-Loving Basilissa Theodora, requests permission to offer his services to the next basileus of Britain and king of the English."

His grandiloquent announcement and splendid appearance threw the guards into confusion. They pulled at their mustaches in uncertainty until their commander came to see what all the fuss was about. He shot a cursory glance at Edmond, whistled under his breath, shrugged his shoulders, and ordered him admitted. After all, the emperor was absent and there was no need to be overly cautious at the risk of offending someone with such an imposing title who was so splendidly equipped. The visitor might well have legitimate business with the atheling who after all was a foreigner with little influence. The officer even thought it politic to personally conduct Edmond to the prince's quarters.

Atheling Edward was not pleased at being disturbed while preparing for his afternoon nap. Confound it, could not these English visitors leave him in peace? As if he yearned to return to their wretched island? He was comfortable in Germany as the emperor's honored relative. He had left England as an infant, and if it had not been for far too many difficult hours spent with a tutor he could not have spoken a word of its language. Even now he spoke it hesitantly notwithstanding that some scholars insisted there was little difference between English and the German of the imperial court.

While the atheling completed his toilet in preparation for the unexpected visitor, he wondered if he might look at matters differently if it were not for a troubling, persistent cough. It reminded him of Henry III's ailment. He shuddered. The emperor's illness was a consideration. If Henry III were not so near death it would be easy to slam the door on these unwelcome and annoying Englishmen. Who could tell what might happen with the emperor gone? A contingency plan was essential. Uncle Edward might be right to insist on his return to England, though he dismissed as absurd the king's contention he owed to it to the memory of his father Edmond Ironside to claim the succession.

"It gives me great pleasure and satisfaction to welcome one of my dear countrymen," the atheling told Edmond in lame English with as much cordiality as he could squeeze out between his thin lips. In spite of himself, he was impressed by Edmond's almost regal martial appearance even if he was too impassive to betray it by more than a mere twitch of the eyebrows.

"My lord atheling, it's a great and warmly appreciated honor for a humble thane like myself to be so graciously and cordially welcomed by my future king," replied Edmond, sinking to one knee and kissing the atheling's languidly offered and limp right hand.

"Not so fast, young man!" Edward scolded, so startled that he broke into a fit of violent coughing. After recovering, he continued hoarsely, "I suspect Bishop Ealdred schooled you to add your persuasions to those he had plagued me with. I am besieged on all sides. No need, I'm convinced it's the best course, considering the sad turn affairs are taking here."

"I have yet to meet the bishop, but if he's trying to persuade your highness to return to England and take up your rightful inheritance, I'll gladly add my voice to his."

Edmond hid his dismay. Edward's appearance and demeanor confirmed the Hungarian court's description. The atheling was a sallow-skinned, wizened little man who spoke in a monotone. His cough suggested he was suffering from a deep-seated ailment. Even as Edmond spoke, the atheling was seized by another fit, and quickly downed some wine.

"You see how it goes with me, Thane Edmond," he gasped while recovering his breath. "I dare not go to England until it's warmer and drier, perhaps in the spring. They say the climate is most abominably wet much of the time and I wouldn't want to worry my friends by falling ill after my arrival." He neglected to add that he hoped by spring affairs might become more settled in Germany and he would be able to judge which was the best way to jump. "You say you didn't come from my good and revered friend Bishop Ealdred. Did Earl Harold Godwinson send you then?"

"Earl Harold? No, my lord, I come by way of Hungary from Constantinople where I was in the service of Empress Theodora."

"Do you know Earl Harold?"

"Your highness asked if he sent me. Is he back in England?"

"Back? I wasn't aware he ever left," the atheling replied in surprise, then chuckled. "Surely, you're not thinking of the sad days when Earl Godwin's family fled the court of my good uncle, King Edward?

Constantinople truly must be at the ends of the earth for you to be so out of touch. It has been four years since Godwin and his family were welcomed back to England after the misunderstanding was explained. It's true the old man died three years ago, but Harold more than fills his shoes, no doubt greatly to the regret of some people."

The atheling's explanation confounded Edmond. There had been vague reports in Esztergom that the Godwinsons had made peace with King Edward, but no one was sure. The Magyars knew very little of English affairs and cared less, scrambling doubtful stories into improbabilities. Edmond discounted all he heard. He was amused to discover that the nonsense he had spouted to Sweyn four years earlier during their confrontation in Constantinople had become reality. He had been almost clairvoyant in foretelling what was actually taking place in England. He pressed the atheling for more details.

The prince related that Godwin and his sons had landed with a large army at Southwark in September 1052 causing the king's supporters to melt away without a fight. King Edward had grudgingly restored all honors, offices and estates to Godwin's family. When the old earl died the following spring, Harold succeeded to most of his property and power. The West Saxon earl's fortunes had been in the ascendant ever since, with King Edward relinquishing the conduct of most affairs to him.

"You can judge how well most of the Godwinsons are flourishing," the atheling concluded. "All but Earl Sweyn, who I'm told went on pilgrimage to Jerusalem to seek absolution for his sins. It's said he died of a fever in a place called Lycia."

Edmond wondered whether this explanation for Sweyn's death was generally accepted. From his standpoint, it was greatly preferable to the truth. If it got out that he had killed Sweyn it would make his return to England all the more hazardous. Dismissing the thought, he chatted amicably with Atheling Edward about affairs in Germany and Hungary while sipping wine. The prince said he had many happy memories of his long stay at Esztergom, and inquired about his old friends there.

A few of the atheling's mannerisms, particularly his hand gestures, reminded Edmond of his own father. The similarity brought home to him that Edward was his nearest living relative, a first cousin, the son of Edwy's brother, Edmond Ironside. A pity he was so unprepossessing. Nevertheless, it was some comfort to realize that to ally himself with the atheling would be to help his own family.

The atheling misread Edmond's preoccupation. "As you may have noticed, I'm far more familiar with the affairs of Hungary and Germany than those of my native England in which you are doubtless more interested," he said apologetically, then snapped his fingers. "I have it.

The bishop of Worcester is dining here today and you should join us. No, I insist, Thane Edmond. I've not learned enough of your adventures and I know the bishop and Lady Agatha will be eager to hear about the court in Constantinople, and especially what you know about Empress Theodora."

The atheling explained that Bishop Ealdred had come on a mission from King Edward and the Witan to renew efforts to persuade him to return to England. The bishop had failed in a similar attempt two years earlier. "I'm tempted to yield to their inducements this time," Edward confided, the wine loosening his tongue. "I've hinted as much to Bishop Ealdred but I don't think he's convinced of my sincerity. All the better, if it helps me squeeze a few more hides of land out of my saintly uncle, King Edward."

Edmond hid his scorn, smiled polite appreciation of the atheling's cunning tactics, and accepted the invitation.

When it came time to sit down for the evening meal, he noted that with the exception of Bishop Ealdred the company was hardly distinguished, the guests being German and French lesser nobles and minor imperial court officials. The higher-ranking noblemen were attending the emperor at Badfeld.

When the wine flowed freely, some guests began to fawn with abandon on the atheling who accepted the excessive flattery with evident pleasure. It struck Edmond that it was probable that when the atheling succeeded to King Edward's throne the Normans now infesting the English court would merely be replaced by another set of foreign predators.

He was more tolerant, even understanding, of the courtiers' similarly assiduous attention to Lady Agatha, the atheling's attractive young wife—a cousin, not the daughter of the emperor as some reports mistakenly had it. Agatha had borne Atheling Edward three children, a son, Edgar, and two daughters, Margaret and Christina, yet preserved a girlish coquetry that was most attractive.

"Come, Thane Edmond," Lady Agatha teased, glancing mischievously at her women companions, "you mustn't deny you've left some dark-eyed Greek princesses in despair at your leaving Constantinople. I don't believe it! A handsome young fellow like you? You must tell us what's fashionable these days, how the finest ladies dress their hair. We must look so backwards to you."

Edmond smiled, resolved to play along with the general tenor of the evening. "Honored lady, believe me when I say that no woman in the Basilissa Theodora's court is superior, even equal, in beauty and accomplishment to yourself or your ladies-in-waiting. I've never been in such charming company, not even in Constantinople."

Agatha laughed with unfeigned pleasure, and urged the atheling, "Edward, when you're restored to your rightful position you must send our young men to Constantinople to learn such pleasing manners. It's evident the Greeks have instructed Thane Edmond in their happy art of graceful dissimulation. I can't imagine a more proficient pupil."

Edmond observed that during the fatuous flow of flattery, flippancy and badinage, Bishop Ealdred sat to the atheling's right without changing expression. He remained grave, ate sparingly, and spoke little. He glanced occasionally at Edmond as if to size him up before approaching him late in the evening.

The bishop opened with an inquiry about Patriarch Michael Cerularius who two or three years before had severed all ties between the Eastern Church and that of Rome. Edmond pleaded ignorance of such weighty religious matters, and could offer not much more than a description of the patriarch's personality from his slight acquaintance with the cleric. When Bishop Ealdred realized he could extract little useful information on the religious conflict he turned to other matters.

"It's not often our young men from England venture so far afield as Constantinople," he remarked. "I suppose the example set by Harald Hardraade in enriching himself in the imperial service encourages some few of the more adventurous souls like you to enlist in the Varangian Guard."

"That's true. My father was poor though a thane, your grace. He left me little of value other than his sword, which I treasure above all else. I had no choice other than try to make my own way in the world and since I could see little opportunity of doing so in England, I left my country to take my chances elsewhere."

"That's understandable. Yet Constantinople seems an unusual place to pursue one's fortune, never mind how tempting its wealth. It's so distant from England one might even say it's at the other end of the world. I imagine few young men would go that far. Most try their luck in Germany, Denmark or even Norway, where customs aren't all that different from ours." The bishop halted momentarily as if to weigh his words, then looked sharply at Edmond as he continued, "Of course, I seem to recall someone telling me of a young fellow like yourself who had thoughts of going to Constantinople for special reasons some years ago."

Edmond replied guardedly, "Indeed, your grace?"

"Yes, I'm sure of it, and now I recall who told me about this bold young man, my dear friend Prior Wulfstan. He had more or less pledged to keep the matter secret, but since he hadn't heard from the youth for a long time he thought it certain he had died abroad so silence no longer mattered."

Edmond was careful to show only casual interest. So Prior Wulfstan had let slip at least part of his secret to Bishop Ealdred. But how much of it?

"It was mere happenstance that Prior Wulfstan spoke to me of this young man," the bishop continued, keeping his eyes fixed firmly on Edmond's face. "We were discussing the atheling's status as the last surviving member of his generation of the race of Cerdic. Prior Wulfstan happened to mention this lad's extraordinary claims, almost surely imaginary yet nevertheless dangerous to public order if anyone decides to make use of him."

"Undoubtedly, your grace," Edmond agreed hurriedly to assure the bishop he understood perfectly. "If the fellow happens to return to England, he'd be a fool to repeat such ridiculous claims. If he has an ounce of sense he'll use whatever wealth he brings back from his travels to purchase a property in a remote county and avoid meddling with public affairs."

Bishop Ealdred nodded approval, apparently satisfied with Edmond's reaction to his broad hint, whether or not he believed him to be the subject of Prior Wulfstan's revelation. It was obvious he suspected without being certain.

Lost in thought, Edmond rode back to the inn after promising to accept the atheling's hospitality again the following day and respond to his offer of a place in his retinue. So the bishop had at least an inkling of his claim to royal descent, whether or not he believed it. It was evident he thought it best forgotten. No matter. If the atheling returned to England and was recognized as King Edward's heir, the Norman danger would be greatly diminished. Edmond decided to accept the atheling's proposal. Once the prince was secure he would leave his service, regain the little estate near Bosbury that had been his father's, add a few hides of land, and live out his allotted lifespan in the obscurity and safety of retirement.

As for his father's deathbed assertion that he "was born to be a king" he would settle for being the monarch of his estate.

Chapter Thirty-Seven

Conspiracy?

A seemingly interminable succession of dreary days dragged through the autumn and into winter at Atheling Edward's pretense of a court at Aachen. Tedious as the atmosphere generally was, it became even duller after the death of Emperor Henry III in early October because his passing entailed a lengthy period of mourning.

Edmond struggled in vain against boredom, the vacuous court routine affording few outlets for his pent-up energy. Fortunately the hunt was among the few activities capable of dispelling the atheling's habitual torpor and Edward soon learned to appreciate Edmond's enthusiasm for and skill in the chase. The prince became as fond of him as his cold nature permitted him to be of anyone. He increasingly called on Edmond if an opponent was needed to play chess or if a discussion turned to military affairs and political matters involving the eastern empire. Lady Agatha also enjoyed Edmond's company, though her limited interests revolving chiefly around women's fashions, household subjects and her children, did little to relieve his ennui. Edmond became increasingly impatient for Edward to make up his mind and leave Aachen for England, so painfully near after their long absences from their homeland.

Edmond being in such a state of mind, it was scarcely surprising that he was stimulated and intrigued when in January he learned of the impending arrival of an emissary from England. It was rumored the envoy was bringing a new proposal from King Edward that might finally convince Edward Edmondson to return home. Since the death of Henry III, the atheling's stay in Aachen was becoming uncomfortable.

Edmond could not contain his surprise when King Edward's representative was ushered into the atheling's presence. "Thane Sebert!" he exclaimed.

"You know me, sir?" The visitor's attention swung from Atheling Edward to Edmond who had recognized Earl Harold's officer though Sebert's formerly ebony beard now was shot with gray. "I don't recall having had the pleasure of meeting you."

"Yet we've served together, Thane Sebert. Like you, I was with Earl Harold when he accompanied his father to Gloucester some years ago,"

Edmond rattled on before halting in embarrassed realization that he was violating protocol by interrupting Sebert's presentation of his credentials. "Pardon, noble Edward, I forgot myself in speaking out with such untimely rudeness."

"Nonsense, no need to apologize, good friend Edmond," the atheling waved good-humoredly. "I'm pleased someone of our court, somebody whose opinion we value highly, is acquainted with Thane Sebert and can vouch for him. As soon as we learn why the noble thane has graced us with his presence you'll be free to chat with him to your heart's content." He nodded to Sebert. "Good thane, to what do we owe the pleasure of beholding you in Aachen?"

"Gracious highness, I bring a letter from my lord, Earl Harold Godwinson." Sebert fished out a rolled-up parchment from beneath his cloak and offered it to Edward. "The earl instructed me to assure you that it is his earnest hope and fondest wish to soon have the opportunity of placing his hands between yours on England's soil."

Edward glanced at Harold's seal, broke it and unrolled the letter. He frowned and pursed his lips alternately as he struggled over its contents, understanding them only in part as he was barely literate. He soon handed it in relief to an attendant clerk whom he trusted to explain it later.

"You have some notion of what the earl has written?" he asked Sebert who nodded. "Well then you may be able to tell me in all honesty— without reservation—about Earl Ralph, whom your lord mentions? Can he be trusted in our affairs?"

After momentary hesitation, Sebert replied cautiously, "I believe he's well-intentioned, your highness, though somewhat over-fond of the pleasures of the table and the chase. He's not particularly ambitious for power and influence in the state, though somewhat avid for wealth and estates. Some say he lacks deep convictions, even that he could be readily manipulated by subtle schemers for their own ends."

"Earl Harold suggests that King Edward is extremely fond of Earl Ralph as his sister's son, which might create further difficulties for us," Edward commented, then asked, "Is that why the few Normans left in the king's court may believe they might be able to secure the crown for him as someone who actually is one of their own even if, like myself, he's a grandson of King Ethelred?" Sebert nodded assent, and Edward resumed. "Earl Harold suggests that the Normans may be brewing a conspiracy, led by my uncle's chamberlain Hugolin, to persuade the king to openly designate Earl Ralph as his successor if I continue to delay my return to England."

"A common report, my lord," Sebert confirmed. "Some suspect it's intended to shroud the Normans' real goal, which allegedly calls for Earl

Ralph to step aside in favor of Duke William upon our king's death. I doubt that. Earl Ralph may not be overly ambitious, but neither is he such a nonentity as to yield tamely to Duke William once the kingship is within his grasp. His claim is indisputably superior to William's even it it's not equal to yours as the son of King Edmond Ironside. If Ralph stands firm, it would be difficult to unseat him. And while most of our people long for your return as King Edward's rightful heir, they'd support Ralph, if reluctantly, rather than accept William of Normandy."

The atheling grimaced. "It's clear I can't afford to delay much longer. I must declare myself one way or the other. How soon do you go back to England?"

"Whenever you wish me to, your highness. I've been instructed to return as soon as you're ready to entrust me with a reply to Earl Harold."

"You'll have it tomorrow. Until then I place you into Thane Edmond's charge since you're already acquainted. For that matter, a letter to Earl Harold is scarcely needed because I've privately assured my royal uncle King Edward through Bishop Ealdred that I'm prepared to leave for England in the spring, God willing."

Edward pulled himself to his feet with a groan, setting off a coughing fit, then added after recovering, "I must leave you now, my friends. Thane Edmond, you'll oblige me greatly by attending to Thane Sebert."

Sebert frowned, shuffled his feet uncomfortably, but composed himself sufficiently to force a polite smile. "I now recall Thane Edmond perfectly," he admitted coldly. "He disappeared rather suddenly after our days together in England."

The off-hand remark revealed the reason for Sebert's chilly manner. He apparently believed Edmond had deserted the House of Godwin during the confrontation with King Edward and his Norman advisors in 1051.

Edmond sought to correct the misunderstanding. "You seem to think poorly of me, Thane Sebert. Do you believe I abandoned Earl Harold after he sailed to Ireland?"

"What I believe? Everyone knows you disappeared after Earl Harold entrusted you with a vital mission. No one ever heard from you again after he left you in Bristol in the expectation that you would carry out his orders. It's obvious you neglected his interests and deserted his cause."

"Is that what Earl Harold believes?"

"What else was he to think?"

An elaborate ivory crucifix lay on a nearby table and Edmond placed his right hand on it as he declared, "I swear by this holy rood that I faithfully discharged my duties after Earl Harold sailed from Bristol. If I failed to succeed it was not because I betrayed him. Furthermore, I did not leave England because I considered his cause hopeless or that I would suffer from my connection to the earl."

"Then why did you disappear when he depended on your support?"

"That I can't reveal, Thane Sebert, but I can assure you it had nothing to do with Earl Harold. I must ask you to take my assurances on faith. It would be prejudicial to others if I disclosed why I left England."

Edmond's earnest manner deeply impressed Sebert who was at heart a fair and judicious man. He scrutinized him searchingly as if trying to read his mind and weigh his soul. All the while, Edmond kept his hand on the cross, lips compressed.

After a struggle, Sebert whispered, "I may choose to believe you, Thane Edmond, but I can't speak for my lord Harold. He was deeply hurt and angered by what he conceived to be a treacherous abandonment by someone he looked upon as a friend. He swore that if he ever met you again he would demand satisfaction with his sword."

"The passage of time may have dulled his anger," replied Edmond. "Even if it hasn't, I'll never draw sword against him."

"Let's hope your resolve is never put to the test. If Earl Harold vows to do something, he never hesitates to do it." Sebert placed a hand on Edmond's shoulder. "If you return to England, I advise you to stay out of his sight until you can lay all the facts before him. If he has a fault, it's that he's slow to forgive, and a man of fearful passions when crossed."

"I'd hoped it would be otherwise," Edmond replied sadly. "Nevertheless, I must risk the earl's anger because I mean to return to England as one of the atheling's court."

"You've committed yourself to Lord Edward then?"

"I'm not his liege man, if that's what you mean, but I serve him freely and with all my heart because I'd rather see an Englishman upon England's throne than a Norman pirate. Atheling Edward is an Englishman, at least by birth if not in his ways, not a foreign interloper like Ralph the Timid or William the Bastard."

"Your words suggest you don't love, or even respect, this prince of ours all that much?"

"I needn't love him to defend his cause. Even to the death if need be, because it's mine and England's as well as his," Edmond declared enigmatically.

Sebert moved closer after glancing around the room to see whether he could be overheard. "Then take care lest the need for your services suddenly disappears. If I read the signs correctly, the Normans around King Edward may not be content with plotting to discourage Atheling Edward from returning to England. They may act to improve Earl Ralph's prospects, and thus indirectly those of Duke William."

"What do you mean?"

"It verges on impiety merely to intimate that clerics, holy men as they profess to be, might contemplate devising a crime so heinous. Yet there's reason to believe the king's chamberlain Hugolin and his good friend Bishop William of London may not be content to rely on God's will to accomplish their aims."

"Are you suggesting a plot?"

"What sort of men of rank are around the Atheling?"

"Mostly German and French knights, none of high rank."

"Are any of them Normans?"

"I'm not sure whether three of the Frenchmen, Jean de Chermay, Henri Bloett and Armand d'Orivalle, are from Normandy. D'Orivalle might be."

"Even the Frenchmen may be suspect. It's certain Hugolin and his allies are not likely to stop at anything, especially if Duke William supports them."

"Then you would advise...?"

"Find out all what you can about these people. Be on guard at all times."

"It sounds like good advice. I'll follow it."

"You'd better do so if you wish to protect the prince from harm. Only the atheling's life stands between the Norman pretenders and the succession."

Not quite, Edmond thought ruefully, but Sebert was correct for all practical purposes. It seemed monstrous to even suspect the Bishop of London of being involved in so ungodly an undertaking as a conspiracy to murder a prince. Yet it was credible. A priest's vestments might not suffice to stifle the predatory instincts of someone a mere three generations removed from pirate ancestry.

Atheling Edward the following day handed Sebert a letter to deliver to Earl Harold. "If God wills, I'll meet with your master before Eastertide. I'll then tell him in person what I now charge you to convey to England, that if Edward Edmondson succeeds King Edward Ethelredson, Earl Harold will be Earl Harold more than ever."

Sebert was momentarily puzzled by the cryptic message, then smiled understanding.

Edmond escorted Sebert into the courtyard for a final word in private. "I'll bear in mind what you've told me. For your part, I'd be grateful if you'd sound out Earl Harold on my behalf and try to soften his attitude. No matter how he responds, however, my regard for him is unchanged."

With Sebert's warning as a spur, during the next few days he looked for indications of conspiracy among the atheling's followers but detected no hint of a plot. There was little reason to suspect the Germans because they hated Normans in general. As for the three French knights he had named to Sebert, all had served Henry III loyally for years before they had entered the atheling's service. Lacking obvious suspects, he decided his sole recourse was to remain constantly alert if he was to counter any threat to the atheling.

A chance remark at a meal in late February drew his attention to one man in particular. The conversation, as if often does among old soldiers, turned to campaigns in which those present had fought. Someone remarked that on occasion treachery had played a vital role in determining the outcome of a battle.

"Nothing can compare to Val-es-Dunes," offered Armand D'Orivalle, a black-bearded, dark-complexioned veteran of indeterminate age whose numerous scars testified to his taking part in many engagements. "You've all undoubtedly heard of Duke William's victory. But you may not know how Ralph de Tesson, lord of Thury, swung the tide of battle in the duke's favor?"

Edmond joined in a chorus urging D'Orivalle to recount the incidents of the famous battle in which William the Bastard, supported by King Henry of France, ten years before had crushed a rebellion of his oft-intractable Norman subjects.

"It'll be a pleasure to retell the story of that glorious day," said D'Orivalle, flattered by the attention. "As you know, the king and duke arrayed their forces near Valmery. Ralph de Tesson, who at the time was lord of the Forest of Cingueleiz, brought one hundred and twenty knights to the field. He swore he would strike Duke William, though he was his liege lord, wherever he found him. But his resolution failed when he saw the duke standing directly opposite him with the battle about to be joined. De Tesson's knights and lesser retainers, terrified of the duke's great power and heavy hand, crowded around to remind him of his homage and plighted faith to William. They argued that he who fought against his natural lord had no right to fief or honor."

Atheling Edward, listening raptly, interrupted D'Orivalle. "There's no gainsaying that. Otherwise there would be no rule or order in the world."

"Indeed so, my lord," D'Orivalle agreed smoothly, "and Ralph de Tesson knew it as well as the next man without having to be reminded he was courting dishonor. But there was also the question of having pledged his faith to the leaders of the rebellion, Viscounts Neal and Randolf, both great and powerful lords. Weighing most heavily on his mind, however, was that he had sworn to smite Duke William wherever and whenever he encountered him on the field of battle."

"So he could not avoid forswearing himself whatever he chose to do," remarked Edmond, keeping his eyes fixed on D'Orivalle.

288

"A less ingenious man might not have found an acceptable solution to such a dilemma," D'Orivalle smirked knowingly.

"Well, what did de Tesson decide to do?" the atheling demanded impatiently. "How did he get out of this quandary?"

"As soon as the battle was joined, he drew his men apart from both armies as if uncertain as to what course he should take. After a delay, he ordered his men to stay put, shouted his war cry, then spurred all alone across the field toward the duke's army. Those surrounding Duke William, believing de Tesson meant to seek his pardon, parted to let him reach their lord's side. De Tesson flicked his glove into Duke William's face, thus carrying out his oath to smite him on the field. I couldn't believe what I was seeing. God knows, de Tesson slapped Duke William hard enough to redden his cheek. Surprised and indignant as the duke was, he immediately forgave de Tesson on hearing his explanation that he was constrained by honor to perform his oath before deserting the rest of the rebels and coming over to support him as his liege lord."

"You must have been quite close to the scene to witness the slap," remarked Edmond. "Were you with Duke William?"

D'Orivalle seemed uneasy. "Close? Well, no, not that close. I was in the front rank of those facing the duke's army and even at a distance I could see what was taking place. No, I wasn't with the duke, though it would've been far better for me if I had been. It was a costly day for me and mine. I lost my little plot of land, and haven't dared return to Normandy for the past ten years."

D'Orivalle's assertion about his misfortune rang sincere, Edmond concluded, yet he could not shake his doubts. The man's eyesight must have been extraordinarily keen to distinguish such detail at the considerable distance likely to have separated the armies before the battle began. It was not inconceivable that D'Orivalle had been among Duke William's men rather than with the rebels.

What was incontestable was that D'Orivalle might have a motive for acting in the interests of the Norman duke regardless of his former allegiance. If a former rebel, he might seek to reinstate himself in the ruler's good graces. If a loyal follower all along, he would either be carrying out the orders of William the Bastard or trying to curry additional favor by anticipating his wishes.

In any case, it would be prudent to keep a close eye on D'Orivalle.

Chapter Thirty-Eight

Death of a Traitor

The atheling's coughing spells became more frequent and protracted as the winter wore on. He was clearly suffering from a serious ailment. The court physician, Master Hermann of Koln, stressed his royal patient's delicate constitution, urged him to curtail physical activities such as hunting, hawking and riding, and prescribed various herbal remedies. Despite the doctor's ministrations, the prince at times was so ill he could not get out of bed for three or four days running. Usually timid Lady Agatha became so concerned she ordered Master Hermann, whom she suspected of being too confident of his own skill, to consult the celebrated Master Pandulf of Ravenna whose professional reputation was unsullied by the recent death of his most exalted patient, Henry III.

After rigorously examining Atheling Edward, Master Pandulf bustled out of the sickroom to report his findings to Lady Agatha and Master Hermann. He declared that "while the disorder is serious, remedial measures if immediately applied, should be highly effective in restoring his highness's health."

"My dear husband's life is in danger then?" wailed the princess, ashen with fear.

"I wouldn't say there's any immediate cause for concern," hedged Master Pandulf. "Not at all. There's good hope if we apply a sound, strict regimen and administer appropriate medication. Herbal curatives are all very well in their way—I applaud my distinguished colleague Master Hermann for resorting to them—but more stringent remedies are required in such stubborn cases. A warm broth of night-gathered snails steeped in dog urine, preferably that of a bitch, or a liberal amount of powdered alum dissolved in mare's milk, is recommended. Once the medicine restores the balance of humors, which I'm confident it will do quickly, a change of scene will hasten the atheling's period of recuperation. Sea air, for instance, should benefit him immensely."

Lady Agatha smiled relief. "My husband has spoken of crossing to England before Easter."

"Splendid, splendid," Pandulf approved. "Lord Edward should be up and about long before then. Once he begins to regain strength, he might benefit from a hunting or hawking expedition on the first fairly pleasant day. Modest activity should do him good."

Though bewildered by the wide divergence in therapy recommended by the two physicians, Lady Agatha and the rest of the atheling's people took heart from Master Pandulf's reassurance. All longed impatiently for relief from the cold, blustery late winter on behalf of the master of the court in exile.

By the time warming breezes heralded the approach of spring, Atheling Edward felt and looked much better, having stolidly endured— or survived—Master Pandulf's radical course of treatment. Nevertheless, even though Edward generally reveled in field sports, he was reluctant to take advantage of the improved weather to resume his favorite pursuits. He grumbled that any exertion still tired him quickly. He thought it best to delay until he had regained full strength. Lady Agatha and his physicians, however, finally convinced him to venture on an outing on the grounds that his health would benefit immensely even if he took just a leisurely ride. While he and some of his companions confined themselves to a gentle canter in the countryside around Aachen, his wife and the other courtiers would go hawking.

The party set out in high spirits in anticipation of a vigorous change from the dreary rounds of a long winter spent mostly indoors. Edmond exuberantly bestrode his Magyar pony that appeared as pleased as its master at the prospect of brisk exercise. Even Atheling Edward, clinging to his charger, was buoyant amidst his retainers as they rode through the city gate out into the still barren yet inviting countryside.

"Come, Thane Edmond, stay with me," the atheling urged. "These physicians may be more skillful than some believe because I feel better than I have in a long time. This fresh, country air is invigorating, a welcome change after being cooped up indoors all winter." He drew a deep breath, smiling gratefully in the realization he could do so without setting off a coughing spell such as those that had tortured him for so long. He touched a spur to his horse's flank, Edmond following suit, and they cantered ahead of the rest of the party, which remained bunched around Lady Agatha.

Edmond glanced back. Lady Agatha's companions were chattering gaily, the men bantering with the princess and her women, content to stay behind the atheling and him, as well as the prince's personal attendant and bodyguard, the Magyar Zoltan who kept close to his master. He noticed that Armand D'Orivalle was not among the company. It was just as well, he reflected, relieving him of having to keep a close eye on the Norman.

Childe Edward, in unusually high spirits, impulsively left the road to cut across a field, Edmond and Zoltan following. The three riders quickly drew away from the rest of the party, which kept to the road.

The atheling was attracted toward a stand of tall trees spread across a few hilly acres. As the acclivity grew steeper, the riders slowed to a trot, then walked their horses into the copse of still barren trees that as yet offered no shade from the brilliant sunshine.

"Blessed Lord, it's peaceful and refreshing here," the atheling commented contentedly as he halted, swiveling in the saddle to survey the view from the hilltop. "I grow weary of the endless chatter of the court," He glanced toward the cavalcade now receding along the road they had left. "Let them enjoy themselves to their hearts' content whether it's hawking or flirting. For once I can say in all honesty I don't envy them in the least."

"I've seen you delight in sport, Lord Edward," said Edmond, patting his pony's heaving flanks. "I doubt anyone enjoys hawking more than your highness does."

"I can't deny I've always loved it," Edward admitted with a sigh. "Perhaps I'll do so again one day. At present, I'm more than content to enjoy the breeze and warm sun, to breathe freely once again." As if to check his optimism, he was suddenly seized with a coughing spell that to his relief was brief and bloodless.

He signaled Edmond to dismount. They left the horses in Zoltan's custody and began to stroll through the little wood. The shouts and laughter of the rest of the party long since had faded into the distance and the only sounds they heard were those of nature, which was just beginning to revive with the approach of spring

They had threaded their way among the trees for two or three hundred yards when Edward stumbled across a fallen trunk. Edmond grasped the atheling's elbow to keep him from falling. "Let's halt for a bit of a rest," his companion suggested weakly as he sank to the ground and put his back to a tree. Edmond remained respectfully standing until the prince urged him to sit down beside him.

"I'd hesitate to admit it to anyone other than you or my wife," Edward confessed, "yet somehow I dread the coming of spring. I have an uneasy feeling it's likely to be an ill-omened adventure I'll be embarking on if I go to England."

"My lord, your uncle King Edward, the Witan and the people will greet you joyfully when you claim your birthright," Edmond protested. "They look to you, the son of Edmond Ironside, as their future shield, their bulwark against the Normans and the rest of the foreign thieves threatening to despoil them."

Edward shook his head. "You think so? I hope you're right. I've a deep concern weighing on my mind. I do feel somewhat better now but there've been times I've despaired, fearing this cough, this ailment, is sapping my strength. I'm scarcely fit to travel. That being so, how can I live up to what people will expect of me in England?"

"Once in London, Childe Edward, you'll draw strength from your many loyal supporters. None can or will dare to oppose you. Your right to the crown is too strong to be contested, and the memory of your father's greatness is evergreen."

"So they still love Edmond Ironside." Edward mused. "Bishop Ealdred told me so." The atheling listlessly plucked at a tuft of yellowed grass. "My poor brother Edmond resembled him, they say. He was a lively boy. It was a great grief when he died at the age of eight in Esztergom. He might have been the one most like my father. I sometimes fear I most resemble our grandfather, the luckless King Ethelred."

"He has been much traduced," Edmond insisted. "He had some ability. Few kings have been so beset by enemies or so often betrayed by supposed friends and allies."

"He may have been more unfortunate than incompetent," Edward admitted. "He was seldom a well man, often ill like myself. There may be a curse on our house. It was an evil day when grandfather Ethelred's half-brother Edward the Martyr was murdered. If it's true that Ethelred's mother, Lady Eldryth, instigated the crime it could explain why her son's reign was so disastrous."

Edmond kept his own counsel though he was tempted to agree. An evil act indeed, and Atheling Edward was not the only one of Ethelred's grandsons to suffer from the crime committed so many years before. He forced a smile. "Come, noble Edward, when your foot touches England's soil your future will seem much brighter."

"Will it? What if Earl Harold chooses to greet me as his father welcomed my uncle Childe Alfred?"

The atheling's suspicion dismayed Edmond. "My lord, don't tell me you believe that old wives' tale. Surely, you don't put any credence in such a vile slander against Earl Godwin."

Edward grimly shook a finger in Edmond's face. "An old wives' tale, you say! It's clear you haven't heard of how Earl Godwin died?"

"What do you mean?"

Edward's feverish account revealed how heavily the matter weighed on his mind. "Four years ago my uncle the king kept the Easter festival at Winchester as has been his custom. He invited many lords, including Earl Godwin and his sons, to share his meal upon the Monday of that holy week.

"Somehow, the talk turned to Atheling Alfred's death. As all the world knows, King Edward never could rid himself of the suspicion that Earl Godwin had a hand in his brother's murder when the prince was invited to return from Normandy after King Cnut's death. When someone mentioned Alfred at the Easter dinner, Earl Godwin angrily protested he had nothing to do with the crime. He seized a small piece of meat and declared, 'If I ever did anything to harm Childe Alfred, may this morsel choke me.' Looking directly at King Edward, he thrust the bit of meat into his mouth. No sooner had he done so than he groaned and slumped face first onto the table, never to speak another word. He was carried to the king's chamber and lay there without uttering a sound until he died. If this was not a judgment before God, there never has been one."

The atheling's impassioned recital horrified Edmond. He could not help crossing himself. Godwin's fate seemed almost irrefutable proof of the great earl's involvement in Childe Alfred's assassination. God must have tired of Godwin's lengthy catalog of crimes, betrayals and lies.

Edmond curbed his instinctive emotional reaction. It was pointless to dwell on something that had taken place so long ago. What mattered was the present and it demanded the return of Atheling Edward to England. He must be reassured that he would not suffer the fate of his half-uncle Alfred, that Earl Harold was thoroughly trustworthy, unlike his often unscrupulous father Godwin.

Even if that were not the case, Harold had nothing to gain from removing Atheling Edward. In contrast, Godwin's rationale for disposing of Alfred had been readily understandable. At that time, King Harold Harefoot, Atheling Alfred's rival for the crown, wanted him out of the way. The current situation was entirely different, King Edward being willing to acknowledge Atheling Edward as his heir.

Edmond attempted to counter Atheling Edward's suspicion by explaining his analysis of the situation.

"So you really believe that we only have to worry about the Normans who influence my uncle?" Edward continued doubtful.

"Don't forget those in Duke William's service, wherever they may be"

"A man who'll stop at nothing and dares everything, I've heard."

"That sums him up."

"Fortunately, none of his people are in my court."

"We can't be sure of that, my lord."

"You suspect someone? His name?"

"I don't know whom to suspect," Edmond replied, unwilling for the moment to direct Edward's attention toward D'Orivalle much as he felt uneasy about the Norman.

Edward buried his face in his hands. Was it fear? Edmond dismissed the suspicion. Fear was unworthy for any man, and doubly so for a son of Edmond Ironside. It would be as if a false coin had been struck from a true die. If not fear, it might be lack of confidence in his own abilities.

The atheling, as he had admitted, might be like his grandfather, feckless King Ethelred, rather than his intrepid father. If so, it was disheartening to reflect that England's hopes rested on such a fragile reed. All the same, with Earl Harold to support him, Atheling Edward might yet meet his country's needs. A high-pitched scream diminishing to a dying gurgle brought Edmond scrambling to his feet and Edward up on his knees. The horrible sounds came from the direction in which they had left Zoltan with the horses.

Two masked men brandishing swords burst into the glade and charged toward the atheling and Edmond. The latter drew his sword and jumped in front of the prince who kept his back to the tree. "Stay behind me, my lord," Edmond cried to the unarmed Edward as he parried a thrust by the leading assailant whose sword was already stained with blood. It was undoubtedly that of Zoltan whose dying scream had alerted Edmond and Edward to the attackers.

"Stand back, thane, and we'll spare you if you leave now," his adversary shouted as Edmond's brisk sword play drove him back and blocked his partner's attempt to get at Edward. "We only want your companion." Edmond heard the prince give way to a fierce coughing spell triggered by the desperate situation.

"My lord, keep your back to the tree and don't despair regardless of what I may say," Edmond whispered when the assailants fell back to prepare for a renewed effort. Even if the prince were armed, Edmond realized, he would have been little help in his weak condition. He addressed their foes, "So you promise me safe conduct if I leave you alone with the atheling?"

"Your horse is where you left it. You're free to go. Don't look back."

Edmond recognized Armand D'Orivalle's voice despite the Norman's attempt to disguise it. He decided to play for time. "If I leave like a coward, I'll be charged with complicity, with having helped betray Lord Edward."

"What makes you suppose he'll be harmed?"

"Why else would you attack us?"

"Enough obstruction! What does it matter to you what we intend? Flee or die! It's all the same to us," roared D'Orivalle, motioning to his companion to renew the attack Both warily advanced on their intended victims.

Edmond's feet left the ground as he lunged forward, his sword leveled horizontally at D'Orivalle as he virtually flew through the air. The astonished Norman could not react in time to defend himself. Edmond's sword point plunged into his belly, touching off a torrent of blood as he collapsed to the ground. Without hesitation, Edmond sprang to his feet as he withdrew the sword and prepared to deal with his remaining foe who was transfixed by what he had witnessed. Edmond gave him no opportunity to recover from shock. He rushed at him, battered down an awkward attempt at defense, and drove his sword point into a shoulder. The wounded man moaned with pain as he slumped writhing to the ground.

Exhausted by his strenuous efforts, Edmond planted his sword in the dirt and leaned on the pommel to regain his breath and survey the bloody scene. He was grateful neither ruffian had been wearing armor or he could not have prevailed so quickly. He tore off the dead man's mask to reveal that it indeed was D'Orivalle. On stripping off the other attacker's disguise, he was confronted by a stranger, a curly-headed lad of about sixteen or seventeen. The wounded youngster looked terrified as he attempted to sit up while stanching the flow of blood from his cut shoulder. "For mercy's sake, help me before I bleed to death," he begged.

"Not until you tell me your name and what prompted you to help this traitor to attempt such a vile crime."

"I'm Pierre D'Orivalle. I but did my uncle's bidding."

The unarmed atheling had only been able to helplessly watch the furious battle even after recovering from the coughing spell, but now intervened. "Here, take this bit of cloth," he said, offering Edmond a scarf from his neck. "See if you can bind up the knave's wound and halt the bleeding."

Edmond slashed the scarf into strips for bandages with which he dressed the wound. The injury was slight, a cut in the fleshy part of the shoulder. The color slowly returned to Pierre D'Orivalle's cheeks.

The atheling looked sorrowfully at Armand D'Orivalle's corpse. "Betrayed by a man I thought a good friend," he lamented. "I can't believe it. Armand, my old drinking companion all these years and once the emperor's liege man. He was almost a brother to me." He was close to tears. "Why did he turn against me? He was forever denouncing Duke William whom he had every reason to hate for taking his lands and driving him into exile after the battle of Val-es-Dunes."

"He might have hoped to regain the duke's favor and his estate by betraying you, Lord Edward," Edmond suggested. "Or he may have been acting for either Chamberlain Hugolin or Earl Ralph in England." He recollected how vividly D'Orivalle had described Val-es-Dunes. He probably had been at the Norman duke's side during the battle rather than among the rebels. "It's even possible he has been in Duke William's pay all along as a spy on your court. His nephew may enlighten us. What say you to that, Master Pierre?"

Young D'Orivalle clamped his lips.

"Come lad, your uncle's dead, nothing you say can help or hurt him," Edmond pointed out. "Tell us what you know of his dealings or it'll be all the worse for you."

Pierre mulled the threat but eventually discretion or fear took over. "I can't tell you much," he quavered. "Uncle Armand sent for me from Normandy a few months ago. He said he'd try to find a place for me in the emperor's court. Nothing came of that. I had to be content with attending my uncle until something would turn up. A couple of weeks ago he ordered me to go to Boulogne and meet a certain Guy de Hauteville who was to give me an important message to bring back to Aachen. I had to wait a few days in Boulogne before de Hauteville arrived. He handed me a sealed parchment, cautioning me to guard it with my life until I put it into Uncle Armand's hands."

"Do you know where de Hauteville was before he arrived in Boulogne?" Edmond demanded.

"He didn't say and I didn't ask, but he might have come from England. He complained of having been seasick, and said he was glad to be on land again."

"The letter might have come from Earl Ralph or Chamberlain Hugolin," Edmond said to the atheling. "If so, it's possible Duke William isn't involved in this attempt on your life. At least not directly." He motioned to Pierre to resume his account.

"I took the letter to my uncle in Aachen and he became very excited while reading it. He thanked me, gave me a couple of coins to drink his health, and said he soon might have another task for me."

"Well, what then?" Edmond urged. "Come boy, your life hangs in the balance. If you tell all without holding anything back, Lord Edward may be inclined to mercy."

The terrified lad continued: "When we set out this morning, Uncle Armand told me he'd gotten wind of a plot to attack Atheling Edward during the ride. He said he suspected the traitor was someone close to the prince, but wasn't sure of his identity. He thought the best course was for us to follow the court out of Aachen, keep watch, and be prepared to defend the prince at any moment. I couldn't understand why we had to put on masks, but he insisted they were necessary. We were to follow the party at a distance, keep the atheling in sight, and be ready to defend him if we detected anything unusual. When Lord Edward left the road with just two companions, Uncle Armand said it was time to act, that the traitor was luring the atheling into a trap. You know the rest."

"You haven't told all," snapped Edmond. "Didn't your uncle tell you the contents of the letter sent him by de Hauteville?"

"Does it matter?" Atheling Edward interrupted. "I've no wish to hear any more. This whole ugly business turns my stomach."

Edmond frowned in frustration. It was important to uncover who was behind the plot but there was nothing to be done if the prince was unwilling to support an investigation. Further proof of Edward's indolent nature, he decided. "Lady Agatha and the others must be wondering where we are," he reminded the atheling. "If you're ready, my lord, we should rejoin them."

"Yes, it's about time we did," Edward agreed, adding, "but what do we do with this wretch and these bodies? How do we explain what's happened?" He was perplexed. "I suppose this scoundrel's life should be forfeit but I've no taste for cutting down a young lad who acted as he did out of misguided family loyalty. It might be best to let him get away free. God knows I myself may soon be in need of clemency."

Edward's decisive manner squelched Edmond's protest even though he would have preferred to question Pierre further. It might be just as well to minimize possible ramifications of the incident by not arousing too much attention even if two dead bodies made it impossible to conceal it entirely. At a nod from the atheling, he helped the still weak Pierre get to his feet as he asked, "Where's your mount?" The youth pointed toward the edge of the copse where Edmond and Edward had left their own horses with the unfortunate Zoltan. Just before they reached the little group of five tethered horses grazing quietly at the foot of an incline, they came across the body of the atheling's faithful Magyar servant.

"My poor Zoltan," the atheling mourned. "You served me long and loyally, to your last breath. God preserve your soul, old friend."

"We owe him our lives," Edmond pointed out. "If he hadn't resisted down to his dying scream, the villains could have ambushed us." He angrily steered Pierre toward his horse, growling, "In the saddle, fellow, and ride for your life. The prince chooses to be merciful but some of his people may not be as obedient to his wishes as I am." He helped Pierre scramble into the saddle, then slapped the horse's rump and it galloped off without a backward glance by its rider.

Atheling Edward pensively watched Pierre depart, then put a hand on Edmond's shoulder. "Noble thane, I can't thank you enough. I thought men like you died out with my father Edmond Ironside. I can never fully repay you, but I'll try to do so once we reach England."

"It'll be reward enough, my lord, to see you there safely. Whoever sent D'Orivalle, whether it was Duke William, Hugolin or Earl Ralph, won't permit one setback to keep him from trying again. You should leave for England as soon as possible, your highness."

"We'll give orders tomorrow to prepare for the journey."

"None too soon, if I may say so. Once in England, the king and Earl Harold will guarantee your safety." Edmond glanced at Zoltan's corpse.

"With your permission, we'd better rejoin the others, Childe Edward. We can send someone from Aachen to fetch your poor servant's remains and those of that scoundrel D'Orivalle."

The atheling somberly agreed as they got back in the saddle. They retraced their route out of the copse and across the fields toward the road on which they had left Lady Agatha's party. They did not have far or long to go. Almost as soon as they regained the road, they met the main body on its way back to Aachen, its gaiety muted by concern over the atheling's unexplained disappearance and protracted absence.

As soon as Lady Agatha saw her husband she cried, "My dear lord, God be praised we've found you. We wondered if you had lost your way, or if you had been in an accident." She rode up to him with a tender look.

He briefly told her about the attack as she listened with growing dismay and horror. "Oh, dear husband, that someone would wish to harm you, you who've never hurt anyone," she murmured, her eyes brimming with tears.

"There are great matters involved, my love," Edward explained. "It's not a few petty hides of land at stake but a kingdom." He wrapped his hands around hers and smiled comfortingly. "Come now, dear Agatha, all's well, so take heart and be your usual happy, smiling self," he added, affecting a light-hearted air. He nodded toward Edmond. "Here's someone who deserves our thanks. Where's your gratitude? Have you no word for Thane Edmond who may have saved you from an early widowhood?"

"More than a word, dearest Edward," she answered with pretended gaiety. "I must ask a boon of you for Thane Edmond who has proved himself so great and good a friend to us. If it's ever in your power, you should compensate him with an ample estate and suitable honors. Even an earldom would not be too great a reward. Surely his modest descent should not bar you from according him the greatest gift in your power."

A shadow momentarily clouded Edmond's face, the atheling mistaking it for humble reluctance to aspire to such an honor. He quickly reassured. "There's ample precedent for such preferment, thane. You wouldn't be the first to climb to a high station from a humble background. I've heard, though I don't believe it, that Earl Godwin's father was a swineherd and, heaven knows, he and his family have prospered mightily."

Amused though he was by the secret knowledge that his birth entitled him to far greater honors than the atheling and his wife could imagine, Edmond replied deferentially, "I'm grateful to you both for your kindness, my lord and lady. My only ambition at present is for the two of you to reach the safety of England as soon as possible."

"Well spoken, my good friend," Edward applauded. "First things first. After all, our promises here in Aachen are worthless but once in England our words should carry weight."

Chapter Thirty-Nine

A Prince Returns Home

B lustery winds and turbulent waters made the crossing from Bruges in Baldwinesland to Dover agonizing for those of the atheling's party who unlike Edmond had little or no seafaring experience. The prince suffered the most, seasickness aggravating his other ills. Edward's coughing spells were frequent and violent, and he once spit up blood until his leech, Master Hermann, sedated him with a herbal remedy.

As the white cliffs of Dover became dimly visible through the dense fog hugging the English coast, Edmond clung to a support in the ship's bow and peered toward the seaport that held such vivid memories for him. He was scarcely aware of the crew bustling about on deck or of the other vessels of the small fleet bringing home England's legitimate heir to the throne after an absence of forty years. Small banners flapped vigorously at the mastheads, their brilliant colors in vivid contrast to the dismal grayness of the April sky whose dull cast matched Edmond's mood. It was only too apparent from Master Hermann's grave face that he was beginning to despair about his royal patient's condition despite the recent improvement in Aachen. Even the imminent return to the native land he had left five years earlier failed to lift Edmond's spirits. He was dominated by a foreboding of impending disaster.

He glanced sympathetically at Lady Agatha who sat on deck in a protective enclosure, her three children huddled around. Her gaiety was obviously forced as she chattered with her ladies in waiting. It was sobering to think she was nearer widowhood than to becoming the Lady of England. Making the situation even more tragic was that she loved her dour, stolid husband. She would be left alone to mourn him and care for their children after his death. Edgar, the eldest, would inevitably become the focus of intrigue as the last known surviving male heir of the House of Cerdic.

Edmond was indifferent to his own future prospects, having become so hardened by the many disappointments he had suffered since that bright and hopeful day when he had set forth from Bosbury on the way to Dover. His sole immediate concern was to present the bill of exchange given him by Constantine IX to a Byzantine banker in London. The emperor's generosity should enable him to buy a considerable property in the vicinity of his native town where he could live out his days in peace and comfort if not in power and glory.

As the ship approached shore, the roar of an enormous crowd gathered to welcome the atheling to Dover roused Edmond from his gloomy introspection. Trumpets blared, drums beat and bells rang in a joyous din. It seemed as if all England had assembled in Dover harbor to greet the prince in the belief that his arrival signaled the nation's liberation from the threat of Norman domination. When news spread that Atheling Edward was finally about to set sail from Baldwinesland, thousands of people from London and Canterbury took the road to Dover that became as crowded as a city market during the earliest spring fair. King Edward appointed Earl Harold to escort the atheling to London with the royal housecarles as well as his own followers.

When the ship cast anchor within a few lengths of shore, Edmond recognized the powerful form of Earl Harold who stood out even amidst the swarm of brilliantly dressed nobles, burghers and soldiers surrounding him.

"What a proud-looking man!" exclaimed a familiar voice at Edmond's elbow. He spun around to behold Atheling Edward's pale face. The prince had ignored his physician's pleas to reserve his strength by remaining abed until it was time to disembark. "Do you recognize him?"

"I do indeed, Lord Edward. It's Earl Harold Godwinson."

"I should have guessed as much." The atheling thoughtfully gazed at Harold as if studying his face, not easy to do at the still considerable distance to the crowd on shore. "It's well this man is friendly to our cause. I wouldn't care to have him for an enemy."

Nor I, Edmond thought, as the atheling's entourage began to disembark to the joy of the tumultuous crowd hailing each arrival in turn. Despite his pessimism about the future he could not entirely suppress his exhilaration when his feet touched England's soil for the first time in more than five years. Once again his eyes were irresistibly drawn toward the vaulting ancient Roman pharos frowning down on Dover from atop the chalk cliffs. It impressed him much as it had when as a country bumpkin he first had arrived at the seaport. How different the circumstances were this time.

The crowd paid no attention to Edmond because the atheling was helped ashore directly behind him. Earl Harold and a delegation of high-ranking nobles rushed past Edmond without a glance in their haste to pay their respects to the prince. Edmond was thankful not to be recognized, yet it was with a shock that he once more heard Earl Harold's familiar deep, melodious voice.

"Welcome to your land and the land of your fathers, Childe Edward," said Harold as he sank to his knees before the atheling who immediately extended his hands to pull him back to his feet. "Welcome, my lord, from a people who have longed for your return all these many years."

"Welcome, Childe Edward!" echoed the enormous crowd, and the cry reverberated all along the streets of Dover. The atheling's eyes misted as he accepted a goblet of wine offered by Harold.

"I've returned home where I belong," he said simply before lifting the goblet to his lips and draining it as the people roared their appreciation.

After Harold had paid homage to Lady Agatha and met the atheling's children, he introduced the most prominent clergymen, nobles and burghers in his entourage to the prince. Edmond was pleasantly surprised at the uncharacteristic charm and patience displayed by the usually reserved Edward despite the pallor and drawn appearance caused by his ill health. His smile, weak though it was, and fitting remarks in broken English captivated his future subjects. He introduced the higher ranking members of his court to Harold, finally coming to Edmond who would have preferred to be ignored.

"Earl Harold, we bid you hold Thane Edmond Edwysson in the highest esteem for we owe our life to this valiant and most noble soldier," he declared earnestly. "His prompt action rescued us from a traitor's attempt on our life."

"So long as he serves Your Highness faithfully and well, we'll hold him in respect," Harold replied stiffly. "We knew Thane Edmond once, or thought we did, and will judge him by his actions in the future as we have done until now by his past conduct."

The earl's ambiguous words and equivocal reaction startled the atheling but he chose not to inquire. Edmond understood, exchanging steely glances with Harold before slightly inclining his head in greeting. It was clear the earl believed he had betrayed or deserted him after having been entrusted at Bristol with the vital commission to his sister, Queen Edith.

When the ceremony of welcome ended, the atheling sagged wearily. Edmond feared he was about to faint. Harold also was struck by the prince's peaked appearance.

"A house has been prepared for your highness and Lady Agatha if you wish to rest and refresh yourselves," Harold informed the atheling. Edward nodded gratefully, and at a word from Harold the housecarles cleared a path through the crowd so the royal party could make its way.

The route was painfully familiar to Edmond for virtually every turn of the winding street brought back a memory of the past. First came the seaside inn at which he had drained so many draughts of ale with that hugely round and jovial sailor, Master Wiglaf. Here he also first had encountered fiery Earl Sweyn whose future was to become so entwined with his own. Sweyn's eventual fate he knew only too well, but where was friend Wiglaf now? He scrutinized the faces in the crowd through which the atheling's party passed. Some of the people looked vaguely familiar but he saw no one he had known well. For that matter, none of the townsmen recognized in this splendidly accoutered and stern young noble the bold lad who years before had led the burghers of Dover in deadly conflict against Count Eustace of Boulogne's arrogant Normans.

Earl Harold halted, indicating they had arrived at their destination, a large ornate dwelling. "This is the house prepared for you reception, Childe Edward," he announced, stepping aside to permit the atheling and his family to precede him through the entrance. Edmond was swept by emotion. Another painful memory evoked! He was about to reenter Osgood's house. This was the threshold at which he had held the dying merchant in his arms. It was under this roof that he had enjoyed a brief burst of happiness quickly swept away by tragedy. Here Adele had flirted with—perhaps even loved—him before repulsing him forever. It was a house of bitter-sweet recall. Edmond numbly followed the party into the great hall where he first had breakfasted with Osgood and Adele so long ago. The huge room was festively decorated, elaborately prepared for a banquet, its rough walls covered once more with heavy, rich tapestries as in Osgood's day. Food and drink was spread out in lavish profusion on a vast array of tables. Earl Harold smiled in complacent satisfaction at the atheling's evident astonishment and pleasure at the sight as he ushered him to the high seat of honor at the head table.

In spite of Childe Edward's delight in such a magnificent reception, his pallor was marked as he sat down in the place of honor with Earl Harold at his right hand and Bishop Ealdred at his left. But he seemed well enough when the banquet began. He conversed genially with those nearby, inquiring about conditions for hunting and other field sports in England. Edmond was seated near enough to overhear the conversation and keep a watchful eye on the atheling's condition.

Scarcely had the first course of the meal been completed, however, when the atheling suddenly groaned and began to cough violently. When his head sank to the table and he began to spit blood, a cry of alarm and horror swept the hall.

"Quick, accompany Lord Edward to the rooms prepared for him," cried Earl Harold, summoning several housecarles to assist the atheling. As Edward was led away, Harold turned his attention to the guests, many of whom had jumped to their feet in consternation and confusion. "Let the feast continue," he ordered. "The prince just needs some rest after such an arduous voyage. I know he wouldn't want us to leave off celebrating his arrival." The crowd complied, but an unnatural hush replaced the earlier gaiety, uneasy conversations being conducted in near whispers.

Master Hermann examined Atheling Edward, prepared a refreshing herbal draught, and suggested that the prince be allowed to rest for a considerable time. He was vague about the nature of the prince's ailment, fending off questions from Earl Harold and Bishop Ealdred as soon as he returned to the hall from attending his patient.

"My lords, it's most likely the excitement aroused by the gracious and splendid welcome prepared for him in Dover has overheated the prince's humors," he explained. "There's also the strain on his constitution from a fatiguing voyage. Yet there's no cause for great concern, no present danger. Some rest and the prince will be himself again."

Bishop Ealdred was not so readily convinced because he had observed the deterioration of the atheling's health during his long stay with the court in Aachen. Nevertheless, at Harold's prompting he attempted to reassure the uneasy crowd in the great hall.

"Good friends, let your minds be at ease," the bishop soothed. "It's merely a passing weakness that has overcome Childe Edward and, God willing, a good rest will quickly restore him to good health. He's somewhat worn from a difficult voyage across a rough sea and our attempts, well-meant as they are, to demonstrate our joy at his return to England. Let us offer our prayers to the Lord Almighty for his speedy recovery."

Most of the crowd departed soon after Bishop Ealdred's reassuring words, and Osgood's house took on the quiet semblance of a hospital— or a tomb.

Earl Harold escorted Lady Agatha into a bower that Edmond recognized with a pang as once having been Adele's.

"My lady, calm your fears," Harold gently reassured the distraught princess who was making a gallant effort to repress her tears. "I'm sure your husband will be much refreshed in the morning after a good rest. Then, with his permission, we'll take the road to London where he's eagerly awaited, especially by King Edward and my dear sister Edith, the Lady of England."

Agatha expressed gratitude with a wan smile, and Harold left her to her women's care. He returned to the great hall where only few nobles remained, Edmond among them, silently standing apart from the others. Harold ignored him to strike up a conversation with one of his own officers, evidently making arrangements for the next leg of the atheling's progress, when a tall young man with close-cut, strikingly yellow hair strode into the room. He was about to address Harold when he halted in astonishment upon recognizing Edmond.

"Thane Edmond, if I can believe my eyes," he shouted with obvious delight. "It's beyond all understanding." He turned to Harold. "Brother, didn't you tell us that you believed Thane Edmond was dead?"

Harold looked coldly at Edmond before replying impassively, "The Edmond you and I once knew and esteemed is dead, brother Leofwine. This man is Kometes Edmond Edwysson, an officer recently in the service of the great emperor at Constantinople."

Leofwine looked bewildered, glancing in astonishment from Edmond to Harold and back to Edmond, who said with a smile, "Your brother is right, Earl Leofwine. The Edmond you see before you is not the Edmond whom you once knew. I am a Roman officer who has chosen to serve Atheling Edward."

After a stiff bow, he left the house and wandered through Dover until he came to another familiar building. After momentary hesitation, he banged briskly on the entrance. A female servant peered out cautiously, then opened the door fully on beholding a smartly dressed nobleman.

"I've come to see Master Aegelsig," Edmond announced.

"My master is unable to see anyone just now," the maid replied, and began to shut the door in Edmond's face. "He's ill abed."

"I'm sorry to hear that but I know he'll be eager to see me if you'll inform him that Edmond Edwysson has returned."

The servant hesitated, then disappeared into the house, leaving the door half open. Edmond impatiently kicked a few pebbles and peered at a dimly-glowing fire banked for the night in the armorer's shop. To his relief, the woman soon returned and led him down a long passageway toward the back of the building and into a richly furnished room. Master Aegelsig was stretched out in bed, so consumed by illness that Edmond almost failed to recognize his old friend.

"Upon my soul, it's Thane Edmond indeed," Aegelsig whispered as he made a futile attempt to sit up. Edmond leaned over the bed and put his arm around the old man's bony shoulders as a support. "Thank you, my lord," Aegelsig smiled wanly. "I never thought to behold you again, dear lad. I feared you were dead, lost at sea or captured by the Saracens as I was in my youth. As you can see, I'm perilously close to being lost myself, God have mercy on my soul."

"Good Master Aegelsig, you'll outlive me by a dozen years," Edmond laughed lamely. Aegelsig shook his head, then fondly looked his young friend up and down as if measuring a customer for a suit of armor.

"It's a good thing I fashioned the hauberk somewhat over large," he observed with a professional air. "You've grown a great deal in the shoulders. I'll wager, though, the hauberk will fit you to perfection now. Yes, my boy, I've kept it safe all these years in readiness for your return. You may not want it now, judging by the quality of that splendid cuirass you've got on." With a wasted, shaking finger, he admiringly traced the delicate inlay of the armor given Edmond by Constantine IX.

"Good friend, I prefer yours," Edmond reassured him. "When I return from London, I'll ask you for it."

"You're bound for London? Then you're with the atheling, may God preserve him for our people's welfare. You must have seen much and done a great deal since we last met, my boy. Come, indulge an old man's idle curiosity and tell me all about it."

Aegelsig listened with wide-eyed pleasure to Edmond's greatly condensed account of his adventures. The old man clenched his fists at hearing of dangers confronted, frowned at setbacks, and rubbed hands in satisfaction at successes, though Edmond was careful not to mention the slaying of Earl Sweyn. "You've done well, my lord, and fortune may at last be smiling on you," Aegelsig exulted. "And you've just begun. Now there's much more to be done. You're in the atheling's favor. That promises much for your future in England."

Edmond nodded agreement, loath to undeceive Aegelsig's optimism. He did not choose to burden a dying old man with the sad truth about the atheling. It was best to change the subject, and no moment could be more favorable for asking a question that had been on his mind all the while. "What of your niece Adele, old friend? Has she indeed taken the veil?"

Aegelsig blinked surprise. "Didn't you know? She did it long ago, my son, long ago. At first I opposed her wishes, but now I understand that what she did was for the best, both for herself and me. I'll need the intercession of her prayers with God, that's certain. I've done a great deal in a long life that requires forgiveness." He sighed deeply, his eyes appearing startlingly large in an emaciated face.

Edmond forced himself to keep his voice level. "Is she still at Wherwell?"

"Yes, she's been there all these years. I hear from her now and then. She's always praying for me, she says. Once, I think, she did ask if I had heard anything of a certain young man whom she knew long ago. The next time I write I'll let her know I've seen him. She'll be glad to hear it so she can pray for him as well. You can depend on that." Aegelsig's voice trailed off as he dozed off.

Edmond took a last lingering glance at the wasted face, then called for the servant. "I must leave. Tell your master when he awakes that I'll return as soon as I can to claim what he's keeping safe for me."

He dejectedly retraced his steps to Osgood's house, taking little comfort in the knowledge that Adele had not entirely forgotten him. She had done well to become a bride of Christ, he reflected. With matters as they were, he surely had far more need of prayers than of a wife.

Chapter Forty

A Final Request

After resting several days, Atheling Edward felt well enough to again set out on the road from Dover to London. The prince stubbornly rode on horseback, defying Lady Agatha's and Master Hermann's protests as they pleaded with him to travel in a litter.

"I'll not enter London on my back or sitting down," he insisted. "The only time I'll let myself be carried is when I go to my grave. I want the people to see me as capable of being their leader, a worthy descendant of King Alfred and his line."

It was thus the people saw him all the way from Dover to London, Earl Harold riding at his right, Bishop Ealdred to his left, surrounded by a detachment of the royal housecarles. The prince clung with determination to the saddle, smiling and nodding graciously to the country folk who lined the narrow road to watch him pass. Only occasionally did a muffled cough reveal his deep-seated ailment as he avoided a protracted fit by exerting extraordinary willpower. Edmond was not deceived, however, observing the signs of pain in the atheling's eyes. The effort was sapping the prince's feeble constitution to the limit.

Archbishop Stigand met the procession in Canterbury to celebrate the mass with the prince in the great cathedral church. He acted as if he did not lie under the interdict of Rome for having supplanted his predecessor, Archbishop Robert, without papal approval and having failed to relinquish his previous benefices. Though it distressed Atheling Edward as a faithful son of the church to permit this pluralist cleric to minister to him, he could not afford to alienate Earl Harold, Stigand's protector. Edward noncommittally participated in the service, saying only what was required of him to the archbishop until the rites were complete. He was relieved to be preparing to resume the road after a perfunctory if polite farewell.

"I mistrust that man," he confessed to Edmond who was helping him into the saddle. "I'm told he's cunning and clever, but much too devious even if he's as learned as people credit him with being."

"What say you, my lord?" asked Earl Harold, who caught only the last three or four words. "You do well to place your trust in Archbishop Stigand. He always has been a staff of support and comfort to my family in our times of need."

Edward realized Harold had misheard his remark. It was just as well. "Yes, I've no doubt the bishop has done the House of Godwin many a good turn. I trust he hasn't lost by it." He drained the stirrup cup offered by Harold, smiled broadly, and gently spurred his horse, only Edmond noticing how convulsively his hands gripped the reins.

The atheling's agitation probably led to the coughing fit that began to rack his frame after they passed through the town of Rochester. It became so severe that he was obliged to dismount and rest on a stool hurriedly brought from the baggage train. Blood came to his lips, and it was as much weakness as Master Hermann's application of a soothing drug that stemmed the outburst.

Lady Agatha, Earl Harold, Edmond and the rest of Edward's retinue were appalled and downcast by this latest demonstration of the prince's debility as they waited until the leech completed his ministrations. Master Hermann drew Harold aside.

"My lord, I can't answer for Childe Edward's recovery if he remains on horseback," the doctor said earnestly. "He's just not up to the physical exertion at this time. He must ease up, make less of an effort. If at all possible, he should ride in a litter the rest of the way."

Harold nodded. "Have a litter fetched from the baggage train, Thane Sexwulf," he ordered. But as soon as the litter appeared, the atheling curled a disdainful lip at the vehicle, and when Edmond offered to help him get into it, shook his head and painfully pulled himself upright from the stool he had been resting on.

"Never!" he rasped defiantly. "You may well carry me out of London after I get there but you'll never bear the son of Edmond Ironside into the city in a litter. I'll ride or never enter at all."

Ride he did, though clinging desperately to the saddle, his lips compressed to hide his weakness and the pain in his chest. He rode through Southwark, then across crowded London Bridge, his horse's hooves clattering upon the sorry wooden structure lined with houses and the ruins of fortifications built partly of stone and partly of timber, damaged during the Danish wars half a century earlier and never completely restored. He rode past the ramshackle booths crowding the bridge, their merchants staring and lifting their fur caps to salute the arrival of their future king.

On he rode through the muddy, crooked streets of the city lined with low-timbered dwellings whose blinds were pulled aside by the curious to witness the atheling's homecoming. He passed the ancient walls attributed to Constantine the Great, noting how worn they were by the passage of more than seven centuries and the destructiveness of man. Similarly decayed was the temple of Diana whose awesome ruins far overshadowed the humble and comparatively crudely-built St. Paul's under whose roof lay the bones of Edward's grandfather, unhappy King Ethelred.

Edward entered the great church to inspect his grandfather's tomb.

"He suffered from much ill-fortune, Childe Edward," Earl Harold commented as they gazed at the royal coffin of stone, covered by a silken pall.

"His misfortunes often were of his own doing," the atheling lamented "He thought too little, he did less than he might have done, and whatever he did, he did too late. At times I fear his sluggish blood courses through my own veins. It would be fitting if when my time comes I were to lie at his side." On that bitter, melancholy note, Edward began to leave the church but paused at the door for a last pensive glance at the shadowy tomb. Edmond thought he heard him promise, "I shall return, only too soon I fear."

They rode in melancholy silence the rest of the way to the great house by the Thames which had been prepared for the atheling and his family. When he was about to dismount the atheling's strength finally failed and he almost tumbled off his horse into Edmond's arms. A renewed effort of willpower, however, restored him sufficiently so he could walk unaided into the mansion after accepting the key from Hugolin, the royal chamberlain, who also brought a message of welcome from King Edward.

"When will my royal uncle be pleased to receive me?" Edward inquired of the official he suspected of being an enemy.

"My lord, he is impatient for you to come to him at Thorney," Hugolin replied smoothly. "As soon as you've refreshed yourself from your long and arduous journey—say within two or three days—he'll be happy to fold you in his arms. He bade me bear his love and that of the Lady Edith to you and to your dear wife and children."

Hugolin's tone seemed entirely sincere, yet Edmond thought it strange that the king had not hurried to London to welcome his nephew and heir presumptive in person, especially since they never had met before.

"I thank the king for his loving words," Edward replied weakly, putting a hand to his forehead. "Assure him that we'll not keep him waiting long. We're just as eager as he is for our meeting."

Whether the atheling spoke in earnest or meant to be sarcastic never became known, because shortly after Chamberlain Hugolin, Earl Harold and the other dignitaries left he again clutched his head, complained of severe pain, and collapsed to the floor. After he was laid to bed, he opened his eyes but remained speechless. A coughing fit soon followed, becoming increasingly intense and he spit blood profusely.

By the next morning it became all too clear this was no passing attack but that the atheling was in mortal danger. It was only extreme weakness that eventually assuaged the coughing spell until he lay totally silent on the bed, eyes closed, his breathing hoarse and labored. Master Hermann tended his patient throughout the night, ceaselessly applying cold compresses to a fevered brow while Lady Agatha, Edmond and a few others kept vigil. The atheling had weakly called for his wife and children during a momentary recovery of speech. He passed his trembling hands tenderly over the brown locks of the frightened and bewildered Childe Edgar, and fondly touched his two daughters on the cheek.

When Master Hermann whispered that all hope was gone, Bishop Ealdred was summoned to administer the last rites of the church. Surprisingly, the atheling rallied sufficiently to understand what was going on and even attempted to sit up. Master Hermann sought to restrain him from the effort but Edward waved him aside. "It no longer matters, good leech," he whispered. "I am approaching my end now and I've something to say that must be spoken." He somehow propped himself up on his elbows and crooked a finger at Edmond. "Come nearer, noble thane, whom I trust above all other men. I owe you much and it grieves me that I must request one more boon from you without being able to reward your devotion."

"My lord, I serve you of my own free will and expect nothing."

"And I've nothing to give you. Yet I must ask you to commend my son, indeed my wife and daughters as well, to Earl Harold Godwinson. Tell him that Childe Edward entreats him to take my dear son Edgar under his protection until the lad grows to manhood. I fear for the boy. He will need a strong arm to shield him from the dangers that are sure to surround him, and that strong arm is Earl Harold's."

"You have my word that I'll bear your message to Earl Harold."

"You'll do me great service then, even greater than you did in defending me from that villain, D'Orivalle. Alas, it's hard to leave good and loyal friends unrewarded." The prince's voice grew weaker. "Tell my uncle, King Edward, only this: atheling Edward desires to be buried beside his grandfather, King Ethelred. Those who were so much alike in life should lie side by side in death."

Edward then lay silent, breathing heavily, eyes fixed upon a gilded cross that hung upon the wall near the foot of his bed until his death agony began. "Father," he sighed as life departed and whether his final word referred to his earthly parent or God none was ever to know.

All in the room knelt as Bishop Ealdred said a final prayer for the dead man before placing coins over his eyes after which the courtiers filed out to leave Lady Agatha in private with her husband's corpse. Edmond retired to the common hall to be ready to respond if Lady

Agatha called for him.

Several hours passed before the princess regained her composure enough to attend to the most urgent matters. She summoned Edmond who found her already clad in mourning garb amidst her similarly dressed ladies.

"We spoke glibly of earldoms when we were still happy in Aachen and could look to the future," Agatha began mournfully. "Unfortunately, my noble friend, such hopes lie cold and dead with my dear lord and husband. I can promise you nothing but I must humbly beg you will carry out his dying request for the respect he had for you, if nothing else."

"My lady, depend on me to try do so," Edmond replied but felt it incumbent upon him to add, "You should know there's a coolness between Earl Harold and myself that may render me an indifferent emissary in such a great matter. It may be that another would serve you better."

Agatha was startled but shook her head. "Indeed, I'm sorry to hear that, but if Childe Edward placed great trust in you I can do no less. I know you won't fail us. Repeat my husband's plea to the earl. If he is a good man, as I believe him to be, we can trust to God for the rest."

"Well said, my daughter," interjected Bishop Ealdred who had just entered the room. "We'll add our prayers to yours. I'm not without influence with Earl Harold who is a good son of the church, all the more since he was healed so miraculously at Waltham. I'm sure we can join forces to influence him to act as your son's guardian in fact if not law."

"We shall do so, lord bishop," Edmond declared. "You've no real cause for fear, Lady Agatha. There may be differences between us, but I know Earl Harold to be a just and trustworthy man though at times he may seem hard and stern."

Despite his confident words, it was with foreboding that he attended Atheling Edward's funeral. The prince was entombed beside his similarly unfortunate grandfather with the pomp and ceremony usually reserved for a reigning monarch. Much sooner than he could have imagined, Edward was laid to rest beside hapless King Ethelred under the roof of St. Paul's. The atheling's undoing might have been that never in life did he keep a pledge so faithfully and quickly as the one he honored in death, the vow made to return to his ancestor's side.

Chapter Forty-One

Remember!

E arl Godwin's extensive mansion in Southwark did not awe Edmond as it had on his first visit a half decade earlier. To one who had beheld the splendors of Constantinople, the rudely-designed sprawling structure in which he had attended the joyous celebration of the bride-ale of Tostig Godwinson and Judith, daughter of Count Baldwin of Flanders, now looked almost like an overgrown hovel. In addition, the building and grounds suffered from neglect because Earl Harold seldom resorted to his late father's home, using it only on special occasions such as a visit to London requiring accommodations for more than his usual complement of followers.

When Edmond approached the mansion on a cold and somber day early in the year 1057 he expected to encounter Harold's housecarles from Wessex but was surprised to note among them men wearing the badge of Mercia as well as others who were obviously Welshmen judging by their garb and weapons. No one obstructed him, however, and he was readily admitted into the building when he presented his credentials as coming from Lady Agatha, the late atheling's widow. As soon as he entered the great hall where Earl Harold was holding council he discovered the reason for the conglomeration of troops.

Seated at Harold's right was a white-haired, bent old man whom Edmond recognized as Earl Leofric of Mercia. The bull-necked, red-faced noble next to Leofric could only be his son Earl Alfgar, much puffed-up since Edmond last had seen him outside the walls of Gloucester. Alfgar's presence accounted for the Welshmen since he had wed his daughter Aldytha to the Welsh prince, Gruffyd. His son-in-law took advantage of the alliance to send some of his promising young men to learn English ways in Alfgar's entourage. Archbishop Stigand and Harold's younger brothers Gurth, Leofwine and Wulfnoth also were seated at the head table while several dozen other high-ranking nobles and their most trusted retainers crowded the hall.

Few noticed Edmond's unobtrusive arrival because Earl Harold was holding forth in what was an obvious response to a proposal made earlier by someone in the crowd.

"My lords, surely there's no pressing reason to debate such a question at this time, important as it may be someday," Harold was saying. "Our beloved and most pious King Edward has many years ahead of him and no doubt God will provide a worthy heir when the matter becomes urgent, which is far off. Indeed some would say, and I respect their opinions, that Edward Atheling has left to our people a son of royal stock with a strong claim on our fidelity."

"A puny, sickly, unpromising lad who may not survive to manhood," scoffed Archbishop Stigand. "No, my lord, with all respect I repeat what I believe strongly, that we can't put off a decision on a matter of such urgency and importance with vague hopes and by citing claims of royal blood. Our forefathers often set aside princes of the line of Cerdic because they were judged unfit to reign or unworthy of kingship. Too much depends upon our future ruler's wisdom, ability and strength to entrust our fortunes to a child in expectation that in time he will become deserving of our trust."

"What's more," interjected Earl Leofric, "our present perilous situation and the common good demand that the claims of a minor, no matter how just and deeply-rooted in ancestry, must yield to our need for a strong, mature ruler. A powerful sword arm, not the feeble limbs of a boy, is essential to protect our people from the dangers that threaten."

Harold shrugged and spread his hands. "I understand your concern, though I'll stand by what I said earlier. I'm willing to listen to your advice. What course would you prefer to follow? What would you have me say?"

Stigand echoed the final word with a sly smile "Say? Only that since God and man are joined in willing that it be so, yield to our fervent pleas and deeply-considered advice and take the burden on yourself. Who other than Earl Harold Godwinson is fit to lead our people? You stand well with our lord the king, you're back in his good graces, and he is disposed to heed our advice, and even more important to accept the voice of God, which calls for him to recognize you as his heir now that the line of Cerdic has become so fragile."

Leofric intervened again. "As for your brother Tostig, he should remain content with the estates he holds now and those we may assign to him in the future. He already has Earl Siward's lands, with more to come besides, so surely he should be satisfied."

Edmond's disbelief and dismay heightened with each successive word uttered by Stigand and Leofric. Childe Edward's body was scarce laid in his tomb and these vultures were already disinheriting his son. Admittedly, the danger to England was great and the land needed a strong ruler, yet it was unconscionable to set aside young Edgar's legitimate claim so flagrantly and unscrupulously as these hard men were bent on doing.

314

He was relieved to hear that others shared his doubts, if for far different reasons. The most vocal objection came from Earl Alfgar who became even more flushed than usual as he banged meaty fists on the council table. "Nay, by the holy rood, this is too much! I'll not hear of it!"

Harold scowled at Alfgar and toyed with a dagger while Earl Leofric tugged at his son's tunic to calm him, then asked in a level voice, "What won't you hear of, cousin? Of Harold Godwinson rising to the kingship of England? I'm not surprised the possibility disturbs you. I can guess what you've left unsaid, that Godwin's son has no more right to the kingship than does Earl Leofric's or—to put it another way—that Leofric's son has as much right to reign as does Godwin's. Am I not right? Well, it's true, which is why I don't wish to say more just now. We've no reason to quarrel. Let's remain the good friends we've always been."

Leofric rushed to Harold's support, admonishing Alfgar, "My son, I know it sits hard with you, but we can't avoid the issue. If we allow this matter of the succession to the kingship to drift much longer others may choose for us to our great regret. Indeed, it may require much blood and silver to defend our rights. Now is the time to come to a decision. We must support each other for the common welfare, and Earl Harold is the only man who can unite our people. He has won King Edward's trust. He has inherited the vast estates and great power of my old friend Earl Godwin. There's no one else who can even hope to successfully oppose Duke William. Be warned, the duke made it only too evident on his visit to England several years ago that he longs to rule us. There's no doubt the Witan will support Earl Harold, and we can't afford to wait for Childe Edgar to come to man's estate. Our need is too urgent. Only Harold can save us."

"Wisely spoken," declared Archbishop Stigand. "What more need be said? We're all agreed our best, perhaps only, hope lies in Earl Harold." He lowered his voice to admonish, "Friends, let's keep this matter among ourselves until the time is ripe to reveal our decision. Meanwhile, we'll continue to work toward the common goal."

Even Earl Alfgar nodded grudging support as the assemblage thundered approval of the prelate's advice. As for Edmond, he recalled when Prior Wulfstan first had broached to him the possibility that Harold might aspire to succeed King Edward. It was a bitter thought that Harold without the shadow of a right should press so near England's throne while he could not even permit himself the luxury of such a dream though his claim was far superior.

His musing ended when Harold, finally aware of his presence, addressed him with obvious contempt, "What, your master just buried, and you've hurried here to dance attendance on us?"

Edmond had been prepared for a hostile reception but bristled nevertheless. Scowling, he instinctively placed a hand on his sword hilt. "I've come to perform my final obligation to my lord, Edward Atheling. He charged me on his deathbed to deliver a message to you as his last request, Earl Harold. As for myself, I seek nothing from you or any man. Furthermore, I neither desire nor need any lord's support or protection."

Edmond's ringing defiance startled Harold into a placating if haughty gesture. "Well, well, you're somewhat too quick to take offense. Calm down and deliver your message. We're prepared to listen if you speak on behalf of Childe Edward whom we esteemed greatly and whose death was a sad blow to us all."

"My lord, I consider it a great honor that Atheling Edward designated me to deliver his final words to you, indeed to all England. His last request was this: 'Commend my beloved son Edgar, indeed my dear wife and daughters as well, to Earl Harold Godwinson. Inform him that I trust him to protect and cherish Childe Edgar until he reaches manhood and can lay claim to what is his rightful station by birth, tradition and the customs of our people.'" Edmond paused, his eyes sweeping the crowd of nobles to gauge their reaction before meeting those of Harold who immediately looked away.

A brief silence ensued, terminated by Harold's demand, "Have you discharged your commission? Is there more?"

"Yes there is, my lord. The atheling added, 'My son will need a strong arm to protect him from the dangers sure to threaten, and that arm belongs to Earl Harold.'"

Harold frowned, then threw himself back in his great chair. Earl Leofric stared disapprovingly at Edmond while Earl Alfgar and Archbishop Stigand exchanged cynical glances. A growing murmur swept the room. Edmond was irritated but reined in an urge to condemn the assembly's disdain for the atheling's final request.

Harold again broke an awkward silence. "Childe Edward feared for his son's life? God knows the boy has nothing to dread from me, I assure you, Kometes Edmond, or Thane Edmond, as you called yourself formerly, though by what right I'm not certain. I've no designs against this orphan lad's life or liberty and I'm sure neither do any others of this noble company assembled here. Yet there may be evil-minded people..." His voice trailed away significantly.

Edmond seized on Harold's suggestion. "Indeed, Earl Harold, there are people to be feared..." but was cut off in mid-sentence when the earl raised a hand in warning.

"Say no more, Kometes," snapped Harold. "I don't want to hear unsupported accusations." He paused to carefully choose his next words. "I'll tell you this much. If it remains in my power to assure his safety, Childe Edgar will grow to manhood and Atheling Edward's daughters will find suitable husbands when they come of age to wed. What more can I promise? Do you seek anything else?"

"I've carried out my lord's bidding. The rest is in the hands of God." Edmond turned to leave, choked with indignation against these arrogant magnates who so pointedly ignored Childe Edgar's indisputable claims. They were clearly determined to deny him the lad his patrimony. He was silent until Harold's parting words angered him beyond control.

"I'm surprised you've asked nothing for yourself, which is just as well," Harold commented dismissively.

Edmond spun about angrily. "No, I seek, ask and want nothing for myself. I came to speak solely on behalf of Childe Edgar, the son and heir of Edward Atheling. To my sorrow and dismay, I've learned that I've come too late and in vain for the prince is sold, bought and cast aside in spite of his dying father's pleas.

"I'm only too well aware there's nothing that I, a humble thane, can say or do that will change your minds. But let me warn you, my lords, it's an evil day for England when you so callously disregard a royal father's appeal to support his son's undoubted right. Your conduct bodes ill for the future of our land and people. The crown of Alfred and Edmond Ironside won't sit comfortably on a head other than Childe Edgar's in defiance of our ancient laws and customs."

"Enough! You've had your say," Harold thundered, touching off an echoing outcry directed against Edmond by the rest of the assembly.

"I've not finished, and I intend to have my say come what may," Edmond shouted over the uproar, then waited until the clamor died down so he could be heard. "I beg you not to abandon the path of righteousness and honor, and of loyalty to the blood royal. True, Childe Edgar is a child now, but it's your duty and obligation as loyal subjects to shape him into a worthy successor to our long line of kings. It's up to you to make sure he becomes worthy of occupying the throne of his ancestors so that he can maintain the laws and customs of our people. I ask for no more than that."

He was distressingly aware that his fervent speech was being greeted with scornful indifference.

"I can see I'm shouting into the wind, that you intend to set aside Childe Edgar, if not because of malice and ill-will it's from the mistaken supposition that you act in the best interests of our people. Yet Earl Harold, worthy lord that he is—and I hold him in high regard no matter what he may think of me—can never grasp the kingly power so securely as would Childe Edgar. Harold Godwinson does not come of a kingly line and cannot rely on God's support if he usurps the crown. Hear me out—alas, I feel like the prophet Jeremiah—the day that Harold mounts a throne to which he has no right will mark the beginning of an end to England's rule by its own kings."

Earl Harold sprang to his feet, eyes ablaze, the veins on his forehead standing out as if about to burst. Before he could speak, however, a cowled figure came up behind him and placed a restraining hand on his shoulder. Harold spun around angrily, but then to the astonishment of the assembly immediately gave way to the monk who threw back his hood to disclose Prior Wulfstan's gentle features.

Wulfstan walked slowly around to the front of the long table to confront Edmond, then gripped his hand firmly as he whispered, "Remember!"

Struck dumb for a moment, Edmond forced himself to reply. "Yes, I remember." He could not help adding, "Yet, Father, I speak not for myself but for a betrayed child."

Wulfstan smiled sadly. "I know that and God will credit you, but it's best if you don't speak at all."

Edmond bent his head in acquiescence. "It hardly matters. My words aren't heard. I might as well remain silent. There's nothing left for me to seek nor to ask for."

Wulfstan blessed him before retiring to a corner of the hall. On the prior's retreat, Harold cried, "You ask for nothing, proud thane, but I reluctantly give you something I and these lords dearly wish for and none would blame me for taking—your head. Yes, your head! Insolent villain, traitor, renegade.

"You've forfeited your life many times over, and I long to grasp your head to tear out that insolent tongue and gouge those defiant eyes. You forget, scoundrel, that the death of Edward Atheling releases me of my pledge to hold you in good regard." He sprang to his feet to point an accusing finger. "You betrayed me six years ago, Thane Edmond. You betrayed me then, and you betray me again."

Edmond countered Harold's furious attack with calm dignity. "I've never betrayed you, Lord Harold, neither six years ago nor today. I owed you nothing then, and I owe you nothing now. I carried out the mission you entrusted me with. When it failed, through no fault of my own, I considered my obligation to you ended. The reason I left England after that is between me and God. Your unjustified anger against me is between you and God as well."

"So be it," Harold muttered, strangely calmed by Edmond's simple declaration. He sat down before continuing, "Let our accounts be settled by Almighty God for only he knows the truth of the matter. I warn you, though, I never wish to see you again. Go!"

318

Edmond thought better of an impulse to retort. At a nod from Harold, Thane Sebert appeared at his side, and took him by the arm to usher him out of the great hall. Sebert whispered, "Depart, friend, before someone persuades Earl Harold to change his mind and detain you, or worse. Some might consider it best to make certain that what has been discussed here doesn't become common knowledge."

"Thank you, good thane," replied Edmond. "I'll keep that in mind."

Once Sebert had safely escorted him out of the building, he pressed the thane's hand before he swung into the saddle. "Let's part friends, good Sebert. No matter what Earl Harold thinks of me, I've never been false to him."

"I believe you, Thane Edmond. It grieves me to see you and my lord at odds because God knows he'll need all the friends and allies he can summon to his side."

"I agree with you, but the breach is not of my making," Edmond protested. "God preserve you, good friend, and your lord as well. I bear him no ill-will even if I deplore the dangerous and false course he seems bent on taking."

He rode off slowly, picking his way past groups of the retainers of Harold and his allies whose black looks mirrored their lords' hostility toward him.

He did not feel entirely safe until Godwin's mansion was out of sight and he was crossing London Bridge to leave Southwark behind.

Chapter Forty-Two

Full Circle

Edmond concealed his true feelings during Lady Agatha's effusive display of relief and gratitude as he repeated Earl Harold's assurances that he intended to protect her children's interests. It would not do to disclose his frustration and indignation at how coldly Harold and his allies had received him at Southwark. He wished to spare her the shock of discovering that Childe Edgar was being betrayed by those she believed in her naiveté would support his rightful claim to be King Edward's heir.

Lady Agatha shed tears of joy when Edmond repeated Harold's glib reply to her late husband's plea. He was careful to convey only the earl's promise that he would protect Childe Edgar until he came of age and would find suitable husbands for the boy's sisters at the appropriate time. He did not tell her that it was evident Harold's supporters were planning to set Edgar aside. That disclosure would merely grieve Agatha who was powerless to avert such an usurpation. She could have little influence, especially as a foreigner who did not understand England's politics, laws and customs.

"My son's safety is in good hands," she rejoiced in her innocence. "You don't know what that means to a mother's heart." She impulsively grasped Edmond's hands. He drew back as if touched by hot coals. She misunderstood. "Nay, brave, loyal thane, you're much too modest. You've proved my dear Edward's best friend in death as you did in life. I'll never be able to repay our debt to you, but I'll try to make sure you don't go unrewarded. I'll ask the king to grant you an honorable post at court."

To her surprise and dismay, Edmond firmly, if politely, declined her offer, explaining he had decided to return to his home in the West Country. She impulsively drew a gold ring set with a large emerald from her right hand. He hesitated, then accepted it, not wishing to offend. She smiled as he slipped it onto the finger next to the one on which he wore King Alfred's silver band.

Fortunately she was unable to read his mind as he gazed upon the rings, ruefully reflecting they both symbolized failure. The ancient silver band with its legend "AELFRED MEC HEHT GEWYRCAN" might not be as tarnished as it had been when Osgood gave it to him, yet the same could not be said of his ambition of succeeding to the throne of the great king for whom it had been made. As for Lady Agatha's emerald, it glittered as coldly as the empty assurances made by Harold to an unfortunate princess laboring under the misconception that her children's future was in safe hands.

He was in a somber mood when he left Lady Agatha, resolved more firmly than ever to depart from London and to dismiss all thoughts of taking further part in affairs of state. He headed for the Lombard quarter to call on Adelphi of Papia, the goldsmith who served as Constantinople's banker in the city. Adelphi's shop was in an ancient black-timbered house hard by Belin's Gate near the Thames. The building's forbidding aspect proved deceptive when a servant ushered him inside. The ornate if sparse furniture, thick oriental carpeting, and richly-decorated wall hangings would have done justice to the imperial palaces of the Roman capital. A gray-bearded, heavy-set ancient bustled forward to greet him, barking a gruff inquiry as to the reason for his visit.

Edmond almost apologetically handed the old man the crinkled, somewhat tattered and stained bit of parchment bearing Constantine IX's signature and the imperial seal. He half expected the banker to laugh in his face, then show him to the door. To his relief though Adelphi glanced casually at the note as if expecting it to call for a small sum, the large amount shocked the banker to full attention. He attentively smoothed out and reexamined the bill of exchange, then regarded his visitor with far greater respect.

"You must have done the good and great basileus—may his immortal soul rest with God—a signal service to merit so splendid a reward, illustrious kometes," remarked Adelphi as he tugged a bell rope. An elderly clerk materialized and the banker whispered an order. The clerk bowed, disappeared briefly, then returned with several leather pouches from which he poured a flood of gold and silver coins upon a counting table.

Adelphi personally weighed out the coins on a balance until their value reached the large sum specified in the imperial note, then ordered his assistant to check the figures. Satisfied with their accuracy, he asked Edmond to sign a receipt before handing over the refilled leather pouches. While escorting Edmond to the door, he assured him profusely he would be delighted to serve as his agent in London.

"I thank you, signore," Edmond replied. "I shall keep your kind offer in mind, but I doubt I'll have further need of your services. It's not likely I'll ever return to London, and certainly not to Constantinople."

"God be with you then, Kometes Edmond," said the Lombard, adding a parting caution, "and take care wherever you're bound for because the roads are not safe."

Edmond knew that without being told. Traveling all the way across England was sure to be dangerous, especially if anyone should suspect he was transporting a small treasure. Well, he would have to trust to luck and his strong right arm.

The next day he purchased a sturdy Flemish draft horse, which dwarfed his Magyar pony, and piled his belongings on the larger beast, concealing the money pouches under the ordinary baggage. He then set out for Dover, though the seaport was in the opposite direction to his eventual destination of western England. He had promised Aegelsig to return for the splendid armor the smith so lovingly had fashioned for him, and he hoped to learn whether Adele remained at Wherwell. He would visit the convent if she was still there. He pushed his horses to the limit, fearing that Aegelsig, so desperately ill at their last meeting, might have succumbed in the interval.

His spirits sank as soon as he approached Aegelsig's shop and became aware of the unnatural silence. Where was the customary din, the harsh clang of metal hammering upon metal, the angry hiss of water turning into steam? He knew instantly the master armorer was no longer alive.

"My dear master died this morning, Thane Edmond," lamented the tearful apprentice who opened the door. He recognized Edmond from his visit two weeks earlier when he had arrived in Dover with Atheling Edward. "He suffered so much in his last hours that—Christ forgive me for saying so—his passing was a blessing."

With bowed head, Edmond followed the lad into the chamber where the body was laid out. To his surprise, the armor and weapons made for him by Aegelsig were displayed on a table next to the deathbed. There were the gilded helmet, the kite-shaped shield, the lightweight hauberk, the ponderous battle-ax, and the glittering, magnificently damascened scabbard with its tri-lobed, jeweled sword.

The apprentice perceived his astonishment. "It's strange, isn't it," he remarked. "My master ordered these brought to him for a last look. He gazed long and hard on them. He insisted it was his finest work, and indeed I've never seen better even from his hands. That's saying much because he was the master of the trade, that's certain."

"Did he tell you anything else about this equipment?"

"He charged us not to let any of it out of our sight and keeping until Thane Edmond Edwysson arrived. You've come to take it, haven't you, Thane Edmond?"

"Yes."

"Then it's yours, my lord. Master Aegelsig ordered that when you came—he hoped soon—all should be given you," the apprentice replied, then recalling another injunction of his late employer, searched under his tunic. "This bit of parchment as well," he added, offering a note.

Edmond took it, asking, "Can you read, lad?"

The apprentice shook his head.

Edmond unfolded the chit to read: "Son of Childe Edwy, my beloved lord and master, as you know I expended all my skill, such as it is, to the utmost to shape this armor and weapons so they would be fit for a king. Even on my deathbed, when only truth will serve, I am convinced I was obeying God's will. Accept them in the spirit in which they were fashioned and in which they are offered, Childe Edmond. There will come a time when you will employ them to defend the right conferred on you at birth by God and the laws and customs of our people. I made them for a king's use and I know that a king will wear and wield them. I have done my duty to my dear lord's son. Pray for my soul, which I shall shortly yield to God's grace and charity."

Edmond sighed and told the apprentice, "You've done well, son, to preserve your master's note for me. A dying man's last request deserves all respect. As for this marvelous equipment, I accept and treasure it though I doubt I'll ever need to use it." Tossing the lad a silver penny, he took a last look at Aegelsig's disease ravaged face, wondering what vision or delusion could have prompted those strange final words so reminiscent of his dying father's statement, "You were born to be a king, Edmond."

He remained long enough to attend the funeral the next day. Aegelsig was laid to rest in the church cemetery near the grave of his old friend Osgood before Edmond rode out of Dover a suit of armor the richer and a friend the poorer.

The convent at Wherwell was much enlarged since Edmond's previous visit though he was hardly aware of it. New buildings heightened the impression of abundance and wealth the convent made on even the least discerning wayfarer. Several nuns occupied with their outdoor tasks furtively glanced at the powerfully-built young nobleman who rode past them toward the convent astride a strange, small pony that bore his weight with remarkable ease, while a large Flemish horse loaded with armor and baggage trotted behind. Edmond was unaware of the stir he was causing as he rode toward the stables. He pulled up when a stablehand appeared to receive his instructions. Dismounting, he tossed the groom a coin and headed for the main building.

After a brief parley with the doorkeeper, he was admitted into a cubicle to await the abbess. She was a small, elderly nun whom he recognized from his previous visit as King Edward's sister Elfrida and, though she did not know it, his own aunt.

"You've been sent by Earl Harold?" she asked, frowning. There was something familiar about Edmond though she did not recognize him.

"No, my lady, or rather as I explained to your doorkeeper, I've served him but I come on my own behalf. I know you can't possibly remember, but we've met. My name is Edmond Edwysson, a thane of Bosbury."

"I thought I'd seen you before, but I don't recall the circumstances," she replied. "Please forgive an old woman's failing memory."

"I was here six years ago. I delivered a message from Earl Harold Godwinson to the Lady of England."

The abbess smiled. "Now I remember. The young man with the sad face." She looked searchingly at him. "You've changed a good deal, my son, but you're still sad at heart, it seems. Not that you should be. This is a time to rejoice, God be praised. The Lady Edith and my brother, King Edward, live in amity again. Earl Harold can have no cause for complaint."

"I don't come from him this time, Reverend Abbess. I come on my own behalf. I have a boon to ask of you. With all respect, and with your permission, I would like to speak to one of your nuns."

Abbess Elfrida looked at him in astonishment, then snapped her fingers. "Now I have it. You're the young man for whom Sister Ursula prays."

"Sister Ursula?"

The abbess was amused. "I forget. You knew her as Adele, of course."

"Yes, reverend lady. Osgood's daughter. Will you permit me to speak to her?"

"Only if she wishes to see you. If she does, nothing easier. She's in the writing room. She has been my clerk four years now. A wonderful woman, true to her vocation and to God, but burdened by a grief that even years of prayer haven't sufficiently eased." The abbess paused to consider, looking speculatively at Edmond. "You're not here to reopen those wounds?" She caught herself. "No, that was foolish of me. How can you help doing so if she agrees to meet you again. Your presence is enough. Do you bring bad news?"

"Her uncle, the armorer Aegelsig, just died."

Abbess Elfrida crossed herself. "She has been expecting that. She had prayed for him daily since hearing of his illness." She began to leave the room but paused. "Why do I hesitate? God will care for his own. I'll send Sister Ursula if she agrees to see you." She glided out of the room. Edmond soon heard approaching footsteps. Light as they were, they resonated like hammer blows to him. His throat became dry and eyes moist when a slender figure wrapped in nun's habit entered the room.

"Adele!" Her name floated like a sigh from his lips.

"Sister Ursula," she corrected softly, and he fancied a trace of the sparkling mockery that formerly had spiced the sweetness of her voice.

"It's good to see you again, Sister Ursula," he said gravely, gazing upon her.

"It's good to see you too, Thane Edmond," she countered, but only with her voice, averting eyes from his burning glance. "You've traveled a great deal, I've heard. Did you get to see Duke William in Normandy?"

He was almost as touched as amused. "You recall our conversations then?"

"I remember a young girl's foolish chatter in her father's garden at Dover. Yes, and I don't regret it." She sat down and regarded him seriously. "But you didn't come here after all these years to reminisce about such nonsense, pleasant as it might be to do so."

"And why not!" His flippancy drew a smile before he resumed in a serious tone. "No, I came because all these years I've been troubled by a question I've been unable to dismiss despite my best efforts."

"I don't know if I should permit you to ask that question, or any other," she replied in alarm, looking away again.

"Yet I must ask." He sank to his knees, hardly knowing how to begin, but finally steeled himself. "Adele, tell me why you turned against me, why you abandoned your family, wealth and material comforts for dedication to the service of God. Commendable as it may be in the eyes of the church, it lacks the fullness of life."

She looked at him sadly. "Edmond, I once told you that I could give you no answer other than to say I have consecrated myself to Christ to obtain forgiveness for my shortcomings."

"That's no answer," he cried, springing to his feet. He turned toward her almost in hostility. "All these years I've questioned myself endlessly as to what I did that you couldn't forgive, something that caused you to turn your back on me and abandon all the bright hopes we had for the future. I returned to Dover to claim you for my own after Earl Harold sailed to Ireland. I was stricken to the heart to find you gone, that you had fled to a convent to avoid me. What caused such a change in your feelings toward me between those happy days in your father's house and my return?"

She was too choked up to reply immediately, tears filling her eyes. After an interval she gasped, almost as if speaking to herself, "Oh God, I must tell him otherwise I won't be able to live in peace with myself." After she regained control, she wiped away the tears and her voice was steady. "Thane Edmond, I may have come to love you dearly at one time. If when my father was murdered you had said, 'Come, go with me,' I would have done so even though I felt partly responsible for his death. I would have found it impossible to refuse you even if it had meant becoming only your hand-fast wife, no more. But when you didn't speak, when you left me in Uncle Aegelsig's care, I had time to consider.

"There was also a letter which my father had given my uncle a day or two before his death, almost as if he anticipated his fate. He instructed me to obey my uncle in all things if anything should happen to him. He spoke of you, cautioning me not to let myself be drawn to you because such an attraction could bring me nothing but grief. He explained you were fated to dedicate your life to a cause in which I could have no part and which made a lawful union between us impossible."

She raised a hand to prevent Edmond from interrupting.

"No, I have more to say. Don't forget I know your secret. I know who you are and what you seek. My father reminded me for your sake as much as for mine. There could be no true marriage between us because such a union might stand in the way of one more advantageous for you in pursuit of your quest. How could a king's grandson wed a humble merchant's daughter?" Tears again filled her eyes. "When I read my father's letter, I knew I must obey him," she resumed after regaining her composure. "Much as I loved you, I had to refuse you. I meant to stay with my uncle the rest of my life, but God willed otherwise. Uncle Aegelsig urged me to marry Heinrich of Bremen, a worthy man no doubt, but I couldn't become a wife to him after having known you. In spite of my uncle's pleas, and to escape his persistent urging, I decided to consecrate my life to Christ."

She rose to leave but Edmond reached out and pulling her toward him cradled her face in his hands and gazed into her eyes.

"Adele, I'm sure you and your father intended to act for the best. Thank you for answering a question that has troubled me so long. Yet I fear Osgood and you have deprived me of the only comfort that might have redeemed an empty life. I've given up my hopeless quest and plan to withdraw from the world's temptations and struggles as you have done. No, I don't intend to retire into a monastery for I lack a religious inclination. I'll live out my days near Bosbury as my father did."

She opened her mouth as if to protest but thought better of it.

"You could have shared a simple life with me and made it happy for us both," he continued. "It's too late now, I know. Yet I shall always think of you, and I hope that from time to time you'll remember me and those few happy days in Dover."

She whispered hoarsely, "I'll always think of you, dear Edmond." As she glided toward the door, she turned to breathe a final, heartfelt, "Good-bye, my love," before vanishing from sight.

He scarcely heard the abbess reenter, nor her severe words. "I was wrong to permit you to see Sister Ursula. May God forgive me!"

"No, you were right to let us meet," he insisted. "I feel better for speaking to her, and I believe she does as well."

"She's so distraught," sighed Elfrida. "She took the news of her

326

uncle's death even more to heart than I thought she would."

"Her uncle's death?" Edmond repeated in consternation. "Heaven forgive me! I forgot to tell her."

Abbess Elfrida stared at him in wonder. "Then what caused her so much grief?" she demanded, softening when she saw how miserable he looked. "No, I'd just as soon you didn't tell me. As for her uncle's death, I'll inform her."

"I'd be grateful, Reverend Abbess. You've been most kind. I'll bother you no longer. You can rest assured I'll not return to trouble you again."

"Wait! Not so quick! Won't you accept some refreshment in the refectory before you leave?" she asked, her customary hospitality surfacing despite her suspicion that he had upset Sister Ursula.

He refused politely, bowed out of the room, and reclaiming his horses at the stable resumed his journey, heading westward after one last glance back at Wherwell.

Sunk in gloom, he took little notice of the countryside or the towns and villages he passed through as he followed a winding course across England toward Bosbury. Somehow, despite his inattention, he escaped encounters with any of the many outlaws frequenting the roads. At length, the well-remembered cottages of Bosbury finally came into view. Almost instinctively, he took a familiar path leading to a tiny cottage not far distant from the village.

Smoke curled from an opening in the roof and for the first time in several weeks Edmond felt a spark of joy. As he approached the building, a well-known figure emerged from the doorway and ran toward him.

"Thane Edmond! Thane Edmond!" Godfrid shouted. "You've come at last."

Chapter Forty-Three

Reunion

"An evil omen, a warning from heaven, no doubt of it," agreed the corpulent, grizzled old tinker, cocking a bleary eye at the hairy star whose brilliant tail stretched like a bridge across a cloudless evening sky. "My father, God rest his soul, oft told me that when he was a boy in the days of luckless King Ethelred just such a star shone before Sweyn Forkbeard's Danes landed to ravage our poor folk." He shuddered while comforting himself with a long pull at a tankard of ale.

"Ne'er mind your old father's days, good tinker," growled Ealmer, a surly churl, as he gazed in awe at the comet. "What's it signify now, that's what we want to know. Surely the Danes aren't coming back to harass us again?"

The tinker spat on the ground and look scornfully at the small huddle of drinking companions gathered outside the tavern. "I know Bosbury's at the ends of the earth, that's certain, but you can't be all so ignorant of what's happening elsewhere. Haven't you heard King Harold has summoned the fyrd and long ships? And bastard Duke William is gathering an army and a fleet in Normandy? There's even talk of that old berserker King Harald Hardraade stirring in Norway preparing to fall upon us poor folk."

"Come, good tinker, do you take us for witless cattle?" snapped Ealmer. "We've heard somewhat of such matters, and it may be that our thane will answer the new king's call." His face mirrored his confusion and concern. "Troubling times are coming fast and hard, sure to get worse. Good King Edward dead in January—Christ comfort his saintly soul—with Harold Godwinson in his place, and now—just three months since—there's talk of war and the like, which can do none good and cause harm to all."

"Only fools would expect anything else than trouble when a king dies," snorted the tinker. "There's many who hold Harold has no claim to be king, and then there's the sacred oath he swore before Duke William." Draining the tankard, he led his companions into the inn from which they had emerged for a glimpse of the heavenly phenomenon.

"Harold swore an oath, you say?" piped up a yeoman. "What did he swear to?"

"Swore over the holy relics of goodly saints, no less," the tinker explained. "Duke William contends that King Edward—his cousin, he says, though, I don't understand how a bastard can claim such kinship— promised him the succession. To make sure of Earl Harold's support, he demanded he swear to uphold his rights. Harold did so, taking an oath over holy bones some two years ago."

"Did he? Where?" Ealmer asked.

"Duke William's court in Rouen. You may ask how Harold happened to be there when it was probably the last place he intended to go. He went out to sea with his warships when a surprise storm drove his vessel upon the rocks. When he was rescued, to his further misfortune he found himself in the power of Count Guy of Ponthieu. God knows what harm Count Guy might have done to him if Duke William hadn't demanded Harold's release. The duke had to threaten Count Guy before that rapacious and bloody lord agreed to turn over such a valuable prisoner. When Harold was brought to Rouen, William demanded that he take an oath to support the duke upon King Edward's death before he would agree to let him return to England. Some say he did so willingly, being grateful to Duke William, others insist he feared being held prisoner indefinitely, and that he swore the oath without intending to honor it."

"What do you think, good tinker?" Ealmer demanded.

"Why even a fool would realize that he swore out of policy rather than gratitude. He knew Duke William would never release him if he thought him a rival for our kingship. Of course, if Harold had known holy relics were hidden under the sacramental table at Duke William's orders, he might not have pledged his word no matter what."

"If that's so, it was a vile trick on the Norman's part, and King Harold did right to disavow an oath exacted by force and under false pretenses," cried Ealmer.

"You might well say so," approved the tinker, adding, "What's strange is that all fell out as some soothsayers foresaw, though I put no trust in any such foolery and never will. King Edward died four and twenty years after he became king in 1042 and now Harold is our lord, all oaths and promises to the contrary."

"It's wonderful how you traveling folk keep up with all that's happening," Ealmer sighed admiringly. "If it weren't for folks like you passing through, we in Bosbury wouldn't know much of what's going on in the world."

"It's true that a wandering tinker's life has its blessings," the fat man admitted while hungrily devouring a chicken leg. "Not that getting rich is one. I've had little business in the way of mending pots, pans and such like today. By the holy rood, much as my old bones ache, I'd better move on if I am to keep body and soul together."

Ealmer sympathetically scratched an ear even while reflecting that the tinker's vast girth indicated he had no trouble keeping his body satisfied. "You might try Thane Edmond's hall," he suggested. "Hundreds of folks live on his lands, and there's bound to be plentiful work for you there."

"Thane Edmond, you say?" the tinker mused. "A common name, but years ago I knew such a one. A likely lad, he was, poor fellow." He sighed, crossing himself. "That was long ago and he's dead, no doubt, God rest his soul. All the same, your advice is good. I'll venture to the thane's hall in the morning."

"You'll get a hearty welcome," Ealmer assured. "Thane Edmond and his people are good hosts to all travelers, whatever their station, noblemen or churls. He's always eager for the latest news from other parts. You'll be sure of a hearty meal, a full flagon, and a friendly hearing."

"I can empty the table and fill the ears as well as any man," the tinker promised with a chuckle. "And I drink more than most, that's certain."

He was not disappointed the next day. A throng of eager women carrying cooking wares that needed mending and men with damaged farm tools responded to the bellow advertising his services as soon as he approached the cluster of buildings around Thane Edmond's hall. He set to work immediately, and soon sweat was pouring down his fat cheeks. Nevertheless, he was able to chaffer with the circle of curious children and aged idlers that gathered around to watch his handiwork.

"The other good wives are keeping me so busy it'll be some time before I get around to the lady of the manor's articles," he remarked to a young woman as he handed her a mended pan.

"No fear of that," she laughed. "Our thane has no wife, more's the pity."

The tinker looked up in surprise. "Not even a handfast one?"

"Not even such a shameless hussy. Not that there aren't a few wenches I know of around here who'd be glad to settle for that if he just would ask them."

"You'd be the first of them, wouldn't you, Maud?" a graybeard teased.

The girl blushed and stamped her feet in embarrassment. "You've no cause to say that. I'll be married or remain a maid," she shouted as she ran off.

The tinker ignored the by-play to ask the old man, "Your good master must be young then?"

"Young? No, I wouldn't say so, but not so old either." The old churl wrinkled his brow. "I suppose he might have been born in the days of King Cnut, not all that long before his son Harold Harefoot became king."

"In his thirties then. A good age." The tinker banged a rivet to secure a pot handle. "There's heat and vigor in a man then. It's strange your lord wouldn't want a woman at such a time of life. Maybe he's too proud to marry beneath him. A freeman's daughter or a churl's might not suit him, and no doubt there's few women of higher station to choose from in these parts."

"It may be as you say," the old man agreed. "Then again I've heard that Thane Edmond traveled all over before he settled here. He could've brought a wife home with him."

"Stay, there's your answer," the tinker exclaimed triumphantly. "A traveling man soon learns he moves fastest with the lightest load. I discovered that when I was young, but to my sorrow when matters were past mending. I married my Hilda before I took to the sea." He sighed deeply, either because of regret over having wed at all or in recalling Hilda's once irresistible charms. "Every time I returned home I rued the unhappy day I married that shrew. Yet, God rest her troublesome soul, she has been dead these three years and it's wicked, if tempting, to abuse her memory."

"So you've been a sailor," said the churl. "Thane Edmond will welcome you all the more heartily. He takes pleasure in visitors who've traveled much as you must have done. He's not a man to stand on ceremony no matter what a man's station in life, tinker or lord."

"That's encouraging. For my part, I love nothing better than to swap stories with someone who has seen something of the world. Your lord has traveled much of late?"

"He has been here among us a good many years now. If I remember rightly, he came here to stay soon after Atheling Edward of good memory died and hasn't left since."

"Why that's been nine years or more," the tinker exclaimed. "And you say he has been living here without wife or woman all that time." He whistled surprise.

The old man shrugged. "Just so. It's said he returned with a treasure in gold and silver, having been gone for years after Thane Edwy died. That was his father, one who left him nothing but a small cottage and a hide or two of land. Now Thane Edmond owns I don't know how many hides in all directions. His great hall is the finest in all these parts, some say. He spends most of his days hunting and hawking and leaves the management of his lands altogether to his worthy steward, Master Godfrid."

The old man prattled on about Thane Edmond and Godfrid but the tinker's mind was elsewhere as he continued his labors. He was impressed by the visible prosperity of the estate, the abundance of well-fed cattle and sleek horses, and the cheerfulness of the churls and villeins. He had witnessed a great deal of poverty and sullen misery during his wandering trade and it gladdened his heart to see there was still an area where the common folk enjoyed peaceful prosperity.

At twilight, it was with heavy feet but a light heart and dry throat that the tinker, exhausted by his long day's labors, entered the thane's hall. A good place near the head table at which the thane customarily sat was quickly found for him. Everybody was eager to hear the latest news from around the country. Thane Edmond was not back from the hunt when the meal began, and the tinker quickly demonstrated that when it came to a trencherman Bosbury had never seen his equal. He was well on his way to proving he was no laggard at drink either when there was a stir at the entrance and the company rose in respect for the arrival of the lord of the manor.

The tinker pulled himself erect with great effort and a loud groan to peer in the direction of the commotion. He could not see the thane's face at first because the lord was bent over to scrape mud from his clogs. It was only when the thane straightened up that the tinker got a good look at him. Despite the lord's joviality as he jested about his poor luck in the field that day even a casual observer might have been struck by the evident melancholy of a countenance to which the advancing years had lent a natural majesty and strength although depriving it of the bloom of youth. It was a face that would have demanded attention even among the great magnates of King Harold's court.

As the tinker gaped in astonishment, the thane tossed his brown bearskin cape to a servant to reveal shoulders that had become even broader without the rest of his body losing the easy grace that had always been among his characteristics.

The tinker took all this in at a glance, then as if demented let his tankard clatter to the floor, and to general wonderment rushed upon the thane to enfold him in a bear hug while shouting, "Thane Edmond! Thane Edmond! Dear boy, bully boy, is it really you?" At that ear-splitting bellow, Edmond's sudden shock evaporated and he laughed uproariously as he furiously pounded the fat old man's broad back. "Wiglaf, old friend, it's you! I never thought to see your big, ugly face again. It does my heart good though." He held the tinker at arm's length to look him over before adding, "What's an old sailor, an old pirate, doing so far from the sea?"

"Sailor no more, my lad. I've turned an honest tinker these ten years or more since my good Hilda—may she have no cause to nag anyone in heaven, or wherever she may be—badgered me into giving up the man-hungry sea after Master Lewin and his crew were lost in a storm."

"Then Master Lewin is dead, like so many other good men I've known," Edmond sighed in regret while leading his old friend to a seat next to his at the head table. "Well, we can drink to his soul and theirs. You and he were good friends to me at a time when I would've been in a sorry plight without assistance." He smilingly nudged Wiglaf. "I forget, you may have given up ale as well as the sea and I'll have to drink for both of us to our departed friends." He roared as Wiglaf replied with a shudder at the mere thought of abstinence and gave it the lie by draining a full tankard at one swallow.

"There's your answer," Wiglaf grunted, wiping his mouth on a sleeve as he gestured for a refill. "What about you, Thane Edmond, how have the years dealt with you since we parted so long ago at Bristol?"

"Not unkindly, old friend. I prosper as you see." Edmond answered without much enthusiasm. Wiglaf sensed his diffidence but was shrewd enough not to pry into the cause. He instead began to divulge the stock of news he thought would be of interest to Edmond and the rest of the gathering in such a remote area.

"So it's true, as I've heard, that both Duke William and Harald Hardraade are hoping to unseat our new king," Edmond remarked after hearing Wiglaf's colorful account of the preparations for an invasion of England being made both in Normandy and in Norway. Rumors of the threats had penetrated even to Bosbury, but not in such detail as Wiglaf gave. The scope of Duke William's plan, which included papal support and recruits from all over Europe, shocked Edmond. "I should have expected it," he reflected. "Whatever else can be said of Duke William, none can accuse him of lacking energy and ability. He means to make good his claim to the kingship of England. As for Harald Hardraade, I'm not so sure what he really seeks. It's said he believes our crown devolved on him through a compact made between his kinsman Magnus, with whom he ruled Norway, and our King Harthacnut thirty years ago. They agreed that whoever outlived the other could claim the vacant throne. Because Harthacnut died first, Haardrade considers himself Magnus's heir to England as well as to Norway. I suspect, however, he would settle for less, perhaps only whatever booty the old pirate's long ships can carry home to his kingdom."

"It seems to me that King Harold Godwinson's brother Earl Tostig is playing the most cunning game," Wiglaf ventured.

"Cunning, yes, treacherous and ungrateful almost beyond belief as well. Is it true he's in league with Duke William against his own brother?"

"Aye, he has been furious since Harold had him outlawed after his people in Northumberland rebelled against his tyranny. He took to the seas with his long ships to seek an ally against the king and may have found one in Duke William."

333

Edmond was grave. "The situation is grievous for Harold, indeed for all of us. Duke William and his cutthroat Normans are menace enough. Add the thousands of adventurers William is recruiting from all over Europe, Tostig's ships and men, as well as the pope's support, and Harold will be hard pressed to win through."

"And then there's Harald Hardraade," Wiglaf added. "If you remember, I once served under him and know him for a devil in a fight."

"I heard much of him in Constantinople. When I was there, mothers still were terrifying their children by threatening to turn them over to Harald Sigurdson. A fine soldier without equal in hand-to-hand combat, people say, but lacking the capacity to plan. He'll hit and run like any Viking."

"You've forgotten what I told you about the birds and the castle in Sicily?"

"No, I recall your amusing account. That was clever, but it takes more than trickery for a general to prevail against superior enemies over a long campaign." Edmond stared moodily at his ale. "We've fallen upon evil, dangerous times, old friend. Who would've suspected when I returned to England with luckless Atheling Edward that some day we'd face so many enemies abroad? If only Childe Edward had lived to succeed King Edward. No one could have questioned his right."

He regretted the plaint even as it left his lips. Regret was useless. Strange how a succession of unexpected events had combined in Harold's favor until recently. First came Atheling Edward's abrupt death. Then Earl Ralph, King Edward's nephew, also died to remove another plausible claimant to the succession. Next, Earl Leofric breathed his last, bequeathing his earldom of Mercia to his son Alfgar, who vented his jealousy of Earl Harold and his brothers by harrying their subjects. It took a sound trouncing by the Godwinsons, and a brief banishment, to make Alfgar submit to Harold and regain his estates. Then came a campaign against the Welsh in which Harold and Tostig, earl of Northumbria since Siward's death in 1055, cornered and killed troublesome King Gruffyd, curbing their power for decades to come.

After the success against the Welsh in 1064, Harold's power and influence reached to all corners of England and he was king in all but name, virtually assured of the throne upon the death of King Edward. That came on the fifth day of the new year of 1066. A short time later, Archbishop Ealdred of York crowned Harold, bypassing Archbishop Stigand who lay under the interdict of Rome despite his claim to the see of Canterbury.

Even as Harold reached the summit of his ambition, fortune showed him a glimpse of its harsher side. Brother Tostig so infuriated the people of Northumbria by harsh justice and heavy exactions that they drove him out of the earldom in favor of Earl Morcar, a son of the recently deceased Alfgar. Another of Alfgar's sons, Edwin, succeeded him as earl of Mercia. The power of the house of Leofricson was expanding at the expense of the Godwinsons. Harold recognized and countered the trend by taking for wife Aldyth, sister of Edwin and Morcar as well as the widow of the unfortunate King Gruffyd. As for Tostig, despite the pleas of their mother Gytha, Harold outlawed him to propitiate the Northumbrians and to gain the support of Earls Morcar and Edwin.

Affairs in Rome also went badly for the new king with the election of Pope Alexander II who was indebted to the Normans for support. At the instigation of his archdeacon, Hildebrand, he not only refused to recognize Stigand's claim to Canterbury but ruled that Harold had perjured himself by violating the oath worn over holy relics at Rouen to support Duke William's rights to the kingship of England. The pope went so far as to call for a virtual crusade against Harold and Stigand.

Harold's grip on the throne was shaky, Edmond reflected with a satisfaction of which he felt ashamed but could not suppress. Not only were two armies preparing to invade England, but Harold's brother was a traitor, Rome was allied with his most dangerous foe, and the Leofricsons, the most powerful family in the country next to his own, were in possession of half of England and hungered for even more.

A lesser danger, though not to be totally dismissed, existed in the person of Edgar Atheling, regarded by some as the legitimate successor to his grand-uncle King Edward. The young prince lived in Southwark, and might become a convenient focus for malcontents to rally around against Harold.

As Edmond saw it, King Harold's greatest resource, one that might enable him to prevail over such a formidable array of enemies, was the man himself. A skillful general and inspirational leader, courageous and determined, Harold could conceivably lead his people to triumph over all his foes.

Edmond sought to convince himself that it was all the same to him how matters turned out. He would take no part in the coming struggle. After all, if anyone sought to bring him to account for disregarding the summons of the fyrd he could cite his virtual outlawing. Harold had threatened him the last time they had met so memorably when he had gone to Southwark on behalf of Lady Agatha, Childe Edward's widow. He would stay on his estate, devote himself to the hunt, and let events unfold without drawing sword either for or against King Harold.

Despite his resolve, he was uneasy. If Harold fell to either Duke William or King Harald Hardraade, England would lie open to devastation, plunder and rapine by a horde of foreign adventurers who would leave no corner of its territory inviolate. Much as he felt justified in resenting Harold's hostility, he realized how inexorably the hopes of a free and independent England were linked to the king's survival. He was torn by inward turmoil, aware of his true duty, yet unable to respond.

All this went through his mind as he half-listened to Wiglaf's chatter. He was recalled from his musings by Godfrid's arrival. As he approached, the steward was surprised to see the hulking Wiglaf sitting in such easy familiarity next to his master.

"Greet Master Wiglaf, an old and true friend of mine," Edmond urged, telling Wiglaf, "This is Godfrid, my steward and good right arm."

The two shook hands before Godfrid began to fill his platter. He was much altered since his years with Edmond in Constantinople and the eastern lands. Instead of a stripling, Wiglaf beheld a mature, solidly built man whose one good arm rippled with muscles as if to compensate for the crippled other member. No one now dared refer to Godfrid's handicap even in jest. And though he was stern and rough in anything concerning his master's interests, the churls and villeins on Edmond's lands respected him as a just and moderate overseer.

"Have you heard, my lord, that our neighbor Thane Aelle has taken thirty of more men to join the king in Winchester," Godfrid remarked after making a good start on a leg of lamb. "They say King Harold is assembling an army and a fleet greater than any ever seen before in England."

"He'll need every man, every ship," Wiglaf commented.

Edmond's noncommittal expression concealed his inner struggle over whether he should rally to the king's support. He dismissed the urge, still stung by the memory of his last interview with Harold. He would stay put no matter what. He owed Harold nothing.

Chapter Forty-Four

The Call of Duty

T he harvest was bountiful and game ran thick in the forests around Bosbury in the portentous autumn of the year 1066. Neither common folk nor master had cause to complain, the first gratefully reaping the abundant fruit of their labors, Edmond returning home heavily laden from every hunt.

It was a good life and Wiglaf was content to share in it, having accepted Edmond's invitation to abandon his wandering tinker's trade and remain for the rest of his days on his old friend's estate.

Yet whenever they met for meals in the great hall they became ever more disturbed about the events taking place at the far distant centers of power. News came rarely, and then it was only sketchy, but the reports indicated that almost certainly Duke William and Harald Hardraade soon would invade England. Their attacks could not be delayed much longer if they were to take place that year. The onset of winter would shield England from harm until the following spring.

The latest news to reach Bosbury had been of a sea battle between King Harold's ships and those of Duke William, which had been broken off by a storm before either side could claim victory. A more serious concern for Harold, however, was the shrinking of his army because of a shortage of provisions, and the anxiety of many of his recruits to return home for the harvest.

"Some say Earl Harold has only about half the men he had after he summoned the fyrd," noted Edmond. "If that's true, he'll be hard put to give battle to Duke William when the Normans land." He stared glumly at the brightly polished armor given him by Constantine IX, which hung on the wall behind his great chair. Godfrid himself burnished it at regular intervals, refusing to delegate the task to a subordinate.

"If that's so, the Norman dogs might be able to rattle our bones as much as they like," replied Wiglaf, swirling the ale in his tankard.

"If only I could do my part to help flay those pirates," Edmond burst out, thumping the heavy table until it rattled. "How I long to be at Harold's side." He clenched his fists. "If it weren't for his hostility and threats at Southwark..." He lapsed into a moody silence.

Edmond's eruption of frustration muted the usually lively conversation in the great hall until a clatter of horse hooves and the furious barking of dogs signaled the arrival of someone in the courtyard. A slender, dark-haired young man of about twenty rushed into the room and slumped wearily to a vacant seat at the head table.

"Elfwy Aellesson, if I'm not mistaken," exclaimed Edmond, recognizing a neighboring thane's son. "Quick! Something to eat and drink for the lad." He waited patiently until the youth took two or three bites and a long pull of ale before asking, "Why are you back so soon? Has your father left King Harold's army?"

"He's still with the king, Thane Edmond. They're on the march to the north and Father sent me home to fetch another twenty men. I thought I'd take advantage of your hospitality before I continued to our lands."

"Marching northward? What has happened? Is Harald Hardraade landed?"

Elfwy stared in astonishment. "Didn't you know? He landed ten days ago with a great host and Earl Tostig at his side. Earls Morcar and Edwin confronted them in battle at a place called Gate Fulford, but were driven off the field and fled into York. The Northmen are besieging the city even now unless, Heaven forfend, it has already fallen."

Edmond leaped to his feet, with Wiglaf, Godfrid and the rest of the company following his example.

"Then Harold marches to the rescue?" Edmond sputtered. "What about Duke William? There's none to confront him. He can land unopposed wherever he chooses with none to guard the coast in the south and east. He can attack at any time."

"There's talk he's ready to sail any day now," Elfwy confirmed. "But King Harold had no choice. He had to hurry north to drive off Hardraade and Tostig."

"Yes, there was nothing else he could do," agreed Wiglaf. "Duke William may be more to be feared, but the threat from the north is immediate. If Hardraade prevails all may be lost anyway. Harold had no choice. Whatever the risk, he has to drive off the Northmen before he can return south to confront Duke William's army."

Edmond stared blankly at the armor hanging on the wall, barely aware of the excited chatter around him as Elfwy Aellesson related all he knew about the descent of Harald Hardraade's great fleet in the north, and his victory over Earls Morcar and Edwin. He was stirred to his depths by the sudden shock of realization that he could no longer sit idly by while such great dangers threatened his people and country. England was in terrible hazard of falling either under the harsh Norman yoke or being subjected to widespread rapine and plundering by Harald Hardraade's ferocious Northmen.

All the illusions and mental safeguards Edmond so carefully had fostered over the years to shield himself from emotional involvement in his country's affairs crumbled in the face of the threats now confronting his people. An overwhelming desire to join in the struggle swept over him. His strained relationship with King Harold no longer seemed to matter. It made no difference now that he himself, Edmond Edwysson, in his heart and by custom the true king of England, was barred by force of circumstance from the crown that was his by right. It no longer seemed important that victories over the invaders would benefit a usurper who stood between him and his birthright. All that mattered was that the country was in danger with invaders poised to seize England's wealth and to enslave its people. If ever duty and conscience united to call upon him, it was now. Swept by emotion, he began to reach for the armor on the wall but changed his mind.

"Godfrid! Godfrid!" he shouted. "Fetch the armor and weapons made for me by Master Aegelsig. I shall wear English gear in England's cause." He explained to the astonished Wiglaf, "Old friend, I've made up my mind. I must join King Harold. This is no time to nurse old grievances and stand aside."

Wiglaf heaved himself upright. "I've been longing to hear you say that, Thane Edmond," he roared, gripping Edmond's right hand. "I esteem you all the more for deciding to forget the wrong done you."

"You'll come with me?"

"How could you doubt it?"

"We'll form a little army of our own," Edmond laughed, thumping the old sailor's broad back. "You and I and brave Godfrid with forty of our stoutest lads. It'll be just like the old times in Dover, eh Wiglaf?"

"We'll give those bastards, Normans or Northmen, a good trashing just as we did Count Eustace's men that day, my lord," Wiglaf bellowed as they clashed their ale tankards before draining their contents. All those in the hall followed suit amidst cheers, which soon became gasps of admiration when Godfrid returned with two villeins loaded down with the armor and weapons Aegelsig had made for Edmond.

Edmond drew the magnificent sword from its jeweled scabbard, and grinned as he held it high so all could see it. "Not the worst of gear for a country thane, would you say, good friends?" he shouted, then ordered, "Godfrid, you know what to do. Assemble your men with provisions enough for a month in the field. We march at dawn."

He had not been so exhilarated since the final moments of the desperate battle against the Petchenegs that had ended in disaster. In a burst of jubilation, he again waved the sword over his head. He felt as he had on the day fifteen years before when he had led the townsmen of Dover against the Normans. Wiglaf ducked in pretended alarm when he swung the sword in an arc before laying it down in order to try on the armor.

It was no longer slightly loose as it had been the first time he had tried it on. Now it was snug without being restrictive. It was as if Master Aegelsig had anticipated the time he would have the greatest need of it. After strapping on the sword belt, he took up the ponderous battle-ax with his right hand and the kite-shaped shield with his left. Aegelsig's armor and weapons felt a little strange because he was accustomed to the Roman gear, yet they were more appropriate to the present situation.

Let the Normans come, he bristled. They will pour from their ships to swarm onto England's soil, swollen with confident insolence, mistakenly believing their chief enemy to be Harold, son of Godwin, whom they considered an usurper. But they will also be met by Edmond, the true seed of Cerdic, the son of Edwy, grandson of King Ethelred and nephew of King Edmond Ironside. William the Bastard will discover he is opposed by a true descendant of the great Alfred, a soldier who knows what it is to contend against a superior force. Let the Norman dogs land. King Edmond will drive them back to their ships or die in the attempt. He spun the battle-ax in his hand and laughed loudly. On impulse, he drew the ancient silver ring from his finger and handed it to Godfrid.

"Polish it, Godfrid," he ordered. "It must glitter in the sun so the glint catches every man's eye. Make the inscription stand out: "AELFRED MEC HEHT GEWYRCAN."

Godfrid examined the ring in wonder. "Alfred? What Alfred, my lord?"

"You'll know in good time and soon, my faithful friend," laughed Edmond. "I'll explain to you, too, Wiglaf, and to all my friends and loyal retainers. Alfred ordered this ring made, and it's mine by right of inheritance. All I can say at this time is that we must be ready to march at dawn."

He visited his father's grave that night. It was a few score yards from the great hall, at the foot of an ancient oak. Edmond gazed at the simple inscription "Edwy" carved below a crude cross upon the tombstone. It was the sole identification of a son of King Ethelred and the brother of King Edmond Ironside.

"No doubt my bones will soon lie in a grave as obscure as this one," he reflected. "Yet Father said I was born to be a king, and I'll die as a king should even if I'm only one to myself."

He knelt and bowed his head to recite a short prayer, then walked slowly back to the hall where he fitfully awaited dawn, unable to sleep soundly. The night seemed interminable. It was almost with relief that he was startled out of a brief doze by a growing clamor of shouts, laughter and clatter of weapons as his men assembled in preparation for the march. They stamped their feet in an effort to shake off the morning chill, and the steam of their breath mingled with that of their horses. He quickly joined them to approvingly watch Godfrid scurry about to make sure every man was fully armed and provisioned for the long march to join the king's army in London.

He was confident his men would stand up well to the trials of combat, having diligently trained them during the past nine years. He had taken special pains with the archers and axmen, drilling them endlessly in the use of their weapons, regarding them the backbone of any English army if it was to withstand the Norman's customarily furious charges. He was pleased to note that Godfrid had made certain the armorer's wagon and the supply carts were fully stocked, thus avoiding the frequently haphazard preparations of most English levies. On inspecting his little army, he was able to compare it favorably with the much larger, battle-hardened force he had led against the Petchenegs.

He was satisfied that all was in good order by the time Godfrid reported, "We await your orders, Thane Edmond."

"Have the men make their farewells, and then we set out."

He swung easily into the saddle of his favorite stallion Ironside while struggling to keep from laughing as Wiglaf desperately heaved his enormous bulk onto a huge draft horse. It was the only animal on Edmond's lands that could conceivably bear his weight for any time or distance.

"No sad good-bye for me, Thane Edmond," the sailor remarked as they beheld the tearful parting of the women with their menfolk. The sons and husbands bore up stolidly, assuring their mothers and wives they would soon return.

"No sad good-bye for me either, friend Wiglaf," Edmond echoed soberly, his thoughts ranging back to days long gone. His last, most poignant good-bye had been uttered nine years earlier. Yet he could not help wondering what it would have been like to part from Adele now. Would he be able to go with such a light heart?

He shook off the somber thought, checked the elevation of the sun, and ordered, "Godfrid, assemble the men. We march!"

The men fell into line after scrambling onto their sturdy little ponies. A nod by Edmond, a command by Godfrid, and the little force of forty-three men got underway. It would head southward from Bosbury toward the ancient Roman highway that ran to the east, then follow the road across southern England to London.

Edmond's great hall and the surrounding cluster of cottages quickly vanished from sight, soon hidden by the gently rolling hills surrounding Bosbury. For a time all that could be heard was the steady trot of horses and muted chatter and laughter until one of the men broke into song and others joined in a chorus.

Chapter Forty-Five

Nest of Traitors

As Edmond's troop arrived in the outskirts of London, news spread of the fierce battle won by King Harold's army over the invading Vikings several days earlier, far to the north. Edmond's relief was tempered by reports of ominous developments much closer to the city. Even as the people celebrated King Harold's triumph over Harald Hardraade and Earl Tostig at Stamford Bridge near York, news spread of the landing of a powerful Norman force on the south coast.

Harold allegedly had killed his renegade brother with his own hands, while a fatal arrow had brought the giant Norwegian king crashing to the ground for the last time. Yet the people's joy was brief, changing quickly to alarm when it was confirmed that Duke William of Normandy had disembarked with a great army at Pevensey in Sussex on September 28, or Michaelmas Eve, only a day before Edmond's little troop arrived in London. Near panic ensued at reports of the Norman marauders spreading death and destruction throughout the villages and manors near their landing site.

"King Harold will hurry back with his army from the north to try to block the Normans' advance on London," Edmond predicted to Wiglaf and Godfrid. "We must decide whether to wait until Harold's army arrives or venture south on our own to reconnoiter. We might be able to discover the enemy's strength and plans."

Wiglaf snorted disapproval. "By all the saints, Thane Edmond, I wouldn't await King Harold here, not if he is as ill-disposed to you as you know him to be. He might be tempted to let anger rule him in London, imprison you or worse, something he probably wouldn't risk doing when he comes face-to-face with the Normans. Then he wouldn't want to weaken his army on the eve of battle."

Edmond pulled at his chin. "Well thought of, old friend. That makes good sense. Yet I wonder whether Harold and his advisors will decide to move immediately against Duke William. It's obvious the king has to block the routes to London, but prudence would dictate avoiding a pitched battle until he can gather reinforcements. It would be foolhardy to risk all while his army remains weakened from the battle up north as well as desertions during the return match to London."

Wiglaf nodded. "He must have lost many good men at Stamford

Bridge. From what I've heard, the slaughter was cruel on both sides even though we drove off the Northmen, God be praised."

A bystander volunteered, "Some say that so many of the enemy were cut down that those who fled the field were too few to man more than a handful of ships for the return to Norway. They had to burn most of them. It's said only twenty-four long ships put back out to sea again of the two or three hundred in the Northmen's fleet."

"That may be so," Wiglaf admitted, "but our people also suffered a great many dead and wounded, and no doubt there have been many desertions since. The king might be in no position to march against the Normans until he can gather more men."

"That would make it all more prudent to avoid battle for the time being," Edmond said, but frowned as he added, "I fear, however, that Harold and some of the young firebrands around him will be impatient to challenge the Normans as soon as possible. As I remember Harold when we first met, he was never overly cautious. He might decide to move immediately to keep the Normans from harrying our people and spreading devastation as they're said to be doing."

"He wouldn't be that foolish, would he, Thane Edmond? That would be inviting disaster."

"He may believe he has no choice because he can't be sure of holding together even the small army he's bringing south," Edmond speculated. "Many of the fyrd have been in the field since they were called out in the spring, and may try to slip away to reach home for the harvest. The levies from Sussex and Wessex probably fear for their kinfolk and property, and with good cause. They'll be eager to return home to defend them from the Normans."

"You speak as if you're convinced King Harold won't hesitate to advance on the Normans at the earliest opportunity?"

"I'm almost sure of it, Wiglaf, much as I fear such reckless haste would result only in disaster. He may have no alternative. Harold also may believe that if he allows the Normans to harry the south without trying to intervene, those of our people who are already unhappy with him may join Duke William. It's even possible that those who support Childe Edgar's claims against both Harold and William might turn to the duke in hopes he would raise the lad to the kingship rather than seize it for himself."

Wiglaf scoffed. "Surely, no one would be fool enough to think the Norman bastard is looking out for anybody's interests other than his own."

"You and I know better, old friend, but as I learned among the faithless people of Constantinople, where treachery is a way of life, the greater the fool, the more likely he is to deceive himself into committing treason," Edmond replied with a wry smile, then paused to reflect. "Speaking of Childe Edgar, I really should play my respects to his mother, Lady Agatha. It wouldn't surprise me to find her, or rather her advisors, preparing to take advantage of the situation by stirring up some foolery on her son's behalf."

He decided to call on Lady Agatha. As he led his troop into London, the turmoil in the city was appalling. The narrow, slop-puddled streets and lanes were choked with wandering armed men. Agitated citizens frequently gathered in clumps to discuss the latest reports and rumors. Edmond's well-disciplined body of men attracted great attention, some mistaking it for the vanguard of the royal army returning from the north. The populace was obviously anxious for Harold's quick return to protect them from the Normans. Nevertheless, it was evident they had little stomach for defending themselves. Edmond sensed they were unlikely to resist Duke William for any length of time if the king failed to arrive quickly and stiffen their resolve.

An air of expectancy gripped him as his troop approached the bridge over the Thames near which lay the mansion assigned to the atheling's widow and children by the late King Edward. His suspicions were soon confirmed. The grounds of the mansion and the surrounding area swarmed with armed men, more than he had encountered while passing through London. He estimated the total at more than three hundred.

Undeterred by suspicious glances and scowls, he unhesitatingly led his band of two score men into the courtyard. On dismounting, he was immediately confronted by an officer of Lady Agatha's household who frowned as if uncertain as to what to make of this unexpected arrival. Edmond recognized him as Gosric, a Mercian thane who had accompanied Lady Agatha and her husband on their return from exile. Gosric clearly did not immediately recall the newcomer.

Edmond offered a hand. "Thane Gosric, I can't say I'm surprised you don't remember me after all these years, but I trust Lady Agatha will know an old acquaintance who wishes to pay his respects."

Gosric tapped his forehead. "Now I recognize you. By the holy rood! It's Thane Edmond, my beloved late master's friend. I would've thought you..." His voice trailed off in embarrassment.

"Dead?" Edmond laughingly finished the sentence.

"No, no, God forbid!" Gosric hastened to assure. "It's only that it has been so long since we last saw or heard of you." He lowered his voice. "We thought you might have forsaken us, but thank the Lord you've not gone over to our enemies. It's good to see you with so many brawny lads. No doubt you've come at our lady's call on behalf of Childe Edgar. God knows she'll be much encouraged."

Edmond preserved a noncommittal expression as he cautioned

Godfrid to make sure his men did not scatter, then with Wiglaf on his heels followed Gosric into the building. The great hall was crowded with prominent men, though he noticed that most of them were wealthy burghers and clerics rather than high-ranking nobles. Lady Agatha stood at the center of a large group, chatting with a hooded churchman whose back was turned to Edmond. There was something vaguely familiar about his stance, but Edmond failed to get a good look at his face before he drew the hood tighter and moved away as if to conceal himself in the crowd.

Lady Agatha was much as Edmond remembered Atheling Edward's widow from their last meeting nine years earlier. She was still attractive even if the intervening years had stolen some of the fullness of her cheeks and dulled the gloss of her hair. He was gratified and flattered by the sudden change in her expression when she recognized him. Her almost desperately serious and intense concentration gave way to a quick smile of delight. She sprang forward, hands outstretched, and almost purred, "Welcome, dear Thane Edmond, welcome back. You've always served us well, and after all these years you've returned to aid my dear son as you helped his unfortunate father."

Edmond bowed low to conceal his confusion as he pressed her hands. "My lady, I've come to pay my respects as befits an old servant, a friend if I may call myself such."

"I see you've kept the emerald ring I gave you," she noted, glancing at his hand before continuing with the subject uppermost on her mind, heart and lips. "I know you've come to help my son redeem the promise made to you by that traitor Harold Godwinson who has stolen a crown to which he has no right. Didn't that impostor pledge in your hearing to protect my son's interests until he grew to manhood?" Her eyes blazed with righteous indignation at the injustice she believed to have been committed against Childe Edgar. The room fell silent as she cried, "Yes, Thane Edmond, you can testify more truly than anyone to the falsehoods and broken vows with which this dastardly son of Earl Godwin has betrayed our people and deprived my son of his rightful inheritance. That's why you've joined us, isn't it, to right a wrong against our people and against God?"

The princess's fervent appeal stirred Edmond even if it conflicted with his sober grasp of reality, the hopelessness of her son's cause. Her sincere warmth and justified outrage expressed in her impassioned tone were touching all the same. How could he disclose that even though he sympathized with her, he was determined to support Harold Godwinson? It might be kind to soothe her with assurances of compassion before departing on some pretext to join the king's army for the confrontation with the Normans. There really was no alternative.

Still, it might be even kinder to learn what she and her advisors were plotting, and attempt to dissuade them from a rash action.

"My dear lady, it's just as I said, an old servant, a friend if I may name myself that, thought it his duty to call on you and his master's son, Childe Edgar," he said smoothly. "I've heard nothing of your plans."

She smiled understandingly. "You wish to know what we expect of you before you commit yourself? What of your companion?"

Edmond glanced at Wiglaf. "I trust him as if he were my brother. More so," he added, recalling Tostig's treachery toward Harold.

"I'll take your word for it. Then listen. We intend to assemble a large force so that whatever the outcome of the struggle between Earl Harold and Duke William—if Harold leaves London to oppose the Normans in Sussex, as seems likely—we can take control of the city and declare my son Edgar the rightful king of England. Of course, we shall act with the support of the Witan and many of London's most influential people.

"If William prevails and Harold falls, it is sure to help our cause. No loyal Englishman would hesitate to support King Edgar of the true line of Cerdic against a foreign usurper. On the other hand, if Harold drives off the Normans, the victory is likely to cost him so dear he'll be hard put to defend himself against us, the more so because many of the people around him would desert his doubtful cause if they had a legitimate leader to rally around.

"And here's that leader," she cried, with a dramatic gesture of her outstretched right arm toward a slender young man who entered the hall at that moment. Childe Edgar was accompanied by an elderly man of distinguished appearance whom Edmond recognized as Prince Andras of Hungary, a distant relative of the princess.

Edgar's resemblance to his late father was remarkable. Not altogether to the good, Edmond thought. There was that same weakness around the drooping mouth, a hint of sullen acceptance, of lack of firm purpose. His eyes were decidedly similarly dull. His entire appearance was unpromising, Edmond concluded, even as he took the boy's limp hand and bowed, before Lady Agatha introduced him to Prince Andras.

"Ah, no doubt you've come to join us, good thane," Andras greeted warmly. "I should have known that an old friend like you would be among the first to respond to Lady Agatha's summons. You're sorely needed because there'll be some warm work before this is over. There aren't many men of rank among us who've had your military experience. I recall that the late atheling couldn't praise you too highly."

Edmond hardly heard Prince Andras's flattery, being distracted by the reappearance of the hooded clergyman whom he had noticed earlier as strangely familiar. The clergyman ended the mystery by lowering his hood to reveal the well-known features of Archbishop Stigand.

Edmond was startled to see the archbishop of Canterbury. Stigand's desertion would be a serious blow to King Harold. The cleric long had been one of the major bulwarks of the House of Godwin. He evidently had finally wearied of a series of rebuffs by Harold, the most serious coming when he was shunted aside for the coronation rites, an ancient prerogative of the see of Canterbury.

"Earl Edmond, you're welcome," said Stigand, advancing to press Edmond's hands. "I may freely call him earl, may I not, my lady?" he asked Lady Agatha. "You can see that our appeal to the citizens of London, nay of all England, supported by the rights of royal birth, a just cause, and favored by the blessings of the Lord, has drawn many of the worthies of this kingdom to gather here in support of Childe Edgar.

"You need have no fear, my son, that you will incur the wrath of heaven for ignoring any oath of fealty or pledges you may have made because they were falsely exacted by an usurper. Truth and Christ march beside us to restore a rightful king. Honors and broad lands await you after our triumph when this worthy youth sits on the throne of his ancestors, the great Alfred and Edmond Ironside."

Appalled as he was at Stigand's betrayal of his former patron, King Harold, Edmond was aware that this was no time for recrimination. He mirrored the archbishop's ingratiating smile as he cast about for some means of extricating himself and his men from the danger they faced if Lady Agatha's supporters suspected them of intending to join Harold's army. Outnumbered as they were, they would be slaughtered on the spot. His only hope of escaping lay in hoodwinking Lady Agatha, Archbishop Stigand and the rest of those assembled in the hall to plot against Harold.

"Your grace, like you I uphold the indisputable claims of birthright to the kingship of our people," he replied with disingenuous irony. "No one can deny that Childe Edgar, the son of Atheling Edward, the descendant of a long line of kings, deserves support against an unworthy usurper. I intend to make every effort to ensure that England's throne will be occupied by someone who is worthy by descent to wear the crown. I'll neither hesitate to act nor waste your time with empty words. I propose to set out immediately with my men to help the rightful heir regain the heritage of his forefathers."

"Spoken like a prophet of old," cried Prince Andras, glowing with pleasure at Edmond's apparently forthright declaration. The assembly of notables joined in the applause, rounding it off with cries of support for Childe Edgar.

Grasping his sword hilt, Edmond continued, "Within the hour I will lead my men toward Pevensey where the Norman invaders have landed. We must discover all we can about Duke William's intentions and the size of his force. I'll report to you as soon as possible to help you complete your plans."

"Splendid!" shouted Prince Andras. "This is what we've been looking for, a man of action and decision to spur our cause, a doer rather than a bandier of glib promises. What more can we ask for than such an ally? While Thane Edmond reconnoiters in the south we can arouse our supporters to oppose Earl Harold's entry into London."

Lady Agatha joyfully clapped her hands, and a buzz of excitement swept the hall. Even Stigand looked pleased.

It was to cheers, cries of encouragement, pledges of support, and backslaps, as well as to his great relief, that Edmond and Wiglaf were finally able to make their way out of the crowded hall and the building. Godfrid had kept his men in good order in the courtyard so the little troop was able to reassemble and march off without delay.

On reaching a safe distance from the mansion, Edmond could afford a sardonic smile. He had fooled Stigand, Lady Agatha, and the rest of the conspirators against King Harold. Fooled them superbly. Not that there was great credit in such a mean achievement. He was almost ashamed. Poor deluded fools, to think he would join in such a futile enterprise, one that could only result in assuring Duke William of total victory. How could anyone imagine that the ruthless Norman invader would consent to placing a powerless, weak stripling on a throne that was his own for the taking? To anyone other than the conspirators, it was clear that the only choice lay between Harold and William. To betray Harold was to betray England.

Though estranged from Harold, Edmond considered him the lesser of two evils. There was no alternative to supporting the capable son of Earl Godwin against a foreign aggressor. As for Childe Edgar's cause, it was hopeless, especially with the Normans already landed on English soil. Much as Edmond regretted having had to hoodwink Lady Agatha, he had no compunction about having deceived devious Archbishop Stigand. His remorse over Agatha was balanced by the satisfaction of having outmaneuvered the unscrupulous prelate. He salved his conscience with the reminder that he could not have extricated himself and his men from the nest of traitors without dissimulating. His men would have been massacred to no purpose.

Satisfied he had acted correctly, Edmond led his troop southward toward the area now reportedly under the control of the Normans. He would be prepared to join Harold's army when it followed, as he was sure it would.

Chapter Forty-Six

Harold Gains an Ally

S moke was still curling into a leaden autumn sky although a day-long drizzle had tapered off by late afternoon when Edmond led his men into the courtyard of a vast three-winged manor house that lay in near ruins. Only a solitary howling dog and the dolorous grunts of two or three swine that had escaped the foraging Normans broke the silence of a scene of devastation. The manor's residents apparently either had fled or been carried off by the foreign raiders except for a middle-aged man whose corpse swung by a rope from an oak tree. Scorched legs and blistered bare feet testified that he had been tortured.

"Have that cut down and buried," Edmond instructed Godfrid as he vaulted from the saddle to inspect the building and grounds.

Godfrid detailed several men to carry out the task while the rest of Edmond's company slumped to the ground, exhausted by the forced march that had brought them from London almost to the Sussex sea coast. Accompanied by Wiglaf, Edmond cautiously picked his way through the smoldering wreckage of the manor house, which obviously had been thoroughly looted before being set afire. He was pleased to discover that the south wing was not so damaged as the rest of the structure and would provide shelter of sorts for his men.

"We'll stay here," he told Wiglaf. "The Normans are unlikely to return after what they've done. They've carried off or destroyed everything of value."

On Edmond's return to the courtyard, Godfrid was ready to report, "The body's disposed of and the pickets posted."

"Well done. Have the men eat, then let them spend the night under cover in there—" he indicated the west wing "—until dawn when we can reconnoiter the enemy's whereabouts and strength."

Edmond bolted down coarse bread and cheese, moistening the cold rations with a swig of ale. Wiglaf shared the frugal meal though he grumbled at the small beer ration. Edmond chuckled, crooked a finger at one of the older men, "Aelle, you'll accompany us," then set out with the churl and the sailor toward a cluster of cottages near the manor house. It was important to gather as much information as possible before sunset.

With Edmond in the lead, the three men trudged along a narrow path past the huddle of deserted little dwellings by whose yawning doors lay items of abandoned household goods testifying to the haste with which the occupants had fled. The cottagers probably were hiding in the nearby forest and brush, waiting to make sure the Norman marauders had left before returning to their homes. The slender trail, not much better than a cowpath, continued past the hamlet into a nearby range of low hills from which Edmond intended to survey the area further south. By the time they reached the summit of one of the taller rises, Wiglaf and Aelle were winded. Edmond ignored their discomfort to eagerly scan the southward prospect.

"To the right, look to the right," he urged, indicating a declivity separating two hills through which the trail continued its winding course. "See the glint of steel there. Armed men, if I'm not mistaken."

"Normans!" Wiglaf exclaimed, shading his eyes. "Men on horseback, escorting wagons, as best I can judge. If it hadn't been for the rain, they'd be raising a cloud of dust. Probably loaded with loot."

Edmond nodded. "At least two or three score. Too far ahead for us to assemble our men and intercept them before it becomes too dark."

"Thieving dogs!" spat Aelle, a hand reflexively going to the bow slung over his shoulder. Edmond made a restraining gesture.

"It's too bad they're out of range," he remarked. "At least, we know in which direction they're heading." He continued to survey the area, but other than an occasional hare or game bird there was little sign of life in any direction. "Let's return to the manor."

A surprise awaited them. Godfrid was sitting in the courtyard by a serviceable if scorched table rescued from the wreckage. He was impatiently observing a bedraggled elderly thrall scouring the last particle of food from a wooden bowl with his dirty fingers. "Hold on, man, there's more if you want it," he cautioned the slave before becoming aware of Edmond's return. "We found this knave skulking in the brush, my lord. He claims to have been a scullion in this household. Says the estate belongs to a king's thane, one Edward Athelstanson."

"Has he told you anything useful?"

"These people were warned the Normans might be coming in this direction, but the thane is in the field with King Harold and no one knew what to do. Not even the steward, the man whose body we found. The steward wanted to arm some men, but the servants and churls ran off with the women and children. This fellow insists he stayed to help the steward hide or carry off the valuables, but the Normans arrived before they were able to get away."

"Poor Letwold!" the thrall moaned. "An honest, good man for all that he was the steward, kind and just in his dealings. Oh Lord, what they did to him! How he screamed when they burned his feet." He shuddered, burying his face in his hands.

Edmond decided he had to be firm, even rough, to get anything out of the man, and demanded gruffly, "What about the Normans? Come, man, tell me how many were here. Don't you know? Are you a fool, fellow?"

The slave despairingly spread his hands. "Sixty, seventy, maybe a hundred. I'm not good at counting, lord. They came upon us before we knew what was happening, before we could get a good look at them." Tears streaked his soiled face. "Poor Letwold! How could he hand over the thane's silver when there was none? They didn't have to torture him, kill him."

"What else did they want?" Edmond prodded harshly. "Did you hear anything about their plans? Think, you misbegotten knave, remember what they said, what they talked about. I'll have it out of you if I have to use the lash."

"They didn't speak proper," the thrall whined, terrified by Edmond's threat. "It was that foreign gibberish they used, not honest words like we speak. How could a poor Saxon thrall like me know what they were saying?"

"Fool, wasn't there something worth remembering. They must have spoken English to you and the steward."

The man brightened. "They had to, didn't they? How else could we know what they wanted, lord? I recall now, they were putting hot coals to Letwold's feet, and he was screaming but wouldn't tell them where there was silver. He couldn't, could he? One of the Normans, a knight he was, put his fingers to his nose and cursed. He said it would be a hard task for even ten thousand men to conquer such a folk if all were as stubborn as Letwold, and he wished Duke William had brought that many with him from Normandy."

"There's something worth knowing," commented Wiglaf.

Edmond nodded grimly. "Worth a great deal, indeed. All reports have put the Normans' strength at upwards of twenty thousand men. Yet ten thousand or fewer seems more likely, considering the difficulty of transporting an army even that large with supplies and horses across the sea. We must get word to King Harold."

"You'll be putting your head on the block, Thane Edmond," Wiglaf warned. "He may carry out his threats against your life. The risk is too great."

"I'll have to take the chance, though I think the king will stay his hand until matters are more settled. It's vital to get this information—if what this thrall says is true—to Harold. The king's decision on whether to confront the Normans now or later may depend on his knowing their numbers."

Accordingly, after resting his men overnight at the manor, Edmond led them toward the Roman road to the east that ran southward from the London area to the Sussex coast. He was sure King Harold and his army would follow the ancient highway toward a confrontation with the Norman invaders. When his troop was within a mile of the road, he sent out scouts to watch for the king's army, then set up camp in a secluded glen.

Several days passed before a scout reported the approach of the vanguard of the royal army. Leaving Godfrid in command with instructions on what to do in the event he was unable to return, Edmond set off with Wiglaf to attempt to confront King Harold. They went on foot in order to avoid detection by the army's flankers until the last possible moment. He and the old sailor would hide in the brush bordering the high road until the king came within sight, then seek an audience.

By the time Edmond and Wiglaf were able to reach the thick vegetation alongside the road, the vanguard was receding southward and the main body of the army was marching past, with the royal housecarles preceding the king and his highest-ranking officers. The celebrated standards of the Fighting Man and the Golden Dragon of Wessex soon came into view, pinpointing the location of the king, still several hundred feet away. Edmond was pleased to note that the housecarles were in good spirits despite the rigors of the long march. With only a brief pause in London, the royal army had come all the way from Stamford Bridge far to the north in less than a month.

Ansgar the Marshal, commander of the housecarles, and Thane Sebert rode side-by side, just preceding the royal party. Sebert was somewhat grayer and heavier than when Edmond last had seen him nine years earlier, but held himself as erect as ever in the saddle. Just behind him came King Harold and his brothers Earls Leofwine and Gurth, the three riding abreast. Edmond was struck by how greatly Leofwine resembled Sweyn, though broader in the shoulders and lacking his late enemy's cynical and sardonic curl of the lips. Gurth was shorter but stocky and powerfully built. The king, stern and unsmiling, rode between his brothers, carelessly holding the reins with one finger in obvious preoccupation. A group of nobles and prelates followed the Godwinsons, the most conspicuous being richly attired Earl Waltheof, a slender youth whose father, Earl Siward, had ruled the north before Tostig's brief and calamitous rise to power.

On the king's approach along the road, Edmond and Wiglaf emerged from their hiding place and scrambled up the embankment of the highway to intercept him. An alarm sounded, and a dozen guards led by

Ansgar the Marshal drew swords to cut down the intruders, but on realizing that neither Edmond nor Wiglaf had a weapon in hand permitted them to advance within a few paces of Harold before blocking the way.

"What's the meaning of this, Thane Edmond?" Sebert demanded, immediately recognizing his old friend. "You know you're not welcome in the king's sight."

Edmond glanced at Harold before replying. The king stared coldly at him. "I've important information to convey to his majesty, Thane Sebert."

Harold's expression remained unchanged as he spoke in an even tone, "I don't know these men, Thane Sebert. What do these strangers want of us, and how dare they interrupt our march?"

Sebert slid his sword back into its scabbard with an ill-concealed grin of relief at the king's restraint. Even Leofwine permitted himself a smile before resuming a stern expression in keeping with Harold's severity. Edmond stepped toward the king, returning Harold's steely look with equal coldness, though reassured by the turn the situation had taken. "My lord king, I bring you important information about the enemy. I also offer my services and those of my friend, if they're acceptable to you."

"We'll judge that after we've heard what you have to say," Harold snapped. He listened without comment until Edmond completed his report, then reflected, "Only ten thousand men, if what you and the thrall who told you that can be relied on." He studied Edmond's face before adding in measured words, "I don't know you, and prefer not to hear your name, but you look like an honest fellow, a worthy thane." He remarked to his brothers, "See how mistaken it would have been to delay in London while Bastard William and his brigands spread death and destruction without hindrance among my good people of Sussex. William must have fewer than ten thousand by now, a force we can match and surpass with the levies that will join us before we give battle. And that doesn't include the forces our good friends, Earls Edwin and Morcar, are bringing to our support from the north. We must attack the enemy as soon as possible before they're able to strengthen their positions and receive reinforcements from abroad." His attention returned to Edmond. "Are there just the two of you?"

"Lord king, I've forty brave, well-armed lads camped nearby, stout fellows all of them. They've come to fight for their king and homes."

Harold glanced even more penetratingly at him, then slapped his horse's rump. "Did you hear that, brothers Leofwine and Gurth? Here's fair addition to our growing power while all this time the enemy must be wasting men in forays and foraging." He signaled to Ansgar the

Marshal and Sebert to get the army under way again, then spoke to Edmond. "If your report proves true, and we overcome the Normans as I'm confident we will, we'll find both time and place to show our gratitude. For now, summon your men and fall in at the rear of the column. We must push forward. We may be able to surprise the enemy and descend on them before they expect our coming."

Edmond and Wiglaf quickly returned to where they had left their little troop, reassembled it, and joined the rearguard of the king's army on the high road. They fell into line to the cheers and good natured raillery of what was largely a motley force composed of local levies from the south of England, many of them poorly armed with clubs, scythes and other farming equipment but nevertheless buoyed by a fighting spirit that would have done the formidable royal housecarles proud.

After riding several miles with the rearguard, Edmond was surprised and pleased to be joined by Thane Sebert who clearly had dropped back specifically to talk to him.

"By the mass, you come in good time, friend Edmond," began Sebert. "Just when the king has great need of every man he can summon to his support. This is no time to nurse old grudges. How long has it been since we last saw one another? Nine years? I never thought we'd meet again, nor—to tell the truth—did I hope to for I feared the king's wrath against you for what he considered desertion, if not treachery."

"I never betrayed him," protested Edmond.

"I believe you, but the king was deeply offended and hurt when you left him. What surprises me," admitted Sebert, "was to see how calmly he reacted to your reappearing without having obtained his consent or forgiveness. He's readier to forget old scores than I thought possible."

"He needs all the help he can get just now, from any source, friend or foe," reminded Edmond. "If, God willing, we defeat the enemy and survive the coming battle, I'll not linger in hopes of receiving his grateful thanks."

Sebert laughed. "That may be just as well if you value your life. Still, you're slighting the king. He's much changed since his younger days. A great deal calmer, more reasoned in judgment, slower to take offense, always willing to listen to good counsel and to seek compromise. I'm confident that if we drive off the Normans, as we did Harald Hardraade, and the king establishes his power firmly, he'll rule England more wisely than any of his predecessors since King Edgar a hundred years ago."

Edmond changed the subject. "Is he determined to give battle immediately?"

"Yes, though he listened patiently to those among us who advised him to remain in London and appoint Leofwine and Gurth to lead the army against Duke William. He replied that the cause was his, and that he owed it to God and to his people to defend it with his own body. I believe he was also distressed by the devastation the Normans are spreading among the people of Sussex."

Edmond shook his head. "It would have been wiser to hold off until he assembled more men and Edwin and Morcar were with him. There can't be more than seven or eight thousand men in this army, if that many."

"Many of the king's council would agree with you," admitted Sebert. "They pleaded with my lord king to wait until he could gather in all the levies and was sure of Edwin and Morcar, that is if that pair is trustworthy. The king contended, with some reason, that if Edwin and Morcar turn against him it would be well to have disposed first of the Normans before having to contend with traitors.

"There's also the fleet, Thane Edmond. In addition to this army, we've troops aboard ships that are sailing toward Pevensey. If the weather holds, they should be able to land enough good men in the rear of Duke William's army to give him something else to worry about."

Sebert's exposition of the situation was broken short by the arrival of a royal aide who summoned him to the king's side. Scouts had reported that a small troop of Norman horsemen had been seen directly ahead on the road, observing the approach of the English army, then had ridden off in the direction of the town of Hastings. Clearly, all chance was gone of catching Duke William's army by surprise. Nonetheless, Harold urged his men to quicken their pace in hopes of being able to engage in battle before the Normans were fully prepared and had taken up a strong position.

Scattered fighting, however, began to break out even on the march as small bands of Norman cavalry began to harry the English column. Soon a series of fierce skirmishes raged along a line roughly perpendicular to the southerly direction of the advance, many in wooded areas where contact was difficult to maintain. After a while it became apparent that the Normans were content to harass the advancing English while falling back in good order toward their main encampment in the vicinity of Hastings.

After landing at Pevensey two weeks earlier, Duke William had immediately ordered the erection of one of the three prefabricated wooden castles brought from Normandy. He placed a small part of his stores and supplies in it, then marched eastward from Pevensey to Hastings where he set up the other two forts on a mound and surrounded them with ramparts and ditches. The structures served as refuges in case of adversity, as well as headquarters from which to send out the foragers and raiders who were spreading terror throughout the countryside.

The Normans established other outposts, the most heavily-manned being on Telham Hill, about seven miles from Hastings. This was the northernmost of a series of low hills extending from the southeast toward the north that was interrupted for about five hundred yards by a ridge perpendicular to its general direction. This ridge, later named Senlac or Sangue Lac, Lake of Blood, by the Normans, was formed and placed by nature almost as if intended to serve as a barrier across the path to London.

When the English approached, the Norman observers on Telham Hill notified Duke William who was near Hastings. He received the report while gathered in a tent with his council of prominent nobles, among them his brothers Robert of Mortain and Bishop Odo of Bayeux.

"He's coming on like a madman, you say?" frowned William, leaping to his feet and calling for his armor and weapons. "I wouldn't have thought he'd be in such a hurry after what must have been a costly victory at Stamford Bridge. They say he lost many men."

"It'll be three or four days before he can give us battle, if then," estimated Bishop Odo. "He'll have to rest his army after such a long, tiring march, and he'll surely wait for reinforcements. He must be aware by now that there's no chance of catching us off guard."

"God's blood! A near thing, though." admitted William. "If I hadn't decided to recall most of the foragers this morning we would have been caught with half our men absent." He slipped into his hauberk and contemplatively gazed at his scabbard. "Brother, I think you're mistaken. Harold will launch an attack tomorrow."

"What makes you think that, my lord?" asked Walter Giffard, one of the duke's most trusted advisers.

"It doesn't make sense, good brother," interjected Robert of Mortain. "His allies, Earls Edwin and Morcar, must be on the road to join him. He'd be a fool not to wait for their arrival."

"Splendor of God!" the duke bellowed. "That's the point, that Edwin and Morcar are coming. Allies? He can't trust them, and rightly not. He's anxious to meet us before they have a chance to betray him."

Bishop Odo drained a flagon of wine and let a thin smile flicker as he observed, "You didn't ask for my opinion, my lord, but I too would have guessed he'll advance against us tomorrow."

William strapped on his sword belt. "Yet perhaps we can parley first and gain some slight additional advantage. To tell the truth, gentlemen, it'll go hard with us if Harold wins the day."

"Thanks to you, dear brother. You would play Caesar and burn our ships as he did," growled Robert of Mortain.

"We'll have no need of them, one way or the other, Robert," William laughed grimly. "If we win the day, England is ours and we remain. If we fall, we'll get as much land as I'm told Harold gave Hardraade and Tostig, seven feet for each grave. Come, let's go for a little canter and see if Harold comes on as quickly as our scouts suggest he's doing."

Accompanied by fifty knights, the duke and his brothers quickly covered the seven miles to Telham Hill. Even as they reached the top, the sun glinted off the spears of the thousands of advancing English on the ridge to the north as if in sparkling defiance to the Norman invaders.

"Look, my lord!" cried William FitzOsbert, commander of the detachment posted on Telham Hill. "Look at the ridge over there, look toward the north. See the English racing out of the forest toward the ridge like bees returning to their hive." Indeed, from a distance the English army resembled a swarm of insects as it poured out of the woods to occupy the prominent rise. The rays of the setting sun sparkled off their armor and weapons as a line of burning metal quickly spread across the entire extent of the high ground.

Duke William thoughtfully observed the English take their positions before issuing an order to FitzOsbert. "You must hold this hill until morning while we transfer most of our army from the shore to this point. This is where we'll make our stand. If the English charge down from the ridge our horsemen can cut them apart. If they chose to hold the high ground, why we must smash upward at them until we can lure them down."

"Their ground is well chosen," remarked Bishop Odo whose occupation of a see did not deter him from gaining the military expertise customary for Norman prelate-warriors.

"The English usurper is an able soldier," replied William almost admiringly. "Even if the battle goes against him, Harold can fall back into the forest unless we can cut him down where he stands or block his line of retreat." He made a quick decision. "We must make a final effort to gain our ends without risking all on the edges of our swords. We might be able to convince the English that justice and the hand of God support our cause and claim, just as the pope has declared."

He beckoned to a monk standing nearby. "Hugues Maigrot, we appoint you to carry a message to Harold Godwinson. Yours will be a holy mission, blessed by God, for if it succeeds we can avoid much bloodshed and save many lives."

Chapter Forty-Eight

Royal Defiance

In keeping with the traditional strategy of occupying the high ground in preparation for battle, the English army under King Harold on October 13 was engaged in constructing a palisade of pointed stakes interwoven with osier plaits, and in digging ditches at the foot of the broad and steep hill. The barriers were intended to hamper the enemy, whether light-armed and heavy-armed foot or heavy cavalry, if the Normans attempted to charge up the long slope leading down from the height to the bottom where began the opposing rise of Telham Hill. The English also dammed several small streams to conduct their waters into the valley to supplement its natural bogginess and render the footing even more treacherous.

On the reverse slope of the ridge behind the English lines the light-armed support troops were excavating trenches and setting traps to provide additional obstacles against the Normans in the event the main body of Harold's army was forced to withdraw into the nearby forest of Anderida. Edmond's contingent from Bosbury, which was stationed on the right flank of the massed English army drawn up as three sides of a square to hold the entire length of the plateau, was busy with this labor when Thane Sebert unexpectedly appeared on a tour of inspection.

Sebert glanced around approvingly, remarking, "You've accomplished a great deal quickly," then swung from the saddle to greet Edmond with a firm handclasp. "It's well you've wasted no time. There's little doubt the Normans will attack in the morning."

"How goes it with the king?" asked Edmond.

"Much the same as when you met him on the road. Somewhat more thoughtful and reserved than he usually is. Perhaps the Norman monk upset him more than he let on."

"The Norman monk? What monk? What happened?"

"Duke William sent a delegation led by a monk from his entourage, one Hugues Maigrot, to parley with King Harold and his council," explained Sebert. "What he brought, however, was not so much an offer to reach a fair and peaceful settlement as an arrogant demand for our king to surrender on William's terms.

"The monk's insolence, or rather his master's, was beyond all belief. Hugues Maigrot began by styling Duke William king of England and basileus of Britain, then calling our good king merely Earl Harold. Those among our people who understood French were outraged, some even threatening the monk, but King Harold didn't change his expression in the least though he must have been angry. He was content to urge Maigrot to get on with what he had to say."

"And that was..." Edmond prompted when Sebert hesitated momentarily as if unable to bring himself to repeat the monk's delivery of Duke William's message.

"In a torrent of words—you know the fashion of such envoys—he demanded that King Harold immediately surrender the kingship to Duke William, alleging that King Edward had pledged the succession to his master. If King Harold was in doubt as to what course to take, Duke William called on him to refer the decision to the pope. As if the pope, who has supported William all along even to proclaiming a crusade against our king, would be impartial! Furthermore, if King Harold was unwilling to accept either of his demands, William declared he was ready to meet him in single combat to settle the matter between the two of them."

Edmond was appalled. "What barefaced arrogance! Surely, King Harold wouldn't agree to any of that? He must have rejected all three proposals."

"What else? The first two were laughable. As for the third, single combat to decide the kingship, how could Harold, the choice of the Witangemot, reject and betray his people and England's army by hazarding their fate on his single arm, great warrior though he is?"

"He can't and shouldn't, of course," agreed Edmond warmly. "As I see it, all this doesn't change a thing, nor should it deter King Harold from defending his rights and people." He plucked a blade of grass and chewed it, his gaze wandering toward the sea of Norman campfires glowing on distant Telham Hill.

Sebert looked searchingly at him. "I'm glad to see you agree that our king was right to reject any compromise and to defy the Normans. All of our lords, officers and officials during the council held after the monk departed supported the king's action in charging Hugues Maigrot to bear his refusal to Duke William."

Edmond roused himself to reply, "Yes, Harold acted as a king of England should in rejecting such outrageous demands. I'd have done the same if I were in his place. But surely, you didn't come here merely to tell me all this, not that I don't appreciate your keeping me informed."

"True, I bear a command from King Harold to his loyal subject Thane Edmond of Bosbury. He requires you to be at his side when the Normans attack, as he expects them to do tomorrow morning." Sebert hesitated, uncertain whether to say more.

Edmond stared at him. "Did he explain why he wanted me, of all people, a humble thane from the West Country with little influence and a handful of men?"

"No, he didn't, and strangely, for whatever reason, he didn't even speak your name, though I understood immediately whom he meant. He just told me, 'Thane Sebert, I would have the thane who accosted us on the road, the one accompanied by the fat old sailor, join us here among our lords and royal housecarles. Summon him.' That's all he said. I know he expects the Norman assault to be heaviest in the center and may consider your experience in the eastern wars will be useful."

"No doubt that's the reason, and I'm honored by his confidence," replied Edmond smoothly. He wondered whether the real occasion for the surprising summons was that Harold did not trust him, or even hoped that in the heat and confusion of battle he would be rid of someone he suspected of being a dangerous enemy. Edmond sighed in resignation. The king had nothing to fear from him. His dreams, hopes and aspirations were long dissipated. Come what may, Edmond Edwysson was resolved to give his life if need be on behalf of this usurper of his birthright, if only because his duty to his people overrode all personal considerations.

"I'll accompany you now if you're returning to the king," he told Sebert. "I'll be at his side when the battle opens, and my life is at his command."

Asking Wiglaf to accompany him, and leaving Godfrid in charge of the little troop from Bosbury, Edmond rode alongside Sebert toward the looming heights on which King Harold was camped with his lords and officers of state amidst the royal housecarles.

Wiglaf's uneasiness manifested itself in a whisper as they approached the king's headquarters. "You're putting yourself in the lion's mouth," he cautioned, but Edmond merely laughed.

When they arrived upon the summit of the ridge, they were surprised to discover that Hugues Maigrot had returned during Sebert's absence bearing another proposal from Duke William. The meeting between the king's party and the Norman envoys had just begun as they approached.

"What's it this time?" Sebert asked Ansgar the Marshal when they joined a group of nobles and royal officials assembled in a respectful circle around the king and the Norman delegation.

Ansgar brought him up to date in an undertone, "They've just offered King Harold the sub-kingship of all the lands to the north beyond the River Humber and to Earl Gurth all the estates their father, Earl Godwin, once held in exchange for recognizing Duke William to be king of England."

The Godwinsons' reaction to the proposal was immediate. Harold and Gurth broke into scornful laughter at what they considered an absurd and patently fraudulent offer, clearly intended to be unacceptable.

"Does your master think we're craven fools?" Harold thundered. "Inform Duke William that all we require of him is to depart our kingdom at once, return to his rightful patrimony, and leave our people in peaceful possession of what belongs to us."

Hugues Maigrot reacted with a theatrical display of outrage as if his master had been insulted beyond endurance. Throwing up his hands in a dramatic appeal to heaven, he cried, "Earl Harold, as God is my witness and Christ is our benefactor, I call you a perjurer and a liar for you have sworn upon the bones of saints everlasting fealty to Duke William. Even now in his tent Duke William has in his possession this pledge of yours, signed by your hand and attested to by many noble lords at Rouen as well as by Bishop Odo and Abbot Lanfranc. For this perjury, His Holiness the Pope has issued a bull of excommunication that Duke William has also brought with him. The interdict of the church falls on you and all who aid your evil cause. Everlasting fire and damnation unto the day of judgment will be yours."

The monk screamed his final threat and some of the more pious among the English squirmed in discomfort. King Harold remained grimly and sternly defiant.

"Brothers," he began calmly, the word undoubtedly embracing all those of his people who heard him, not only his siblings Gurth and Leofwine. "Brothers, it would be false of me to deny I've sworn fealty to Duke William, but it was under duress, constraint and misrepresentation. I can't, won't believe that such an oath could be binding in the eyes of either God or men, but still I rue it much and will do penance in this world and the next as God is my witness and as I declare freely to you all.

"Yet I cannot, nor must not, yield the lordship of England to Duke William for it is neither mine to give nor his to take. It belongs to you, the people of this fair land, to those that sit in the Witangemot, and those in my army who now are prepared to yield their lives if need be to assure that the choice made by the blessed King Edward of hallowed memory on his deathbed be honored.

"More than that, even were I to yield myself to William, it would be a sore day for our people. Let this monk confess to you what William has promised his captains and knights, and those other bandits he has gathered from other lands to plunder us. Is it not so, monk? Deny it if you can. Deny that your bastard master has told his barons that they will become earls and his common soldiers that they will be knighted if they overwhelm us. Have not our possessions, our lands, our cattle, nay for

361

that matter our very wives and children, already have been divided up among these foreign thieves?" Harold paused to see what effect his words were having on his supporters, then continued, "As for the bull of excommunication that this bandit duke has brought along in his saddlebags, let me tell you what it's worth. No more than any other words of the forsworn apostate, that anti-Christ who gained the throne of St. Peter through deceit and usurpation and rattles the keys of heaven as if he were a common gaoler rather than the representative of Christ on earth. Let our churchmen, our Archbishop Stigand, our Bishop Elfwy tell us what we owe to God, not some rapscallion in Rome. God knows I've been there and understand well what deviltry and faithless behavior is practiced in that city.

"Take this message to your master, monk: I stand here on this hill and await your coming. We make neither peace nor truce nor treaty with you, and the only land of ours that we will freely yield is a half foot less than what was required to bury Harald Hardraade. God will smile upon us and bless our cause for we never have done aught but what we thought would be pleasing in his eyes."

Sebert looked searchingly at Edmond to see how his friend responded to the king's fiery and pious exhortation. Edmond was lost in thought, and Sebert would have been startled if he could have read his mind to discern a compound of pride and bitterness contending for domination. There was bitterness at the casual, almost flippant, way in which Harold had so lightly passed off the accusations of perjury and treachery leveled against his seizure of the crown. Yet there was pride in how stirringly a king of England had challenged the pretensions of his nation's enemy with the only reply Edmond considered it honorable to return to the arrogant duke of Normandy.

Sebert broke in on his thoughts. "Was it not a noble answer? His bold words put the heart back into our men, as did those of Bishop Elfwy when he supported the king by denouncing the papal bull, and setting it at nothing."

"The good bishop did that?" Edmond asked, and Sebert nodded. "Well then, our cause is God's as well. What's left other than to make good the king's defiance and drive the Normans into the sea."

Chapter Forty-Eight

The Death of Kings

The sun gradually shed its veil of morning mist during the course of its regal ascent of the mid-autumn sky to cast a honeyed glow upon the metamorphosing yellow, red and brown foliage of the primeval forest of Anderida as the day advanced from dawn to halfway toward noon on the 14th of October in the year 1066.

The assembled divisions of the English royal army, hallowed by the mass at sunrise, took up their positions along the entire length of Senlac on the orders of King Harold's council of war. They were massed in a very dense grouping to form three sides of a square, and to leave no part of the plateau undefended. The king with his brothers and chief nobles and officials took up a prominent position at the midpoint of the ridge beside the royal standards of the Golden Dragon of Wessex and the Fighting Man. The lofty emblems of England's rulers fluttered defiance at the Norman invaders from behind a living wall of royal housecarles under Ansgar the Marshal. The king's guards, clad in glittering gilded hauberks, kept their shields closely interlocked.

Thane Sebert led the men of London who were placed to the right of the housecarles, as were the levies from Wessex, many of whom often had shed blood on behalf of Earl Godwin, the king's father, and for Harold himself. To the left was the fyrd from East Anglia and Huntingdon, which comprised the largest complement of the army.

Just where the slope began its rise, ahead of the great mass of warriors defending the ridge, were posted the men of Kent. They were reinforced by those fierce and loyal Danes from the north who had anticipated their sluggish earls Edwin and Morcar by joining in King Harold's return march to the south from Stamford Bridge.

A sprinkling of light-armed thralls from Sussex was distributed among the other units to stiffen their doubtful resolve. A small force of archers was stationed at the center, with other bowmen placed in the woods flanking each end of the ridge where they were protected by ditches, traps and trees from a charge by the Norman horsemen.

All in all, Edmond thought, the English army was well-positioned to defend the high ground, the heavily armored infantry protecting what seemed an almost impregnable center while the more mobile light-armed foot soldiers guarded the wings.

King Harold called his final council in preparation for battle under the shade of a massive hoar apple tree near the royal standards. The king was on foot, his helm-bearer at his side, with the pennon of the Fighting Man flapping in the breeze over his bare head. Next to him were his brothers Gurth and Leofwine as he exhorted a group including Ansgar the Marshal, Thane Sebert, Earl Waltheof, Bishop Elfwy, Edmond and a dozen other high-ranking prelates and noblemen.

The king once again outlined the reasons why he intended to let the Norman take the offensive, laying particular stress on the enemy's greater mobility. The invaders fought on horseback while the English were accustomed to dismounting and fighting on foot. Harold cautioned, "On no account allow your men to descend from the high ground to pursue the Normans if they retreat unless and until you have my authorization. Let the enemy charge up the slope against our shield wall and exhaust themselves. We'll cut them down. Let them come at us again and again. When they're worn down, then it'll be time enough to begin the chase."

He let the warning sink in before continuing. "They may feign flight in an effort to lure us into pursuing them down the slope. Let them flee. Most likely it'll be a ruse to draw us into a trap. If we hold firm, they'll continue to attack until they realize they can't dislodge us from our position, or until they suffer such heavy losses that they'll lose heart. So long as we hold this ridge the advantage is ours. If we drive them off, they may be doomed. Duke William has burned his ships and can't return to Normandy without being helped from abroad. Even if he is able to retreat to the seashore, he may not escape because our fleet is on its way to cut off all assistance from Normandy. Bastard William must prevail or perish. So it is with us, my loyal lords and faithful subjects. We must hold firm or fall where we stand. God and right support our cause. The Lord will steel our hearts because we defend what he has granted us in his merciful providence.

"Remember! Let us yield to bastard William and his bandit rabble only what we so willingly surrendered to Harald Hardraade and his Norsemen pirates. Let us divide our lands, which is what William intends, and assign an equal share to each of his thieving vassals. We'll grant six feet of our holy English soil to every invader though none of them is entitled to an inch of it. More they'll never need!"

Even the Normans on Telham Hill, five hundred yards away, could hear the thunderous roar that greeted Harold's rousing and defiant call to battle. The invaders responded instinctively and instantly with their customary battle cry of "Ha Rou! Ha Rou!" and the clashing echoes reverberated from one hill to the other.

Edmond, wearing Aegelsig's superb armor, addressed Wiglaf who stood beside him and brandished a ponderous battle-ax as if it were a twig. "Old friend, do you recall when we first fought these Normans at Dover?"

"How could I forget?" snorted the old sailor. "What a drubbing we gave those misbegotten dogs, and we'll hand them a worse hiding today, God willing."

"I don't doubt it," said Edmond softly. "And if all of our people are half as stalwart as you, good Wiglaf, we're sure to prevail. But there's always a chance we won't succeed, and it's even more likely that some of us won't survive the battle. If I fall, there's something I'd like you to do for me."

"Thane Edmond, you know you've but to ask."

"This goes beyond friendship, Wiglaf," said Edmond earnestly. "I've never mentioned this to you, but before that clash in Dover poor Master Osgood gave me this ring." He lifted his right hand to display the silver band on the ring finger. "This bit of silver, Wiglaf, is more precious than you can imagine. If I fall in battle, take it and give it to King Harold. Bid him read the inscription. He'll understand what it signifies."

Wiglaf scratched his head in puzzlement, unimpressed by the battered old ring whose inscription he could not read, but indicated he would honor Edmond's request. Satisfied, Edmond turned to Godfrid whom he had ordered at dawn to join him with the detachment from Bosbury.

"Did you hear what I said to Wiglaf?" he asked. "Godfrid, you who've been like a son to me, remember what I asked of him. If Wiglaf is unable to carry out my bidding, you must perform this final task for me."

"Surely, there'll be no need for that, my lord," replied Godfrid confidently. "But if there is, God forbid, I promise I'll do my duty."

A tremendous roar from the English army cut short the conversation. The clamor was touched off by the martial blare of brass horns setting the Norman cohorts into motion. All eyes turned toward Telham Hill to witness the first division of the invading force pour into the valley separating it from Senlac and form up parallel to the English right wing. Simultaneously, the second division, larger than the first, took up a position confronting the English left wing. Each division was comprised of archers in the front line, mailed foot and spearmen in the second, and in the third the armored knights perched heavily on ponderous horses and brandishing swords, battle-axes and maces. The two divisions comprised the duke's confederates, adventurers gathered from all over Europe with the promise of English loot and under the reassuring aegis of the papal blessing of William's equivocal cause.

The first two units were quickly joined in the valley by William's third and most formidable body, the chivalry of Normandy under the duke's personal command. Here rode men bearing names that were to become as familiar as household words in England's annals, such as Montgomery, FitzOsborne, Mortimer, Gifford and many more. Over their helmeted heads fluttered the papal gonfalon under which Duke William, with Robert of Mortain and Bishop Odo of Bayeux at either side, stormed eagerly into battle. The great body of men wheeled into the center of the valley, then spread out until it covered the ground between the wings to create a seamless front. As it formed up, the Norman churchmen and camp followers occupied their army's former position on Telham Hill to observe the impending battle of whose outcome they had no doubt.

After Edmond inspected his troop of two score to make sure his men were ready for combat, his gaze wandered to the enormous gnarled hoar apple tree under whose branches King Harold had just spoken so inspiringly. There was something vaguely familiar about it. With a start, he suddenly realized why. How could he have forgotten? It was the very tree against whose trunk he had rested his back while eating a frugal meal of bread and cheese during the eventful trek from Pevensey to London fifteen years earlier.

He circled the tree trunk, carefully examining its bark. Yes, it was still there. He could just make out faint traces of the single word he had carved into the wood, the name Adele. He whispered it, "Adele." The remembrance was painful, recalling as it did a joyful period of youth, beauty and unclouded hope and ambition. How lovely, how alluring that impish face! He could not repress a sigh of regret for what had been and what might have been.

Strange that he should think of her at a time like this. How different everything could have been if she had not rejected him so unfairly, so cruelly! Or would it? Could the actual realization of love and hope ever have matched the imagined delights of the dream? Or would it have turned bitter as most hopes and aspirations do? Does not every man mentally fashion an ideal mate and seek a woman of flesh and blood to fit the pattern only to suffer disappointment either because of deception or disillusion? Was it not the same with any ambition, whether to possess a crown, a fief, a horse, or a patch of land? Does any achievement ever approach expectation? He sighed again, before laughing ruefully at himself. He shook off the strange mood, and strove to forget Adele.

"Up shields!" rang a command passed along the ranks, and a roof of leather and metal went up to defend the English from death hurtling from the sky as the Norman archers opened the battle by loosing a cloud of arrows. Despite the protective ceiling, enough missiles penetrated to cause numerous casualties among Harold's troops The Norman archers continued the barrage until it became evident that the expenditure of thousands of projectiles was not breaking up the enemy formations. As for the English bowmen, their smaller volleys were no more effective in discouraging their foes.

When the arrows stopped descending, there was a brief interval of relative calm as if each side was contemplating its next action. It was soon signaled by the trumpets, which proclaimed a Norman charge. A massive wave of horses, men and steel began to surge across the autumn-browned slope beneath Senlac toward its heights bristling with the English. The attack was conducted at a measured pace as if to build up momentum until a single rider broke away in advance of his compatriots, spurring his mount as if feverishly impatient to encounter the enemy.

A powerful baritone voice rose melodiously above the clatter of hooves and jangle of arms as the solitary rider chanted "The Song of Roland", and played the juggler with his sword and lance until he reached the English front line. Bracing himself, he plunged his lance into a Kentishnan's breast, then cut down another with his sword before his foes recovered from their astonishment at his daring to drive lances through his chain mail. Thus fell Taillefer, Duke William's minstrel, meeting the hero's death he so often had sung about in courtly entertainment for his master's pleasure.

As Taillefer's body slumped from the saddle to the ground, the main body of Normans burst upon the line of English standing shoulder to shoulder across the front of Senlac. Sword, lance, battle-ax and mace struck an unearthly metallic clangor from shields and chain mail in a dissonant hammering. The seemingly irresistible force exerted by the massive wave of charging heavy cavalry nevertheless soon was spent against the unyielding shield wall. Hundreds of men and horses fell victim to the English, and the foot of the rise soon really deserved the name of Sangue Lac, or lake of blood. Decimated, temporarily discouraged and in disarray, the Norman left wing retreated down hill in order to regroup. Many of the Normans were funneled into a series of ingeniously concealed fosses by a coolly directed counter-charge of the English. The Normans' terrified and screaming horses stumbled and rolled into the ditches, many of the riders either being crushed under the weight of their mounts or battered to death by their pursuing enemies' battle-axes. The few who during the charge had succeeded in cutting their way through the ranks of the Kentishmen in the center and even somehow surmounting the palisade were cut to pieces by the housecarles.

Despite the failure of the Norman charge, the English also suffered heavy losses. And even though the Normans had been repelled at least for the time being, they were able to avoid a total rout chiefly because of the leadership of Bishop Odo. The warrior prelate, mounted on a white horse and wielding a mace, urged, cajoled and threatened the demoralized survivors of the opening assault to reassemble and prepare for a greater effort to drive the English from the ridge.

For a quarter of the day, from mid-morning to mid-afternoon, the battle raged almost ceaselessly with neither army able to gain a clear-cut advantage despite a fearful expenditure of life. The English stubbornly beat off one Norman cavalry charge after another. Between the furious mounted assaults, foot soldiers and archers carried on the fighting, offering little respite for either defenders or attackers. As heavy as the English losses were, dead and wounded piling up at a grisly rate in front of, along and behind the shield-wall, that of the Normans was even more severe. The strength of Duke William's army was clearly waning as the day wore on. A hedge of mangled bodies of men and horses surrounded Senlac, and the plain turned into a boggy red mire, tinted grotesquely by the blood of the dead and wounded.

During a lull in the battle, King Harold surveyed the nightmarish scene with a practiced soldier's eye from the top of the ridge, cradling helm in left elbow and with right arm around brother Gurth's shoulder.

"The enemy can't keep it up much longer," he remarked. "We've lost many good men, God knows, but they've suffered even more. If William can't break through our shield-wall by sunset, he'll be hard pressed to renew the attack in the morning, especially if Edwin and Morcar arrive to reinforce us." A wistful smile replaced his stern expression. "How well our men have fought, even the thralls with their farm implements. The discipline has been remarkable. The housecarles, yes, I expected no less, but I feared the fyrd might abandon all restraint and rush after the retreating Normans, especially when the enemy gave way after that opening charge."

"They've fought nobly, brother," agreed Leofwine, standing with Edmond at Harold's left. "They believe in our cause and their king."

"I doubt if the noble deeds done at Maldon were more glorious that those of this day, much as that battle has been so deservedly sung about," mused Harold. "Yet even greater effort will be needed before this bloody day is done if we're to conquer."

"You think they'll come at us again?" asked Gurth, peering toward the Normans reforming their depleted but still formidable ranks in the valley.

"I know Duke William. He'll come at us again and again even if he's forced to crawl uphill with a dagger between his teeth," replied Harold grimly.

"Why don't you withdraw with the housecarles into the weald, royal brother, and rely on Gurth and me to carry on the fight?" suggested Leofwine. "Surely, you've done more than enough to satisfy duty and honor. It's foolhardy to continue to risk your consecrated life and your subjects' fortunes. When reinforcements arrive—if Edwin and Morcar do come—you can rejoin us to crush the Norman curs for good."

Gurth eagerly voiced his support. "Leofwine's advice is sound, lord king. What he suggests is prudent and makes good sense. Why risk everything in one battle?"

"No! Here I stand or fall, England's true and rightful king," declared Harold. "I'll not be branded a coward as well as a perjurer by these Norman bastards. God will help me to defend my rights and those of our people."

He was interrupted by shouts from all points. "The Normans come again!"

A cloud of arrows signaled the opening of another assault, taking a fierce toll of the English ranks, with Leofwine being one of the victims. The king's brother fell with a groan, an arm reaching out to clutch at Edmond's hauberk, then flailing feebly as he sank to the ground with the shaft imbedded in his right eye.

"Brother!" lamented the king as Edmond bent down over Leofwine, then reported mournfully as he met Harold's inquiring glance, "He's dead, my lord."

The king kissed his brother's forehead, made the sign of the cross over his corpse, then repressed all further show of grief. There was no time to mourn with the Normans again hurling themselves with almost reckless abandon against the shield-wall. The melee raged even more fiercely than earlier as if the invaders were convinced they must prevail quickly or perish in the attempt. The fighting was most ferocious on the English left, which the Normans were determined to break through whatever the cost. Their losses were appalling, and suddenly it seemed they had lost all heart. They turned in flight as if panicked. The men of the fyrd, seeing them turn their backs, believed victory was in their grasp. Enraged with the frenzy of combat, they abandoned all caution and discipline to ignore their leaders and pursue the escaping enemy. They thundered down the slope after the Normans, past the ditches and traps, heedless in their fury.

"God save us!" cried King Harold on realizing what was taking place. "What possesses Thane Cedric? How often have I cautioned him to keep his men in check. Send word he must beat them back even if he has to use his sword on his own people."

The order was not only too late but futile. Neither Thane Cedric nor a score of officers like him could stem the wild, undisciplined rush of the English fyrd after their apparently demoralized foe. As the Norman right wing pursued by the English rushed back down into the valley, Duke William swung his center in their direction. With resounding cries of "Ha Rou!" the Norman heavy cavalry rode down the surprised and terrified English foot levies, slaughtering them by the hundreds and forcing the survivors to flee for their lives into the surrounding forest. Only a pitifully small number of those who had rushed down the slope regained Senlac, and the shield-wall continued to shrink under the Norman battering.

King Harold looked on in rage and despair at the destruction of his army's left wing as it was ground to pieces. Even worse, the scene soon was repeated on the right flank when the Normans again lured the English down from the heights with a feigned flight, followed by an irresistible onslaught of the cavalry under Duke William. As before, hundreds of Harold's men ran to their destruction on the points of Norman lances or were crushed by the hooves of their ponderous chargers. Few escaped to return to the ridge or to find haven in the forest.

Now the battle on the slopes of the ridge and in the valley was fragmented into a number of isolated hand-to-hand combats as small bands of the English struggled to reunite with what was left of the bulk of Harold's army. The king's force was reduced in effective strength to the surviving housecarles and a few hundred other men who had cut their way through the Normans to rejoin the royal standards.

Duke William now felt so certain of eventual victory that he abandoned all restraint and the husbanding of his reserves. He threw his entire army into assault after assault in the face of sharp resistance by the housecarles whose billets and axes sheared off innumerable Norman lances and hacked hundreds of horses from under their riders. Between charges, the Norman archers wreaked havoc. Despite the upturned shields of the English, the missiles took a severe toll, the ranks of the housecarles thinning noticeably though their shield-wall remained unbroken.

During a brief respite between enemy attacks, King Harold leaned wearily against the trunk of the hoar apple tree and raged against the impetuous folly of the levies who had rushed to destruction. "They've lost the day for us, Gurth," lamented Harold. "They've lost England. There's little left for you and me other than to die with Leofwine."

"We can die well, brother," came Gurth's calm rejoinder.

"Die well we shall indeed," echoed Harold. "We know how to die, as witness those rash fools who've doomed our cause." His voice rose. "We know how to die with honor, and so we will."

Those who heard his words took up the pledge, "We'll die with honor," until the Normans looked about in some alarm in an effort to discover what caused the uproar. Some even feared that in spite of their duke's assurances the expected reinforcements for Harold's army were approaching under Edwin and Morcar.

But there was no sign of help for the English, and the Normans renewed their attacks with even greater vigor, sensing the end was near. One of the charges was led by a richly-armored knight whom Edmond and Wiglaf recognized as an old foe.

"Look! It's our old friend from Dover, Eustace of Boulogne," shouted the sailor as he and Edmond braced themselves for the attack. Edmond ordered the men of Bosbury to take up a position in front of the shield-wall so they could meet the enemy head-on. When the Normans reached the top of the slope, Edmond's troop momentarily encircled Count Eustace. The count desperately fought his way out of the trap, however, and turned tail with his surviving men. Wiglaf led a pursuit, followed by some of Edmond's men and a group of blood-maddened housecarles. The Normans gave way to the counterattack and fled downhill. Edmond attempted to recall those charging after the enemy, cursing Wiglaf for his folly, but they were out of control. The blood lust spread, and within a short time almost the entire English royal guard, which had held its position so steadily and courageously all day, abandoned the shield-wall to race after the Normans.

Edmond saw Count Eustace swivel about in his saddle to mock his pursuers. The taunts succeeded in enraging the English even more, and there was no restraining them as they poured down the slope onto level ground. As soon as the majority reached the meadow, a trumpet blast sounded. Suddenly those in flight parted ranks to the right and left and a wedge of mounted heavy armed men stormed through the gap. The counterattack was led by Duke William himself. His first victim was Wiglaf who took the full force of a sword thrust into his broad chest without even a murmur.

"God rest your soul, old friend!" cried Edmond who from a distance saw his old companion fall, he himself not having reached the foot of Senlac. He was soon in the thick of battle, however, striking out in rage and sorrow, but the pressure of the Norman advance forced him back up the hill with the retreating housecarles. The royal guard quickly reformed a shield-wall, recalled to their duty by King Harold, Gurth and Ansgar the Marshal. So fast did they gather renewed strength that the Norman charge lost impetus, and the knights fell back with Duke William in order to reform once more at the foot of the ridge.

"Ha Rou!" roared William. "To me, men of Chaux! To me, FitzErnies and Montgomery! Once more up the hill, men of Normandy!" A thousand heavy armed foot soldiers charged at what remained of the English palisade, trampling it into the blood-stained mud. They seized all the ground between the foot of Senlac and the top of the ridge where the remaining English were gathering around the royal standards, King Harold, Edmond and their other surviving leaders.

"My lord king, look!" shouted Edmond. "Gurth and Ansgar are cut off!" Harold swung toward where his brother and the marshal, with sixty or seventy men, were trapped in a pocket by the enemy at the foot of the ridge to the right. They resisted with desperate ferocity, but it was evident they would soon be overwhelmed.

The king determined to save his brother and led two hundred men, almost half of his remaining force, in a downhill charge. The momentum of the rush by the heavy armed housecarles, their axes hewing a bloody narrow path through the Norman ring, carried them to Gurth's side, but not before Harold was wounded in the thigh by a lance.

"The king is down!" screamed the English who saw him fall.

"Harold is dead!" joyfully shouted the nearby Normans.

It was not so. The housecarles, led by Gurth and Ansgar, carried King Harold uphill with them as they conducted a difficult and costly retreat back to their remaining comrades atop the ridge. At the king's request, they set him down beside the standard of the Fighting Man. A physician determined he wound was not serious, staunched the flow of blood, and provided a makeshift bandage. "It's only a scratch," said the king dismissively, and after a brief rest pulled himself to his feet, resolved to fight to the end.

Encouraged by the king's fall, the Normans sought to end the battle, dispatching two thousand men against the barely three hundred survivors comprising that iron circle of English gathered around the standards. Duke William and Bishop Odo led what they hoped would be the final charge, sword and mace swinging in fearful rhythm to cut down the exhausted remaining housecarles.

Gurth broke away from the ranks to oppose the duke in a desperate effort to cut down the Norman leader. He managed to momentarily drive back William with the ferocity of his charge before a powerful blow of Odo's mace struck him on the helm, stunning him for a fatal sword thrust by Roger de La Isle. Roaring with grief and rage, King Harold hacked down three Norman assailants in an effort to reach his brother's killer or to confront Duke William but the press was too thick. Nevertheless, the Norman duke and his prelate brother were forced to give ground.

Edmond fought at Harold's side, delivering blow for blow, while desperately attempting to rally the housecarles to restore a protective iron ring around the king. But it was all to no avail. Another Norman sword found the king's side, and Harold fell beneath the standard of the

Fighting Man. This time it was obvious he was mortally wounded. Edmond and Ansgar the Marshal knelt at his side while the tumult continued to rage around them a few steps away.

"Ansgar, my faithful marshal," gasped the king, blood frothing from his lips. "All is lost. I go to join my brothers in heaven."

"Don't attempt to speak, my lord," cried Ansgar. "Save your strength, royal Harold. The physician will attend to your wound. If we can hold on until nightfall all may yet be well."

"Alas, it'll come too late for me," groaned Harold. "All is over. Yet to secure a place in heaven and enjoy God's forgiveness and eternal grace, I must speak one more thing." With great effort, a shaking right hand lifted feebly to touch Edmond on the chest. "I know you, Edmond, son of Childe Edwy. I know your royal birth. Bishop Wulfstan disclosed all to me." Harold turned to Ansgar. "Here's your true king, born of the line of Cerdic. Hail royal Edmond, undoubted king of the English, basileus of Britain."

They were Harold's last words.

Ansgar remained on his knees until the king drew his final breath, then closed Harold's eyes as Edmond, overcome by mixed emotions, watched with bowed head. When they rose, Edmond drew the silver ring from his finger and silently showed it to Ansgar who read the inscription, "AELFRED MEC HEHT GEWYRCAN," in awed astonishment. The marshal murmured, "This must be the ring of our ancient rulers. Tradition holds that King Edmond Ironside wore it at Assandun. It's said to have disappeared at his death."

"I'm his nephew, the son of his brother, Childe Edwy," explained Edmond. He suppressed a powerful impulse to laugh at the bitter irony of the situation. For many years he had dreamed of having his royal status recognized, and now Ansgar had done so, but on the brink of disaster. As for the silver band, it could only serve to make his death at Norman hands more certain. What hopes and dreams had it not stirred when at Osgood's bidding he first had removed it from a nail in the merchant's house?

He shook of the mood of regret, despair and foreboding. It was no longer a dream. For the moment, whatever fate held for him, he was king in Ansgar's eyes as well as his own. Harold's dying confession and declaration had confirmed his right to the crown, as had his father's mysterious words so long ago, "You were born to be a king."

"I need no proof of your right other than the word of my king," declared Ansgar, breaking into Edmond's thoughts. "Surely, he would not have risked his immortal soul with so great a deception as he lay dying. Hail, King Edmond!" He placed his hands in Edmond's and swore fealty.

All the while the ring of housecarles around Edmond, Ansgar and King Harold's corpse, now covered with a cloak, shrank to a small circle around the hoar apple tree but still held somehow under repeated Norman onslaughts.

During a brief cessation of combat, Ansgar ordered the housecarles to form a circle around him as he stood with the apple tree at his back, Edmond at his side and the body of King Harold at his feet. He grasped Edmond's right arm and raised it high as he proclaimed "The king is dead! The king lives! Hail, King Edmond! Hail King of the English! Hail heir of Alfred and Edmond Ironside!"

The astonished housecarles stared in wonder at Edmond, then cheered in acclamation to signify their acceptance. Moved to the core of his being, Edmond yielded to a wave of emotion to seize the standard of the Fighting Man and wave it overhead, drawing another roar of approval from the royal guard.

"King Edmond bids you defend the sacred body of King Harold and the honor of the English," he shouted. "If need be, we'll die before we yield to these Norman curs. Let us conquer or perish as Englishmen should in defense of their country."

After he and Ansgar positioned the pitifully small remainder of the once great English army for a last-ditch defense, he whispered to Godfrid who had been at his side during the entire dramatic turn of events, "Godfrid, you've been like a son to me all these years. You've been an obedient and faithful squire. Now you must obey what may be my final order. You must live on. I want you and Ansgar to attempt to join those who've been able to escape into the weald."

"No, my lord king, let me remain with you," pleaded Godfrid, almost in tears. "I've sworn to serve you, come what may."

"You've also sworn to obey me, whatever I demand," Edmond reminded.

Godfrid bowed his head, gazing mournfully on the ground while Edmond informed Ansgar of his decision.

"Honor bids me to stay with my brave men until the end, whatever the outcome," protested the marshal. "Duty requires me to defend my king with my life's blood."

"Honor and duty also require you to obey our orders, whatever they are," Edmond thundered. He gently put a hand on Godfrid's head. "The sun is about to set, dear lad. I may be king only till night, but to you, Ansgar and all those who fight at my side, I'll always remain a king, if only in memory. Live on, my boy, to recall Edmond Edwysson's brief but not inglorious reign. Go with Ansgar as you love and honor me."

Godfrid silently and tearfully wrung Edmond's hand, then slipped away with Ansgar down the reverse slope of the ridge. They were able to elude the patrols and reach the safety of the dense forest with a desperate dash before the Normans could intercept them. Edmond saw Godfrid disappear, then took up his sword in his right hand, grasping the standard of the Fighting Man in his left, and awaited the next enemy attack.

Duke William led what he hoped would be the final onslaught upon the slender cordon of housecarles collected around Edmond, King Harold's corpse, and the royal standards. The Normans now totally encircled the remaining English, rendering it virtually impossible for anyone to escape into the forest as Godfrid and Ansgar had done. When the attack began, William himself cut down the last two foes between his escorting guards and the fluttering symbols of English rule. He wrested the Golden Dragon of Wessex from a wounded housecarle who had been defending it until Robert of Mortain struck him with his mace.

The slaughter was furious, the Normans by sheer numbers overwhelming the housecarles, few of whom had strength enough left to resist for long. The first Norman to confront Edmond was a foot soldier whom he cut down with a single sword stroke. He felled two more as Duke William, grasping the Golden Dragon, paused to take in the scene, eyes glittering with the fury of combat. "Ha Rou!" the duke shouted in jubilation when he recognized King Harold's body outstretched on the turf.

Edmond heard the duke's war cry and spun about immediately, almost intuitively recognizing William. He was aware of being possessed by a frenzy such had overcome him during the battle against the Petchenegs on that other hill in distant Dacia. His mind swirled with the words so often recalled but never realized until just now: "You were born to be a king."

Yes, he was born of kingly blood and now he was the king, and he would die as a king should. Here stands Edmond Edwysson, king of the English, basileus of Britain, heir of Alfred and of Edmond Ironside. Here stands the king amidst a circle of heroes, the blood of enemies flowing at his feet. Here stands the king, the symbols of his rule fluttering in the twilight breeze. Here stands the king, the heir of Harold Godwinson, the banner of the Fighting Man in one hand, a regal sword in the other.

"Yield the banner, Saxon!" shouted Duke William. "Lay down your sword! I'll spare your life."

"Yield!" Edmond laughed scornfully. Yield! The king of the English may die but never surrender. Harold had shown the way. Yield? God knew the struggle had been desperate and all was lost. He never had thought he would gain the crown, but once it was in his grasp he would not surrender it. Yield? He had yielded too much in the past—land, love and high rank—to surrender what he finally had gained that day.

"The banner will serve as my shroud, bastard of Normandy," he retorted. "I hope to wrap you in it as well before I fall, lord pirate."

"I'll kill the insolent fool," shouted Walter Giffard, one of the duke's escorts. He dug spurs into his horse's flanks to charge at Edmond, but a wave of the duke's hand pulled him up short.

"No, it's up to me to seize the standard, and I claim the honor," cried William. He swung from the saddle, disdaining the advantage of being on horseback against a man on foot. Sword in hand, he approached Edmond, who planted his back against the trunk of the hoar apple tree.

"Will you surrender?" asked the duke, and when Edmond shook his head, demanded, "Your name, before I kill you. The splendor of your equipment shows you're a man of rank, but I don't recognize you. Who are you? What is your station?"

"Edmond, rightful king of England," rang the proud, defiant reply.

The duke shook his head. "What mockery is this?" he muttered as he gripped his two-handed sword to attack after commanding his escorts to stand aside.

Edmond skillfully beat back his assailant's opening strokes, but was hampered by his stubborn and proud insistence on wielding his sword with one hand while grasping the Fighting Man with the other. The effort tired him, and a thrust by William penetrated his hauberk, drawing a gush of blood. The standard slipped from his hand to be caught by Duke William before it struck the ground.

As Edmond reeled, growing faint with loss of blood, he groped with failing sight for the support of the ancient tree trunk. He no longer could read the name scratched long ago on its bark yet sighed, "Adele!" before his father's deathbed revelation echoed for the final time: "You were born to a king, Edmond, you were born…" His hand slipped from the tree, and he slumped to the ground next to King Harold's body.

Only Duke William had heard his dying words.

FINIS